GIRL FRIENDS

Alex Dahl

HEAD
ZEUS

An Aries Book

First published in the UK in 2024 by Head of Zeus Ltd,
part of Bloomsbury Publishing Plc

9 7 5 3 1 2 4 6 8

A catalogue record for this book is available from the British Library.

ISBN (PB): 9781801108331
ISBN (E): 9781801108348

Cover design: Matt Bray | Head of Zeus

Printed and bound in Great Britain by
CPI Group (UK) Ltd, Croydon CR0 4YY

MIX
Paper | Supporting
responsible forestry
FSC
www.fsc.org   FSC® C171272

Head of Zeus Ltd
First Floor East
5–8 Hardwick Street
London EC1R 4RG
WWW.HEADOFZEUS.COM

To my girl friends

Part One

'Keep your friends close and your enemies closer.'

–Sun Tzu

Part One

Prologue

Bianka

Can Xara, Ibiza

Charlotte comes to slowly, though Bianka is increasingly persistent in her attempts at rousing her, slapping her cheek at first gently, then firmly, audibly. She's on her back on the floor of the farmhouse, her white linen dress smeared with vivid blood and vomit. She opens her eyes briefly, then throws up again, a splash of thin green bile and wine. Bianka helps Charlotte into a half-sitting position, holding her tight to her chest, the way a mother would an injured child.

'We're going to get through this. I'm going to help you. Wake up, Charlotte. Charlotte, can you hear me? Here, sit up, oh no, hey it's okay, I've got you. I'll never let you go, Charlotte. Never.'

Bianka glances around the room. How are they going to get out of this? There has to be a way. At least Bianka is sure of one thing – this will bring them closer together. It has to.

Charlotte makes a low growl, then coughs repeatedly. Her throat must be sore from the shouting and vomiting.

Her glossy brown hair flows loose around her shoulders and into the narrow space between them like slivers of silk, and Bianka gently smooths it down. The long metal pin that held it up in a twisted coil is in Charlotte's hand, its entire length slick with blood. Bianka pulls away slightly and sees that Charlotte's eyes are fully open now and taking in the impossible and shocking scene.

When she's certain Charlotte is able to sit unaided, Bianka releases her from the half-embrace that was propping her up.

'No,' Charlotte whispers as she recognizes the lifeless figure by the door; dead, beyond any doubt. It's the absolute, empty stillness that gives it away, and the sliver of white beneath half-open eyelids. Bianka's stomach turns, and she's overcome by a vicious nausea, her heart racing.

'Yes,' whispers Bianka, catching a fat tear rolling down Charlotte's cheek with her fingertip. 'Oh, Charlotte, what have you done?'

One

Bianka

She's imagined this moment over and over for several months, but when it comes, she still feels unprepared, and a bolt of anxiety rushes through her, settling in the pit of her gut like a cool, hard fist. The house is mostly empty, their personal belongings in transit. All she needs to do is take a couple of steps across the hallway, strangely uncluttered now, then step out through the open door to where Emil and Storm are loading suitcases into the waiting taxi. Storm looks wan and suddenly much younger than his sixteen years, and for a moment Bianka feels bad for all the times she's looked forward to the time when she wouldn't need to deal with him every day. That time has come and, in a couple of minutes, a blue school van will pull up at the curb, ready to take Storm and his extensive equipment to his introductory summer camp at his new boarding school.

But it isn't saying goodbye to Storm that Bianka finds unsettling, it's the frightening nature of making a change this big, of turning her entire world upside down. She swallows back tears at the thought that their house will just stand there, like an empty shell, all the memories of life as she's known it for over a decade fading slowly. Who knows whether they'll ever return? At least they're not selling it or renting it out, so they'll have the option to go back, but Bianka knows all too well that big changes are rarely reversible, no matter the intentions. She resists the urge to turn back around to look at the house that gave her shelter and security – a home – when she needed it most. She smiles at Storm, who has placed the last of the suitcases into the boot of the car, but he turns away, and she can tell he's embarrassed by the sheen of tears in his eyes. How do you say goodbye to a child you've raised but who often feels like a stranger?

Bianka feels a little faint, so she gets into the back seat of the taxi and closes the door with a soft click, staring down at her hands, avoiding the eyes of the driver in the rearview. Through the open window carrying a soft, warm June breeze, Bianka can pick out snatches of conversation between father and son.

'You're going to love it.'

'What if I don't?'

'I know you will.'

'Well, it's not like you've left me much choice. The slopes aren't that great in London.'

'Just give it a chance, Storm. We'll see you in two weeks.'

The van arrives to take Storm to the school high up in the mountains a couple of hours north of Oslo, where several of the other kids are also on national teams for skiing and other sports. The Olympic Factory, they call it.

Bianka watches out of the corner of her eye as her

husband hugs Storm. She doesn't get out of the car for a final goodbye – she decides to spare them all the awkwardness – and settles for a little wave. Emil says nothing as he gets in next to her and watches the van with Storm inside pull away and turn left at the end of the quiet residential road. Their taxi begins to move just as a light rain starts to fall, and only then does Bianka turn around at the last moment to look back at the white wooden house with its shiny black roof and small, well-kept garden dominated by the apple tree, reaching its long, gnarled arms across the lawn.

Emil takes Bianka's hand, and she lets him hold it, sneaking a sideways glance at her husband. He's a handsome man but somewhat bland; pleasant enough to look at but easily overlooked or forgotten, she always thought. With age, he's grown more commanding, and his tall, lanky body, which once made him look gangly, now comes across as fit and athletic. After all these years of marriage, it still sometimes strikes Bianka as improbable that Emil would be the man she'd tie herself to. And yet, here they are. Just the two of them. And the day has finally come – the day they embark on the adventure of a lifetime.

Bianka spends the first few weeks driving slowly and carefully up and down the beautiful, serene streets of their new neighbourhood, memorizing their unfamiliar names; Clifton Road, Lauriston Road, Berkley Place, Lingfield Road, Edge Hill… She familiarizes herself with the one-way streets, the big new car, and driving on the left side of the road.

Before moving here, Bianka had been to London a couple

of times before, but it was years ago and she'd only done the typical touristy things in central London – shopping on Oxford Street, lunch in Covent Garden, a show in Leicester Square. A few months ago, during the winter, Emil and Bianka had flown over for a quick visit just after the job offer had come, and while she'd thought Wimbledon seemed pleasant enough, the short time had passed in a blur of house viewings and Uber rides and client dinners in fancy restaurants in Mayfair with Emil's new associates at Norbank.

Now, it doesn't take her many days to fall in love with Wimbledon Village. It seems to Bianka to be the perfect place – the embodiment of everything anyone could ever want – safe and quaint with a village feel but on the doorstep of one of the world's most exciting cities. The people look sophisticated and quietly wealthy, not dissimilar to those in the upmarket Oslo suburb they've just arrived from, but vastly different from Bianka's own beginnings. Even at home in Norway, she'd never quite felt like one of them. Might it be different here? She can feel the old Bianka and her boring life in Oslo slither off her like the discarded skin of a snake, and she realizes that all the worry was for nothing; she can do this – start over, make a new life for herself.

The house the company have provided on Dunstall Road is gorgeous, the kind of house anyone would fantasize about living in: vast and half-timbered with red-brick foundations and lovely, rambling gardens bordering Cannizaro Park. If only little Bianka could have seen herself now – living like a queen in London and not even having to work for it. Or slightly older Bianka – the incarnation of herself who had believed she'd never have anything worth having, after everything she'd lost.

She begins to unpack as soon as their belongings arrive from Norway, making the big, part-furnished house feel like a real home, with their smiling faces beaming from photographs placed around the living spaces, their art hung from the walls. She places Storm's belongings into the smallest of the spare bedrooms downstairs and shuts its door firmly behind her – it's not like he'll be spending a lot of time here between school terms and all the international travel he does as one of the most promising Super G stars of the Norwegian national youth team.

Today is a Monday, the first of June, and even at nine in the morning, it's getting warm. After Emil has left for the office in the City, Bianka sits for a long while on the terrace steps, drinking tea and enjoying the garden. She tries to imagine what the future will hold, how the new life will shape up, but draws a blank. They've agreed she doesn't have to work during the years they'll spend in London; Emil makes more than enough money for both of them and thinks Bianka 'deserves to explore what makes her happy' after over ten years in a job that hardly felt fulfilling. The problem is that Bianka has very little idea what might make her happy, and she already misses the daily routine of getting up and going in to the office, even though she resented it for years while she actually had to do it.

After less than a half hour she feels bored and decides to walk across the common and pick up dinner from one of the delis in the village. She passes people with dogs straining at their leads; mothers pursuing their little charges across the vibrant green, dewy grass encircling the pond;

some school kids from one of the nearby private schools in gym kit, their chatter drowned out by the rumble of regular planes on approach into Heathrow. She smiles to herself that she is suddenly here, in the midst of all of this. She stops to look at the window displays of several of the upmarket boutiques on the high street and notices a group of Norwegian women sat drinking coffee at a café. It feels strange to hear her mother tongue here, as though nothing from her home country could exist here in this new world.

Bianka takes a couple of steps closer so she can overhear what they're saying. Unfortunately, it is uninteresting, like snatches of other people's conversations usually are. They're talking about a fundraiser at school, how to sell more cakes, how difficult can it really be to ensure everything is not only gluten-free but vegan, too, and why can't the mothers of the senior school step up a little more? Bianka sneaks a glance at them. There are four of them, all groomed and blond and tightly botoxed. They wear variations of the same outfit: skinny jeans, ballerina shoes and floaty white blouses. A passerby might be forgiven for thinking that Bianka is one of them; she looks unmistakably Scandinavian in her colouring and most likely a little out of place in her brand-new London life. And perhaps Bianka will become like these women; ladies who lunch, whose husbands head in to the City every day while the wives spend their money in the suburbs, passing time until afternoons spent ferrying the children from their private schools to horse riding or tennis lessons or theatre club. With both a Norwegian primary school and the larger Scandinavian International School just down the road, Wimbledon is filled to the brim with Scandinavian expats.

She buys dinner from the deli, stops into a couple of designer boutiques, then picks up a chicken halloumi baguette and a coffee to go from Gail's and walks back home the same way she came. Soon, she'll hopefully have some friends to sit at the cafés with.

In the afternoon she takes a long bath with a glass of white wine, looking up at planes streaking across the sky through the domed skylight in the master bathroom. She reads an interiors magazine, and after, feeling inspired, decides to move the furniture around in the living room. She drags the sofas around so that they face each other rather than stand next to each other in a corner of the room, and places a low marble coffee table in between them, then a bronze vase filled with white roses on top. When she's finished, she sits down and waits, but as the minutes and hours drag by, she feels increasingly lonely and annoyed. Why hasn't Emil come home yet? It's past seven and dinner is long ready, as in heated up. Of course she's well aware that working hours are longer in London than in Norway, where it is completely normal to leave the office at four on the dot, but she didn't anticipate just how long the hours would be or how displaced she'd feel.

Relax, she tells herself. *You just got here.*

At seven thirty Emil walks through the door, looking exhausted but elated. Over an exquisite parmigiana she bought from the Italians on the corner and pretends she's made, he talks about his day and his various colleagues, none of whom Bianka has yet met. After dinner, they bring the rest of the wine into the living room, Emil settling down close to Bianka on the sofa when she expected he'd sit opposite.

'It looks amazing, baby,' says Emil, taking in the new layout of the room. 'Oh, by the way – I forgot to say – we've already been invited to, like, five events. One is this weekend. At my colleague Andreas's house. I wondered whether you'd heard of his wife, Charlotte Vinge?'

'No, I don't think so. Why?'

'Apparently she's quite a big deal in Norway. The Keto Queen, she calls herself. I think she's some kind of TV chef. Her show is premiering on Streamstar in the UK in English and they're throwing a big party.'

'Wow. Ok, sounds nice.' Emil picks up the TV remote from the table in front of them and switches on the TV. He goes to YouTube and enters 'Keto Queen.' Nothing could have prepared Bianka for what happens next. There she is, back from the dead, leaping to life on the screen, only it isn't her, of course it isn't. And yet, there is something so similar about this woman that Bianka feels instantly and deeply affected. Her heart doubles its pace in her chest and she consciously works on keeping her expression neutral. Emil must notice it, too, but how could they possibly acknowledge it? Bianka sneaks a glance at her husband but his expression is seemingly unperturbed. They watch Charlotte Vinge talk about the apparent horrifying effects of consuming carbohydrates as she sears a steak to perfection, her beautiful face breaking into frequent, mesmerizing smiles, deep dimples studding her smooth, tan cheeks, until Bianka can bear it no longer and gently takes the remote control from Emil's hand and switches the TV off.

'Interesting niche to build a career in, isn't it?' says Emil, and Bianka watches him carefully as he speaks. He really does seem completely unaffected by Charlotte Vinge. A part of her wants to allow the tears that threaten to burst free from deep inside her loose, and ask her husband whether he sees what she sees – the impossible – *she's* back. But she decides to say nothing, all the better if he doesn't notice what she sees. She feels herself nod.

'She was a newly qualified doctor, Andreas said. And decided to start this Keto Queen thing instead. Apparently makes a killing.' Emil chuckles.

'I can't wait to meet her,' says Bianka, and in this moment, the new life in London, the new start, and the new Bianka, take on a new meaning altogether.

Two

Charlotte

The lawns roll out from the wraparound teak terrace, vibrant green and lush after the recent rains, and a large marquee has been erected to the side of the pool. The lawn on the other side of the pool has been made into a dance floor, especially commissioned for events like this. A little over the top perhaps, but I won't have it said that Charlotte Vinge doesn't know how to host a party, and this is a once-in-a-lifetime event, after all. I watch as the enormous screen is stretched across the terrace at the back of the house, and positioned at a perfect angle for the crowd to see from where they'll stand in the garden. I picture my face filling the screen, following the Streamstar UK logo. I smile to myself and swallow back a lump of nerves in my throat. No time for that.

The caterers busy themselves setting up the food stands and unloading the crates of champagne, plunging the bottles into ice buckets behind the bar inside the vast, domed marquee. There's sashimi and carpaccio and oysters and huge slabs of Gruyère and Roquefort, all keto, of course, though I'm not going to make a point of it. I don't need to; everybody knows that carbohydrates aren't served at this house.

I step off the terrace and onto the striped lawn, which Andreas insisted on cutting himself this morning. I must admit he did it well, though I wasn't at all sure he'd be able to as I watched him from the terrace, pretending to answer emails on my phone, fighting the urge to scream that it didn't look straight enough or that he'd missed a spot.

Andreas has sidled up behind me and slips his arms around my waist, pulling me into a close hug. I'm a little surprised, he's not exactly the cuddling kind.

'Hey babe. So, tell me, what are you freaking out over right now?'

'I'm not freaking out.'

'Charlotte, I know you. I can read your stress levels purely from the set of your jaw. You're looking pretty stern.'

He grabs my chin and pinches it lightly before kissing my cheek and I laugh in spite of myself.

'Well, it's hot today, there's sashimi and oysters, they could be left at the wrong temperature and become dangerous, they could cause food poisoning, who knows how much experience these guys have ensuring the correct amount of ice, I've never used them before, though they were recommended by Silje Evensen—'

'Charlotte. Seriously. You need a drink. Here, come with me.' Andreas pulls me across the lawn to the marquee, where a couple of waiters who look around the same age as my thirteen-year-old are placing champagne glasses on a starched white tablecloth in a crooked line.

'Can you please make me an Arctic Kiss?' I ask but am met with blank stares. 'It's the signature cocktail of this party, so perhaps it would be good if you knew how. There, look over there on the drinks blackboard.' I point at the cute French-inspired blackboard where I've listed the drinks on offer in careful calligraphy. My friends always wonder how I have time for all this stuff, but really, it's simple – I *make* time. Besides, you can sleep when you're dead. One of the waiters nods and sets about making my drink. One part vodka, two parts Dom Perignon, a dash of fresh lemon juice, hardly rocket science. I roll my eyes dramatically at Andreas, who chuckles infuriatingly.

'Remember what I said. Have a few drinks, just relax. This is meant to be fun. This is your moment, Charlotte.'

'Relax? The entire Scandinavian community of London and half of the UK's top TV people are about to descend on my garden and you're telling me to relax?'

'Charlotte, we've talked about this. These people are all coming because of you, and your amazing achievements. Remember that. You know most of them anyway; they're your friends. Think of them as individuals, just one friend after another. No reason to get all worked up over having your girlfriends over and getting smashed on champagne on a beautiful summer day.'

'I just want it all to be perfect.'

'It *is* perfect. Like always. And like you.' My husband does know how to say the right thing.

'Mmm.'

'By the way, I invited my new boss, Emil – I think I mentioned him the other day – and his wife, Bianka. With a k. Biank-*ah*.' Andreas says this woman's name a couple of times, ending it with a dramatic *ah* sound and laughing.

'Okay, whatever, that's fine, of course.'

'They've just moved here, so it would be nice to introduce her to some of the ladies.'

'Yeah, sure, if I remember, but it's not like I don't have quite a lot on my mind today.'

'I know, babe. Just, you know, the husband is the new CEO at Norbank, so it would be good to get in there with the wife.' I nod. I get it. Andreas and his scheming. It's always the same thing: *be friends with this wife, and that wife, let's have these goons over for a snooze fest of a dinner party*. I thank my lucky stars that I'm self-employed and eternally removed from the excruciating dullness of office politics. 'Be nice, honey,' he continues. 'You know it's not that easy being new in another country.'

I glance around at my house and my huge garden and suddenly a vivid image comes to me of the first time I ever saw it, six years ago when we arrived in Wimbledon from Oslo. I felt like a fish out of water, having had to leave everything behind and uproot my children, even quitting my job as a newly qualified doctor so that Andreas could pursue his dream in the City. I thought I'd never be happy here, but then I was swept into a wonderful, tight-knit community and decided to start a keto blog which ended up changing my whole life because, well, I suppose everybody needs something to do with their time. I became the Keto Queen, and, I suppose, some would say – the queen bee of the Scandinavian community of southwest London. I do remember those early days, though; especially the feeling of being completely unmoored from everything that had tethered me in my old life.

I snap back to the present and look from my house, by now a much-loved home, and up at the sky. A dark, bulbous cloud appears as if from nowhere, blocking the sun and casting dark shadows across the garden. I glance anxiously upwards – even a single drop of rain could ruin everything. I don't understand where this giant, terrible cloud has come from. The weather report said clear skies and twenty-three degrees all day—

'Charlotte. Stop it. Even you can't control the weather.'

But I want to. I want to control everything.

Andreas squeezes my arm and winks at me, then disappears off somewhere. I make my way back to the marquee and watch carefully as another apparently pre-teen waiter makes me another Arctic Kiss. I knock it back in a few big glugs, feeling the alcohol mercifully warm my insides. The guests are arriving in thirty minutes and my to-do list is substantial: make sure the kids are appropriately dressed and prepared to greet the guests on arrival, check on all the orchids positioned around the house, inspect the glasses to make sure none carry a half-moon lipstick stain from some other event – that happened once and, needless to say, was very upsetting.

I start upstairs, where the kids slouch silently on the sofa in the TV room behind their respective screens. Oscar's shirt has a stain on it. Madeleine is wearing jeans and a crop top and says 'Lol, no,' when I tell her to change immediately. My son knows better than to argue with me when I place a fresh pink shirt on the sofa next to him, but my daughter just stares at me defiantly and doesn't even back down when I give her the Look.

'Give it a rest, Mum,' she says. 'Seriously, you'd be so much more fun if you weren't so highly strung all the time.' Madeleine gets up and pushes past me, leaving her iPad playing its endless stream of TikTok videos on the table.

Everything goes to plan. Of course it does. The secret to a successful party is quite simply to think of every last detail, every single moment, so that there are no surprises. I really hate surprises. People arrive, bearing flowers and gifts and fawning over the house and the kids, who, to their credit, manage to greet everyone politely, even looking fairly groomed. The waiters circle the crowd smoothly, refilling glasses and offering canapés. Andreas and I talk to a couple of his colleagues and their wives, people we've known for years, and I even feel myself relax a little. My two best friends in London, Anette and Linda, have arrived, and we spend a long while, just the three of us, in a quiet spot at the bottom of the garden, perusing the crowd and the surreal event this actually is. It's so crazy to think that the blog I started as a bored expat housewife has grown into one of the biggest starch-critical blogs in the world, five cookbooks, a range of own-brand keto products, my own Norwegian prime time cookery show and now, the jewel in the crown – a major deal with Streamstar in my adopted country.

'You got this,' Linda says, squeezing my hand as the massive screen flickers to life and the orange Streamstar logo appears, followed by the trailer to the *Keto Queen* show, renamed *Viking Keto* for the UK market. The crowd cheers and a blur of faces turn around to locate me. Jax Myers, head of international development, raises his glass to me in a little private toast as the me on the screen launches into a punchy monologue about the evils of grains and pulses. 'Beans!' I scream from the screen, my amplified voice booming across the lawn. 'Only touch them if you want to flood your system with phytochemicals. All you actually need is *this*. And I'm going to show you how to change your life, Viking Keto style.' I'm holding up a huge slab of marble-veined rib eye steak, grinning widely, before dropping it down into a smoking pan.

After the trailer, there is thunderous applause, followed by loud chatter and more drinks and I lose Anette and Linda in the crowd. Andreas swoops in and plants a hard kiss on my cheek, and even the kids rush over for a hug. Andreas stays close to me as I move around the garden, speaking to old friends and industry contacts. He is noticeably in a supporting role this evening, letting me guide the conversations and laughing whenever I say something moderately funny; it's like he's switched on in a way he isn't behind closed doors, when we're alone, stripped of alcohol and fancy outfits and the upbeat company of others. He is like he was when we first met and I feel a stab of longing for the way he used to be with me, back then, because today, in this moment, it's just for show.

I nod at whatever my husband is saying, and take another glug of my Arctic Kiss, feeling pleasantly buzzy by now, and turn my eyes back to the laughing, smiling people that have descended on our garden to celebrate me, the sun bouncing off their Rolexes and huge diamond studs. The women are mostly dressed similarly to me, in white summer dresses, accessorized with discreet gold jewellery, diamonds, and coloured enamel Hermès bracelets. I scan the crowd gathered on the lawn and every single woman is wearing a variation of this Scandi-Sloane uniform. Except for one.

She's tall and very striking, with a wild halo of blond curls framing a tan, fine-featured face. She's wearing a bright-red trouser suit, casually unbuttoned to reveal a very low-cut silk camisole. She looks stylish and sexy and very out of place in the conservative white cotton dress crowd. She also looks like she couldn't care less about blending in, walking confidently toward us on towering gold Valentino shoes, watched by literally everyone.

'Oh, here they are. Bianka. Emil. Welcome, both of you. So glad you could make it.'

Bianka leans in and kisses my cheek, and it's a real kiss, not an air kiss. The way she smiles at me is genuine and open, and for the first time in ages I feel completely out of my depth in someone's company. I'm reminded of being back at school and suddenly being spoken to by one of the cool kids several grades above. I'm not often in the company of someone who doesn't seem to care about conforming, especially not here, with my mummy friends and Andreas's finance buddies – a sea of conformist conservatives.

'Charlotte. I'm so pleased to meet you. I'm a really big fan. I've followed you for a long time, and your approach has just made me feel so amazing.' One of the things I've often found strange as I have become increasingly high-profile, especially in Norway, is that it's like another version of me exists and always walks a few steps ahead of me, and it's this Charlotte people think they know. Bianka may have seen me on TV and smiling from the cover of my books. She knew how I talked and laughed and moved before we'd ever met, and yet I know nothing about her. Looking at her, I suddenly want to know everything. Bianka seems like the kind of person who brings a special energy to a room. I can tell that others notice it too; people glance over constantly as though needing to know where she is and whom she's talking to.

'What are you drinking?' asks Bianka, peering into my half-empty cocktail glass.

'An Arctic Kiss. Vodka and champagne, with a splash of lemon.'

'Sounds odd.' She laughs, and so do I. 'Can I try?' She takes the glass from me before waiting for a response and takes a little sip, her lips pressed to my lip gloss stain on the glass. Not afraid of germs, it would seem. She wrinkles her nose and shakes her head, reaching out to grab a glass of champagne from a passing waiter. Her husband and mine have faded into the crowd somewhere and I want to keep Bianka close to me; there's something about her and her energy I want to be near. She stands very close to me, though there's plenty of space on the lawn. I want to ask her a million questions, like why did you choose that outfit, how many times have you been in love, do you really feel as calm and confident inside as you look, what are you afraid of, does your husband make you laugh, like, really laugh?

I glance back up at her to find Bianka looking at me intently, her expression hard to read, perhaps wistful or slightly melancholic.

She leans in close before whispering straight into my ear. 'You know, you remind me of someone.' Her thick, wild hair comes to rest across my shoulder like a soft cashmere shawl and I have the sudden and strange sensation of wanting to touch it with my fingertips. I wait for her to continue, but just then a waiter steps directly in front of us and thrusts a tray toward us laden with canapés of salmon roe atop sliced cucumber. I shake my head, but Bianka takes two, sliding them both into her mouth and winking at me.

'This is all so perfect. A lot of prep must have gone into this,' she says when she's finished chewing. I want to ask her who I remind her of, but it's as though the strange feeling of intimacy that passed between us when she drank from my glass and whispered in my ear is gone and we're strangers again.

'Oh. Thank you. You know what it's like.'

'What's it like?'

'Oh. You know. Hosting events like this.'

'Nope. No idea.' She laughs, making several heads turn.

'No?'

'I'm not really much of a hostess. The idea of a bunch of people in my house is super stressful. I make Emil do everything. By the way, I love your house, it's just so beautiful.' Bianka glances appreciatively at our house, softly lit now although it is still light outside, long streaks of pink and violet dragging across an indigo summer sky. I try to get my head around what she's just said, about making her husband, the new CEO of Norbank, do everything when they have people over.

'I guess I just like it, looking after everyone. It's what I always wanted to do. You know, make sure everyone has what they need.'

Bianka smiles and grabs another couple of canapés from

a passing waiter and pops them in her mouth, one after the other. 'And who looks after you?'

It's a strange question and one I don't know how to answer. I get the feeling that Bianka does this, consciously cutting to the bone to ask what she really wants to know, to hell with convention and small talk. *Who looks after me?* Nobody looks after me, though I haven't really thought of it like that before. But it's true – I'm a wife, a mother, and a business owner. I look after everything and everyone all the time. No wonder I'm a control freak. Maybe my face shows that the question's hit home, because Bianka gives my arm a firm squeeze and smiles gently at me, a smile that suddenly makes me want to cry. I want to steer the conversation onto safer ground.

'How are you finding Wimbledon so far? Isn't it just the most fantastic place?'

'Oh yes, it's lovely,' says Bianka. 'And everyone seems so nice.'

'Yes, it really is the best community,' I say, my thoughts darting to when we had just arrived and I was welcomed so generously by Wimbledon's Scandi ladies. 'You must come to Scandi Ladies Night. And Thursday coffee in the village after drop off. And we could do lunch sometime.' I feel a little self-conscious even as I speak, like I have no friends and am way too eager to make Bianka one.

'Sure,' she says, and flashes me that wide smile again. 'I'm going to do a little round, say hi to everyone. Catch you later.'

'Wait,' I say, and she stops and turns back to me with a little exaggerated twirl, like a ballerina. 'Who do I remind you of?' Bianka laughs, a deep rumble erupting from her, and she takes several steps closer before leaning in to whisper in my ear. I laugh too; she's just so commanding. I take a sip of my drink and her breath brushes the hair around my ear when she speaks.

'This woman I used to sleep with,' she whispers. I splutter, spraying Bianka's cheek with champagne and vodka. She throws her head back and laughs again. 'Best sex I ever had,' she adds, much louder, and I sense the people standing close to us turn at the mention of sex.

She moves into the crowd, stopping several times on her way over to where Emil is standing amid a group of guys, talking and laughing, everyone's eyes on her still. I'm so shocked, I can barely move, but more than that, I suppose I'm amused and fascinated because I burst out laughing and I can't stop for a very long time, even when I get drawn into conversation with a group of ladies I know from the PTA at school, who are the radical opposite of Bianka; conventional, modest, boring.

It's past two a.m. and in my walk-in wardrobe I slip my dress off and hang it back up among the many similar white dresses. Andreas is in the bedroom, and rubs his face, looking exhausted and a little unsteady. I've always loved these moments with my husband, when we're finally alone after a party when everyone has gone home and we share a little gossip and debrief. They remind me of when we were first married, though almost everything else feels different now. Today was a big success, everyone said so, and like any good party it went on into the early hours, getting a little rowdy at the end, when Anette insisted on tequila slammers until Linda and her husband Richard eventually dragged her into a taxi.

Andreas and I go into the bathroom and stand at the side-by-side washbasins, our eyes meeting in the mirror.

'So. What did you think of Bianka?' asks Andreas before inserting his toothbrush into his mouth.

'I thought she was... interesting. She's certainly different.' An image of Bianka appears in my mind again, laughing unselfconsciously at my surprise at what she said. *This woman I used to sleep with...* I feel myself blush and bend down to splash water on my face. I wonder what Andreas would say if I told him what she said, but I know I won't.

Andreas nods, circling his mouth with the toothbrush, little bubbles appearing at the edges of his mouth. After a long while, he spits, rinses, then speaks.

'I mean, what's the story there? I wanted to speak to her more but there were so many people to catch up with that I didn't get a chance. Did you notice how much attention she got? It was like everyone was watching her.'

I nod and Andreas smiles at himself in the mirror, his straight, white teeth glinting.

'Yeah, I noticed that,' I say. 'She really is quite different. It was as though she just appeared from another universe. I can't really put my finger on it. It's like she just doesn't have the same references as my usual crowd, or that she doesn't care, rather. She was quite refreshing.'

Refreshing feels like a rather big understatement. I keep replaying in my mind the way she looked at me, and the brazenness of what she said. Usually, I'd instinctively dislike someone who takes up that much space, but there was something about Bianka that brought balance to her way of being; I think it was her perceptiveness, her fine-tuned ability to really see someone. Yes, that's it – I felt really seen by her. I glance at my husband and he meets my gaze in the mirror. I put my arms around his bare waist from behind and rest my head on his back. I want him to turn around, and respond to my touch. And yet, he never does. Like I knew he would, he breaks the embrace by removing my hands, turns me around to face him, then pulls me in for a quick hug.

'I'm heading to bed,' he says. I take a step closer, perhaps emboldened by Bianka's way of being, and place my hand on Andreas's chest, just above his heart.

'I'll be there in a sec,' I say. 'Don't go to sleep.'

I leave the bedroom and walk quickly across the cool parquet, then down the stairs. I can't go to bed without my little ritual, not even tonight when I'm happy and exhausted and still a little drunk. Downstairs, I turn off all the lights in my usual order, except for the gold antique window lamp which belonged to my mother. I always keep this light on. I stare into its bulb for a long moment, letting its light imprint itself on my retina, then I hurry back upstairs, irrationally uncomfortable at being in the vast space of interlinked living rooms in near darkness. In the bedroom, I slip beneath the covers and cozy up to Andreas.

'Hey baby,' I whisper, letting my right hand travel from his waist down across his buttocks, but even though I've been gone less than a couple of minutes, my husband is apparently already fast asleep. I feel the usual pang of disappointment – it's been so, so long since he's touched me. I lie back and watch the moon weave in and out of fast-moving, gauzy cloud, listening to the soft murmur of Andreas's breath.

Three

Charlotte

I wake after what can't have been more than a couple of hours of sleep. I feel surprisingly okay. I'm used to little rest and a full-on, productive life. I can hear the faint hum of family life from downstairs; our au pair Ayla will be busy getting the kids fed and off to school, and Andreas will have left already. I have a quick shower and by the time I've gotten dressed the house is quiet. I drive to the shopping centre by the train station and park my car, then I hop on the first Waterloo train, and manage to find a window seat. I watch the suburbs streak past in a blur of grey and brown outside, droplets of rain gathering into little rivers on the window glass. I look at my face reflected back to me, my hair still wet and my face bare of makeup, and am pleased to note that in spite of the very late night and the numerous drinks, I still look fairly fresh-faced and definitely younger than my forty-two years, no doubt thanks to my strict regime, which I have turned into a very successful career. And Botox, of course; lots of it.

The TV studio is in Vauxhall, just yards from the train station, and I'm greeted with hugs from the team, and a huge black Americano is shoved into my hand as they get to work on my face and hair. I pinch myself, glancing around the set as the team prepare me for the camera. Quite the contrast to the early days of my keto journey, when I struggled to find a decent mayonnaise without the satanic seed oils and realized I'd have to make it myself. And here we are today, about to shoot the ad for my own-brand version, which will launch at Waitrose next month.

Shooting the ad takes all morning and the director, Jules, keeps telling me to 'switch it on'. Take after take, I walk into the room clutching the bright-pink pot of my mayonnaise and say the same sentence: 'Believe me, you haven't had mayo until you've had *my* mayo.' And again and again, Jules shouts, 'Cut.'

'I'm wondering if what's missing is a sense of fun. You know, spontaneity. We need it to be just a little more peppy. Do you know what I mean?'

I nod, though I don't exactly know what he means. I open my mouth to object, to say that my mayo definitely isn't about fun, it's about quality and, frankly – skinny. My company, at the end of the day, is always going to be about skinny. Then something occurs to me: How about if we could make skinny fun? It's the eternal struggle in my industry – control and discipline aren't exactly synonymous with fun, but what if we could angle it so the consumer feels it could be?

Suddenly, Bianka appears in my mind. How would this ad look if it was *her* own-brand mayonnaise, if *she* was the

Keto Queen, not me? I imagine she'd make it peppy. Fun. I decide to take a leaf out of her book.

'I'm ready,' I say to Jules, who's peering at the reels on his Mac, frowning. 'You're right,' I continue. 'We need to make it lighter, more sassy. Like this tube of mayo is the thing that makes an otherwise rigid diet feel indulgent. Fun.'

'Yes,' says Jules, excitement in his eyes. 'That's it exactly.' I stand up and release my hair from its usual tight bun, letting it flow around my shoulders. Jules whistles softly and laughs.

'Can you give me a red lip?' I ask the makeup artist, Elias, who's Jules's boyfriend. He nods excitedly and begins rifling through his arsenal of lipsticks before settling on a bold scarlet.

'Let's do this,' I say when he's done, lingering for a moment in front of this new me in the mirror. I realize that I look much more like my mother, who was never afraid of taking up space and was no stranger to a bright-red lip, but instantly swat that thought away.

The camera starts to roll and Jules counts down from five. Instead of the scripted line, I improvise. In my mind, I see Bianka, laughing unselfconsciously, claiming the centre stage at a party full of strangers, blatantly ignoring the unspoken dress code and drinking from the hostess's glass without even waiting for permission.

'Are you ready to feel like you're breaking all the rules? Isn't it time to bring *fun* into keto?'

'And cut,' shouts Jules, theatrically clapping his smooth, well-kept hands, face beaming. 'Nailed it. You should do carefree and sexy more often. Suits ya.'

I laugh and hang out with the crew for another hour, before checking my phone – it's been hours since I even glanced at it and I need to ask Ayla to handle dinner and take Oscar to tennis practice. There's a friend request on Facebook from Bianka Langeland and a message on Messenger reading *So, when are we going to hang out?* I place the phone back in my bag and smile at Elias, feeling my face flush behind the veneer of the thick foundation.

Four

Storm

The plane takes off with an unexpected lurch followed by several minutes of noticeable turbulence, and though he noticed a brisk wind when he stepped out of the school bus which had brought him to the airport, Storm sits up straighter in his window seat at the back of the plane and presses his face to the plastic glass to calm his suddenly racing heart. After a couple of minutes, the plane turns sharply west, giving a clear view of central Oslo, and Storm busies himself picking out the landmarks he knows: Tryvann tower in the woods at the top of the city; the museum island of Bygdøy with its real estate coveted by Norway's billionaires; the huge, symmetrical Vigeland park dominating the western city centre. From his vantage point and thanks to the beautiful weather, Storm can see all the way to the mountains north of Oslo, and he's able to pick out one of the distinctive peaks not far from his school; it has a curious, twisted summit, making it easily recognizable.

Storm reflects on the two weeks since his father and

Bianka moved to London and sent him to school in Lillehammer. He'd both wanted to go and felt resentful at having to, especially since Bianka had seemed so excited about the opportunity in London. His father had at least had the decency to hesitate over the job offer and what it might mean for his son, who not only still lived at home, but also had a place on the Norwegian national Super G ski team and most certainly wouldn't be able to come with them for such a move. And Bianka had seemed like she couldn't get away from Oslo, and her job, and – Storm supposes – her stepson, soon enough.

The last two weeks had been good. Great, even. He'd found that in spite of his reticence it felt right to be surrounded by other kids pursuing their sport at the same level as him. For years, he'd been used to being the odd one out at his old school, the one who had to miss classes for weeks on end in the winter when he travelled to various locations for competitions. When his classmates listened to the slow Texan drawl of Miss Kemp in English class or copied Mr Eskildsen's incomprehensible geometrical shapes in math class, Storm would be hurtling down a mountain in Courchevel or Innsbruck or Cortina, closely watched by Europe's sports media. In PE class at school, he'd often have to go for a gentle jog or do adapted exercises to avoid sustaining a freak injury in an innocent game of softball. But now, at the new sports college, Storm finds himself surrounded by others like himself, kids who'll compete at the world championships and the Olympics, and who are as focused and diligent as he is.

He's enjoyed being out of the city, too; it has felt like getting rid of an annoying bottleneck in his life – the constant driving between his home in the capital to the cabin in Valdres where he trained as a boy with his father almost every single weekend. As the flight settles into a smooth purr at cruising altitude and Norway's jagged south coast disappears from view, Storm tries to imagine what the next few days might hold. He's never been to London before; he has never really been anywhere that doesn't have freshly prepped world-class powder.

His father parks almost self-consciously in front of a grand house with creeping ivy and merrily lit windows overlooking a charming garden. It occurs to Storm that this is the first time he's seeing his father and stepmother's home, and that they have a new life entirely removed from him now. As they approach the front door, it swings open inwards and there stands Bianka, wearing a strangely dressy light-blue outfit and high heels, beaming. Storm brings to mind the tired-looking Bianka who worked full time in an office in Oslo, rarely seen without jeans and sneakers.

'Storm,' she coos, and pulls him into a hug. 'Welcome. Let me show you your room.'

He steps into the house and takes in the black-and-white tiled floor, the heavy chandelier spilling light into the furthest reaches of the room, the carved wood staircase disappearing into the gloom of the upper levels of the house.

'Over here,' she says, opening a door off the hallway. Storm steps into a small, unadorned room, the kind usually used for storing boxes or perhaps turned into a guest bathroom, though it has a lovely view of the garden, now shimmering softly in the late-afternoon light. He feels

Bianka watching him as he takes in the room, scanning his face for a reaction, but he gives her none.

'Uh, honey, I thought we'd put Storm in the big green room upstairs. Opposite us,' says Emil.

'No,' says Bianka. 'He'll be much more comfortable down here. You know teenagers; they need their own space.'

'B, I'm going to put him upstairs. I've already prepared it for him. He gets plenty of space to himself these days. Come on, Storm.' Storm turns away from Bianka and follows his father up the stairs and feels his heart pick up its pace in anticipation of Bianka's reaction, but she says nothing. The room upstairs is huge and airy, with unbroken views across the back garden which borders what looks like a huge park or a nature reserve. The bed has been made up with his familiar favourite childhood bedsheets and it's this detail that gives Storm a lump in his throat.

'Check it out,' says his dad, pointing to two huge cardboard boxes standing next to a beautiful shiny wooden desk over by the windows. 'A surprise for you.' He catches sight of Bianka's look of shock; she clearly had had no idea Emil had gotten him something. He walks over to the boxes and opens them. The first contains a gaming monitor, the one he'd wanted for Christmas but didn't get, and the second contains the newest, just-released PlayStation console, almost impossible to get hold of in Norway.

'Wow,' says Storm.

'Yeah. Wow,' says Bianka and walks out of the room.

The sound of angry voices, or one angry voice, rather, travels through the big house all the way up to Storm's bedroom.

He listens to music while playing FIFA but every now and again he removes an AirPod to check whether they're still at it. He feels a rush of anger at the sound of Bianka's shrill voice, and another at the meek murmur of his father in the few gaps Bianka leaves him to speak. He knows that they're fighting about this evening's dinner party at the house of his father's colleague. Storm has said he won't go and Bianka is throwing shitfits about it. What he doesn't understand is why she can't just leave him be. He's not some trophy Bianka gets to drag along and show off, and he's most definitely not *her* trophy.

It goes quiet. Storm listens for a long while but the house is quiet and the only sound is the tinny voice of Vinni, still playing from his headphones. She'll have gotten her way, she never stops until she does. He imagines her in this moment, in the bathroom, getting started on her meticulous grooming routine. She'll stand in front of the mirror, a self-satisfied smile playing on her lips, before applying mascara with a trembling hand, anger still coursing through her. She'll tease her unruly hair into a carefully arranged mess that apparently is supposed to look like she's never brushed it. She'll paint her lips with a slick of bright-red lipstick, a shade so far removed from the natural palette of human lip colours that it looks completely ridiculous, just another of Bianka's many attention-grabbing tricks, thinks Storm. He shudders at the thought of his father pressing his lips to hers, which he seems to want to do all the time.

Just like Storm knew she would, when she is completely ready, she calls his name in her singsong voice, as though she isn't quite aware that he'll have heard the past hour's tantrum. As though he still lives under her roof. Storm shudders at the thought and he feels a sharp yearning for his room at school, overlooking the slopes of Hafjell, shared with a nice golfer called Albert, from Bergen.

Her voice rises up the stairs to where he sits, first once, then twice more, a vein of irritation apparent in the third attempt. He has his headphones in but their volume is muted. He will make her come all the way up, her face reddening with the effort, haloed by her bouncy platinum curls. She'll knock briefly once, then burst into the room as though hoping to catch him at something unsavoury, like rolling a joint or watching porn. He'll be slumped over in his chair, pretending to be listening to music and that he hasn't heard her repeat calls. He'll smile blandly at her in the way he knows infuriates her, just the way he used to at home in Oslo, and rise slowly, following her down the hallway, shuffling his feet.

Instead, it's his father that comes. His face bears an expression of exasperation.

'Storm. Come on. Bianka has been calling you. We're leaving.' Storm removes his earphones and focuses on keeping his face open and amiable.

'Hi, Dad. Oh, sorry. I didn't hear her.'

'Storm.'

'What?'

'Can you just try not to frustrate her? Please?'

His father glances at his outfit – slouchy sweatpants and a faded grey T-shirt with Pete Davidson's face stretched across his chest – but says nothing. Storm follows behind Emil down the stairs, steeling himself for the moment he comes face to face with Bianka. She's standing by the entrance door, looking at her own reflection in the mirror in the hallway. She's wearing a green dress, the colour of poison, thinks Storm.

'Nice dress,' he says, unable to keep the sarcasm from his voice, and Emil shoots him a sharp glance.

'You look beautiful, baby, as always,' says Emil, and wraps his arms around Bianka from behind.

'He's not wearing that,' Bianka says to Emil as though Storm isn't standing right there.

'Storm, I think your, uh, Bianka's right. It's probably a good idea to change.'

'You said I could wear this.'

Bianka rolls her eyes at Storm, then sweetens her expression and looks up at Emil. 'Honey, please. Surely we should all dress vaguely presentably.'

Storm slowly walks back up the stairs, taking care to hold his head high; he knows it infuriates Bianka that she never gets a real rise out of him. Showing his fury would imply he cares on some level, and Storm quite simply does not.

It's not far, but they take a taxi as Bianka won't walk. Storm stares out of the window at the unfamiliar streets, and the pubs with their outdoor terraces overflowing with people who seem to have stopped by on the way home from work. There's a buzzy atmosphere, far removed from the quiet suburban streets of Slemdal where he grew up, or the mountains of Lillehammer where he now lives.

The people whose boring dinner he's being forced to attend are clearly quite well-to-do; as the car turns down another residential road, Storm notices that there aren't any smaller terraced houses or semi-detached ones like the ones he saw on the way here, only huge villas set back from the road in lush, vast gardens with pristine lawns and manicured hedges. Storm peers out the window as the taxi comes to a stop in front of a particularly impressive house, its blond stone facade beautifully lit by expensive-looking spotlights. They are buzzed through the gate and he waits for Emil and Bianka to start walking up the gravelled driveway before following them several steps behind. As they approach, the door swings open and two women beam at them. On closer inspection, Storm realizes they are mother and daughter, and the daughter is hot as all hell.

She smiles at him and he returns her smile, feeling a flush of heat creep up his neck, and is suddenly grateful to Bianka for basically forcing him to change clothes. He can't even bear to think how awkward he would have felt turning up at this girl's house in sweatpants and a stained T-shirt with Pete Davidson's goofy grin printed on it.

'Hey, I'm Madeleine,' she says.

Storm shakes Madeleine's mother's hand, then greets Madeleine with a little wave.

'Storm,' he says.

'I know,' she says, giggling nervously, and he realizes that most Norwegian kids his age probably have heard of him at this point. She leans in and gives him a quick hug, leaving a fresh floral scent in the air. Storm's heart lurches in his chest. He feels hugely more positive about the prospect of dining at his father's business associate's house.

'I'm so glad you came,' says Madeleine, out of earshot of the adults, who have continued down the hallway into a reception room where Madeleine's father is wrenching the cork off a bottle of champagne. 'My family is, like, insanely dull. And the other kids here are equally dull.'

'Uh. Yeah. My family too,' says Storm.

'At least your mom looks super cool. Mine is all prissy and uptight. She always wears some variation of the same thing.'

'Oh,' he says. He's going to need to up his game here and work on his conversational skills if he's going to impress Madeleine. He follows her awkwardly into the kitchen where a younger kid is watching something on an iPad, but looks up to give them a quick wave.

'Let's hide out in here until it's time to eat,' says Madeleine, flashing him another one of her wide, brilliant smiles. 'Want a drink?'

'Sure.'

Madeleine opens the refrigerator and takes out two cans of Coke Zero. She pours them into wine glasses, expensive crystal ones similar to the ones Bianka kept locked away in a cabinet at home in Oslo. She clinks her glass softly against his and takes a sip.

'You know, I was really psyched you were coming. Like, I knew who you were and everything, and my brother idolizes you. He's really shy, that's why he's just hiding behind the screen. Right, Oscar?' The boy's face darkens into a deep red and Storm feels bad for him. He smiles and waves at the younger boy, who drops his gaze back to the screen. 'What you did in St Anton was, like, beyond sick,' she continues.

'Uh. You heard about that?' He feels stupid as soon as he speaks and his cheeks grow hot.

Madeleine laughs, not unkindly. 'Storm, everyone heard about that. It was all anyone could talk about for weeks.'

Storm supposes this is true. He did, after all, get invited to the royal palace on his return to Norway, so the king could personally shake his hand at an event for extraordinary people in sports and culture.

'Um, so, yeah. Thanks. It was, uh, pretty cool, I guess.' Storm can feel himself blush even more as he speaks and realizes just how far out of his depth he is. He's never taken much interest in girls up until now, except to perhaps notice who he finds remotely attractive, but he's never felt this intense awkwardness around anyone before.

Madeleine's mom, an energetic-looking angular woman with thick dark hair piled atop her head, comes to tell them that dinner is served. In the dining room, there are two tables, one for the adults and another for the kids. Storm is relieved to not have to sit anywhere near Bianka or his dad. Other guests have arrived too, a woman with a red-haired daughter who's much younger than the other kids, and a couple with a son around Oscar's age. Madeleine sits next to Storm, pulling her chair closer to his. Throughout the meal, the little red-haired girl peers down at an iPhone barely concealed beneath the tablecloth. The younger boys speak quietly but animatedly among themselves.

'Geek fest,' whispers Madeleine, though she doesn't need to lower her voice – the adults are several bottles of wine in by now and laughing constantly and raucously, Bianka's voice rising above all the others with her shrill, hollow laugh.

'Watch my mom pretend to eat,' whispers Madeleine, her eyes glinting conspiratorially. Storm looks over at the main table, and, sure enough, Madeleine's mom really is pretending to eat – she's squared up her duck breast into tiny little pieces she pushes around on her plate, in and out of the jus, then pretends to take a bite, but the piece of meat is still speared on the fork and brought back down to the plate. She repeats the charade again and again. 'Fascinating, huh?'

Storm smiles and nods. 'Why does she do that? The food is so good. Like, I never get food this good at home. Or at school.'

'Because she's an obsessive control freak who structures her entire life around being skinny.'

'Woah. That's, uh, not great.'

'Nope.'

Bianka, on the other hand, is chewing merrily and taking big gulps of her wine. Whenever Madeleine's mom speaks or turns toward her, Bianka smiles slowly, tilting her head, or laughs loudly at the most moderately funny little comment.

'Total mutual fangirl vibes going on there,' says Madeleine.

'Mmm,' he says.

'Like, my mom hasn't shut up about Bianka since they met. It's Bianka this, Bianka that. She refers to her as Beautiful Bianka. How cringe is that?'

'Yeah, that's fucked up.'

'My mom thinks she's so *interesting* and *different*, apparently.'

'Yeah, Bianka says the same about your mom. And my dad says she's, like, stopped eating carbs or whatever.' They both giggle.

Storm follows Madeleine's gaze over to Bianka, who's sitting facing them but hasn't looked toward the kids' table a single time that he's noticed. Bianka's eyes are locked on

Madeleine's mom. *Beautiful Bianka*. Storm tries to see her as others might, as interesting and different and beautiful, but no matter what, he can't compute that someone would refer to Bianka as any of those things, especially beautiful. Or maybe he just can't see past what she's like inside to be a fair judge of the outside. But they go hand in hand, don't they? Storm thinks they do, in any case, and what he likes about Madeleine is that her undeniable outer beauty is enhanced by the mischievous glint in her eyes and her frequent, unselfconscious laughter.

Madeleine's mom, too, Storm recognizes as beautiful. She's a petite woman and almost regal in the way she carries herself, the kind of person who holds the attention of a room without having to try. He knows who she is, because since he's arrived in London, Bianka hasn't shut up about her 'NBF'. When he stared at her the first time she said it, she helpfully translated for him, explaining it means New Best Friend, in case he didn't know. And every time she says NBF, Storm cringes all the way down into his core – do fortysomethings really have to adopt the slang abbreviations of Gen Z? Can't she just refer to her as, *Charlotte, a new friend of mine.*

The plates are cleared from the table by a young woman and the adults stand up unsteadily and file outside onto the terrace. Through the windows, Storm can see the flash of several lighters, then the pinprick tips of skinny cigarettes moving around.

'Urgh, seriously, she barely eats but has no problem lighting up. So gross,' says Madeleine, walking out of the dining room and down a long hallway, motioning for Storm to follow. 'Come,' she says, 'let's fix ourselves dessert.'

***

In the attic, among carefully labelled and stacked cardboard boxes, Madeleine and Storm sit close together, leaning their backs on the cool stone chimney that runs up through the house. From a plastic bag hidden in one of the boxes, labelled 'winter boots', Madeleine retrieves a packet of gummy bears and a big tray of ultra-processed American cookies with rainbow-colored chunks of marshmallows embedded in them.

'I have to hide these from my mom,' she says, pinching a cookie from the tray after offering them to Storm.

'Would she go crazy?'

'Yeah, totally. You know, she's the Keto Queen and, oh boy, do we all know it. No carbs allowed in this house.'

'What, none at all?'

'Nope.'

Storm picks up the bag of gummy bears and realizes they're marijuana gummies.

'Woah, where did you get these?'

'Internet. Have one.'

'My dad would go so crazy.'

'So? He'll never know.'

'What would your parents do if they found them?'

'My mom would go way crazier over the cookies, believe me. The gummies are sugar-free.'

'That's fucked up.'

'Yeah. Aren't most people's parents fucked up, though?'

'I guess,' says Storm, feeling the gentle and almost instant release of the marijuana spread out in his system, loosening him.

'Yours does seem pretty cool, though.'

'Bianka's not my mom,' he says, his voice suddenly loud in the hushed, cosy space.

'Oh. I just assumed… I heard your dad say "our son", like, whatever.'

'Yeah, they do that.'

'Do what?' Madeleine's pretty, gentle face looks puzzled.

'Pretend like my mom doesn't exist.'

'So… Where is your mom?'

'She died when I was three.' Storm realizes he's never told anyone this before. His friends at home have always just known, and it's never come up with his new friends at school – when they're there, it's as though home and family and everything outside of their bubble just ceases to exist.

'Woah. That's fucked up.'

'Yeah.'

'I'm so sorry.'

'It's okay.'

'Can I ask what happened to her?'

'She died in a freak accident in the mountains near our cabin in Valdres. Lost her footing and fell down the side of Rasletind mountain.'

'Oh my God.'

Storm nods. It feels good to talk about what happened to his mother; he never feels like he can bring her up at home and his father and Bianka never mention her at all.

Madeleine picks up his hand from where it lies on the dusty floorboard, then quickly releases it, as though it was a ridiculous impulse. He takes her fingers again and smiles at her. She smiles too, and Storm mentally high-fives himself.

Five

Bianka

The opportunity presents itself in a little lull between dessert and coffee. The kids have disappeared off somewhere and Charlotte has gone into the kitchen, from which Bianka can make out the rise and fall of her voice as she gives instructions to her au pair. Bianka excuses herself and stands up slowly, well aware of her unsteadiness from the amounts of wine consumed at dinner. It felt like every time she'd taken a couple of sips from her glass, it was smoothly topped up, making her lose track of how much she'd actually had.

She steps into the large hallway, where a stunning staircase wraps itself around a central gallery and, after glancing around, makes her way up to the first floor. There is a landing halfway up where the stairs branch out left and right, with large windows looking out over the lawns, and she can hear the men chuckling on the terrace directly below. She imagines observing last weekend's Streamstar party from up here, a little bird watching the moments unfold as she met Charlotte Vinge for the first time. She could tell immediately that the chemistry she'd hoped for carried through from fantasy into real life, and that Charlotte was immediately taken with her. Or her carefully honed persona, rather. It was working out well so far, this new life.

Upstairs, there is a long corridor carpeted in a plush, thick beige and Bianka wonders how anyone with children could manage to keep it looking pristine. After making sure she's alone, she moves quickly down the corridor to the master bedroom; it doesn't take a rocket scientist to surmise it'll be the biggest room at the front of the house. If she's interrupted by anyone, she'll say she felt unwell and decided to look for somewhere quiet to lie down for a minute. The room is huge and hushed, decorated in muted, grown-up shades of taupe. Bianka feels a pang of disappointment; she hoped that Charlotte's bedroom might reveal something surprising about her, something that would penetrate the gilded picture painted of a high-achieving perfectionist. She'd hoped for a daring nude on a wall or an unmade bed or a pile of dirty clothes in a corner, but there is none of that. It looks like a hotel room.

Bianka walks over to the window and peers outside. She can make out Charlotte's voice outside, too – good. But she doesn't have long; someone will come looking if she doesn't return in the next few minutes. There's a built-in vanity table opposite the bed, with a little dusty-pink silk stool that looks like nobody has ever sat on it, but Bianka sits on it now, feeling a deep thrill spread out in the pit of her stomach at the mischief of it. She opens the three drawers of the table in turn. In the first she finds a few expensive sample-sized face creams. In the second, a ring with a large diamond solitaire, casually deposited in a drawer. In the third, a tangle of slinky necklaces. Bianka glances around again, holds her breath, and separates one, a plain silver chain, from the others. She slips it into the cup of her bra, where it can be hidden, warmed by her breast.

She picks up a photograph of a much-younger and less polished-looking Charlotte and angles it to better catch the sliver of light from the hallway. She closes her eyes and makes sure she retains the image and can still see her beautiful face in her mind. Then she takes a picture of it on her phone, to be sure. The resemblance that initially caught her attention is unnerving, though it's diluted a little in mannerisms and ways of speech – and it's at its clearest in photographs.

'What would you say if you could see me now?' whispers Bianka into the heavy, discreetly fragrant air of the bedroom, feeling silly for speaking out loud, but continuing nonetheless. 'Oh, baby... I think you'd laugh, at the absurdity of it all. At me, of all people, in a crowd of bankers and their spoiled wives. Wouldn't you? I try to remember your laugh, but I can't.'

Bianka places the picture down in the exact same position it had stood and wipes a single tear meandering down her cheek. Enough. She meets her own eyes in the mirror and has to consciously adjust her expression back to 'fun, outgoing, centre-of-attention Bianka'. That's who she is now.

Then she goes back downstairs, the necklace coiled around itself and pressed tight against her breast.

Six

Charlotte

I sit down at my vanity table, wiping my makeup off with micellar water as Andreas steps out of his pants and loosens his tie.

'I thought that went well,' I say and smile at him in the mirror.

'Yeah, definitely. I think everyone enjoyed themselves.'

'So, what do you think of Emil now he's been at the office for a couple of weeks?'

'He's cool. Definitely knows what he's doing. He's a funny guy, though, isn't he? Hard to read.'

'In what way?'

'Just, he seems so relaxed and easy going privately. You know, the way he is with his wife and son – it just seems like he's happy to go with the flow. But at work, he's much more authoritative. He's only been at Norbank a few weeks but is already talking of ways of "streamlining operations" and "optimizing output". That obviously means cuts.'

'You think?'

'Oh, yeah.'

'Well. It's not like they'd ever get rid of you. I mean, you're indispensable.'

'Charlotte, if there is one thing I've learned, it's that nobody is ever indispensable. Especially once you start getting very expensive.'

'I'm seeing Bianka again at some point this week. I guess I can fish around a little for more information.'

'I doubt she'd know anything. And besides, it would come across really obvious. Honestly, the best thing we can do is to solidify a good friendship with them outside of work. And that doesn't feel like much of a chore. I think they're both pretty cool.'

'Yeah.'

'You like her a lot, right? Bianka?'

'Yes. I like that she's a little different. She just doesn't seem to care about all those little social rules the rest of us spend so much time on. I'm planning on introducing her to some more people in the next couple of weeks. I imagine it isn't that easy to meet people when you don't have kids at the school.'

'Good. Actually, do you know what I was thinking? Why don't you invite her to Ibiza with the girls?'

My mouth literally drops open at Andreas's suggestion.

'What...' I whisper.

'Don't look so utterly horrified, babe. Just a suggestion. I think you'd benefit from some fresh blood in that group of friends.'

'I...' I actually struggle to find words, which doesn't happen to me very often. Every year for years now, Linda and Anette and I go to our house in Ibiza the third week of June and open it for the season. It has long become a tradition, one we cherish increasingly for every year that goes past. It started with Anette and I when we both still lived in Oslo, and then Linda started joining us after we reconnected when we'd all ended up moving to London. Though many people associate Ibiza with partying, we lie low and focus on re-centring ourselves during this short break from our gruelling lives in Wimbledon. We do yoga every morning on a wooden platform overlooking the Mediterranean. We eat simply and spend long afternoons on the terraces, journalling and dozing. We go out for a couple of early, casual dinners at the local beach clubs.

'Andreas, that's not possible. We have a tradition. I'm not going to suddenly invite a fourth person none of us know well – it would give the whole week a completely different vibe.'

'Exactly. Might be fun.'

'The week in Ibiza isn't about fun.'

'Why not?'

'Andreas. Let's just drop it, okay? I like her. Let's totally have them over for dinner again and, I understand that it would be a good idea to be friends with her. But she can't come to Ibiza. Obviously.'

'Charlotte, all I'm saying is, maybe you should let loose a little more. You're only just forty, but you and your girlfriends sometimes behave like you're a decade older. You're allowed to just… have some fun. Bianka would help with that; she seems pretty wild.'

'What does that even mean? Maybe I should let loose a little more?' I'm super loose. Relaxed as all hell. I have so much fun with my girlfriends that there is simply no way

I can squeeze in any more fun. How dare Andreas suggest that I need to have more fun? Has he even seen my social schedule? He shrugs and leans in to peck me on the cheek but I'm trembling with fury at his words.

Maybe you should make love to me a little more, I think to myself, watching my husband disappear down the hallway toward the spare bedroom. And he has the nerve to say that I behave like I'm a decade older. I go after him. He turns around in surprise when I place my hand on his bare lower back. I pull him close and kiss him hard on the mouth, prizing his mouth open with my tongue but he pulls back and looks at me.

'Charlotte, what are you doing?'

'I think you should come to bed with me,' I whisper, pushing my lower body, clad only in a silk camisole, into his. 'I think you're right, about having more fun. Let's have some fun.'

'Babe, it's almost one a.m. on a school night. I have meetings all day tomorrow.' My husband leans in and gives me a chaste, brotherly kiss on the cheek.

'Why don't you sleep in with me tonight? Andreas, come on. Please. I'd like that.'

My husband sighs deeply, as if asking him to sleep beside me is such a chore. 'Charlotte, you know it's best if I go down the hall when I'm going in to the City in the morning.'

Alone in bed as usual, I can't sleep. Thoughts chase through my mind like little storms; how did we get here, to a place where we don't share a bed during the week because Andreas needs his 'rest'; where the mention of having fun hits home so hard because I know it's true, that my life is predictable and controlled and ordered, with little room for spontaneity or so-called fun. If I'm honest, the idea of fun terrifies me, and doesn't sound like fun at all. It seems synonymous with breaking rules and slipping up and losing control – my very idea of hell. When I try to picture what fun might look like, I see things like the strobing neon lights of crowded nightclubs, feeling the beat of the music reverberate throughout your body so you can't help but dance. Or nights in sweatpants on the sofa, eating pizza straight from the box, followed by pick-and-mix candy, and beer, even. Not that I would ever do either of those things.

Besides, those are hardly fun activities, just dirty and chaotic. But I see Bianka, too, in her crazy vermilion trouser suit in a sea of prissy white cotton dresses, her wild platinum curls standing out among the poker-straight, honey-blond hair of everyone else. And tonight, at dinner, the way she looked at me as though I were an amuse bouche when she sat back down for dessert, making me suddenly aware of the tiny hairs down the length of my spine, standing up.

In the morning I run, circling Cannizaro Park several times, and though the weather is lovely, there is thick mud in parts from this week's rain and by the time I finish, I'm filthy and lethargic. Anette and Linda are waiting for me in the café of the hotel lobby, where we meet at least three times a week after drop-off. I sink into the plush seat and as soon as he sees me, the waiter sets about making what I always have – a double black Americano. No cheat days for the Keto Queen. I've summoned Anette and Linda here; we weren't due to meet until tomorrow but I knew this couldn't wait – Ibiza is coming up. I've been up all night turning Andreas's suggestion over and over in my head. At first I thought it was utterly insane, quite a shocking suggestion, but the more I considered it, the more I recognized that the strange feeling in my stomach was unmistakably excitement at the prospect. I tried to imagine the usual set-up; Anette, Linda and me whiling away the days in cushy, slow luxury with interiors magazines, expensive albariños and tons of yoga. I don't want that, not anymore. I've realized that Andreas is right – we need to mix it up a little. We need to have fun.

'God, you look wiped,' says Linda, who of course looks as serene as always.

'Mmm,' says Anette, shooting a rather horrified glance at my mud-splattered yellow tights. 'Did you fall over?'

I pick up my coffee and take a long, delicious sip, and then smile graciously at my girlfriends.

'So. I've been thinking. We need to finalize plans for Ibiza, and—'

'What is there to plan?' asks Anette. 'Same procedure as always, presumably?' Linda nods eagerly, almost aggressively, as though suggesting any changes at all might make her snap.

'Well. Yeah. Largely.'

'Largely?' An ominous flatness creeps into Anette's voice.

'I was thinking it might be fun to mix it up a little this year. I'd like to invite Bianka Langeland to join us.'

'What?' screams Anette.

'What?' whispers Linda, her sweet face suddenly very pale. 'Mix it up. Fun.' She repeats my words as though she's never heard them before.

'Yeah. Come on, guys. We don't want to grow stagnant, right?' Anette keeps opening and closing her mouth but she says nothing. Linda's eyes have filled with tears. 'Look,' I continue, taken aback by this extreme reaction, 'trust me on this one. I think it would work out really well. Bianka is so lovely and I really think she'd bring some fresh energy to our group and to the trip. Remember when the three of us went together for the first time? That was actually kind of random, too, and look how well that worked out.' I take a sip of my coffee and smile my brightest smile at Anette and Linda. Linda peers into her green tea and Anette looks as if she is still completely unable to speak. Then, slowly, she stands up and gathers her stuff together.

'Anette? What's happening? We need to talk about this,' I say. But she's walked out, her long, skinny legs covering the lobby of the Cannizaro Hotel in just a few furious strides. I raise my eyebrows at Linda, throwing my hands up in the air at the sheer ridiculousness of it all. We're planning a girls' trip to my house in Ibiza, not debating membership of the UN Security Council.

'I'd better, uh—' whispers Linda, indicating toward the doors, and standing up. She looks like she's about to have a seizure from sheer stress. 'I'm going to make sure Anette's okay.'

And so I find myself alone. I sip my coffee and replay the whole scene in my head. It's true that this trip has been a long-standing tradition between Anette, Linda and me, but this extreme resistance to change is something else entirely. I'm now totally sure that Andreas is right about inviting Bianka and I won't be made to feel bad about it. I pull out my phone and message her.

Hey, how's it going? Want to meet up?

She replies after just a few minutes.

Sure. How about we step outside the box? Meet me in Leyton at 7.

My heart begins to pound hard in my chest at her reply. I've lived in London for almost seven years and haven't exactly explored the city much. I tend to hang out in Wimbledon, Richmond, Chelsea and Kensington, so I have to look up Leyton on the map. I get the bill and half-run back to the house, feeling energized again at the prospect of meeting Bianka this evening.

Seven

Charlotte

She's waiting for me outside the Tube station at Leyton, a place I've never been before. Leyton is miles away from Wimbledon, and I'm intrigued, though not surprised that Bianka suggested meeting here. She told me the last time we met that she wants to 'get beneath London's skin'.

When Bianka explained that we were going to an avant-garde gallery opening out here, I was both unnerved and exhilarated in equal measures. Usually, when I meet with friends, it's to drink coffee in one of the bijou, self-conscious coffee roasteries in the village, or for a glass of wine on the King's Road or Mayfair, places we've come with our husbands and their work associates, and sometimes return to with our girlfriends.

Bianka is leaning against the side of a building, her face lighting up in a slow smile as she watches me approach. I imagine that most people waiting for someone would while away the time scrolling on their phone, but I suppose Bianka isn't most people; she just waits, seemingly without hurry or annoyance. We hug, and she links her arm through mine as we walk up toward the gallery opening, which is being held in what looks like an industrial warehouse wedged in between tall apartment buildings with hundreds of little balconies.

'So. Are you into art?' asks Bianka as we approach the warehouse.

'Yes,' I say. 'Well. I suppose you could say I grew up surrounded by it. My mother was a painter.'

'Oh, wow. That's very cool.'

'I—' I start to speak, but as has often been the case when it comes to my mother, I'm unable to continue, I just can't find the words. Bianka seems to notice and smoothly deflects.

'Here,' says Bianka, handing me a glass of lukewarm prosecco in a plastic glass. 'Oh, wow,' she continues. 'Check this stuff out. So beautiful. I've been wanting to see this for such a long time. Adler Heung was featured in *The Hub* magazine last year and I was just blown away by him, so when I heard he was coming to London this month, I was pretty excited.' I take in the pictures, and try to articulate some thoughts that would suggest that I'm someone who frequents art galleries and have an opinion about their offerings. They're evocative and laced with a savage beauty I can't quite describe or even process inside my head, but I find myself transfixed by his use of light.

There is a big crowd consisting mostly of trendy-looking people much younger than us, and suddenly I feel dowdy and outdated in my Ralph Lauren blouse and high-waisted jeans. Bianka looks like she belongs here with these fashionistas, dressed in a backless black dress and scruffy boots, her hair loose and wild. Her body is lithe and firm; I bet she finds it easy to maintain thanks to keto, as so many people have discovered. She said that I'm the one who got her to try it and that she loved it so much that she's stuck to it ever since. Still, I imagine she and I are quite different – Bianka strikes me as someone who eats for enjoyment, who unapologetically and unselfconsciously enjoys sex, who sees her body as a vessel for enjoyment. I want to be like her. Around her neck is a simple thin silver necklace, unadorned by any charms, and it looks really effortless and cool; though I have many similar necklaces, I would never have thought to wear one like that, just on its own.

We circle the room, then Bianka tops our glasses up to the brim from an abandoned half-full prosecco bottle on a table in the far corner.

'Let's get out of here,' she says, and though I'm surprised, I follow close behind as she pushes her way through the crowd, toward a side entrance. We step out onto a quiet residential street, and though the sky is totally dark now, the air is still warm.

'Hot in there,' says Bianka, and takes a sip of her prosecco, glancing down the empty street as if trying to think of what to do next. I don't want the night to end, to get back on the Tube and then in an Uber, to unlock the door to our house, I want something to happen, an adventure. And Bianka herself feels like an adventure. 'Let's walk,' she says, gesturing to a sign that reads Leyton Jubilee Park. We pass a primary school and a closed café and then the park is there, like a dark, unexplored country. I raise an eyebrow; I don't know this neighbourhood or how safe it is in the evening – is it a good idea to walk in the park at night drinking prosecco from open plastic containers? But I wanted an adventure and more time with Bianka, so I smile and fall into step with her as we head down a wide, gravelled path bordered by woods, past a playground, and a mini golf area.

'Tell me more about yourself,' says Bianka, stopping on the path before sitting down on a bench. I sit down beside her and she's staring at me as though I were an incredibly interesting creature, not an overworked, often-sad, exhausted mother of two and a wife who hasn't had sex with her husband in a very long time. It's as though she can read my mind because she reaches out and places a small, warm hand on my wrist and squeezes it. It feels like an oddly intimate thing to do, and like a gesture of real care, making me remember what she asked me the very first time we met at the party, *Who looks after you?* I feel embarrassed at the lump in my throat, the sheen of tears that spring to my eyes. I don't know what's happening. I'm not upset; I'm not the kind of person who loses control of her emotions and blubs to a stranger, but I'm also not someone who spends much time thinking about how or what I feel. Bianka doesn't look surprised or horrified at my strange display of emotion, triggered by an innocent request like 'Tell me about yourself'.

I decide to tell her something I never talk about, even to my closest friends.

'When I was fifteen my parents got divorced and my mother moved to Ibiza and basically never came back.'

'Wow,' says Bianka. 'The artist.'

'Yep. She was Spanish. Born on the island.'

'So what did you do?'

'I stayed in Norway with my dad. He was so broken and I didn't want to leave my friends. I threw myself into my schoolwork and just never stopped until I'd achieved everything I wanted. I was terrified of people feeling sorry for me. I still am.'

Bianka nods. 'So you ploughed all your efforts into achievement?'

'I suppose so. But I missed my mother so much.' I pause, thankful for the darkness hiding my burning cheeks. I have never spoken of that time or of my mother like this to anyone before.

'Where is she now?'

'She died a few years later, when I was twenty.'

'I'm so sorry.'

'Yeah. Thank you. It is what it is. But losing her is the hardest thing that ever happened to me. I used to lie awake at night wondering if it might have been different if I'd gone with her to Ibiza.'

'You can't think like that.'

'But I do.'

'How did she die?'

'In her sleep. Her heart just stopped. She was only fifty.'

'Jesus. I can't even imagine what that must have been like for you.'

I nod. It's true – she can't possibly imagine what that was like for me, I don't think I've ever met anyone who could. We fall silent for a long while; there doesn't seem to be anything more to say, though the silence is a peaceful, intimate one, not awkward or uncomfortable. Eventually I continue because I realize that for the first time, I feel comfortable talking to someone about her. Most of the time I just block her out.

'When I was small, she'd cry when I cried, and I knew

that she truly felt what I felt. When she laughed, she laughed loudly and made everyone else laugh, too. I took after my calm and quiet Protestant father. And yet, as a child, I adored my mother and it felt like an open current of energy ran between us, a strong, unseen channel of communication known only to us.' Since she died, I've never allowed myself to wallow in emotions or pay that much attention to feelings. I choose to be cool, calm, and always in control.

But now, just for a moment, I let in her memory, for the first time in so very long, and I can practically see her: walking up the path from the beach to her little finca farmhouse in the late-afternoon light of high summer, carrying a couple of rocks smoothed down by the ocean, picked from the surf. Her black hair, streaked silver, is piled atop her head and her bare face is the deep brown colour of someone who spends their life outside, gardening and painting. When she sees me, her face breaks into a brilliant smile, and it's the smile that gets to me – that I'll never see it again, that I'd forgotten it, or repressed it – that it was here, all along, inside me.

I snap out of the image and look into the clutch of tall, dark trees, and beyond, the colossal concrete apartment buildings at the far end of the park, asymmetrically lit, then at Bianka, whose face is shimmering in the soft light.

'I bet your mother would be very proud of you,' says Bianka, gently touching her plastic glass to mine before taking a long sip of her prosecco.

'Thank you. It helped to have my children. To feel truly rooted to someone again.'

'They seem like really great kids. And it looked like Storm and Madeleine took quite a shine to one another.'

We both smile.

'It did.' I can think of worse potential boyfriends for Madeleine than Storm Langeland, Norway's biggest youth ski star. 'Oh, I've been wanting to ask you more about Storm. He's just incredible, so impressive. Oscar idolizes him. What he achieved in St Anton was unbelievable.'

'Yes. He's very driven when it comes to the skiing. He's not like that at home, though. At all. He's usually throwing stuff around or playing Fortnite.' We laugh and the atmosphere between us feels light and conspiratorial, the shared experience of motherhood an instant bond. 'I've always imagined it must be amazing having a daughter.'

'It is. Terrifying, too.' I think of my daughter, my sweet and strong Madeleine. I think of her when she was a chubby, happy baby, with a bald head and toothless grin, and it never fails to give me a chill to take in that it's fifteen years ago. I'd give anything to hold that little baby and her brother in my arms one more time, to go back and really drink them in, instead of wishing them older or wallowing in exhaustion. I often feel like the best time of my life is already over, that it evaporated with the children's childhoods, and that the rest of my life will be a monotonous slog toward the horrors of old age and, eventually, death. I've seriously considered having a third child in an attempt to hold onto my youth but that's hardly the best reason to bring a new life into this world, and besides, I couldn't bear another nine months of obesity followed by what can only be described as attempted murder trying to get the baby out. Besides, my husband would have to have sex with me for another baby to even be a possibility, and he's making it pretty clear that he doesn't want to do that.

I feel Bianka's eyes on me, and again I have the feeling that she is truly interested in hearing about me.

'Terrifying how?'

I swallow hard and mentally return to the conversation about daughters.

'Well. Just... I guess I found being that age pretty difficult. So now I find myself constantly looking for signs of the same kinds of struggles in Madeleine. I know it's unfair, but it's impossible not to.'

'Difficult because of your mother?'

I nod. Again, I feel myself divulging something to this woman I have never told anyone, in fact, something I've spent the last two decades denying, even to myself. 'I coped with it by developing a serious eating disorder. My whole life became about control.' It still is, and sitting here with Bianka in the soft grey evening, in a random park across town, the ever-present hum of London like a backdrop to our conversation, I sense that she knows this, that she gets me in a way nobody ever has.

'That must have been so hard for you.'

I pause. It must have been, I guess, but I realize I have no idea, and no language for talking about it; I just never allowed myself any space to dwell on those years.

'I don't remember that much from those years.' I feel uncomfortable now and want to change the subject. It's as though I've suddenly emerged from a deep sleep only to realize that I've shared my deepest secrets in that unconscious state, leaving me exposed and vulnerable. But I can't deny it also felt good to talk about it. 'To be honest, the thing that helped in the end was keto. That's probably why I'm so obsessive about it. I feel like it saved me. It gave me something to do, firm boundaries, control. I love knowing exactly what I can and can't do all the time.' It's a deflection, but it's also the truth.

'How did you go from a teenager with an eating disorder to Norway's biggest lifestyle blog to a TV show and a bestselling range of own-brand products, though?' Bianka reels off my achievements in an exaggerated voice, making us both laugh.

'I'd wanted to be a doctor, so I went to med school, but I was in total denial about my own struggles. Then I had the children just after I qualified and got sucked into the storm of motherhood for years. I was going to start working when they were both in nursery but then Andreas got the transfer to London and I realized it was a good time to take some time to get myself healthier, in both mind and body. I got even more serious about keto and started blogging about it, and it just took off from there, really.'

'So you built an empire out of your fucked-up teen years. That's impressive.'

Bianka looks at me deadpan and I stare back, not sure whether to take offence. She's touching on a real truth; that my impressive career is in fact a veneer for my deeply ingrained and much-courted eating disorder. I might pretend that Keto Queen is all about optimal health and the best way of eating for our physiology, and the results speak for themselves, hence its success. I know deep down that it's more complicated on a personal level, but does it matter? I like to think that what matters is that I maintain a healthy weight and that my passion for a ketogenic lifestyle has blossomed into a successful career. And yet, sometimes I feel like such a phony and I yearn to tell someone that in spite of the fact that I make a living off my innovative and elaborate low-carb recipes, making a point out of turning pretty much anything keto, all I actually eat is steak and cabbage. I'm literally terrified of anything else and go to great lengths to conceal that these are the only two things that pass my lips. I consider telling Bianka but decide against it.

'I'm sorry, Charlotte,' she says. 'That probably came out wrong.'

'No, it's fine,' I say, and it is – in fact, it's incredibly refreshing that Bianka just says it as it is. 'You're absolutely right – I built an empire out of my fucked-up teenage years.'

Bianka clinks her glass against mine again and then we both erupt into laughter.

'I'm sorry you had to deal with all of that,' she says when we finally stop laughing and just sit side by side, smiling in the dark, pleasantly tipsy. She places a hand on my wrist and just lets it linger there, stroking the skin beneath the sleeve of my silk blouse. It feels deeply intimate and comforting, and suddenly I feel teary again.

'It's okay. It is what it is. I'm sorry to be such a mess; it really isn't my usual style to be all weepy and...'

'Please don't apologize. You're allowed to be a whole person, you know. I'm not only interested in the shiny, perfect Charlotte Vinge. I want to know the real person.'

It feels as though her words heal something that came loose inside of me a very long time ago and I realize how much I've missed having a very close friend. I do have Anette and Linda, but we never have conversations like this. We talk about kitchen refurb inspiration, our kids' achievements, Gucci belts, where to eat out in Cannes, that kind of thing. We don't talk about how we feel or how we came to be who we are. I feel a bolt of gratitude for the unexpected appearance of this woman in my life.

'Enough about me,' I say, as we start walking back toward Leyton and the Tube – it's getting chilly and our glasses are empty and tomorrow is another hardcore day with a photoshoot and a book signing. 'I want to know about you.'

'What do you want to know?'

'Just… everything. Like, tell me about the woman I reminded you of. You mentioned it the first time we met.'

'Ah.' Bianka chuckles a little. 'I've been waiting for you to ask about that. The look on your face was priceless.'

'So…?'

'She was my girlfriend. For years. Ended in tears.' I try to process this information and feel like I have a hundred follow-up questions, but Bianka swiftly changes the subject.

'You know, I lost my mother when I was very young, too.'

'Wow. Oh, my God.'

'Yes. So I understand how you felt. What you said really resonated with me. About having them one day, and the next they're gone forever.'

'What… What happened?' Bianka tilts her head back as though she is trying to stop tears from running down her face, and maybe that is what she's doing, and a splash of moonlight spreads out across her features. 'I mean, you don't have to tell me, of course.'

'I'll tell you another time,' she says, looking back at me, her eyes huge and sad. 'But I do understand.'

I nod.

She stops for a moment under a streetlight and just looks at me, smiling, the sadness of moments ago dissolved. The atmosphere between us feels charged, like there is something intangible between us that I can't grasp. The only comparison I have is to when I first met Andreas, when every thought of him brought a delicious shiver chasing the length of my spine. I imagine Bianka taking a step closer, then another, cupping my face with those soft, warm hands, and am surprised to realize I want her to; I want there to be nothing unsaid between us, no distance at all between her and me. I feel confused by this; I'm a married woman, I love my husband and our family. But I haven't been touched for so long. Nobody has looked at me like this for a long time. Until Bianka. And I want her to.

'Bianka,' I say, my voice light and soft, my heart beating hard and fast in my chest. 'I wondered about something. Every year, a couple of friends and I go to my house in Ibiza the third week of June. A girls' trip. I think you should join us.'

Eight

Bianka

Bianka feels a wave of annoyance as she presses *Start video call* on Skype, but it dissipates at the sight of Dr Matheson. In spite of everything, the therapist has a calming effect on her. Bianka sits all the way on the edge of her seat, leaning forward toward Dr Matheson. She keeps her hands tightly clasped in her lap to keep herself from wringing them. She has to use a lot of effort to appear vaguely calm and in control of herself, to not come across as too intense.

'I met someone. A woman. A new friend. She's… I need to talk about her. I can barely think of anything or anyone else. Not gonna lie, it's thrown me. At first, it was very obvious what drew me to her so strongly and instantly. It was like a bolt of lightning. She reminds me of someone.' Bianka has to swallow hard several times before continuing. '*Her*. You know who I mean.'

'Mmm.'

'So, at first, I thought it was just that – a painful reminder. Looking at her was like looking at everything I've lost and feeling like I could have it back. But then it became obvious that it was more than that. One person can't be another, right? And that's a good thing. She's special and she doesn't know it which makes her even more special. I can't think about anything else, it's as though she fills me up in all the spaces where before, there was nothing.'

'Nothing?'

'Yes, nothing.'

'But *you* were there. In those spaces. Inside yourself. You were already filling them. It was never nothing.'

'I guess. It's just… I've always felt so empty.'

'Yes, it's a feeling we've returned to many times.'

'And then suddenly, there she was and it's like being filled with this soft, glowing light. It's like being in love, only better.'

'Better?'

'Yes. Surely, female friendship is one of the strongest human connections there is.'

'Well, the bonding between women can feel as powerful and intense as falling in love.'

Bianka closes her eyes. She feels the burn of excitement and trepidation in her stomach, from speaking about it. She knows, indeed, that the connection between female friends can be so intense it blurs boundaries, all of them – even the ones that keep us safe. It's like a powerful love affair that sidesteps the natural distance between men and women, eviscerating that sliver of difference that is necessarily there even in the very closest of heterosexual relationships. And sometimes, like love, it can turn dark. Toxic. Dangerous. Bianka knows this right down to her bones.

'Yes.'

'I told her about what happened to my mom.'

'What did you tell her?'

'That I lost her as a child.'

'Did you tell her everything?'

'No.'

'Bianka. It sounds to me like you need to be a little bit careful here. And that this relationship might trigger some of the underlying challenges we've been working on together.'

'No, it's not like that. This feels good, and healthy and like being ignited.'

'You spoke earlier of the intensity of this new connection. Of feeling filled up where there was emptiness before.'

'Yes.'

'Isn't that where things have gone wrong before?'

Bianka closes her Mac and stands up to walk over to the window of the study. In spite of the therapy session, which she always finds emotionally draining, she is grateful to be here, in Wimbledon, in her new life, free of the old one. She shudders to think of her daily routine back home in Oslo, for so many years, and of how she'd felt like a domestic prisoner.

She'd come home from work and immediately have to start cooking for Emil and Storm, making sure they got enough performance-boosting protein, when really, she'd have quite liked to throw a fucking frozen pizza in the oven. She often tried to imagine the looks on their eerily similar faces at the sight of the small, soggy disk scattered with plastic-like faux-cheese. Only, it would never have happened – Bianka knew what was expected of her. Next up – laundry;

the endless cycle of Storm's sports clothes spinning in the machine before hanging to dry. If she was going to describe the soundtrack to her life, Bianka would have to say it was the whoosh of the washing machine. Once, she dreamed she fed armfuls of Lycra into the hot, hungry mouth of the fireplace instead of the washing machine, its synthetic fabric crackling and producing an odious black smoke.

When the job offer from London came, Bianka was only too ready to escape. She had always known deep down that she wasn't designed for the old kind of life: a comfortable, socially acceptable life in the suburbs, working part-time in an unfulfilling job and succumbing to outdated gender roles to please a man who thinks being a feminist means agreeing that women should be able to vote and not much else. She couldn't quite grasp what kind of life might have suited her better, and therein lay the problem; whenever she's tried to explore herself, she's come up against that vast, familiar emptiness. Even as a child, she'd found it hard to express herself in ways that seemed to come naturally to the others, struggling to answer questions such as *Which do you prefer, blue or green? Do you like ice cream or cake? Which boy is cuter, this one or that one? What do you want to be when you grow up?* The other children seemed to have a sense of self that effortlessly delivered the answers to such questions, whereas when Bianka tried to decide what her general preferences were, she just came up against a milky void. So she turned to other people; watching them and mirroring back their opinions and desires, needing them to fill her up.

Bianka allows her mind to return to the other night, to the slow walk through the dark park and the moments on the bench, how Charlotte's presence had made it feel like an occasion touched by magic. Charlotte, like almost everyone else, liked talking about herself and hadn't needed much encouragement to open up. Bianka felt genuinely sad for her because it was obvious she'd not had anyone else to really talk to. She'd watched her speak, drinking in every facial expression and mannerism, consciously committing them to memory so she'd be able to return to them in her mind, while listening intently, a skill she'd perfected years ago. Making someone feel truly seen and heard is half the battle, ideally complemented by the perception of shared experiences. Chemistry is the other half, and that one is harder to create, but is usually achievable with good mirroring; most people experience chemistry when they are basically interacting with themselves.

Bianka had narrowed her eyes in sympathy, nodded in all the right places, smiled gently as tears sprung to Charlotte's eyes, touched her wrist to assess whether the other woman was comfortable with physical touch. She was initially surprised, but open to it for sure; starved even.

Bianka begins to walk slowly around the house, fluffing cushions and tweaking curtains and wiping down a couple of surfaces. She thinks back to the moment when Charlotte invited her to Ibiza. It was so delicious, so perfect, that she'd known instantly that she'd never forget it.

For every slow minute sliding by, she reminds herself that this time next week, she'll by flying off to her absolute dream destination with Charlotte Vinge. What a turn life has taken. It's a shame Charlotte's insipid girlfriends from the Streamstar party will be there, too – but Bianka isn't daunted by a couple of droll suburban tagalongs.

Nine

Storm

He'd been surprised when his father had agreed to let him spend the night alone at the house in Oslo – the flight would land at ten p.m., missing the last available pickup service from school.

'You're almost seventeen and obviously I trust you,' his father had said, placing his hands on Storm's shoulders, then drawing him into a hug as he dropped him off at Heathrow. 'Just don't attempt to cook anything.'

Walking through security and scanning the monitors for the right gate, checking and rechecking his digital boarding pass, Storm had felt pretty grown up. He'd also felt sad; it was still new and unfamiliar that Emil would leave the airport and go back to his life, a different life altogether than the one Storm was a part of. They'd discussed the possibility of Storm returning to London in just over a week – he'd be off his training schedule for a summer break, and when Emil had seen Storm hesitate, he'd added that Bianka would be flying off to Ibiza. Plus, Storm is more than a little keen to see Madeleine Vinge again.

He finds his seat at the front of the plane by the window and recalls the feeling he'd had that evening after the dinner when he'd met her for the first time.

The house on Dunstall Road was completely quiet and the usual faint noise from the traffic on the A4 had died down, and Storm lay still and alert on top of his bed in the green room, still wearing his smart Ralph Lauren shirt and chino trousers. He didn't want to take them off, signalling the end of the evening; he wanted to hold onto it for a little longer. Madeleine circled round and round in his mind, like a bird high up in the sky, impossible to catch and impossibly beautiful. He imagined running his hands through her glossy light-brown hair and pressing his mouth to her soft, pink lips. He felt himself blush again in the dark at the thought, and at the memory of the long moment in the attic space when he held her hand, blissfully high and a little braver for it. He felt like a different boy than the boy who'd woken up that morning, the boy who really only ever thought of skiing and FIFA. Was this what it felt like to become a man? He closed his eyes and smiled and, for the first time in as long as he could remember, Storm felt free and happy, and the loneliness he usually felt at home was gone, if only for a while.

He feels it again now as the plane takes to the sky, marking the end of his first trip to London. The rest of the weekend had crept by slowly, spent with his father running around Wimbledon Common and taking a train into the city to look at all the sights, most of which feel like a blur in Storm's mind. The Tower of London, London Eye, Madame

Tussauds, the Shard, and Buckingham Palace; Storm had dutifully perused all of these sights and more, taking a few pictures here and there, constantly checking his phone for a new message from Madeleine.

In Oslo, it's still light outside at eleven when he walks from Slemdal metro station to the house. People sit out in gardens in the gentle, warm evening, laughing and clinking glasses together. Storm tries to pretend that this is like all the other times he's walked home on a summer evening, that his father is at home watching TV or tidying up the kitchen before bed. But it feels nothing like before; it feels like years later even though it's only been a few weeks, as though he's a man returning home from war, the same on the outside but fundamentally altered within.

He pushes the door open but it meets resistance – a pile of newspapers, flyers, and letters have accumulated on the doormat inside and Storm wonders whether his father has forgotten to redirect the mail. He kicks his shoes off and is about to head into the living room to relax for a while in front of the TV when a plain white envelope on the top of the pile catches his eye. It's addressed to him. He picks it up and turns it over to open it, but when he reads the name of the sender at the back of the envelope, his heart skips several beats in his chest and he drops it to the floor in shock.

Ten

Charlotte

The last couple of weeks have just flown by with all the excitement of discovering a new London with Bianka. The gallery opening in Leyton and the slightly frightening and emotional walk in the park was followed by a Caribbean street food festival in Hackney, then a tarot reading in Dulwich at a woman's tiny flat that was decorated almost entirely in purple silk. Bianka apparently discovered her on Instagram.

I smile to myself at the memory – Bianka and I have known each other only a few short weeks but it feels like we've already covered a lot of ground. And today is a special day. My alarm rang at 5 a.m. and I practically leaped from bed, I've been looking forward to this day for so long. Throughout winter, when the bone-chilling, grey cold settles on London, and throughout the endless rains of spring, I have looked forward to this every single day. Our annual girls' trip to Ibiza. This year it's even more exciting than usual because Bianka is coming with us.

I apply my makeup carefully, enjoying the deep silence of the house and the first, bright rays of the late June sun spilling onto the terracotta tiles of the bathroom. I can't quite believe that when I remove my makeup this evening, I'll be at Can Xara, my beloved house on the northwestern coast of Ibiza. Going there always gives me a thrill, but never have I felt it more than today. Our first trip came about many years after my mother died, when my kids were small, and Andreas and I discussed selling the property I'd inherited since we never used it and it was just standing there. I'd found it too painful to go there and to sort through my mother's things, putting it off for years. Then a generous offer for the house came and since Andreas would stay at home to look after the kids, Anette offered to come with me to help sort things out. Within days of being there, I knew I would never sell it, that the place still held within it an unbreakable bond to my mother.

Why don't you build a modern, sleek villa up there on that hill? Anette asked and I shielded my eyes and followed the direction of her pointed finger to the natural plateau further up the steep hill, and it was as though I could actually see it there – the house that would embody my own dreams as much as the ancient rambling finca had embodied my mother's. I designed the house myself and two years later, it stood there, exactly as I'd envisioned it – a long, white-and-glass structure that was built to merge with the landscape and looked like it had sprung forth from Ibiza's very core like a desert flower.

And in the many years since, Can Xara has brought more peace and joy to our family than I could ever have anticipated. After we moved to Wimbledon and grew close to Linda, who'd once been a casual acquaintance in Oslo, she too started to join us. And every year the three of us count down to this day, and every year our trip has more or less followed the same rhythm. It has never occurred to us to bring our partners or invite anyone else on this week away, so it came as no surprise that it didn't go down especially well when I broke the news that I'd invited Bianka to join us. I didn't think they'd be that negative, though – not even Anette, who can be more than a little territorial and feisty. A couple of days after the fiasco at Cannizaro, when she just walked out without a word, she called.

'I just don't understand why you'd even try to fix the least broken thing in our lives,' she said. I explained and she listened and in the end she pretended to be okay about it, because, really, what choice did she have? We're in our forties and generally try to avoid throwing our weight around when we don't get our way. It's cuter to just smile graciously. Besides, it's my house, and my decision – and we all know that at the end of the day.

I drive fast down the empty streets to Anette's house on Calonne Road, and she's already outside, waiting on the curb. She's wearing a floaty orange kaftan I recognize as one she picked up at a market in Sant Joan de Labritja last year, which perfectly complements her vivid copper hair. The overall effect is that of a commanding, flickering flame. Anette air-kisses me and we set off. We're giggling and beaming at each other; we both know exactly how much we have to look forward to. I feel almost euphoric to leave my family and work behind, if only for a week. The monotony of parenting, the endless demands of work – I often feel like I'm trapped in a washing machine, spinning on the fast cycle. I manoeuvre the Range Rover onto the A4 heading toward the M25 and Heathrow, urging the accelerator with my Valentino-sandaled foot.

'Aren't we picking up Linda and Bianka?' asks Anette.

'Nope,' I say. 'Linda is driving herself because that's much easier from Cobham. And Bianka's husband is driving her because he's off to Copenhagen for a meeting.'

'Ah. Not gonna lie, this is going to be interesting.'

I glance at Anette and smile and though she smiles back, there is something slightly confrontational in her eyes. Anette is my best friend from school, we've known each other since our very first day of primary, aged six. We've always been close and, even as adults, our lives mirror each other's in many ways. Anette runs her own law firm and is married to Mads, one of Andreas's university friends and long-time colleagues at Norbank. When Andreas got transferred to London, Mads and Anette followed just months later and thank God for that. We do a lot of couple's things together, and Anette and I remain as close as we have been since childhood. If I have a problem, it's Anette I call. If I need to just forget everything, even calorie-counting, and just get drunk, again it's Anette I call. But while Anette and I live similar lives and have many shared interests, we don't have the kind of friendship that is built on a deeper emotional understanding, the kind where we just 'get each other' implicitly. I've never even thought about this, or known we were missing such a connection, because I've never had it before. Until Bianka.

'Yeah. Yes, it will be great for you guys to get to properly know each other.'

'I mean, she's got to be something rather special to get an invite to our week, so my expectations are naturally sky high.' This sounds exactly like the subtle threat it is and I feel anxiety stir in my stomach at the thought of Bianka and Anette having some sort of bitch-fest power struggle on this trip.

'Anette. Be nice, okay?'

'I'm always nice,' she says breezily. This is such a blatant lie that we both burst out laughing. Anette did not become a successful lawyer by always being nice. She's referred to as 'the shark' or 'the rambunctious redhead', both of which Anette considers huge compliments. 'So. What makes her so special?'

'Oh, well, I'm not sure she's that special. She's just really nice.'

'Must be, considering the amount of time you've spent with her recently.'

'Anette. Stop being so jealous. It was actually Andreas who suggested that I invite her.'

'Ah. I see. So this is basically a strategy invite.'

'No. No, Anette, actually not at all.'

'I'm sure it doesn't hurt to do what Andreas suggests, though, right?' Anette keeps her voice breezy, but there is a clear tone of malice beneath it.

'That's not fair. I wouldn't have invited her unless I really wanted to.'

'And why is that?'

'I feel like she gets me in a way that nobody else does.' Boom. That shuts her up. And it's the truth. Of course the idea came about when Andreas suggested it – it obviously can't hurt to be in with the boss's wife, but that's not at all why I invited her. I invited Bianka because nobody has ever made me feel that I'm interesting for *me*, rather than for what I do or produce or achieve.

It's still early, not yet 7 a.m., but traffic is building on the M25 heading north and we slow to a crawl for a long stretch. Anette has fallen into a sulky silence thanks to my comment about my unique connection with Bianka. As we approach the airport, I glance at Anette again – she's leaning her head against the window, eyes closed. I don't feel bad; thankfully we have the kind of friendship where we can speak up when something bothers us, but I'm aware that we've started our trip on a slightly charged note and I want to fix it. All I want for this week is peace and laughter. *Fun*.

'Come on,' I say, as I painstakingly begin the process of reverse parking the beast that is my car in a narrow bay. 'I think you guys are going to totally love each other. I've told Bianka so much about you and how you are my absolutely best friend.' This is partially true at least; I've mentioned Anette several times, but Bianka always seems much more interested in hearing about me.

'Yeah. I'm sorry. I didn't mean to be bitchy about it. I'm looking forward to getting to know her. She seems like an interesting person and you're right: it's sometimes a really great idea to bring in some fresh blood.' I nod and smile at her and in this moment everything feels restored. I'm about to get out of the car when I notice that there is a sheen of moisture in Anette's eyes and that she's trying to hold back tears.

'You okay?'

'Yeah. No. Actually, no. There's something I need to tell you, Charlotte.' I sit back in the seat and shut the door with a soft click. I stare at her, waiting. I feel a tremor of anxiety; Anette is not the kind of person who'd announce needing to talk about something unless it was something quite serious. 'Mads and I are divorcing,' she says, voice trembling.

'Oh. Oh, no. I'm so sorry, Anette. What has happened?' I am blindsided by this. Anette and Mads are so established as a couple in my eyes that I'm actually unable to picture them apart.

'Well. The girls are pretty much grown up now. Earlier this year I had a breast cancer scare. I didn't tell you about it because I freaked out so completely and was in total denial, but the experience really changed me. When the results came back and I realized I'd be okay, I decided I wanted to live differently. And eventually I came to the conclusion that it's better to leave than live a life of pretence.'

'I guess I didn't know it felt like that for you. Like pretending.'

'Oh, Charlotte, come on. I'm forty-one and haven't slept with my husband in as long as I can actually remember. He only cares about work and drinking beer with his friends and running in the woods.' Sounds familiar. I feel uncomfortable, because Anette and I live similar lives, something that Anette is now denouncing as pretence. 'You know what Mads is like,' she continues. 'Nice enough but just on a different planet. I want someone who truly wants me. Who doesn't turn away from me in bed or kisses me with dry lips clamped shut.'

My mind darts to my husband's brief, chaste peck on the cheek last night when we said goodnight and goodbye, before he headed off down the corridor toward the guest room.

'But Anette. Isn't that what most marriages are like eventually?'

'I don't know but I don't want that. I looked at him one night when the girls were both in bed and I'd finished the endless tidying after yet another dinner party. He'd fallen asleep on the sofa and was snoring so loudly. I noticed then how fat he'd gotten; like a pot-bellied old man, and I just thought, this is what the rest of my life is going to look like if I don't do something.'

'But... Won't you lose the house?'

'I'm a divorce lawyer, Charlotte. If anyone gets to keep the house in proceedings, it would be me. But we might have to sell. And here's the thing, at the end of the day – it's just a house, right?'

I think of my own house and I feel numb with terror at the idea of boxing all of our possessions and watching them being loaded into a moving van, presumably to be driven off to some soulless apartment somewhere, with a galley kitchen and a cramped balcony overlooking a main road. I'd probably have to leave London, even – returning to Oslo like a complete and utter failure.

It's just a house. It's not just a house, though. Not for me. It's the physical symbol of security and safety and I couldn't bear to lose it. I realize I've unleashed an anguished little sob and remember that this really isn't about me. My marriage is rock solid and I'm not going to lose my house. I'm not going to lose anything. And now I need to be here for Anette.

'Of course. You're right. It's just a house. The most important thing is that you're happy.'

'Yes. It really is the most important thing. I just can't face another decade of facade living, of going through the motions and giving my one life up for a man who doesn't seem to give a flying fuck about me.'

'Oh, but Mads loves you so much, Anette. It's always been so obvious. I thought you guys were super happy and—'

'That's just how it's looked. From the outside. It's different, at home. And between us.' I nod and refuse to allow myself to draw any further comparisons to my own life and marriage. I'm being ridiculous by feeling so affected by this; it's nothing to do with me.

'I'm really sorry, honey,' I say. 'Please let me know what you need right now and how I can best be there for you.'

'To be honest, I just want to forget about it for a week. I haven't told Linda yet. And since I don't know Bianka, I'd appreciate it if we could just keep this between me and you for now. But if you want to know how to help, there is something I need.'

'Of course, anything,' I say softly, squeezing her hand gently to not hurt her heavily bejewelled fingers. I notice with a jolt that her wedding ring is gone.

'You are officially in charge of keeping me mercifully drunk pretty much constantly for a week, starting now.' We both laugh.

'Let the games begin,' I say, slamming the car door shut

and together we march toward the terminal building, linking arms and laughing.

Walking into Heathrow, clutching the handle of my wheelie bag, Anette marching self-confidently alongside me toward where Bianka is standing at the end of the security line, I feel suddenly way out of my comfort zone. I do childhood friends, rock-solid marriage, impressive career, super mum. I don't really do new friends or merging my different worlds. Looking back at the past month and the fact that I've spent every free moment with Bianka, I realize that she's hit me like a freight train.

'Charlotte!' screams Bianka when she sees us approach, and throws herself around my neck before planting a sticky crimson kiss on my cheek. She's wearing an over-the-top geometric print red silky jumpsuit and towering platform sandals. Her hair has been teased to the heights and her makeup is immaculate. The overall effect is of a white, middle-aged Beyoncé, in the best possible way. Bianka turns her attention from me to Anette.

'I'm so excited to finally meet you,' says Bianka, kissing Anette on both cheeks. 'I've heard so much about you.'

'We've met before, actually,' says Anette, 'at the Streamstar party.'

'Oh, God, yes. Of course. I remember you.'

Anette nods lightly, then they smile at each other, sizing each other up, before turning to me.

'Where is your other friend, then? Linda?' asks Bianka.

'She's already gone through security and is waiting at the champagne bar.' I find the WhatsApp photo message Linda just sent me and show it to the others – although it's only just gone seven a.m., she's holding a glass of champagne up in a toast, her face beaming.

'God, you ladies don't beat around the bush, do you?'

'Linda is a nervous flier; she can't get on a plane without a glass of wine or three,' I say.

Anette and Bianka then launch into an animated discussion about the merits of geometric print as we get in line for security and I follow behind them, breathing a sigh of relief that they're apparently getting along. The airport is busy as ever this morning and Bianka is sluiced away from Anette and me to a separate conveyor belt.

'She's something else, huh?' whispers Anette, keeping a faint smile on her face, meticulously loading her tray before pushing it onto the belt.

'What do you mean?' I ask.

'I can see why you find her so mesmerizing.'

I open my mouth to say I don't find Bianka mesmerizing exactly, and that that's a bit of a weird way to put it, but Anette has already stalked through the metal-detector gate and the security lady on the other side motions for me to follow. The machine beeps as I walk through, even though I've removed jewellery and my belt. I'm asked to step aside and wait a moment. Bianka comes up to me, a sly smile creeping across her face.

'I'm afraid I'm going to have to pat you down, madam,' she says, winking at me, placing a light hand on my hip. Though she's only joking and I laugh it off, I'm taken aback by the feeling of complicity between us and the fact that I find myself wishing that it is only Bianka and me heading to

Ibiza. Anette is right: I do find her mesmerizing, and being in Bianka's company makes me feel both exhilarated and completely out of my depth.

Eleven

Charlotte

The taxi pulls up to the broad, bronze automatic gate, which slides open when I press the key fob. The driver urges the jam-packed car up the long drive to the property at its crest, high above the azure Mediterranean. As he parks in front of the glass front entrance, Bianka whistles between her teeth and turns around from the front seat.

'Shut up,' she says. 'This is your actual house?'

Can Xara must come across as a very extravagant holiday home to someone arriving here for the first time, and I feel a little embarrassed at how spectacular it really is – I don't want Bianka to think I'm some insanely loaded rich lady who could just point to a house like this in a property magazine and buy it. Because that couldn't be further from the truth. Can Xara is my mother's legacy, the only thing I have left of her.

I disable the alarm systems and we file into the house, dropping our bags to the floor in the hallway and naturally gravitating to the wall-to-wall panorama windows of the main living space, overlooking the beautiful little bay of Cala Azura and beyond the jagged cape, Cala Xarraca. I press the button of the automatic sliding windows and they swiftly open, obliterating the boundary between indoors and outdoors, making the living spaces merge with the giant teak wraparound terraces. We step outside and in this moment, being back at Can Xara is even better than the fantasy I'd built in my head, all those long evenings spent dreaming, because though I'd pictured how good it would feel to turn my face toward the hot sun, drinking in one of the most spectacular views one could possibly imagine, it's impossible to fully evoke all the more subtle details of this magical place: the breeze carrying the particular scent of Mediterranean pine, verbena, hydrangea, eucalyptus, and the occasional drift of marijuana from one of the beach bars at Cala Xarraca, shielded from view.

'Oh, my actual God,' says Bianka, and it's quite sweet, really, how utterly blown away she seems to be by Can Xara. 'What does Can Xara mean?'

'Can means house,' I say. 'I think Xara is a name. Not sure where it came from, to be honest.'

'Wait until you see the pool and the yoga platform,' says Linda.

'I mean, I would literally kill for this house,' says Bianka. I laugh and step onto the lower terraces that lead to the pool area, motioning for the others to follow. Bianka coos some more and then we all just fall silent standing on the wooden yoga platform, jutting over the cliffs on the steepest part of my property, looking out at the calm, patterned sweep of silvery sea stretching out ahead.

***

I show Bianka to her room, a large guest suite opposite the master bedroom. Linda and Anette are in their usual rooms upstairs on the top floor, and we can hear rummaging around as they unpack their suitcases.

'I'm right across the hallway, so if you need anything…'

'I have everything I need right here,' says Bianka, letting herself fall back onto the pristine white bed and smiling up at me.

'Okay, great,' I say and turn toward the door. I'll leave her to get freshened up and unpacked before we head back down to the yoga platform for some stretches before dinner.

'Hey, come here,' she says, patting the space on the bed next to her. I sit down and she pulls me gently back so that I'm lying beside her, looking up at the unblemished white ceiling.

'I'm so excited to be here,' she says, her face only inches from mine.

'Good. Me too. I'm so glad you came. We're going to have so much fun.'

'All the fun.'

'Yep.'

Bianka reaches out and strokes my bare upper arm and it feels like such an intimate gesture I'm momentarily taken aback, but at the same time, I realize it feels good; it's been a long time since anyone deliberately touched me, and besides, I think it's sweet that Bianka is so affectionate. I sit back up after a long moment and slip from Bianka's room but bump into Anette in the hallway.

'Everything okay?' I ask. She nods and smiles, looking

past me through Bianka's open door where she is still lying reclined on the bed, and I wonder whether she was stood there for a while and saw the way Bianka stroked my arm. I feel suddenly awkward and can feel myself blushing so I turn away from them both and step into my room, shutting the door behind me and leaning against it.

At sunset, we sit in a circle on the yoga platform and Linda guides us through a series of slow, deep hatha poses. I focus on my breathing and try to remember when I last did yoga – probably in this exact same spot, last year. Sometimes I feel like my life is so rushed and so demanding day to day that even a task as simple as breathing properly seems insurmountable. Linda knows I struggle to relax and properly guide the air deep into my stomach, and smiles encouragingly at me as I give single-nostril breathing my best shot. By the time we finish, the sun is burning red on the horizon and my stomach growls; I haven't had anything to eat today except for eight unsalted almonds on the plane.

'I'm so ready for a soak in that gorgeous tub,' says Anette, releasing her amazing hair from its tight topknot.

'I'm going to need a nap,' says Linda, yawning as if to justify her need for a little lie-down.

'Dinner will be ready at eight,' I say. 'It's a surprise.' I can't wait to see the looks on the girls' faces when they learn what I have planned. 'We'll be eating at home, but cute dresses are most advisable.'

'Hey, I really want to pop down and see the beach,' says Bianka, slowing down so that we drop out of earshot of

Linda and Anette who have started on the steep path back up to the house. 'Come with me?'

'Sure,' I say. I'd rather spend the next hour pre-emptively burning off dinner's calories in Bianka's company by power-walking down to the beach than scrolling through my phone in my bedroom answering emails, which I know is what I'd inevitably end up doing. I need to let go and trust that Caty, my manager, is completely able to handle affairs while I'm away.

We walk side by side on the narrow path that is fringed by rows of olive trees on one side and a thick, low hedge on the other side, designed and planted to mark the sheer drop of the cliffs. When my mother first came here, she had the hedge put up after 'feeling unsafe walking down to the beach at night', she wrote in one of her many, early letters. She built the whole world of Can Xara for me in those letters, evoking its scents and sights, trying, I imagine, to convince me to come and live here. I wish I had.

I bring my focus back to Bianka and take pleasure in her effusive delight at being here. It makes me wonder whether she perhaps isn't as sophisticated as I'd assumed she was – as lovely as Can Xara truly is, it's not like I haven't seen other equally spectacular homes on this island, in the South of France, or Italy. It occurs to me that as much as I like and crave Bianka's company, I don't actually know that much about her. In London it feels as though we're part of the same world: big houses in Wimbledon and our husbands in the same company, but I don't know much about her outside of all that. It feels as though she is very firmly focused on me, and as much as that's gratifying on some levels, it also means our relationship is necessarily somewhat one-sided.

'So where do you guys usually go in the summer?' I ask.

'Nowhere, really,' she says.

'Oh.'

'Yeah, because of Storm's skiing career, he usually trains throughout summer to build muscle for the winter season so he and Emil head to our cabin in Valdres most weekends to roller ski and run long-distance. And those really aren't my thing, so I've just ended up staying in Oslo. You know, mooching around the galleries, having dinner by myself in restaurants in parts of town I've never been to before, that kind of thing. And moving forward, I guess I'll be doing the same thing, only in London, when Emil travels for work or to see Storm in Norway.'

'Oh,' I say again, sounding like an absolute idiot. I try to imagine spending long weekends by myself in the city when my family is elsewhere, catching up on the cultural scene and eating by myself but find I just can't. 'That sounds pretty cool.'

'It is. I love it. I guess you guys come here for most of summer? I mean, I know I would if I had a place like this.'

'Yeah. We tend to head out mid-July after a couple of weeks in Norway at our summer house in Hvasser. Then we stay until the kids go back to school, but the last couple of years we've cut it short as it's just been unbearably hot in August.'

Bianka nods, but her attention is diverted by the little horseshoe bay we're just arriving at – Cala Azura. Its waters are sheltered by craggy headlands on both sides, and tonight the narrow bay shimmers in shades of bronze and gold with the very last rays of the sun. At the far end is a little boathouse, which still houses my mother's wooden rowing boat, as well as our stand-up paddleboard and various beach stuff. As I knew she would, Bianka gushes about our little cove, saying it's the loveliest beach she has ever seen and asking lots of questions like, *Can you snorkel here? Can I try the stand-up paddleboard?* I answer her questions, but my mind is elsewhere, as it always is when I come down here. It's as though this little bay casts a spell on me and I'm compelled to just walk into the water and let it close over my head.

We walk to the north, where the bay is closed off by the tall cliffsides that separate it from the much more frequented Cala Xarraca. Hardly anyone comes here, mostly because only my property has direct access to it, a fact which is contested by my neighbours, the loaded Parisian Dubois-Joseph family, even though they have unrestricted access across my property on the path that leads to the coves. They've been wanting to buy a big chunk of my land so the coastal path will run across their property rather than mine, and claim it was originally theirs anyway.

For years, they have tried increasingly persistently to convince me to sell and last year they presented me with an offer so high I thought I'd imagined an extra zero in the formal lawyer's letter. Money is clearly no object for these people, but I didn't even tell Andreas how much they were prepared to pay – four million euros just for the land – because I suspected he'd start to put pressure on me to accept. I felt bad keeping it from my husband, but Can Xara is mine, at the end of the day, and Andreas doesn't involve himself in the running of the property beyond showing up a couple of times a year in his Vilebrequins. So I explained to the Dubois-Josephs that no part of my mother's estate is for sale, not now and not ever.

I feel her here: Ximena, my mother. Maybe it's because she was born on the island, or because she died here, but it wasn't until I came to Ibiza that I felt something of her remained in this world, infused into its air bearing the scent of wild thyme and frangipani, or held in the gentle waves lapping at the shore, or in the fading, ethereal evening light. She no longer feels dead to me.

A sound cuts through my thoughts. Bianka says something, and by the bemused look on her face I gather she's repeating it for the second or perhaps third time.

'What?' I say, turning to her and focusing on giving her my full attention. Bianka is pointing to the low, ancient, whitewashed building halfway up the steep hill, between Cala Azura and my sleek modern construction, and only partly visible from the beach. You'd have to know it was there to access it on an even narrower path than the one we came down. The finca sits in the midst of a clutch of lemon trees, beneath the terraced olive trees that grow in neat rows on the hills. Now, in the low violet evening light, the house is only just discernible from the rocks. You'd be forgiven for thinking it was a little shepherd's hut or a storage building or even just a pile of rocks, but up close, it's actually quite large; a three-bedroom farmhouse with unparalleled ocean views.

'What's that little house up there?'

'It's a finca.'

'A finca?'

'An old, traditional farmhouse. It's where my mother lived.' I can feel Bianka's eyes dart from the finca to me and back again but keep my gaze focused on the hillsides, awash in stunning light in shades of purple and red. The spotlights have gone on at the main house on the top of the hill, making it look like a UFO perched there to gain an overview of these enchanted headlands.

'We'd better head back up,' I say. 'We should start getting ready for dinner, really.'

'Can we go see that house? The finca?' The idea of diverting from the main path and heading toward Ximena's farmhouse instantly fills me with a vicious dread. In all the years since I started spending time here and built the new Can Xara, I've only been to the finca a couple of times, and only because it's been absolutely necessary, like when it flooded in a winter storm and its foundations needed reinforcing.

An image appears uninvited in my mind, of my hand reaching out and touching the well-worn, bronze doorknob and pushing the heavy, metal-studded oak door open, revealing the ancient sanctuary my mother loved.

'Um, no, sorry. I… I actually never go there.'

'How come? It looks utterly charming,' says Bianka, narrowing her eyes to get a better view of the house as we start on the steep stone steps rising from Cala Azura back up to the path.

'It's a ruin, basically. I forget it's even there most of the time; I never think about it.' This is, of course, a lie. A big one. But this way, I get to pretend.

I feel a sudden, intense wave of exhaustion. I don't want to think about the finca or explain anything about it to Bianka. I want to lie down on my bed in my sleek white modern box of a house and let tears flow from my eyes into my pillow, if only for a moment. Bianka must sense that I've gone quiet and quickly drops it, mumbling something about 'perhaps another time'. I'm reminded of Bianka's own loss – she told me that night in Leyton that she, too, had lost her mother very young but wouldn't go into the details, and I wonder if she'll tell me about what happened sometime, perhaps on this trip.

I stomp up the path fast, making Bianka half-run next to me. I need to treat this as a workout if I'm going to indulge in both food and alcohol this evening. When my heart races, my mind clears. I keep my eyes firmly on the dusty path, now lit by an almost-full moon appearing above Punta de Sa Creu, sending ripples of light onto the darkened sea. If I looked down to the right in this moment, I'd just be able to make out a small patch of the finca's terracotta roof tiles and the waxy, dense tops of the citrus trees surrounding it. But I don't. I work on getting my pulse racing so it overrides any other feeling, even the burning pain I feel in the hollow of my stomach when I think about my mother and her beloved finca.

Sometimes, if I'm especially drunk or especially sad and in the mood for self-torture, I let myself pretend that she's down there, a couple of hundred yards down the hillside, painting. I can see her in my mind, so clearly then; her skin brown and glowing, her long hair coiled around itself like rope and secured on top of her head, streaks of silver picking up the light. I pretend that I could just go to her if I wanted to.

★★★

I come downstairs just as the intercom rings. I'm wearing a short, ruffled red dress and a full face of makeup – I felt the need for a bit of armour after my walk down to the beach with Bianka. I'd felt strangely tender when we arrived back at the house and sat a long time at my desk in the bedroom, just crying my eyes out. Can Xara seems to have that effect on me; it's as though all my control peels away and the real uncensored me forces her way to the surface.

After, I made myself get in the shower, where I let the water rush down my face for a long time. Now, I feel much better. The girls are all sitting in the living room chatting animatedly, and they cheer when they see me in my dress and high heels. Bianka leaps up and presses a glass of champagne into my hand as I open the gates.

'Who is it?' asks Anette. She, too, is all dressed up in a gold toga silk dress.

'Dinner,' I say, and wink. I open the door and two extremely attractive young men emerge from a white soft-top bearing the neon pink 'Carlo Catering' logo. These guys know how to appeal to the fussy lady eaters of the island, that's for sure.

'Charlotte,' Carlo says, 'so good to see you back in Ibiza.' He takes turns kissing my cheeks enthusiastically. I introduce them to the girls and we all file out onto the terraces and sit back while gorgeous Carlo and his brother Ricky fire up the barbecue and prepare the thick slabs of steak I've ordered. I crank up the music and smoke the thin menthol cigarette that Anette hands me, enjoying the feeling of relaxation spreading through my system from the champagne and nicotine.

The food is exquisite: chargrilled steak and buttered pointy cabbage, just the way I like it. Carlo and Ricky discreetly wrap up and leave us to it and we sit outside in the warm evening for several hours after we've finished eating, sipping wine and laughing. Bianka seems to slot right in with my friends, and I feel relieved the slight tension of this morning seems to have dissipated. Our conversations flit from work to husbands to kids to Ibiza. I think about Andreas, Madeleine and Oscar, how they'll likely be fast asleep, and find that I can't quite conjure them up in my mind; they feel slippery and vague, like people from a dream. I feel so acutely present in the moment with Bianka, Anette and Linda, it's as though my real life has ceased to exist.

Linda stands up and blows kisses to the three of us still sitting.

'Off to get my beauty sleep,' she says as she heads back into the house.

'One more glass of wine, girls?' I ask the others, lifting the open bottle of rosé from the ice bucket and refilling our glasses without waiting for a response.

'What a day,' says Bianka softly. 'I am so grateful to be here. And it's so lovely to properly meet and get to know you, too, Anette.' Anette and Bianka smile at each other, then clink their glasses together in a toast.

'Real life feels so far away,' I say, staring out at the moon-drenched sea and the star-studded night sky, a shiver chasing the length of my spine, though the air is still warm and humid.

'Thank God,' says Anette, and we all laugh.

'Here's to a wild time away from husbands, children, and piles of laundry,' says Bianka, and we touch our glasses together enthusiastically again.

'What happens in Ibiza stays in Ibiza,' I say, and take a sip from my wine glass. As I do, my eyes meet Bianka's across the table and her gaze is intense and charged. I swallow and glance at Anette, who has clearly noticed the fleeting moment between Bianka and me.

'Indeed,' she says. She stands up, covering her mouth and yawning exaggeratedly. 'Bedtime for me, ladies,' she says. 'Be good,' she adds, winking at me as she walks back toward the house. Bianka and I fall silent, perhaps sobered by the realization that we're alone again.

'It's so dark,' Bianka says. I feel confused by the atmosphere between us; the way she looked at me seemed challenging, like she was daring me to do something but I don't know what it is. Or like she can see right through me. I try to make sense of how I actually feel about the current that seems to run between us, but my own feelings are murky and chaotic. I do know that I want to be here with her, mellow and a little woozy in the moonlit night, feeling her gaze on me, a smile playing on her lips, like I am a strange and interesting creature that has never been seen before. An image inserts itself into my mind – I'm in bed, naked, and Bianka is sitting beside me, gazing down at me with that exact same look in her eyes. I feel myself blushing deeply and feel convinced she can read my thoughts. I take another sip of the wine and try to think of something to say, something far removed from the very inappropriate mental picture I just entertained.

'So, tell me more about what you did for work,' I say. 'I mean, I know you worked in marketing but not much more. I feel like we've only ever really talked about mine.'

'That's because yours is super interesting and impressive, and mine was really, really not.'

'Oh…' I begin, and the truth is, I can't really imagine going to work every day in a job that doesn't fill you with passion and enthusiasm. Or not working at all, what the hell would you do with all that time? I almost went crazy when we moved to London and I had nothing to do every day, hence the blog, and the rest is history. I always work on holiday, a few hours each morning at the crack of dawn, and so does Andreas. I can't imagine just sitting around on the beach, and eating, or whatever it is people do.

'No, really. If I told you what I used to do all day, you'd fall asleep right here.'

'Try me. I want to know about you.'

'Okay, so I basically worked in the B2B marketing department of a German white goods company. Much of what I did was pitch their products toward various institutions, like old people's homes, schools, hospitals—'

I mime falling asleep. Bianka laughs and so do I. She's beautiful this evening, more beautiful than I've ever seen her before. She's wearing a plain white shirt and cut-off denim shorts, the only one of us who hadn't dressed up for dinner. I must have forgotten to tell her that we tend to be quite over the top when away together – I think it's true what they say, that women dress for other women, not for men. She didn't seem at all bothered that the rest of us were in heels and dresses while she was casual and barefoot, her hair swept back in a ponytail, face bare of makeup, and this is what I find so fascinating about Bianka – the innate self-confidence she seems to possess. 'Okay, I'll hand it to you, that does sound pretty boring. Have you thought about doing something new now you're in London?'

'Yeah. I just don't know what yet.'

'Well, what's your passion?'

'This feels like a job interview now,' says Bianka, and we both laugh again. 'What's *your* passion, besides keto?' she asks. She's good at deflecting but I don't want to return to me yet. I want to know about her. I just can't quite picture someone as exuberant and charismatic as Bianka Langeland selling dishwashers to retirement homes. I try to picture her sitting in an open-plan office, sticking out like a sore thumb in a row of tired-looking men in blue shirts, but find that I can't. If I'd observed Bianka in a social setting and then been asked to guess what she does for a living, I would have guessed she was an actress, or perhaps a used-car saleswoman or a nightclub hostess; definitely a profession where her luminous personality would take centre stage, unlike what I imagine to be the case in the marketing of white goods.

'Control,' I say, and smile. 'Back to you. What did you want to be when you were a kid?' I ask. Bianka stares into the distance for a long while with a frown on her face, as though she could see a younger version of herself out there.

'I wanted to be a writer,' she says. 'But I wasn't exactly encouraged.'

'Oh. I'm sorry.' I feel a stab of grief, unexpected and sharp, at the memory of how my mother always encouraged me to trust myself and find magic in every day. *You can be anything you want, Charlotte*, she'd whisper into my ear, night after night. 'Do you mean after you'd lost your mother?'

Bianka nods, then tilts her head up to the stars and doesn't meet my gaze for a long while.

'And my father,' she says, softly. I feel a twinge of shock at this information. I wait for her to continue but she doesn't and I don't want to push her to embellish. I can't imagine losing both parents in childhood, or maybe I can. In many ways I did. My father stayed behind, of course, but only in body. His mind and thoughts and love never seemed to belong to me.

'By the way, I googled "Xara" earlier. It means *to set free* in Basque. Isn't that lovely?' I'll allow her the change of subject, considering, but she's caught me off guard and I swallow hard a couple of times, and look away. Of course it does. It was the thing my mother loved the most besides me: freedom. I nod and smile, perhaps a little coolly, and Bianka seems to pick up on the shift in mood and falls silent. I light another menthol cigarette and draw the smoke deep into me, trying to let go of what Bianka said about Xara. There is something about it that niggles me, like I knew this already but can't say how or from whom.

'I sometimes feel like I'll never be happy,' I say, surprising myself and probably Bianka too. 'I work and work and still nothing ever feels enough. I achieve something, and then I just move the bar. At first, all I wanted was to publish a keto cookbook. Then, it was to have my own TV show. Then it was to create own-brand products. And now, five books down the line, a primetime TV show, and a whole range of own-brand products and I feel backed into a corner, uninspired and unfulfilled, you know?' I pause for a moment but decide to keep going because it feels overwhelmingly good to say something that is actually true out loud, to stop pretending and performing, if only for a moment. 'I feel like all the dreams I had have just disappeared, the ones I must have had as a child. I remember a very intense feeling of aliveness back then, like I was fully alert and in the moment, all the time. I never feel like that anymore. I feel disconnected and light-years away, going through the endless motions in the suburbs. I feel like I'm acting out a marriage that isn't mine and that I have no idea who I am anymore.'

When I stop talking, Bianka looks stunned and impressed at the same time.

'Oh, Charlotte,' she says, and I close my eyes, feeling her hand close on top of my own and I decide to just allow myself this moment of feeling taken care of. 'You don't have to live like that,' she whispers.

It's almost three a.m. by the time I get to bed but I feel wired and happy, like I could put on my running gear and go for a long, gruelling run into the southern hills, the only sound in the night my sneakers pounding the dry, crumbling path and the crash of waves far below. Instead of actually doing it, I close my eyes and try to bring the nighttime run to life as much as I can by inventing minute details – the silhouette of the mountains as I head toward Port de Sant Miquel, bats tearing across the sky, the waves slapping against the black rocks of the cape, my heart pounding in my chest like a bouncing ball. I try to evoke the exhaustion I'd feel when I round the final bend in the track leading back up to Can Xara, how I'd stand a while, doubled over, catching my breath, snapping at the fresh cool air. I'm still not tired, though it's been a very long day, and it's like I'm filled with thoughts and impressions that demand to be processed before my mind will shut down.

I think about Bianka sleeping in the guest room across the hallway, her hair fanning around her head, her pretty, animated face peaceful. I smile to myself at how impressed she was with Can Xara; it's really nice when people show appreciation rather than behave all blasé like Linda and Anette, though I suppose to them, this place is beautiful but nothing that special – I am only one of many friends with impressive second homes abroad. It seems like the thing Bianka loves the most about this place is the natural setting and Cala Azura – my favourite aspects too. Though the new house is spectacular, the main event here really is the coastline and the mountains. My mind returns to the moments Bianka and I stood on the pebbled, narrow beach earlier, watching the sun lower itself into the Mediterranean. I felt wired, then, like now, as though all my senses were heightened and every single detail was seared into the pathways of my memory. It's as though Bianka has that effect on me; that being in her presence returns me to a way of being I thought was lost to me – the intense aliveness of childhood we talked about earlier.

I feel my muscles begin to relax and my eyelids feel a little heavier. I can hear the hoot of an animal through the open window and the surge of the waves. I feel a visceral aloneness but also like I'm part of everything, as if my existence was essential and woven into the pattern of the universe. Bianka would like that notion; she likes to talk about things like that, and I'm discovering that so do I. I make a mental note of telling her about it tomorrow and picture the animated glint in her eyes as I speak, how she'll fix me with that clear blue gaze that seems to look through me completely.

As though my body answers not to my conscious demand, but to itself, my hand travels across my collarbone and my breasts, then down the concave curve of my stomach and into my underwear. I can't actually remember the last time I did this, but my touch feels good, just what I need, and as I keep going I grow simultaneously tense and relaxed until wave after wave of total release crashes over me.

Twelve

Bianka

She wakes to the sound of waves crashing onto the rocks far below. The air is cool and fragrant, carrying that scent which by now is both familiar and exotic – thyme, lavender, frangipani, the ocean. At first, she feels disorientated, the sparse and bright unfamiliar room taking a while to register in her mind, then she remembers: Ibiza, the night before, the conversation with Charlotte that went on long into the night. Another Charlotte had emerged from the contours Bianka had built of her in her mind; it was the sensation of unpeeling something and finding something other than what you'd expected underneath. She pictures the vibrant, juicy flesh of an orange emerging from a banana peel and feels instantly unsettled by the image.

I feel like I'm acting out a marriage that isn't mine, she'd said.

Bianka takes a deep breath, clears her mind and places her bare feet on the cool marble floor. The room has nothing in it except the bed, a white minimalist leather chair, and a sleek built-in wardrobe that runs the entire vast length of the wall. Bianka slides it open and there is nothing at all inside. She can't imagine a life without clutter, without odd socks and out-of-season clothes shoved into closets. She supposes that because this is a second home, things wouldn't amass as easily as in a family home, and feels another bolt of jealousy at Charlotte's life. She thought they were the same, comfortably well-off with high-earning husbands; Bianka's is Charlotte's husband's boss even, but she didn't realize Charlotte was clearly next-level rich until she arrived at Can Xara.

She steps out onto the balcony that is constructed entirely from glass to give the sensation of floating in thin air, and though it isn't the first time she's stood here, she feels a deep thrill in her stomach. She squints in the sharp sun, shielding her eyes to try to make out what looks like an animal swimming across the tightly curved bay far below, weaving in and out of the water, dragging up a line of white froth. It moves fast and for a moment Bianka thinks it must be a dolphin, but its movements are too conscious and symmetrical. It reaches the cape on the far end of the bay and Bianka watches as it hauls itself from the sea, its black body glinting in the sunlight. Now there is no doubt that it's a human, a woman in a wetsuit – Charlotte.

Bianka moves quickly around the room, slipping out of her pyjamas and into her bikini, covering herself up with an Ibiza-style fringed white linen kaftan. She hurries downstairs, hoping not to bump into Anette or Linda, but they are there in the open kitchen-dining area, laughing and fiddling with a professional-looking coffee machine. The room is surrounded by floor-to-ceiling windows and has a large skylight, giving the effect of being almost outside, a medley of Mediterranean blues reflected in the glass and metal surfaces of the kitchen.

'Good morning, Bianka,' says Linda. 'Can we make you a fancy coffee? An oat milk turmeric macchiato, perhaps?' They laugh.

'Thank you, I'm okay for now,' says Bianka, though she usually maintains she can't function without the first caffeine hit of the day. 'I thought I'd head out for a walk.' Coffee can wait – she wants to get to Charlotte before she comes back up to the house. She wants time alone with her, doesn't want anything to get in the way of the growing intimacy she shares with Charlotte.

She slips outside and heads to the stone steps that lead from the terrace and down onto the winding, narrow path, cooled by dense pine trees reaching across it as if to keep it secret. Bianka half runs on bare feet, past the guesthouse, past the yoga platform, down through the first terraces of olive groves and almond trees, past the clutch of citrus trees that hide the finca from view. She pauses for a brief moment as the path divides into two, one leading to the coves and one to Charlotte's mother's house, its ancient stone visible through the waxy verdant leaves of the citrus trees only when you know where to look. Bianka wants to see it from the inside, and finds it interesting that Charlotte never goes in there and seems to keep it as a shrine.

She continues on the uneven path, her feet aching from stepping on an occasional sharp stone, and pauses again when the path emerges from the wooded patch and turns sharply down the steep hillside on the final stretch leading down to the sea. She has an uninterrupted view of the bay, from the rocky promontory that separates it from the azure calas to the north, past the little boat whose tin roof glints in the morning sun, to the cape where Charlotte emerged from the sea. There is no sign of her now and Bianka feels a pang of disappointment as she descends the several flights of stone steps that run from the end of the path down onto the rocky beach.

She quickly scans the shore but sees nothing but the sharp rocks rising from the sea glistening in the morning sun and the Mediterranean pines scattering the hillsides towering above the narrow bay. Could Charlotte have made her way back another way? Bianka looks back up toward the house. There are no other properties visible except for one further along and higher up from Charlotte's, but there is no sign of any other point of access to the beach than along the path and stairs she came on. She looks out at the sea again and then she sees it, a pair of black-sheathed arms slicing the water far out, almost by the lighthouse at the end of the cape.

Bianka shrugs out of the kaftan and lets it drop to the pebbled beach. Then, on an impulse, she unties the strings of her bikini and lets that, too, drop to the ground. It feels empowering and the exact opposite of revealing, to stand there naked. She wades into the sea, which is surprisingly cold considering how warm the air already is. She feels her skin pucker into goosebumps but wades further out before throwing herself all the way in, head first. The water is even colder than it felt at first and she emerges, gasping, before propelling herself forward in the direction of Charlotte. Bianka's a fast swimmer and after a few minutes she crosses her trajectory and heads toward the cape, directly intercepting Charlotte, who's making her way back to the shore.

'Hey,' she shouts when Charlotte is within earshot. She turns around slowly as though she isn't sure she really heard someone speak. Before it fully registers that Bianka is out there, right in front of her, kicking the clear turquoise water and laughing, she looks tired and drawn, almost unrecognizable from the groomed and perfectly made-up Charlotte who smiles so confidently at her audience from the TV screen. When she realizes that she's not imagining things, she too laughs.

'Charlotte, hi,' says Bianka, flipping over onto her back and floating. 'I didn't realize you were out here, too.'

'I always swim first thing in the morning when I'm here. Even in winter. God, you must be freezing; you're not in a wetsuit.' Bianka feels Charlotte's gaze on her body and relishes the little moment of shock when she realizes she's fully naked.

'How funny. Me too, whenever I can. I love to swim in the sea. And yes, a little chilly this morning. Excuse the nudity; I thought I was alone.' Charlotte laughs and they swim slowly side by side back to the shore. Bianka can tell by Charlotte's red, splotchy cheeks and jagged breath that she's nearing exhaustion. On the beach, they flop down side by side on their fronts on a narrow sandy patch. Charlotte tactfully avoids looking directly at Bianka, and Bianka wonders whether Charlotte has actually seen another woman completely naked this close before.

'How is it possible that we didn't even know each other six weeks ago,' says Charlotte, angling her beautiful face toward the sun.

'I know,' says Bianka. 'It really does feel like we've always known each other.'

'Yeah, it's crazy, isn't it? Listen, Bianka, thank you for the talk last night. I thought about it in my room after, that I haven't ever really talked to anyone in years, the way that you and I do. Not even Andreas. And about, uh, Andreas, I feel like I might have overshared a little bit. I didn't mean to give the impression that our marriage isn't solid or whatever. I'd had too much to drink, and—'

'Charlotte. Don't sweat it. I didn't think that at all. I don't even remember exactly what you said. Besides, what you said about everything at home feeling really far away resonated with me too.' Charlotte smiles gratefully and Bianka returns it, before gazing back out to the sparkling sea. Cala Azura is so beautiful she feels she could almost cry.

'Thank you for saying that. I guess I didn't realize it feels good to just talk about stuff.'

They fall silent for a while, watching a wide-winged bird swoop down low to the surface of the sea and emerging with a twitching little fish. 'Being here, I can't help but think about my mother, you know? It's like she's here, in everything.'

'I don't think you ever told me her name. What was it?' Bianka watches Charlotte's eyes travel from the sea and up into the hillside behind them, where her mother's house sits in the midst of its old citrus tree grove, only the chimney and ivy-clad archway visible from the beach.

'Ximena.'

Bianka repeats it.

'Hee-*men*-ah. I don't think I've heard it before.'

'Her name used to annoy me. When I was little, I just wanted her to be like all the other moms at school. You know. Prim Oslo West ladies with pearl earrings and blown-out blond hair. My mom was like a little Spanish hurricane, all flower prints and gold hoop earrings and bright-red lipstick and loud laugh.'

'She sounds very cool. Like you.'

Charlotte nods pensively. 'Oh, I'm not cool. And I'm nothing like her, at all. I'm the most average person ever.'

'I very much doubt that. I don't think there's anything especially average about you.'

'Well, you don't know me very well.'

'Yet.'

Charlotte nods and laughs and their eyes meet and it happens again; that slight shift in the atmosphere between them, when the air becomes charged. Charlotte seems to sharpen her senses and takes Bianka in more consciously, really considering who the person lying next to her is.

'I feel as though you know so much about me already. And I still don't know that much about you.'

'Well. You can ask me anything you want.' *I just might not answer*, thinks Bianka, careful to maintain a relaxed smile.

'What was your girlfriend like?'

'My girlfriend?' Bianka returns her gaze to the sea, its surface still and clear.

'Yeah, you mentioned that you'd had a girlfriend at university.' Bianka gets the impression that Charlotte had been wanting to ask about this, waiting for the right moment. She's pleased that this is something she's curious about; she's been waiting for her to ask. And she's been thinking about what she'd say when the moment would come. And what she wouldn't.

'Yes. A very long time ago now.'

'So what was she like? And what happened?'

'She was a bit like you.' Bianka watches Charlotte carefully, her heart beating faster at her own words. *She was just like you,* she should have said. Charlotte looks surprised but not horrified. Rather, a faint smile plays on her lips.

'Really?' Charlotte laughs a little, then flicks her long, wet hair over her shoulder in a move Bianka interprets as quite consciously suggestive.

'Mmm,' she says. Then she stands up, facing Charlotte directly for a long moment before picking up her bikini from the sand, then putting it back on. 'Let's head back up, shall we? I think the others are making breakfast.' Charlotte looks momentarily confused, then disappointed.

'I was just getting warmed up there,' she says.

Bianka starts on the stairs cut into the limestone cliffs, then turns back to Charlotte with a big smile.

'Come on,' she says, taking her hand and pulling her gently along. When she releases her grip, Charlotte doesn't, not for several long moments.

Always, always leave them wanting more, Bianka thinks to herself, and powers up the hillside toward the house, not looking back, feeling beads of sweat run down the back of her neck and in between her breasts, her heart pounding hard in her chest.

Thirteen

Storm

He wakes late with a start, and for a long while lies in bed, disorientated, looking at the soft light streaming in from the window blinds, but then he remembers it's the first week of the summer holidays and he's back in Wimbledon. And this time, it's just him and his dad. He smiles to himself. He stays in bed for ages, scrolling on his phone, enjoying the thick, pleasant silence in the house, as profound as if the house has been sealed whole into a soundproof cocoon. His dad is probably in his home office, tapping numbers into his phone or speaking into his headset to someone in Sao Paolo or Tokyo or Reykjavik, but it's Bianka's absence that makes all the difference. Usually, she manages to create noise of some kind almost all the time. If she's not shouting, she's laughing shrilly, or speaking loudly on the phone, or hoovering, or moving furniture around, or emptying the dishwasher in the demonstrative, passive-aggressive way of the extremely hard put-upon. She never seems to just *be*, in the way that Emil is, or Storm himself.

Storm pulls on a clean pair of boxers and a T-shirt, fished from the still-unpacked suitcase open on the floor and heads downstairs. The scent of eggs and bacon wafts toward him from the kitchen and as he gets closer, he's surprised to hear his father humming loudly to the song on the radio, some vintage country tune. He searches the unfamiliar cabinets for a bowl and the box of cornflakes. He feels light, happy, energized at the thought of the empty, quiet days of holiday stretching ahead. Now all he has to do is work up the nerve to call Madeleine Vinge.

'We should hang out sometime,' she'd said, offering her smooth, tan cheek for Storm to kiss when he was leaving. And since then, they've been texting back and forth constantly. At the thought of hanging out with Madeleine in person again, his heart seems to drop into the hot pit of his stomach.

His thoughts are interrupted by his father's soft chuckle. 'Earth to Storm. I repeat, Earth to Storm,' says Emil.

Storm snaps out of his dream-like state reliving the moment his lips grazed Madeleine's dry, soft cheek and he stares at his hand pouring milk all over the table, missing the cereal bowl by several centimetres. His cheeks flush and he instinctively glances around as though Bianka might be there after all, ready to start screaming at him. Ever since he was little, whenever he's spilled something, she's gone ballistic. But now she isn't here, and nobody starts yelling. Instead, his father swiftly mops up the milk with a cloth, before wringing it out and repeating.

'You were light-years away there, kiddo,' he says when he's done, sitting down across from Storm who is chewing his cornflakes slowly, his pulse still pounding in his ears from the stress of the spillage.

'Mmm.'

'Good thing your mother wasn't here,' Emil says, chuckling again, as if the way Bianka behaves toward Storm is remotely normal or amusing. Storm looks up abruptly, making Emil glance away. He doesn't say what he wants to say – *She's not my mother, please, please stop calling her that* – but he keeps fixing his father with a cool glare.

'I need to ask you something.'

'Okay.' His father has the decency to look nervous now, realizing he definitely hit the wrong tone.

'Why don't you say something to her? Why do you let her talk badly to you, and to me, over every little thing?'

'Storm, I—'

'No, seriously. Why do you put up with her bullshit? And why do I have to?'

'Your m— Bianka does a lot of stuff for us, Storm. She, uh, works very hard for me and you to have a good life. She loves us and just... just gets frustrated sometimes, I guess.'

Storm rolls his eyes incredulously. It's as though Bianka has actually cast a spell on his father and no matter how unreasonably she behaves or how extreme her demands become, Emil never questions her. 'Okay. So let me ask you this. Why is the atmosphere so much better when she isn't here? And have you even noticed how different she is around other people? It's like she has this whole persona that just comes out.'

Emil sighs and after a long while, nods. 'Look. I don't think that's quite fair. But I'll talk to her. I do agree that she can be, uh, unusually reactive at home.'

Storm nods. They sit a while in silence across from each other, Storm chasing a couple of limp leftover cornflakes around in the bowl with his spoon. He breathes consciously through wave after wave of bitter anger at the thought that it could be like this, all the time – Emil and Storm. Storm and Emil. He contemplates whether now is the right moment to broach the subject of the letter, but decides against it. It feels like too big a conversation for early in the morning. Besides, Storm wants to work out how he himself feels about it before discussing it with his father. And if there's one thing Storm has learned as a result of his skiing success, it is not to be overly reactive. Even when something unexpected and shocking happens – especially then. It could end up costing you everything.

'Hey,' says Emil. 'I was thinking we could do something together this weekend, just the two of us. How about we drive down to Brighton? Check out the beach and the nightlife? I hear it's buzzy and we need to start exploring a bit more of the UK.'

Storm nods, but feels strangely distant.

In the car, the atmosphere between them is light again, the conversation about Bianka forgotten. Storm briefly wonders what she's doing in this moment, whether she's thinking of them at all. Then he wonders what Bianka even thinks of the life she shares with him and his father; she's never, in all the years he's known her, seemed especially happy.

As they head south out of London, a sudden rainstorm slows traffic down until it gets so bad that they can hardly make out the road and they have to slow down to a crawl with the hazards on. For a long while they sit there listening to loud music as the rain slams against the windscreen,

Storm's favourite playlist of Norwegian hip-hop. The rain eventually lets up and Emil turns off the hazards and urges the Tesla into the faster lane, which is moving properly again now. Storm turns down the volume dial on the radio and clears his throat. His voice comes out loud and clear, as though he's been planning to say this, though he hasn't. In fact, he's never asked before, not like this – directly. But since the letter arrived, he realizes that he wants to know more.

'Dad. I need you to tell me about my mother.'

Emil glances at his son and for a moment, Storm tries to picture himself the way his father must see him in this moment. No longer a little boy, Storm is as tall as a man, though his lankiness gives away his youth. He has dark-brown eyes, unlike Emil's steely blue ones, and an unruly mop of thick dark-blond hair. Emil doesn't look surprised or annoyed; he must have anticipated that the day would come when Storm would start asking proper questions about his mother, and not be satisfied with the vague answers he'd been given in childhood.

'Of course. What do you want to know?'

'More. What she was like. I feel – I feel as though I only know her name and what she did. Not who she was.'

Emil nods, then begins to talk, and when he speaks of her, Storm notices that his father's face lights up in a way he's never seen before, as though there is an extra switch inside him that has just been flicked on for the first time.

'Well, she was really funny. Nobody has made me laugh like she did. She loved to travel. That's one of the things I've thought about after... After what happened. That I'm glad we made time to travel as much as we did. Her favourite was India, for all the reasons that it was probably my least favourite – she loved the colours, the smells, the chaos, the noise of Mumbai and Kolkata. And the humid heat of the countryside. We went twice, before you were born.'

'Do you have pictures?'

'From India?'

'Yeah.'

His father hesitates and keeps his eyes firmly on the busy road. They're just coming into Brighton and Emil manoeuvres the car across a busy roundabout. The rain has let up completely and a brilliant sun is reflected in puddles and windows, and the streets are filled with swarms of young people smiling and talking, mostly walking in the direction they're driving, toward the beach. Storm stares at them; it feels safer than looking at his father, and besides, he's fascinated by the sheer crowds. He's not used to them, having grown up in quiet Norway. He wonders if that is one of the things that fascinated his mother about India.

'Yes. I do. I – uh – put them away up in the attic, years ago. But I do have them.'

'I want to see them.'

Emil hesitates again, but after a quick glance at Storm's face, realizes he's absolutely serious and nods.

'Where are they now, exactly?'

'I – I believe some of them are in London at the new house. In the attic. We had almost everything personal from Oslo shipped here because the company paid anyway, so—'

'Why weren't there ever any pictures of her at home?'

'You know your, uh, m—, uh, Bianka, felt a little strange about having lots of pictures of her around.'

'And I feel a little strange about the fact that, thanks to

her, I've only ever seen a few photos of my actual mother. We never even speak about her.'

'I'm sorry, Storm. I know I haven't always handled it very well. I've never known how to talk about her with you. It has sometimes just seemed better to wait for you to ask. That's what the child psychologist said, too.'

'Well, I'm asking now.'

'Yes. And you can ask me anything you want about her. I want you to know that.'

'Okay, tell me more.'

'Well. She was quite geeky, too, and collected lots of little trinkets from our travels, everything from ticket stubs to faded rocks that had once been part of temples, you know, that kind of thing.'

'And where is all of that stuff?'

'We, uh, had to get rid of quite a lot of it when we moved to Slemdal. After she died.'

'We.' Storm can feel his father shoot him a sharp glance. Emil chooses to ignore the little dig and continues speaking of Storm's mother as they come to a stop in a gridlocked line of traffic queuing for an underground garage by the beachfront. The water is a gorgeous shade of blue, the beach is busy, and the atmosphere is relaxed and happy, a contrast to the conversation Storm and his father are having.

Emil's face is bright and animated as he speaks of Mia, telling Storm about the time she tried to convince Emil to move to Italy, and the time she hitchhiked to France with a friend, and the time she bought a boar's head at an auction on a whim. When he finishes speaking, they've just parked, Emil squeezing the big Tesla into a spot so small Storm has to climb over and exit from his dad's side. As they emerge back into the bright daylight and head toward the beach, Emil looks crestfallen and drained, but from the way he spoke of Mia, it is clear to Storm that he really loved her and needed to speak about her as much as Storm needed to hear about her.

It's late when they pull back up to the house in Dunstall Road. Storm feels exhausted, even more so than after a day of training – it's as though his body doesn't know how to cope with a few days off.

He bids his father goodnight and slips upstairs, finding his way in the dark without switching the lights on. He's gotten to know the house now and knows how many steps he needs to take before feeling for the door to his bedroom. He slips into the unmade, cool bed and is drifting off when he's brought back by the buzz of the phone on his nightstand. He grabs it and peers half-heartedly at the screen, probably just yet another inane Star Wars Snap from Albert, but as he takes in the words he sits up straight, blinking at the text.

Hey you. When can we hang out? I've missed u, from Madeleine Vinge.

Storm pretend-punches the air in the dark room, lit only by the glare of the screen, then he falls asleep smiling.

Fourteen

Charlotte

It's late afternoon and we're drinking wine by the pool, when we hear the sound of drums climbing the hillsides around Can Xara.

'What is that?' asks Bianka.

'It's, like, a weekly thing, I think – a bunch of people gather on the beach down at Benirràs at sunset and play drums. There's a pop-up mojito bar and it tends to get a little crazy,' I say.

Bianka sits up and cocks her head to better catch the sound. 'Sounds fun. Can we go?'

'We went once, years ago, and honestly, it's a bunch of weird, stinky hippies worshipping the moon. That kind of thing,' says Anette.

'Just my vibe,' says Bianka, and we all laugh, but I don't think she's joking.

'I'll go down there with you if you want,' I say.

***

Down by the coves, a giant bonfire has been built, ready to be lit when the sky is properly dark. The atmosphere feels electric, with hundreds of people laughing and swaying to the rhythmic beat of the many drums playing. It makes me feel suddenly emotional to be here, like my ties to the island are deepening and I'm inching closer to who I really am. Or maybe it's because I'm here with Bianka and her very presence makes everything feel heightened and different. Since we've been in Ibiza, this has intensified even more and I'm realizing that I want something more from Bianka than just friendship. But what does that mean for my marriage and for my life? Since Anette shared the news of her divorce and dismissed the way she – and by extension I – live, there is a part of me that feels like it's waking up to the possibility of other ways of living. Could I, too, be free? And what does it mean that I find myself this attracted to a woman? I thought I knew everything about myself. I thought I was in control. When I try to think whether I've ever experienced this kind of attraction to a woman before, I realize that I've never really stopped to consider how I feel at all. Besides, does it even have to matter that much? After all, we are in Ibiza, worlds away from real life. Perhaps I could allow myself to just have a little fun. And Bianka is my idea of fun.

'I'll get drinks,' says Bianka, slipping into the throng of people standing between us and the mojito bar. I watch her walk over to the pop-up bar and she is instantly drawn into conversation with a couple of guys as she waits. She says something animatedly, then throws her head back, laughing, her distinct voice slicing through the incessant thud of the drums.

One of the guys who is standing with his back toward

me seems to explain something to her, gesticulating enthusiastically, his thick, dark hair flopping around with the effort, and I watch Bianka follow his pointed finger across the bay with her eyes. It's obvious the men are enchanted with her and I feel a twinge of jealousy. Bianka laughs some more, then returns with two huge mojitos.

I take the drink and inch closer to Bianka, wanting to show the guys, and the world, that she's here with me, then feel instantly ridiculous. Bianka is obviously entitled to engage with other people in whichever way she wants. But every time she looks at me, or leans in to whisper something in my ear, or places her little warm hand on my wrist to iterate a point, I feel something deep inside, something I don't quite understand, both frightening and irresistible at the same time. *Fun*, I tell myself. *That unfamiliar feeling is fun*. And maybe I just need to let go and allow myself to have some without overthinking it.

I reach out and take Bianka's hand. She laces her fingers through mine and we stand like that for a long while, swaying to the beat with the crowd that is made up of people from all over the world, mostly young and beautiful and rich, drawn to Ibiza not just for her beaches and parties and drugs, but for her mythical and deeply spiritual core. As I stand here on this beach, a small part of a human horseshoe curved around the roaring bonfire they've just lit, watching the last rays of the sun bleeding into the sky, listening to the drums, Bianka's hand snug and somehow inevitable in my own, I feel what my mother must have felt: a homecoming, an undeniable connection to something bigger than myself. I've always avoided that kind of thing, the suggestion that life could be about more than what we can see and touch;

it reminds me too much of Ximena and her spiritual quest, which ended in tragedy.

We ride the moped home on the narrow road rising and falling through the dark hills, the scent of verbena and wild rosemary permeating the humid air, my arms tight around Bianka's waist, the soft sound of my laughter swallowed up by the drone of the Vespa's engine. Bianka drives deliberately slowly, and by the time we reach Can Xara, it's late, past midnight, and Linda and Anette are nowhere to be seen.

It's me who stops on the path up to the house, it's me who softly whispers 'hey' into the dense air that's alive with the chirp of cicadas and frogs, and it's me who steps closer, then closer still, then leans in to softly kiss Bianka on the lips.

Fifteen

Bianka

For Bianka, being in bed with Charlotte feels like travelling back through time, to when she wasn't broken and empty. To the only time she felt whole.

She's just like Bianka expected, beautiful, a little shy, playful.

The moment they kissed felt inevitable, like it had to happen, and yet Bianka was impressed that Charlotte actually went ahead and made a move. Since the moment they met, a fantasy of kissing Charlotte and discovering every single part of her has played in a constant loop in Bianka's mind. And yet Charlotte has been hard to read and Bianka couldn't quite tell if she was just elated to have a new, close friend, or if their intense connection merged into sexual attraction the way it did for Bianka. As Charlotte releases Bianka's breasts from her bra and begins to kiss them softly and enthusiastically, it's very obvious to Bianka that it does and she has to pace herself, manage the wild beat of her heart, because she is both intensely here in the moment with Charlotte, and suddenly back in the past, in the only space she has ever truly felt something. She closes her eyes and lets herself just breathe and live and enjoy.

She wakes with a jolt and for an instant she fears that it was all just a dream, that Charlotte could only be hers in a fantasy world. But she's here, sleeping softly beside her. Bianka moves away from her a little to get a better view in the shaft of moonlight shining into the room from the huge windows. She sits up, drawing the bedsheet up to her chin, and watches Charlotte. She can't help the tears, then. It's too much, too overwhelming. Her thoughts race, image upon image settling on top of each other, blurring reality and fantasy, past and present. Charlotte is so still that for a moment Bianka imagines that she's dead, that Bianka has killed her in her sleep without remembering. Would she perhaps even be capable of such a thing? She fixes her gaze at a spot on Charlotte's bare chest but in the meagre light she can't be sure she's breathing, or if she's even alive.

'No,' she whispers. Bianka reaches out and lightly places her finger against Charlotte's neck just beneath her jawline and instantly finds a throbbing, strong pulse.

Charlotte shifts in her sleep at Bianka's touch, and Bianka's heart is thundering in her chest. She moves closer to Charlotte; so close, her features grow blurred, and then she wraps herself into her arms in a tight embrace, chasing away disturbing thoughts of death, focusing on the steady, calming thud of her lover's heartbeat.

Sixteen

Charlotte

I wake in the night and the air is cool, the fan whispering from the ceiling. There is another sound, a rhythmic beating sound, and I remember last night, the magic of the drums reverberating around the bay at Benirràs, the blood-coloured sky and lavender sea; it's as though its sounds and moods have been trapped inside me. I turn toward the windows to see if I can make out whether it's dawn or still the middle of the night, and it's only as I move my head that I realize I'm not alone. Moonlight spills into the room and illuminates the woman in my bed. Bianka. She's naked, with a sheet draped across her waist, her unruly blond curls fanning out around her head like a halo, her puffy lips open as she sleeps, her teeth glinting in the moonlight like a string of pearls, and behind them, a sliver of wet, pink tongue. When I slept, my head must have been pressed up against her bare chest – the sound I heard was her heart beating. I sit up slowly, careful not to rouse her.

I feel panic starting up in the pit of my stomach, then

spreading through me at the sight of her in my bed. My palms are slick with sweat and the fine hairs at the back of my neck prickle and stand up, my breath coming short and fast. I think of Andreas in this moment, peaceful and unknowing in our bed at home, our children asleep in their rooms above ours. What have I done?

My heart starts racing as memory returns to me through the lingering haze of all the alcohol, in little pieces that slot together to form a series of images. Panic gives way to a deep thrill as I remember the way I took Bianka's hand and we pressed up against each other in the throng of people at Cala Benirràs, feeling bold after several mojitos. And when we kissed... The kisses quickly deepened from careful and soft to intensely passionate so that I was pushed up against the whitewashed wall of Can Xara, my shoulder chafing against the concrete, before we quietly slipped upstairs into my bedroom.

I leave the bed and cross the room to the bathroom. I close the door, then switch on the light. When my eyes have gotten used to the glare from the spotlights, I stare at myself in the mirror. My whole life, I've felt as though I had a solid grasp of who I am, and it always seemed to me that we mould ourselves into who we want to be. It was important to me to be predictable and calm, the kind of person who runs through all the potential pros and cons before making a decision. The kind who creates a good life for herself and works hard at sustaining it. I've never believed that we just wake up in the perfect circumstances; we have to plot and plan and create them, and then, once we're happy, we have to do everything we can to hold onto it.

I eat carefully, to maintain that level, empty feeling

that makes me feel safe. I do everything one should do to run a successful business; I treat people fairly and with kindness, and pay my taxes on time. I take my role as a mother seriously, trying to be an example for my children to follow. I invest in my marriage, ensuring Andreas gets enough care, enough conversation, enough freedom. I'd make sure he got enough sex, too, if only he wanted it. And then Bianka walked into my life and threw all of it up into the air. I suppose I could go back out there and speak to her gently and clearly, explaining that I got carried away, that what happened shouldn't have and never can again. She'd understand, of course she would, because what choice would she have? She probably feels exactly the same; after all, Bianka is happily married, too. We got carried away, that's all. These things happen. I've heard similar stories of holiday escapades and much worse from my wider circle of friends and acquaintances. Not ideal, of course, but one might be forgiven an indiscretion or two after what feels like one thousand years of marriage.

I think about what Andreas would feel if he knew that I have slept with someone else, and it's the realization that he probably wouldn't care that much that brings tears to my eyes. I watch a teardrop run slowly down my face, followed by another, and another. Of course I can't know if that's how he would react; it's possible he'd make a huge deal out of it, especially as he might worry about his job, but I don't think he'd care on an emotional level, and it's this distance that hurts me. It's also this that stops me from feeling *that* bad.

I wipe away the tears and stand another long while in front of the mirror. I force thoughts of Andreas from my mind. I try to see myself as Bianka does, because it seems that she sees something other than what everyone else does, even me. But I can't imagine what that is, I only see myself as I always have: a little bland, much like most people, not someone worthy of any particular attention, let alone deep interest and adoration.

I wonder how my mother saw me; I remember how she'd always try to encourage me to think bigger, step outside my comfort zone, dare to dream. *All of the beautiful things in the whole world are inside of you, Charlotte*, she used to say to me when I was little. I take a few deep breaths, watching my bare chest rise and fall, my skin feeling slick with sweat away from the bedroom's air-con. My lips are red from all the kissing. I close my eyes, then turn out the light.

I slip back into the bedroom and when I get back into the bed, Bianka's moved to face me, her eyes open and shining in the soft light, and I let myself be drawn into her embrace. It feels so good, better than any other. Her small, warm hands touch the sides of my face, then travel around the back of my neck into the moist tangle of my hair, slowly working through the knots, then across my collarbone and close around my breasts. Her lips touch mine. I reciprocate the kiss hungrily and any confusion is gone. I pull her on top of me so every part of us is touching.

Afterward, Bianka sleeps in my arms and I lie awake, watching the first pink rays of the sun pierce the morning sky. When the sun itself appears on the horizon, casting slivers of pale golden light onto the smooth, whitewashed walls, I gently untangle myself. I pad across the room and grab the wetsuit from the bathroom before walking quietly through the house and outside onto the terrace. I stand facing the sun, feeling its faint warmth, then I head down toward the sea.

I swim fast, nudged by the current toward the cape, and even though my arms ache and my body feels a little slow from lack of sleep and alcohol and all the sex, I can't stop smiling.

The four of us do yoga on the platform in the late afternoon when the air begins to cool. I'm conscious of my movements and expressions, as though Linda and Anette can guess just from looking at me that Bianka and I spent last night passionately making love in my bedroom. I'm noticing things I wouldn't usually, as if my senses have been magically heightened; the countless nuances of the sea leaping onto the rocks across the bay at Punta de Sa Creu, the way the air sweeps across the bare skin of my arms, the loud chirping of birds rarely heard in Oslo or Wimbledon. I have the strange feeling, sitting here in the lotus position, closing my eyes, succumbing to the calm of yoga – something my mother loved – of the distance between us being bridged, that I might embody more of her than I thought, and that that could be something beautiful. I open my eyes and meet Bianka's who is sitting across from me, looking straight at me. When our eyes meet, she smiles a suggestive little smile just for me and a current of electricity shoots up my spine.

'Namaste,' says Linda, standing up slowly, a serene look on her face. She puts the incense burning on the brick wall out with her fingertips and turns to the sea. 'Now let's start drinking.' We all laugh and roll up our yoga mats. We've managed to secure a reservation at El Cielo, apparently one of northern Ibiza's coolest beach restaurants, just a quick Vespa ride through the hills to Port de Sant Miquel. I've been wanting to go there for a long time, but now I feel as though all I want is to stay at the house with Bianka, to return to the intensity of last night and this morning. I can't quite believe everything that has happened since yesterday, and throughout the day I've repeatedly ignored thoughts about home, consciously wrestling my mind back to the here and now. I have the rest of my life to worry about real life and we only have a few precious days on Ibiza.

On the way back up to the house, I fall into step with Linda, and have the sudden strange sensation of finding nothing to say to her. We've known each other for so many years and though ours might not be the most profound chemistry, it's always felt easy between us, nice. And now she feels like a stranger, someone who knows nothing about me or who I actually am, that there is a huge gulf between us that can never be crossed.

'Isn't it funny,' she says, wiping at perspiration dotting her blond hairline as we climb the path from the platform toward the terrace, 'that every time we come here, it feels fundamentally different from the last? How many times have we done this now? Seven, at least? And every trip is easily discernible from the others. Do you remember that year when Anette's kids were being particularly full-on and she just slept the entire time? Or two years ago, when we managed to squeeze it in between all the restrictions? It just felt so amazing to get away then, like I couldn't quite compute that all this was still here and had been all that time when the whole world just shut down...'

Linda keeps talking and I'm pleased she doesn't feel what

I felt, that there's nothing to be said between us, and I make myself nod and laugh as she recounts memory after memory we've built at Can Xara over the years.

I shower and change into a dusty-pink halter neck silk dress that has hung in my closet here for years, unused. It has never felt like it's me, but tonight it does. I coil my clean hair into an updo, securing it into place with a long silver hair dagger my mother gave me the last Christmas she was alive and which I instantly loved. It still feels too warm to wear my hair loose, even in the evening. I apply some discreet makeup, too, wanting to look enhanced but not overdone. I tan easily, probably thanks to my mother's Spanish genes, and already have a golden glow after a couple of days in the sun. When I'm done, I stand in front of the mirror like I did in the middle of the night, again trying to read the woman in front of me. Who is she and what does she want?

An image of Bianka immediately appears in my mind; the way her expression seems to change and deepen when it's me she's looking at. The way she maintained eye contact with me as she inched her way down my naked body, kissing and rubbing and sucking as she went, her blond curls tickling the skin on the inside of my thighs.

Yes, I think to myself. I want Bianka.

We order oysters and sashimi and tiger prawns and when the food arrives it's artfully displayed on ice in towering trays. The restaurant is on Platja d'en Bossa, one of three similar establishments, all popular places to go in summer, when the sand becomes a dance floor after dinner. It's packed though it's still early, just past nine, and the loud lounge music spreads out on the warm air that carries the scent of sea salt and pine trees. Out in the bay, some big yachts are moored, their lights undulating across the darkening surface of the sea.

We sit on low sofas built around a table with a glass fire pit feature in its middle and because Bianka sits across from me, next to Linda, I can barely see her through the tall flickering flames. I feel frustrated and on edge; I don't really want to be here, I want to be back at Can Xara, alone with Bianka, and I find it hard to fully engage in the conversation bouncing back and forth across the table. I just want to stay close to that feeling that has been awakened in me, the feeling of being young again, that anything is possible.

'Told you this place is insane,' shouts Anette to Bianka, as they turn to watch a man who has climbed onto a podium at the far end of the restaurant, from where he sprays the cheering crowd from a magnum bottle of champagne.

'That's the biggest cliché I've ever seen,' says Linda. 'I'd go so crazy if some guy ruined my dress with alcohol.'

'Clichés become clichés because they're true or fun, though, right?' says Bianka. She leans forward a little so we can see each other clearly through a patch in the fire feature. She smiles, then lifts an oyster to her lips and sucks its flesh from the shell, her eyes locked on mine. I look away, take a sip of my mojito, and feel myself grow instantly aroused. It feels strange and somewhat frightening that Bianka suddenly holds such visceral power over me, that a single suggestive glance can produce an immediate physical response. I glance at Anette next to me, but her eyes are glued to the cheering crowd gathering at the fringes of the beach, drifting onto the sand from all three restaurants, bodies pushing up against each other and breaking into dance.

Bianka stands up. 'Come on,' she says, 'let's join them.'

'What? Bianka, no, look, they're all practically kids. They're all in their twenties,' says Anette.

'So?'

'So, we can't just, like, go out there and start dancing in the middle of dinner.'

'Why not?'

'Because…'

'Come on, Anette,' says Linda, her face lighting up at the realization that if you feel like getting up to dance in the middle of dinner, you can actually just go ahead. 'Let's do it.'

I stand up too, because Bianka has already disappeared into the crowd and I want to be where she is.

'Yeah, Anette,' I shout over the increasingly persistent beat. 'We're not that old. And we're in Ibiza.'

Anette reluctantly follows, keeping her heels on – even though they sink into the sand and the rest of us have kicked ours off – and smoothing down her structured designer skirt, glancing around as though someone might lurch at her and drench her with champagne. Linda, Bianka, and I start to dance, feeling the upbeat music pulsate through us, laughing at the energy and exuberance of the crowd, letting ourselves be bumped and jostled and drawn into the spontaneous movements of other groups. Finally, Anette joins in too, kicking her shoes off and unleashing her beautiful auburn hair from its sleek chignon, inspiring the admiration of several young men around us. She realizes this and feels empowered, and I just love watching her let go of rigidity and perfection and that cool detached persona she's honed, probably much like myself. I sidle up to her and put my arms around her from behind and she twerks against me, lapping up the attention and making a couple of guys whistle.

After several songs we let ourselves drift to the periphery of the crowd and back toward our table. A sudden, loud scream cuts through the music and I turn around to see Anette crumpling to the ground. I'm the person closest to her and I rush over to her and take her gently by the arm and she looks up at me, face twisted in a grimace of pain and fear.

'I stepped on broken glass.'

'Oh, my God. Oh no,' I say, helping her sit on one of the sofas as blood gushes from her foot onto the sand. I angle her foot up to the light as Linda and Bianka rush off to get ice and bandages, and there is a big triangular shard of glass wedged deeply into the space between her big toe and its neighbour.

'Seriously. For fuck's sake,' she whispers through gritted teeth.

'I know. I'm so sorry this happened. I'm going to try to gently prize it out, okay?'

She nods, face still pale with pain and shock. Bianka and Linda return, pushing their way through the crowd, carrying a champagne bucket and a first aid kit.

'Why did I agree to something like that?' says Anette. 'It was a really fucking stupid idea to dance barefoot in the sand when we've just watched people like that idiot on the podium.' Bianka says nothing, just hands me the ice, and I press it against Anette's toe, then swiftly pull out the shard, making her gasp. I clean the wound, spraying it with antiseptic, then cover it with three plasters. The crowd has long since lost interest, gathering around a couple of South Americans playing drums further down by the water.

'Time to go home,' says Anette when I finish. Linda nods. I nod, too, assuming that we'll all head back to Can Xara together. 'Unless you guys want to stay behind, of course.' It feels like there is a slightly challenging tone in her voice and I'm sure Bianka and Linda hear it, too, but Bianka smiles and nods.

'Yeah, I mean, I'd be up for staying a little longer.'

'I think I'm ready for bed,' says Linda, probably quite aware that as she drove the Vespa with her and Anette here, she'll need to drive it back. Linda isn't drinking much at all on this trip due to the hormonal injections she's taking for IVF.

'Charlotte?' Bianka and Anette say my name at exactly the same time.

'Yeah. I, uh…' Anette is looking at me somewhat coolly. Bianka raises an eyebrow slowly as I glance from Anette to Linda to Bianka, realizing I'm being asked to choose.

'I should head back to Can Xara with you guys,' I say. 'I'll show you where the first aid kit is at the house. You should probably clean it again before bed.'

'Don't feel like you have to on my part,' says Anette, slowly getting to her feet. Her haughty expression reminds me of when we were children and she'd tell me I had to choose between her and whoever I was playing with. If I wouldn't, she'd spin around on her heel and stalk furiously across the playground, her long auburn hair rippling down her back like upside-down flames as she went. Now, in this moment, I realize it makes me angry.

'Okay,' I say, and give her my best sympathetic smile; gentle and concerned. 'Then I'll stay and ride back with Bianka.' For a brief moment, Anette looks shocked, like she can't believe I'd cross her, but I don't back down. We are, after all, in our forties now, and I don't think I need to feel bad about doing what I'd actually like to do.

'Come, Linda,' says Anette, hobbling away from the table, supported by Linda who glances back at us, an uncomfortable and slightly unreadable expression on her face.

It's past one a.m. when I pull off the road onto the track leading through the pine forest to Can Xara. I kill the engine a little distance from the house so we don't wake Linda and Anette. As if we already agreed it, we walk around the side of the house, onto the terrace and down the steps leading to the olive groves, and the finca, and the beach. I feel as though every sensation is heightened, as though all my cells and synapses have been activated, a feeling I could only compare to the hours after giving birth when I was spent and sharpened in equal measure, when the world looked suddenly and eternally different. I don't want this night to end and it seems as though Bianka feels the same way; she didn't hesitate when I continued on the path down toward the beach.

We stand close together and watch little waves surge across the pebbles in the moonlight. There is the pulsating sound of techno music somewhere in the hills, as though it were coming from within Ibiza herself, but it must be coming from the Parisians at the neighbouring property.

I've never come down here in the middle of the night before. I try to imagine this moment with Andreas instead of Bianka but it isn't the kind of thing he'd do; he's particular about sleeping before midnight so he's ready to run at seven. And I'm not sure that the silver-speckled sea and the silhouette of the craggy hills and the whisper of a breeze would feel as beautiful to Andreas as it does to me in this moment. My husband isn't an especially sensitive or reflective man; he's a pragmatist, a man who prides himself on being straightforward and uncomplicated.

Bianka puts her hand on the bare skin of my lower back, inside my silk dress. She lets it run slowly upwards across my skin until it reaches the metal clasp of my bra, which she undoes smoothly. Bianka moves so she's standing behind me and now both of her hands are inside my top, cupping and caressing my breasts while she nuzzles my neck. I lean back into her, and close my eyes. Perhaps it's because I'm wired the way I am, being such a control freak, I can't quite relax into the moment, just giving in to the pleasure of Bianka's soft lips and hot breath on my skin. She must sense this, that my mind controls my body, even now, especially now, because she turns me around, her hands still holding my breasts. I lean in to kiss her slightly parted lips and the moment feels too intense unbroken. I need to close my eyes rather than look into hers, but she takes a light step back, making me hold her gaze. Then she drops into a kneeling position slowly, her bare knees finding the soft sand in between the pebbles.

I remain standing in front of her and Bianka's hand travels slowly up the inside of my thigh until it reaches my underwear. She rubs me through the thin material, making me groan. She slips one finger, then two, past the sliver of cotton, inside me, before slowly pulling my underwear down. I step out of it and kick them in a tangle on to the sand. Bianka looks up at me, a wide smile spreading across her face, then she leans in and closes her lips against me.

And in these moments I feel an intoxicating sense of freedom, a sensation that nothing exists beyond Bianka and me, and beyond Ibiza.

Seventeen

Storm

Everything is neatly boxed and labelled with the shipping company logo that brought their stuff to London. They spend a long while reading the labels, until they come across a few in the far corner beneath the skylight, labelled 'DIY Cabin'. Storm looks at his dad and slowly raises an eyebrow, but Emil pretends like he doesn't notice and busies himself opening the boxes. Inside are several shoe boxes overflowing with photographs, as well as a couple of leather-bound albums. Storm swallows hard, and tries to summon that feeling he gets when he stands ready at the top of the run, waiting for the flag to drop; it's as though a vast cave of steely focus opens up inside him.

Storm sits down on the floor beneath the skylight and his father hands him the first box of pictures. He sifts slowly through them, holding them up to the sunlight in turn. There are pictures of Mia as a child, Mia with Storm, Mia on their trips to India, and on the beach in Santiago de la Compostela. It seems to Storm that she crammed a lot into a short life. Maybe, on some level, she'd always known she'd die young. He considers saying this to his father but then feels ridiculous; it's not the type of conversation they have. They talk skiing, logistics, school, gaming, pocket money. Storm sneaks a few glances at Emil looking at the pictures – he looks weary and old, quite unlike the young man beaming at the camera in the old photographs.

There's a picture of Mia with her parents. Storm realizes he looks just like his grandfather. Now's his chance to gently broach the subject of the letter.

'What about my mom's parents? My grandparents?'

'Uh. What about them?'

'Why don't we ever see them?'

'I don't know really. We lost touch in the years after Mia died. It was very hard for them. She was their only child.'

'But didn't they want to see me?'

'I'm sure they did. They sent cards and things. Then it stopped quite suddenly. I imagine it just became too difficult.'

'Where are they?'

'What?'

'The cards.'

Emil glances around the vast attic space. 'I don't know in this exact moment, Storm. But I can have a look another day, see if I can find them.'

'I bet Bianka doesn't know you've kept all this stuff and brought it all the way to London.'

Emil shrugs, then nods, rubbing at his puffy eyes. 'Let's keep it that way,' he says, his eyes pleading with his son. 'It's just not worth the hassle.'

***

Storm brings two plastic boxes of pictures downstairs to the green bedroom, taking them over to the desk, then drawing the heavy curtains shut as though someone might be standing outside looking in. He looks through every single one of the photographs again, trying to commit his mother's face to memory, so it might appear in his mind suddenly, taking on a new life. Since the arrival of the letter and the realization that something has been hidden from him, it's as though Storm's interest in Mia has been woken up. Until recently he's not given her absence as much thought as one might have expected; besides, it's been made perfectly clear at home that there's no point in dwelling on her death, and bringing her up in conversation has certainly never been encouraged.

He finds the picture of his mother with her parents again and studies it for a long while beneath the bright bulb of the lamp on his desk. Their names are Einar and Frida. There really is a striking resemblance between his grandfather and himself, something to do with the eyes and the deep dimples. Mia looks like her mother, a kind-looking woman with neat, white shoulder-length hair and darker, perfectly arched eyebrows framing a bland but pleasant face. Mia looks absolutely nothing like Bianka, who seems to feel the need to make every occasion about herself. Mia looks natural and a little shy, frequently gazing at Emil or her mom or into the distance, not prone to squarely locking eyes with the lens as Bianka does, evident in all the rows of pictures of her and Emil displayed on every shelf and available surface of the living room.

Storm carefully places all the pictures back in their boxes, besides one, his favourite, a picture of Mia stroking an elephant's trunk in India. She's clearly unaware the picture is being taken and is looking into the animal's huge eye, a look of pure joy and awe on her face. She has an expressive and lucid face, one that seems to reveal something of the soul; looking at her, Storm feels close to her. He places the picture underneath his pillow before leaving the room.

He's so nervous he can barely walk when he leaves the house and walks up in the direction of the village, as directed by Emil, who'd winked at him when he said he'd be meeting Madeleine Vinge. She's waiting for him on a bench by the lake, holding a cardboard tray with two hot drinks. This makes her seem impossibly sophisticated to Storm, that she'd thought to go and order drinks and bring them here.

'Hi,' he says, and an awkward moment ensues when he sits down beside her just as she stands up to hug him in greeting.

'Hey,' she says, laughing, and to Storm it seems that as long as he can figure out a way to keep this girl around, everything will be pretty great. Conversation flows easily and Storm begins to relax. It was this he'd feared the most – long, awkward silences – but it doesn't happen a single time. Madeleine is funny and engaged and as big of a *Star Wars* fan as Storm, at one point lifting the leg of her jeans to show him her Chewbacca socks. They eat lunch on the pavement of a little Thai restaurant on the high street, before walking down the hill to Wimbledon town, where they catch an early afternoon movie at the Odeon, some

Scottish drama Storm couldn't name if he tried, but which makes Madeleine well up and take his hand in the dark. When they emerge from the cinema, they walk slowly back up toward the village, not wanting the day to draw to an end. In a particularly dark spot between streetlights, Storm musters all his courage and stops walking. Madeleine pauses alongside him, and he can sense her looking at him quizzically. He leans in and kisses her lightly on the mouth, first once, and then again, pausing in between to make sure she's not horrified, but she doesn't seem to be. She stands on tiptoes and wraps her arms around his neck, drawing him even closer, and touches the tip of her tongue against his.

When they finally break apart and walk on, Storm feels overcome with a wild energy, not unlike when he's smashed it in a competition and climbs onto the winning podium, clutching the gold medal.

'Hey, by the way,' says Madeleine when they arrive at the gates to her house, 'I'm coming to Oslo next week. I go every summer for a couple of weeks and stay at my aunt and uncle's house. So we can hang out there, too. If you want.'

'Cool, yeah. I have to head to a summer training camp at school, but I can definitely get away for a bit.'

Eighteen

Bianka

Bianka opens her eyes. In this moment, everything is perfect, and so that is where she will train her focus. Right here, right now.

It's still dark outside, though a faint pink has appeared in the sky to the east. She's in the master bedroom and as soon as it starts getting properly light, she'll quietly slip across the hallway into her own bedroom.

She thinks about how she must be lying in the exact place Andreas usually sleeps, how she is seeing the room and the world outside and his wife from his exact vantage point. The mother of his children is curled into Bianka's arms like a warm little animal, breathing softly and rhythmically, calm in sleep in a way energetic Charlotte never appears to be when awake.

The first rays of the sun reach across the eastern sky and Bianka shifts a little, readying herself to untangle herself from Charlotte, who releases a long, shuddering breath.

'No,' she whispers. 'Don't go.' So Bianka doesn't, not for

a long while. She closes her eyes again and dozes to the feeling of Charlotte's gentle fingertips drawing light circles on her skin.

Anette is reclining on the vast white structured designer sofa in the main living space, her injured foot dramatically bandaged and elevated by a stack of pillows. She's scrolling on her phone and doesn't glance up when Bianka enters the room. Bianka pretends not to notice Anette's obviously frosty demeanour.

'Hi, Anette,' she says intentionally chirpily. She flops down onto the identical sofa opposite, separated by a low jade marble table, the only coloured piece of furniture in the huge room. 'Oh, you poor thing. That looks so painful.'

'Yes, well it is, not gonna lie. Total disaster. I mean, I might as well go home.'

'Oh, no, don't say that. We can do relaxed stuff around here. And take the car when we head out for dinner.'

'Not sure I feel like going out to Ibiza's fancy restaurants with one foot completely bandaged. Besides, I wanted to swim in the sea and now I can't.' Bianka watches as Anette's bottom lip trembles, marvelling at the kind of life where you never experience not being able to do what you want all the time. Bianka carefully arranges her face to one of utmost sympathy and nods.

'I totally understand that. Maybe we could get those hot guys from Carlo's Catering to come back and cook for us?'

'I guess that's a pretty good idea.'

'Where's Linda?'

'She helped me downstairs earlier but went back to bed. The hormones she's on give her really bad headaches.'

'Oh, poor thing. Gosh, it's one thing after another.'

'Indeed. So you and Charlotte have carte blanche to go do your own thing today.' Anette's expression is clearly confrontational and Bianka knows she wants her to say *Oh, what do you mean?* or *Oh, no. I'm so sad you guys can't join us.*

'Okay great,' she says instead, looking Anette square on and smiling brightly, as though she didn't pick up on Anette's snarky undertone. Bianka isn't going to waste a single second on a judgmental, narrow-minded woman like Anette – that much was obvious within moments of meeting her – but Bianka understands the necessity of being friendly with her, otherwise her relationship with Charlotte will suffer. And behind the scenes she can subtly divide and conquer.

Charlotte rides confidently and quite fast, heading south from Can Xara. Bianka closes her arms around her small, firm waist and feels her hair stream out from underneath the helmet, jostled by the wind. When they round the bend and she catches a glimpse of the sea, she can see that it's even windier out there, white-crested rolling waves surging dramatically at the cliffs.

'I want to show you somewhere,' Charlotte said before they set off, instructing Bianka to bring a diving mask and snorkel. Bianka was happy to come along anywhere at all, away from the house and moody Anette and alone with Charlotte. They leave the paved country road they'd been on and head down toward the sea on a dusty narrow track. It grows narrower still until it peters out into a barely discernible path. Charlotte parks the Vespa and they climb down, pulling helmets from their heads and shaking their hair loose, laughing.

'So, care to tell me where we are?'

'You'll see in a sec,' says Charlotte, and after a quick glance up and down the deserted path, leans in and kisses Bianka hard on the mouth. 'I hope we will have this place all to ourselves.' They walk slowly down the path which has been worn into the remote hillsides. Bianka thought Can Xara was unspoiled, but this place is next-level. There isn't a single sign of human presence or activity with the exception of the paths that crisscross the hills and cliffs that stretch as far as they can see. As they approach the sea, Bianka wonders if they're going to have to climb – they are walking along the edge of a cliff high above a tiny, sheltered cove, its iridescent turquoise waters the clearest Bianka has ever seen, even in pictures. The coastline toward the south is broken by huge caves and limestone arches and Bianka feels stunned by its beauty in a way she's never felt anywhere else.

Bianka hasn't travelled extensively like the other women have; at least it seems from the stories they tell that they've spent their lives up until this point in one exotic location after another. Winter breaks in Megève, summers in Cannes and Ibiza, fall break in the Maldives or Tulum, punctuated by endless weekends in London and Paris and New York with 'the girls'.

When all the bad things happened in Bianka's life many years ago, she did fight the impulse to just walk away, to get on a plane somewhere random and never, ever look back. But then, perhaps as a result of never having had a real family to speak of, the urge to have that was stronger and Bianka directed the urge to escape into her new family instead, ploughing all her energy into it. Bianka had focused on simply placing one foot in front of the other, both in her marriage and her role as stepmother to Storm. She just hadn't anticipated it would leave her feeling so dissatisfied. But what could she expect, really, after what happened to Mia? Bianka began to fear that she really was empty inside and not even the unexpected love of a little boy and his kind, devoted father could fix her.

'Look,' says Charlotte, shouting to be heard above the wind tearing across the headlands. 'Down there.'

Bianka follows the trajectory of Charlotte's pointed finger to a vaulted cave with a narrow slash of an opening in the crook of the tiny bay. They reach the end of the path and climb down onto the beach by carefully stepping from one boulder to the next. When they finally reach the patch of fine white sand interspersed with pebbled rocky parts, the wind disappears completely, screaming overhead but never reaching the cove.

The water, too, is as still as a mirror, a strange contrast to the crashing waves beyond the cape. They walk in comfortable silence to the mouth of the cave. Charlotte places her beach bag on the rocks and pulls her emerald green kaftan off, folding it neatly and placing it on a smooth, flat rock. Underneath she is wearing a white string bikini with coloured beads fastened to the strings. She pulls at the string at the nape of her neck, then the one behind her back, and the bikini top drops to the ground. She fixes

Bianka with her gaze, as deep and irresistible as the calm waters of the cove. She pulls at the strings tied into bows on either side of her hips too and lets the bottoms fall from her body. Then she turns around and runs into the water, leaving Bianka stunned and wanting on the beach.

Bianka swiftly pulls off her black T-shirt and steps out of her denim cut-offs. She struggles with the clasp of her bikini top, watching Charlotte swim far out into the bay, frequently disappearing beneath the surface like a big fish. When she's free of her bikini, Bianka leaps into the deliciously cool sea after her. She loves discovering this carefree, playful side of Charlotte; she suspects it doesn't come out very often in her ordered, controlled life at home where the currencies seem to be success, achievement, and appearance.

Later, they lie side by side on the beach, right on the warm sand, holding hands loosely and watching wispy clouds sweep fast across the sky.

'How are we ever going to return to real life?' asks Bianka, turning to face Charlotte, whose expression instantly darkens.

'Don't,' she says. 'I can't even think about it.'

'Like, obviously we have to go back, but can we? Really? It's not like we can ever unknow this.' Charlotte ponders this for a while and when Bianka glances at her again, she realizes tears are streaming down her face. 'I'm sorry,' she says, alarmed.

'No. No, it's fine. I'm just thinking about how you're absolutely right. We can't unknow this and will have to go back into life at home, which will no doubt feel different when you have a fresh point of comparison. I meant what I said the other night. That even though I have a good life in many ways in London, I don't feel quite alive most of the time. Like less than half of my mental and emotional register is ever activated. Do you know what I mean?'

'Oh yeah.' *More than you could possibly imagine*, thinks Bianka. She half sits, supporting her head with her hand, letting her elbow sink into the soft sand. 'All we have is now,' she says.

'At least we have that,' says Charlotte, eyes shining, raising her arms and locking them around Bianka's neck, pulling her back down into another embrace, making her shift her weight so she rolls on top of her.

The Carlo Catering boys return in the evening. Anette has mellowed and is especially nice to Bianka; perhaps she's clever enough to understand that it's a good idea to stay on friendly terms. Bianka chuckles to herself and eyes Ricky appreciatively as he flips the steak in the air, his biceps flexing. Bianka asks Anette whether, if she wasn't married, would she want to take this guy for a bit of a ride.

Anette responds deadpan, 'I'm getting a divorce, actually. But it's not like I'd want to sleep with some random guy half my age.'

'Why not?'

Anette stares at her, then bursts out laughing and Bianka feels hopeful she's finally winning her over.

Anette is more animated than Bianka has seen her before and is definitely the person driving the rowdy conversation after dinner.

'Okay,' she begins, her light eyes travelling around the table to each of them in turn. 'Let's play a drinking game. Never have I ever. You know the rules, we each say something we've never done and if you have done it, you drink.' Everyone laughs a little and Bianka notices Charlotte glancing over at her, perhaps wondering whether she thinks she and her friends are weird playing this game as middle-aged married women. Bianka winks at her; she doubts they'll surprise her with any juicy stories she hasn't heard before.

'Never have I ever slept with someone more than ten years older or younger than me,' says Charlotte. Nobody drinks except Linda, whose husband is a decade older. 'Okay, your turn,' Charlotte says to Linda.

'Uh, okay. Never have I ever slept with two people in the space of a week.' Anette, Bianka, and Charlotte all drink, then burst out laughing.

'Okay, your turn, Anette.'

'Never have I ever slept with a woman.'

Bianka waits a while, gauging the others, who all seem to have grown still, then she drinks, a deliberately slow and long sip, before placing her empty glass on the table with a little clang. The atmosphere seems to shift when Charlotte, too, takes a big sip of her wine, emptying her glass. Anette's mouth drops open in surprise. Linda looks as zen as ever. Charlotte laughs and Bianka loves this sudden brazen version of her.

The game continues for a long while until eventually, after another bottle, Linda makes her excuses and heads up to bed.

'Poor thing,' says Anette. 'Imagine going through IVF at our age. I'm heading up too.'

Bianka and Charlotte finish their wine and then stand up and, without speaking, head back down to the beach. Later, much later, they return to Can Xara, still mellow from all the wine, loosely holding hands and laughing quietly so as not to wake the others. On noticing that the van from Carlo's Catering is still parked in the driveway, they exchange a confused glance, but when they head upstairs, Ricky, the sexy man child, emerges from Anette's room, fumbling with the buttons on his linen shirt and looking mortified to bump into them. Bianka and Charlotte slip into the master bedroom in fits of laughter.

Nineteen

Charlotte

Two days pass in a blur – it's all about *her*, being close, and closer still. I've never known anything like this before, a quest for complete possession; I've never experienced someone's touch as confident and pleasurable as my own. She kisses my lips raw, she dislodges bubbles of laughter that must have been hiding deep inside of me, so they constantly burst to the surface. I don't think of myself as unhappy but I realize I'm far out of touch with simple joy.

I try to spread myself evenly between my guests, but in truth, all I want is Bianka, Bianka, and more Bianka. Today I made a conscious effort to stay behind at the house with Anette while Linda and Bianka went to the beach. And all the while we sat by the pool, flicking through fashion magazines and sipping rosé, I couldn't stop thinking about my excursion to the sea with Bianka the other night, how free I'd felt zipping up the road, how good it felt when Bianka's hands closed around my waist. And after, in the sea, watching Bianka dip beneath the surface to find me with her tongue, how I closed my eyes and tipped my head back, the sun beating down on my face.

By now, it feels like it's almost a given that Linda and Anette head back to the house after dinner and Bianka and I stay for another round of drinks. Since the night when Anette cut her foot at Platja d'en Bossa, she's been noticeably cool with me on occasion, especially if my attention has been specifically on Bianka. I pretend not to notice – we're presumably all adults here and I'd like to think I'm allowed to hang out with whomever I please.

I watch Bianka carefully as dinner draws to an end, plates are cleared, drinks finished. I'm pleased to notice Linda suppressing yawns before the exorbitant bill is even placed on the table.

'Well, that's a shit ton of money for some chickpeas,' says Bianka, and I can't say I disagree, not that I would ever touch chickpeas. Lou's Ocean Bar is a trendy vegan restaurant a little further down the coast from Can Xara, where people pay for the pretty faces and incredible ocean views rather than the food.

'I thought it was fantastic,' says Anette.

'Me too,' says Linda. I stare at the sea, at ripples of darkness twisting into its depths in between the last splashes of deep-amber sunlight fading on its surface.

Bianka drives again tonight. She seems to enjoy the Vespa and the undulating, bumpy road through the hills to Can Xara, and though we stayed for another couple of drinks after dinner, it's still early and my heart sinks at the thought of yet another day here almost being over. I've been trying to steel myself for our time at Can Xara coming to an inevitable end and yet, I can't bear to think about returning to London. How it will even be possible. With the exception of my children, I feel as though I wouldn't care if I never went back to any of it.

I'm so deep in my own thoughts that I haven't noticed that Bianka has pulled over by the side of the road and that the steady drone of the Vespa's engine has been replaced with another sound. Bianka smiles and lifts the helmet off my head and I recognize it now – it's the same haunting music that was playing the other day when we were down on the beach in the moonlight. It's a kind of lounge music with a woman's deep vocal overlaid on an insisting beat and a catchy hook, and judging by its loudness we can't be far from its source.

'House party,' says Bianka, grinning widely. I glance around, trying to gauge exactly where we are. The stretch of road looks vaguely familiar, but so does every road around Can Xara. 'I think it must be the property next to yours. You said they were French, right?'

'Uh, yes. Hey, Bianka, look, let's head back to the house.'

'*Pourquoi?* There's a party here somewhere. We should join.'

'We haven't been invited. Also, we've had an ongoing dispute with them, it's not like I can just gate-crash their party. To be honest, I'm a little surprised they're even having a party. They're quite elderly. Maybe they've rented the house out.' I try to summon Anne-Marie and Louis Dubois-Joseph to mind, but I haven't seen them in many years. We may be neighbours but both Sa Capricciosa and Can Xara are big estates with a lot of land and it's not like we bump into each other randomly.

I had the impression that the Dubois-Josephs were quite friendly with Ximena in the years before her death, when she first moved back to the island, but for a long while now Andreas and I have endured an exhausting legal dispute with them over the path that leads down to Cala Azura. I replace my helmet and get back on the Vespa. We're just moments from home and it feels more tempting to sit upstairs on the roof terrace with one last drink than to gate-crash their late-night party.

'Come on, Charlotte. Don't be such a party pooper.'

'No, Bianka. I'm really sorry, but there's just no way I can go there.'

We hear another sound insisting itself into the gaps in the music; a car is approaching. It's a green-and-white taxi from Eivissa, and from it spill three beautiful, flamboyantly dressed young women, laughing and chattering. They catch sight of us standing by the roadside, dressed in pretty dresses, and one of them, a stunning mixed-race girl with huge diamond earrings and blood-red lips, hooks her arm through mine and drags me along as though we are old friends. Bianka laughs and catches up, looping her arm through my other arm, and a guard waves us through the gates of Sa Capricciosa with barely a glance.

It's my first time inside the Dubois-Josephs' property. Sa Capricciosa and Can Xara were constructed before the headlands of Punta de Sa Creu and Punta Xamena were made into a national park, and I suppose it won't hurt to finally see the house. I've only caught glimpses of it from my morning swims across the bay.

The music is so loud it feels as though it enters my body, becoming part of me, overriding my pulse with a new beat. The house is huge and sprawls on several levels around a light turquoise pool; a series of interlinked sections built in the traditional whitewashed Ibicenco style, with roof terraces on which people are dancing.

Bianka merges with a crowd dancing by the side of the pool and drags me along with her, pulling me close and pushing her hips into mine. She laughs and leans in, whispering into my ear, and I am so disarmed by her and by the moment that I can't help but laugh.

Before this trip, I can't remember when I last danced. It's not like Andreas and I go out clubbing in London, though we did when we were much younger in Oslo – it was how we met.

I'd been dragged out to a new club in downtown Oslo by some friends from med school and felt instantly out of place as I took in the grown-up, chic crowd starting to fill up the dance floor. The women had thick, glossy blond hair and almost all of them wore variations of tailored little black dresses. In my quirky pastel slip dress and short, dark bob I felt like Amélie from Montmartre in a sea of Carolyn Bessette-Kennedys. I made myself laugh whenever someone spoke, and made myself dance, though I felt acutely self-conscious and my body felt wooden and lanky.

I became aware of someone's presence next to me after I'd drifted to the edge of the dance floor, in need of a quiet moment to myself.

I can't stop looking at you was the first thing he ever said to me. I liked that. He could have mumbled something about buying me a drink or awkwardly asked my name, but instead he went for the adult, confident approach. And Andreas was adult and confident, even back then, and though he was only a couple of years older than me and my student friends, he was already working and exuded an air of maturity. He felt like coming home.

And now... I glance around at the young crowd exuberantly bobbing around the dance floor, at the inky Ibiza sky pulsating with stars, at the woman in front of me who is saying something to me, her hand warm and firm on the bare skin of my lower back, and I realize I have no concept of home anymore. Andreas, Oslo, Wimbledon, my house, even my children – they all feel light-years away.

'What?' I say into Bianka's ear. I didn't catch a word of what she said.

'I said, check out those guys over there. To the left of the pool, on the white lounge sofa. Yeah, those ones. They're beckoning us over.' I glance at the guys, and they are clearly talking about us, one of them raising his champagne glass to us in a toast. They look like they're in their mid-twenties and are all dressed head to toe in white linen, with soft leather moccasins. Bianka throws her head back and laughs loudly as though I'd said something far funnier than 'what?'. Then she leans in and kisses me on the lips, her hand slipping into the tangle of hair at the nape of my neck, slick with sweat. I'm shocked by the sudden public display of affection and feel a tremor of annoyance that she's only kissing me like this to impress these men. When we break apart, I feel a stunned shift in the atmosphere from the crowd. Bianka keeps dancing, pulling me very close, and it's as though our display gives the crowd a surge of energy because there is a tangible shift in the air, and others too start dancing more closely and suggestively.

She kisses me again and again, so hard that my lips hurt and there is a new aggression in her embrace. She's clearly excited by being watched and as her tongue slips deep into my mouth, I realize that so am I. Nobody here knows who I am, something that no longer happens to me very often, especially in Oslo. I get stared at and approached every time I go to a restaurant or a party, mostly discreetly, but still, the feeling of anonymity is long gone. It's one of the things I've come to appreciate the most about living in London as my profile in Norway grew bigger and bigger. It's easy to forget how much of our freedom is lost when we're known everywhere we go, when a presumed version of us enters every room ahead of the real person.

'Hi, ladies,' says a voice. It belongs to the man who raised his glass in a toast at us. 'Why don't you come and join us for a while?'

'Sure,' says Bianka, before I even have a chance to think.

'I'm Max,' he shouts over the music, and we follow him through the crowd back to the lounge area where several bottles of champagne are cooling on ice in silver buckets. Max pours us each a glass and hands them to us, smiling widely. He seems completely sober, unlike his two friends who have the glazed eyes of the very inebriated. There is something vaguely familiar about him and I wonder if he could be a C-list reality star or something, glimpsed on the cover of a trashy weekly magazine, perhaps; I wouldn't be surprised, he certainly looks the part. The friends are wearing matching pink Versace polo shirts, apparently in a non-ironic way, and they both have neck tattoos of interlinking 'o's.

As I sit down on the soft white leather sofa, I feel a wave of exhaustion and annoyance wash over me. I could be at home by now in my own bed, not gate-crashing the Dubois-Josephs' rave party and drinking champagne with this sleek man child with whom I'm apparently expected to make small talk. I sip the champagne and feel myself zone out as Bianka talks to the guy, only picking up snippets of the predictable conversation. So, have you been to Ibiza before? Have you tried the new place at d'en Bossa? Where are you from? How long are you staying?

'So, are you guys a couple or what?' asks one of Max's friends, who was introduced to us as Ruben, and I realize how stoned he is when he speaks – he can barely string a sentence together.

'Yeah,' says Bianka. 'We're engaged, actually.' She holds up her left hand and shows off the ring on her finger, a large sapphire haloed by pinprick diamonds. An image pops into my head of Emil sinking to his knees in front of Bianka, asking her to be his wife, slipping this same ring onto her slim, pale finger. The thought makes me feel uncomfortable.

'Really?' asks Max, touching his glass to Bianka's then mine, eyes glinting in the low light. 'Well, congratulations to you two beautiful ladies.' Max is old-school handsome with longish dark hair and a deep shadow of facial stubble, with a charming white smile. Another image appears in my head, of Max pinning me down in bed, moving hard but slow inside me, rubbing the skin on my face and chest raw with his stubble. I blush and while I'm sure he would have given me palpitations back in the day, at forty-one I'm sooner seduced by a soft bed and a solid night's sleep than the mere fantasy of bedding a good-looking guy half my age. At least before this trip. I feel disturbed by the image, though; it's as though a part of my mind keeps conjuring up all these scenarios that I can't control.

'What about you guys?' asks Bianka, motioning to the two similar-looking men on the sofa. 'Are you a couple?'

'Ha-ha,' says the especially stoned one. 'You're a funny one, aren't you?'

'Marco and Ruben are brothers,' says Max. 'Silly rich brothers from Sicily. Bad boys.'

'Shut up,' says the same one that spoke before; his brother still hasn't said a single word. 'We're businessmen.'

'By that he means second-generation mafioso boys who haven't ever gotten their hands dirty but like to pretend like they're tough like their old dead daddy. But these guys are more into tattoos and fast cars than knowing where the money that bought them came from. Isn't that right, Marco?' Max refers to the unspeaking brother, who nods earnestly, a blank look on his face.

'So, whose party is this?' I ask, glancing around again, still half fearful I might come face to face with my difficult, persistent neighbours.

'Just some kids',' says Max, and laughs. 'You know the type. Obnoxious billionaire playboys from Paris and Palermo who can rent out a place like this on a whim.'

'Mmm,' says Bianka, as though she knows plenty of kids like that, as though her circle of acquaintances aren't mainly middle-aged Scandinavian bankers in Wimbledon. Bianka and Max keep chatting and I hover at the edge of the conversation, fighting back another wave of tiredness – it's almost one a.m. She makes up one lie after another, seemingly completely effortlessly. I'm both fascinated and unnerved. She tells him that we left our husbands for each other last year, that we live together in Copenhagen, that she's an architect and I'm a chef, and that neither of us have children. She says she's half American and that her mother is an opioid addict living in Fort Lauderdale. Max hangs on to her every word, laughing in all the right places, smoothly refilling our glasses. Marco appears to have fallen asleep, and the other one, whose name I've already forgotten, sits scrolling on his phone.

I'm a little unsettled by the ease with which Bianka creates an entirely new universe, seemingly out of the blue. My thoughts dart to my husband and children at home, as though to reassure myself that they really do exist. Suddenly they don't feel far away or hard to conjure up in my mind, and I am overcome with gratitude and yearning for them. Soon I'll be home. But will it be the same? I drain my champagne glass and place it on the glass table with a loud clang.

'Come on, Bianka,' I say, standing up. Enough fun for one evening. Bianka is in the middle of a made-up anecdote about coming out to her parents and stops mid-sentence, visibly annoyed.

'Charlotte, don't be such a party pooper.'

'I want to get back to the house.'

'Where are you guys staying?' asks Max.

'Charlotte owns the fancy pile next to this place,' says Bianka. I pick up my purse from the table and am already walking away from them, a vein of fury throbbing in my head, pushing my way through the crowd when Bianka catches up with me, grabbing me by the arm.

'Seriously, what the hell was that?' She must see that I'm upset because her expression softens and she gently strokes my arm, but I pull away from her, hugging myself and rubbing my upper arms as though the puckered goosebumps that have appeared on my skin were from cold.

'Bianka, it's past one a.m. I need to get back. Feel free to stay.'

'I thought we were in this together.'

'In what?'

'Charlotte, we're just out, having a fun time, talking to some guys, drinking champagne. It makes me feel young again. You know, like all the doors are still open and we can just go anywhere and become anyone. You don't have to get all Aunt Edna on me.'

'Aunt Edna?'

'Yeah, old and uptight.'

'Bianka. Look. I just found it a little weird. You know, that you just invented all that stuff.'

'It was just a bit of fun. We'll never see them again. Who cares? Maybe let's allow ourselves to be those other people, just for one night. Think about it. Me and you, engaged and free of all ties, living in a cute little apartment in Copenhagen...You have the rest of your life to be a high-strung perfectionist in London.' She very lightly runs her fingertip across my collarbone and fixes me with those clear blue eyes.

I laugh in spite of myself. Maybe she's right; it might be good for me to let go a little.

'Come on. Dance with me. Please.' Bianka smiles her

wide, irresistible smile and holds her hands out to me, her feet doing little salsa steps. Maybe I'm just being silly. Though I don't want a divorce and I am starting to miss my family at home, it has been unanimously agreed that I need to learn about fun. Maybe Andreas wouldn't mind what's been happening between Bianka and me. In fact, I might even tell him someday, and it might inject some new passion into my marriage; I've heard this kind of thing can have that effect. Or not. After all, it's also been agreed that what happens in Ibiza stays in Ibiza. And I'm provably good at compartmentalizing.

I take Bianka's hands and she pulls me out onto the dance floor and very close to her. When she kisses me again, it's softly and gently and I feel the familiar pang of desire in the hollow of my stomach. Before the song is even finished, Bianka takes my hand and we meander through the crowd, across the vast terraces and into one of the several cottages at the edge of the property. Inside, the air is hushed and fragrant, bearing the scent of fig and firewood.

'What... Where are we?' I whisper, my eyes slowly adjusting to the near darkness, broken only by occasional strobing neon lights from the party.

'Shhh,' she says. 'Max said this room would be empty.'

I can just about make out the contours of a four-poster bed made from driftwood, with gauzy linen curtains fluttering on a light, cooling breeze. Bianka presses a finger to her lips and pushes me gently backward onto the bed. A mahogany fan spins lazily from the ceiling, sending wafts of cool air down onto me, but the room is still very hot and when I lie back it spins a little. I've had a lot to drink over the course of the evening. I hear Bianka laughing softly in the near darkness. She undoes the bow on my halter neck then swiftly slips the lightweight dress off my body. She lies on top of me, kissing me deeply while drawing light shapes up the entire length of my thigh. Then she inches down my body, stopping to kiss my collarbone, my nipples, my belly button.

For a while she stops and seems to fumble with something. She's probably taking her own dress off and I reach out for her, but she stops me.

'Shhh,' she whispers. 'Wait. Stay still.' She fumbles some more and then I feel her pour something onto the skin of my lower stomach. I sit up a little and, as a neon pink light sweeps across the room, I watch as Bianka snorts two lines of cocaine off my skin through a rolled-up ten-euro bill.

'Wait... Where did you get that?'

'From me.' A man's voice, from somewhere over by the door.

'What the hell?' I say, and scramble from the bed, covering myself with the top sheet. A match is struck, lighting a couple of candles standing on a shelf above a stone fireplace, and by its light I see Max.

'Don't freak out,' says Bianka, her eyes shining.

'Yeah, don't freak out,' says Max, smiling his boyish, beautiful smile, his teeth glinting in the soft light like little stones in shallow water. He hands me another glass of champagne and leans in to kiss me. Before our lips touch he pauses and pulls back a little, checking if I'm okay. I'm amazed to find I am okay, in fact, I want this – I want to feel his hands on my skin and his tongue in my mouth. Max kisses me and picks me up so I have to wrap my legs around his waist. Then he places me back down on the bed and turns around to kiss Bianka too, while twisting my nipples between his fingertips. He pulls a little pouch out from his pocket and waves it teasingly in the air.

'May I offer you some premium Colombian snow, beautiful Charlotte?' I shake my head and open my mouth to say *No, I've never touched drugs in my life*, but nothing emerges. It's as though I'm mesmerized by the moment, by Max's beauty, and Bianka's, too. And if this is one of the last nights I ever have of freedom, I want the night to last forever. I nod.

Bianka slips out of her dress and lies back on the bed. Max scatters some white powder onto her chest, between her perfect little breasts, then cuts it into lines with a black credit card. He bends down and pulls first one, then another into his nose. He hands the rolled-up note he used to me and I copy what he did, drawing the cocaine into my nostril. It burns the back of my throat and I can't believe what I've just done, but almost instantly I'm filled with a delicious, sharpened feeling. It strikes me that this is how I've wanted to feel my whole life: in control, calm, confident, like the very best version of me.

I watch as Max sits back to look at Bianka and me, lying naked except for underwear, side by side, mellow and waiting. He unbuttons his linen shirt, revealing a tan, wide chest. I reach out for him and run my hands across his warm skin, feeling the fast rhythm of his heartbeat beneath my fingertips. I could still back out. I glance toward the door and imagine extricating myself from this situation and walking through it back into the night, taking the coastal path home to Can Xara. But I realize I don't want to do that. I want to be here. Max lies down beside me and I unbutton his trousers while kissing Bianka. When he's free of all his clothes, I reach down and take Bianka's underwear off, then my own. I am so turned on by the situation, by the sensation of more than one pair of hands on my bare skin, by Max's incredible body, by the sight of Bianka getting up to crouch between his legs and taking him in her mouth, her eyes locked on mine. I start to touch myself and find I'm already very close. I keep going, moaning loudly, then Max pulls back from Bianka and positions me on my back on the bed. Then he's inside me, moving hard but slow, just like in the image I had in my head earlier, and I come faster than I ever have before. After a little breather, I turn over on my stomach and Max enters me again from behind as I go down on Bianka, teasing her with my tongue.

We take several little breaks, sipping from the fragile champagne flutes and doing another line of coke as the sky breaks into deep pinks and purples at dawn, and then we are doing it again in various configurations. The music has died away and when I finally fall asleep, it's to the sound of birds chirping and Max and Bianka breathing evenly on either side of me.

When I wake again, shrill sunlight pours onto the terracotta floor tiles. All of the magic and fun of last night is gone. I feel terrible, worse than I have in all my life. Though I knew they would be there, I'm still shocked at the sight of the two naked people in the bed with me. For almost seventeen years, I have slept next to Andreas almost every single night, waking to the familiar sight of his peaceful, puffy morning face. But today, there's a young man about whom I know pretty much nothing, and another woman. I realize I know even less about myself than I do about them. My mind feels tender and partially blank, but more and more images from last night come back to me – the drugs, the sex, the way the cocaine ironically made me feel like I finally had a steely grip on my life. But today is different; it all feels different now. My mouth is dry and the back of my throat stings from the burn of the cocaine. Tears rush into my eyes as I carefully shift around before getting up. I slip from the bed and into the adjoining bathroom, running the tap full blast to disguise the sound of my sobs.

I sink down on the floor and give in to hysterical, uncontrollable tears. I haven't cried like this in years, or maybe ever. I want to bolt from the Dubois-Joseph property and run through the wild lavender and heather of the hillsides, cutting across to Can Xara along the crest of the cliffs until I reach the finca, and I want to push open the old oak door to find my mother inside. She'd be sitting in front of the open fireplace, reading, her face glowing and breaking into her radiant smile at the sight of me. She'd hold her arms out to me and I'd collapse into them, folding her birdlike body into my own and she wouldn't flinch at my tears, she never did. I'd remember what it feels like to be loved by someone fully and without judgment, and my mother would bring the pieces that have broken loose inside of me gently back together.

When there are no more tears, I get up from the floor slowly. My body aches. I force myself to meet my own eyes in the mirror. The woman in front of me is smirking as though this meltdown is remotely funny. Her hazel eyes are smudged with last night's makeup, much of which has been dragged down her face in sooty rivers. A couple of bruises run across her collarbone. Her arms are very skinny and also bruised on both biceps.

I realize what this feeling is – I feel dirty and unlovable and worthless, things I have always held to be truths about myself, and they are the things I have tried so hard to stave off by being successful, happily married, perfect. But this woman standing in front of me is the real Charlotte, there is no doubt about this. A messy, deviant, and deeply flawed woman who has revealed her dark side to Bianka. I feel repeat stabs of shame: this is a woman who deserves none of her many blessings, least of all her children, who should have been able to trust that their mother wouldn't single-handedly destroy their family for the sake of a sordid sex game.

I take a few very deep, shuddering breaths and try to gain some control over myself and my racing thoughts. I need to take stock, rationally. Is what I've done really so bad? Or is this something I might learn to live with, locked away in the recesses of my memories for the rest of my life? How much harm can it really do there? What I feel ashamed about is my hunger. How much I wanted something I knew was wrong. And I just don't want it anymore, or ever again. I want to go home. Even the thought of Bianka doesn't rouse me now, not even a little; it's as though a switch has been flipped and what felt so incredibly exciting and passionate now feels seedy and dangerous. I bring our intimate encounters to mind and still there's nothing.

I quietly push open the door to the bedroom and glance at Bianka, fast asleep on the bed. A tremor of regret courses through me, followed by a wave of stress. I have jeopardized my sixteen-year stable marriage and the security of my children for this woman. How could I have allowed it to happen? And it was me who instigated it, who took her hand at Benirràs and ran my fingertip around the soft creases of her palm, it was me who didn't flinch when our eyes met, who willed our lips to touch. Bianka hit me like a freight train, like the embodiment of all my pent-up desires, with all the force of resentment, sacrifice, and longing. Again, I think of Anette and Mads divorcing, of their daughters placing their belongings into boxes as the house is slowly emptied into moving vans, a 'Sold' sign stuck into the ground next to the gates. I don't want that for Andreas and myself, definitely not.

I swallow hard. I have to find a way to come back from this, whatever it is, right now. I can still hold onto everything – my predictable, gentle life, my control, my career, it's all still there – at home. I am, after all, not the first person ever to go a little wild in Ibiza. And if there is ever one rule of girl trips, it would be that what happens on a girls' trip firmly stays there.

All I need to do is figure out how to file this away as a little appendix in the story of my life, to reduce it to a sexy, if tasteless, footnote not to be repeated. I have to reframe this in my mind as a one-off wild and deeply inappropriate exploration of another way of life, after which I arrived at the safe and convenient conclusion that, for all its shortcomings and frequent boredom, I actually like my life and want to go back home. If I could make sense of why it happened and what I gained from this, then I can move on, knowing it was worth it and with the motivation to keep it completely quiet. I just hope Bianka will feel the same way, that we can leave everything that happened between us on the island and smoothly return to a drama-free Wimbledon.

I actually think that everything that has happened is a symptom of a massive midlife crisis. It's a strange feeling to realize you've arrived at a stage in life when you have everything you ever wanted, only to find that it isn't enough. That it's nowhere near enough. Can I be forgiven for wanting to feel alive again?

I think about the euphoria of the past few days, and how maybe I just needed to feel like I could still become someone else. I look at Bianka and Max sleeping heavily, a sliver of sunlight slicing the messy bed, and wonder if I already have.

Twenty

Bianka

Bianka wakes to find Charlotte sitting in an armchair opposite the bed, fully dressed in last night's flimsy yellow silk dress, watching her, a hard and unnerving expression on her face. It doesn't soften when their eyes meet like it usually does; rather, it grows even steelier and Bianka sits up slowly, rubbing sleep from her eyes. She feels terrible, naturally, and as fragments of the night before begin to return to her, she suppresses the urge to laugh, if only because of the look on Charlotte's face. It's puffy and patchy with splotches of red, and her expression is etched with regret and even horror. Bianka realizes she's going to need to play this very carefully if she wants to avoid Charlotte slipping away from her. At the thought of losing Charlotte, of not having access to the connection that has made her feel something real for the first time in years, Bianka is instantly sobered. *Could it already be too late?*

She senses a presence next to her and realizes Max is still there, out cold, mouth grotesquely open, his tongue

protruding from between his teeth like a serpent's. A wave
of nausea washes over Bianka but she quashes it, making
herself remember how incredibly hot what happened
between them last night really was. It's obvious that
Charlotte doesn't feel the same way in the cold light of
day. It's one thing exploring a physical relationship with
another woman – a little naughty, perhaps, but hardly
that uncommon, even among married women. But a drug-
fuelled threesome with a much-younger stranger, including
full intercourse? Bianka can see how that might feel like
next-level stuff and how it might call into question certain
truths you may have held about yourself. Now, damage
control is crucial, before Charlotte pulls back further.

'You okay?' she whispers, but realizes immediately that it
was a stupid thing to say – it invites an instant conversation
about all the ways in which Charlotte is most certainly not
okay. Charlotte rolls her eyes and shakes her head curtly,
making fresh tears scatter from her eyes onto the silk dress,
staining it a darker mustard yellow. Charlotte points to
the door and motions for Bianka to get up. She glances at
her watch; it's just past ten in the morning, so they've had
less than four hours' rest. Bianka feels stone-cold sober but
realizes that most likely isn't the case. She places her feet on
the tiles and, as she stands up, she feels woozy and nauseated.
Max shifts in the bed, closing his mouth and pressing his
face into the pillow. Bianka gently pulls the bedsheet from
the bed and he shifts again and groans. She wraps it around
her naked body so she doesn't have to move around the
room completely exposed. Before, Charlotte looked at
Bianka undressed with raw desire, but now it's just a brief
glance and utter disdain. Bianka feels a wild, uncontrollable

surge of fury at the thought of Charlotte extricating herself from their beautiful bubble and has to turn away from her – she can't trust her facial expression not to betray her.

In the adjoining bathroom, Bianka puts her dress from last night back on. She avoids her reflection in the mirror because why would she want to see herself in such a moment?

Charlotte opens the bathroom door without knocking and grabs a monogrammed bathrobe from a hook on the door, putting it on over her dress.

'What are you doing with that?'

'I'm not walking home at eight a.m. in a party dress like a whore.'

'Wow. A little harsh, perhaps. But okay.' Bianka follows Charlotte back through the little bungalow and then outside in the fierce sunlight. The property is deserted and there is no sign of the party that was going strong until just a couple of hours ago. Bianka assumes a team of staff has swept silently through the rooms and terraces, picking up the debris: cigarette butts and bongs and empty bottles and various items of clothing flung across furniture. Charlotte turns right instead of in the direction of the main gate.

'Where are you going?' she says, but Charlotte is walking very fast ahead of her and Bianka can't be sure she even heard. The house stands in huge, carefully kept grounds and a water feature runs down toward the cliffs and the sea below – a series of gurgling fountains passing the water from one to the next leisurely, as though water wasn't a treasured and somewhat scarce commodity here in the barren and remote part of northwestern Ibiza, something which is stated on signs everywhere. *Be careful with your water usage.* Unless you're rich, of course, then you can send thousands of gallons of the stuff down a hillside every hour just because it looks pretty.

The water feature ends in a huge, round mosaic-tiled shallow pool in the centre of a vast lawn hemmed in by hedges as tall as prison walls which seem to mark the end of the property. Charlotte walks determinedly toward the corner where two of the hedges meet and, sure enough, a small door painted the green of the hedges and clad in ivy is embedded in its middle. It's unlocked and Charlotte and Bianka pass through it, emerging onto a path very high up on a hill. Bianka hesitates and shields her aching eyes from the sun. She's lost her sunglasses somewhere, but Charlotte stalks along as though they've gone out for a full-on workout. They're both barefoot, carrying shoes more suited for restaurants and parties than rocky paths. Further down the hillside Bianka spots the outline of Can Xara, and recognizes the little horseshoe bay with the tiny boathouse with its blue corrugated tin roof at the far side, and the distinct cliffs of Punta de Sa Creu.

No wonder the owners of Sa Capricciosa wanted to purchase the land on Charlotte's property – now it's clear to her how it's the only way for them to gain direct access to the sea. It's also obvious to Bianka that Sa Capricciosa must be one of the largest private estates on the island.

'Charlotte, wait, please,' she says when they are getting closer to Can Xara but still well out of earshot, stopping for a moment to catch her breath. Her heart is racing uncomfortably and she can feel the disgusting aftertaste of the cocaine still lingering at the back of her throat. She anticipates several hours of being sick after they get back, her body probably still in shock from last night but currently running on adrenaline. 'Can we talk?'

'I'm not sure there's that much to talk about just now,' Charlotte says, the corners of her mouth dragging downwards. Bianka feels a deep empathy for her and places her hand on Charlotte's shoulder. Charlotte shrugs it off and starts walking again, fast along the perilous path, which is strewn with loose rocks and has several sheer drops; a slip would send you at least a hundred feet down the side of the cliff. These especially dangerous points are marked by a flimsy string, fastened to wooden fence posts inserted into the ground at apparently random intervals. And that's when it happens: a vicious and overwhelming vision that appears in Bianka's mind, making her stop instantly. She sees herself as clearly as though she were watching a film, running toward Charlotte at full speed and using her entire force to fling her down the rocky ravine to the beach far below. She'd scream, but only briefly, joining the screech of the circling gulls. Bianka would watch her body strike against a jutting sharp rock and bounce grotesquely off it with a spray of blood from her head before slapping onto a flat rock plateau next to a little beach. The ocean would wash Charlotte's blood away then rise to drag her to its depths with the tide.

'Bianka. I – I just can't right now. Please just hurry.'

'We need to talk about what happened. And we need to talk about us.' Bianka tries to rid herself of the vision of Charlotte dead and broken on the rocks far below, but she can still see her there, in her mind.

'Us? There is no us. And nothing happened. It was a party that got way, way out of hand.'

'Charlotte. Look. I realize that was a bit... extreme. But we had fun, didn't we? Is that really so bad?'

'A little too much fun, frankly.'

'Why do I feel as though you're blaming me?'

'I don't actually know that much about you or how you choose to live your life, Bianka. But I can tell you, this really isn't my vibe. And I'm feeling as though I've made a couple of really stupid and out-of-character judgment calls this past week and it's time to get real again and cut the crap.'

'What do you mean, get real again? I feel that what you and I have is more real than anything else in my life, and—'

'I'm sorry to be blunt but I need to be very clear here. Me and you is not real. We're Ibiza gone wrong. Everything has gotten completely out of hand and I need to do what I usually do at Can Xara, which is relax, think, re-centre myself, and reconnect. Not take drugs and fuck my girlfriends and random men at parties.'

Bianka watches as Charlotte spins around again and walks away from her, with an unparalleled wild fury. The images of Charlotte crashing onto the rocks and dying flash through Bianka's mind again; the moment her hands make contact with the small of her back, the brief look of surprise, followed by horror on her face, then the freefall through the air. And then – the sickening thud and the burst of blood. Bianka picks up her pace and rushes after Charlotte but by the time she catches up with her, Charlotte is opening the gate at the top of Can Xara's garden and moving briskly toward the terraces, where Linda and Anette are drinking coffee. When they see Bianka and Charlotte approach, they both sit up straight and place their little gold coffee cups onto the table.

'Hey, ladies, whoa, slow down. Where are you going in such a hurry? I think it's only fair to spill all the dirty details,' says Anette, laughing loudly, and when she bares her teeth she looks like a bloodthirsty animal pressing its prey into a corner. Charlotte looks stricken and shakes her head before storming into the house, her bare feet slapping loudly on the marble as she rushes upstairs.

'I wish there were some dirty details to spill but sadly not,' says Bianka, placing her sunglasses on top of her head and meeting Anette's green eyes square on, taking care to appear as calm and composed as ever. 'We grabbed another bottle of wine from the restaurant and drank it on the beach. Next thing we knew, the sun was high in the sky and we were sleeping on the sand like a couple of old drunken bohemians.' Bianka makes herself chuckle a little, but both Anette and Linda just look at her, perhaps trying, and failing, to picture or believe the scenario she just described. Then Bianka rushes inside, charging up the stairs in pursuit of Charlotte. The door to the master bedroom is locked and Bianka can hear the insulated and distant sound of water running somewhere within. She knocks, again and again, but there is no response, only the sound of rushing water.

Back in her room across the hallway, Bianka paces around and around, as though the wild fury she feels inside is actually chasing her through the room. After a while she stops, her eyes scanning the sparse, white space for something she can hurl to the ground to release her furious energy. She settles on a white-and-gold Jonathan Adler vase placed on the little table by the balcony doors, and rips the white lilies from its narrow mouth before placing the vase into a plastic bag she brought for dirty laundry. She goes through to the ensuite bathroom and turns on all the taps and the rainforest shower and when she feels certain nothing can be heard by Anette and Linda outside on the terraces or through the thick stone walls in the master bedroom, Bianka brings the bag with the vase inside down onto the marble floor with all her force, again and again. When she finally stops and peers inside the bag, the vase is not only broken but pulverized.

Bianka feels tears press into her eyes, but she successfully forces them away. She never cries, not ever, and she most certainly won't cry over Charlotte; self-absorbed, insecure, neurotic Charlotte, who seems to be under the very wrongful impression that she can control everything, Bianka included.

'It doesn't fucking work like that, Charlotte,' she whispers out loud, her voice drowned out by the gushing water. *You might think you control everything, but you'll never control me. It's quite the contrary.*

Now, it's time to calm down and recover her position. Bianka knows all the way down to her bones that she will. It's Bianka's way or nothing. It always is. She smiles at herself in the mirror, carefully honing her expression until she feels satisfied it's gentle and soft – the expression of a kind, concerned friend.

Twenty-One

Storm

Storm spends a week at summer training camp, but his head is miles away, his mind filled to the brim with Madeleine. He suddenly understands why athletes are discouraged from dating, and consciously ploughs all of his efforts into the rigid program. He has to if he's going to bunk off next week when Madeleine's in town. Every morning, the alarm sounds at six. After a quick breakfast of plain porridge, he and the two other ski guys in his year rush out into the woods bordering the school in Lillehammer's eastern suburbs, accompanied by their gung-ho trainer Bojan, a one-time Serbian Super G Olympic gold winner.

'Faster,' Bojan screams, his deep voice hollering down the hillsides.

After, Storm spends a couple of hours in the gym doing targeted exercises to maximize muscle strength. Then, in the afternoon, he has another session with Bojan, on roller skis on the smooth cycle tracks of the Gudbrandsdal valley. And throughout every gruelling session, Storm Langeland thinks of one thing: the moment his lips touched Madeleine's, how it had felt inevitable and entirely right.

On the Sunday, he waits until the lull between the afternoon training session and dinner. He has the room to himself – Albert is away at a golf tournament in Canada, and he swiftly packs a little hold-all bag of essentials. He logs onto VY.no and buys a train ticket to Oslo with his own money – he's always been a saver and has accumulated a nice balance after all the sponsorship deals. His father controls his bank accounts, but Storm has access to the current account under supervision, and he knows Emil will never notice small expenditures like a train ticket. Next, he creates a new email address with his father's name on Gmail. He composes an email to school, saying Storm won't be attending next week's summer training camp, and is authorized to leave campus and travel to Oslo to stay with relatives, signing it off with his father's name before sending it.

Madeleine is waiting for him on the doorstep of his house in Slemdal, wearing jeans and a light-blue velour hoody. His heart begins to race as soon as he sees her and she jumps to her feet and pulls him close in a long kiss.

'God, it's good to be back,' she says, as Storm unlocks the front door and motions for her to step inside. 'London seriously drives me crazy sometimes. It's just so crowded.'

'So your parents just, like, let you come here by yourself every year?'

'Yeah, to stay with my father's brother and his wife. They're pretty chill. They had twins last year so they don't micromanage me too much at this point. I have to help them out with the kids in the daytime and stuff while I'm here, though, that's the deal.'

'Cool.'

'What did you tell school?'

'You mean, what did my dad tell school?' He winks at her and hands her a cold Coke from the fridge and it takes her a moment to clock what he meant.

'Oh,' she says. 'Clever.'

They cook together, a simple pasta dish Madeleine would never be allowed to make at home, and laugh until their stomachs hurt at the thought of the Keto Queen's expression if she could see her now, wolfing down farfalle, sitting close together with Storm Langeland at his empty family home in Oslo.

'There's something I wanted to tell you about,' Storm says, when they've finished eating and settled comfortably on the sofa, scrolling through Disney+ on the hunt for a show neither of them have seen.

'What?'

'I... uh, it's, like, a weird family thing.'

'Okay. You can talk to me, you know.'

'Yeah. Uh. I wanted to, I guess.' It's the truth – ever since Storm picked the letter up off the doormat when he first arrived back from London, he's been yearning to speak to Madeleine about it. He senses that she's wise and trustworthy, the kind of person who'd know what to do about these kinds of things.

'What is it, Storm? You're worrying me.' She places a

hand on his wrist and he loves how soft and warm her fingertips feel on his skin. He sticks his other hand in his trouser pocket and retrieves the letter, a little crumpled now from being reread many times. She begins to read it with a neutral expression, but it changes as she nears the end. She reads it again, out loud.

Dear Storm,

We saw your recent interview in *VG Sport*. We've framed it, like all your other ones. Your mother would be so very proud. We're so proud, too, and hope to meet you again someday. Perhaps you've received our letters, and don't feel ready to see us, but perhaps you haven't. We'll never stop writing to you in the hope that we'll reach you, unless, of course, you want us to stop.

Your loving grandparents,
Frida and Einar

'What? I don't understand...'

'They're my mother's parents. I found the letter when I came back after my first trip to London. It's the first one I've ever received.'

'Oh, my God.'

'Yeah.'

'Where have the rest gone? They've clearly written before.'

'That's the million-dollar question.'

'What did your dad say?'

'I didn't tell him. But I did some digging, fished for information. He told me that they had been in touch for the first few years after my mom died, but then suddenly stopped contacting me. Either he's lying or Bianka has intercepted their letters.'

'Fuck.'

'Yep.'

'You have to go see them.'

'You think?'

'Without a shadow of a doubt.' Madeleine places the letter gently on the table, then takes one of Storm's hands in both of her own, kissing its palm. Then she places it above her heart and keeps it there for a long while so he can feel the thud of her heart through her light summer blouse.

The next morning

The return address had been carefully written on the back of the envelope – Mosseveien 270 F, across town on the waterfront beneath Nordstrand, according to Google. If he cycles now, he'll be there in half an hour, but he decides to Google Earth the property first to see what it looks like. The cottage sits right on the Oslo Fjord on the lower side of Mosseveien, a major road leading southeast out of the capital. It's a cute white property in the traditional Swiss style that was popular in Norway at the beginning of the last century, complete with wood carvings and snug verandas. It even has a long jetty that hovers out over the water. It looks idyllic, peaceful. As he zooms in as far as he can, he can just make out a decked terrace that runs around the waterfront and an outdoor kitchen and dining area overlooking the dark-blue water. Storm wonders if his mother spent her early life here, diving off the jetty, swimming with friends to the small islands nearby. He wonders if he's been before, as a child, but he feels as though he's looking at the house for the very first time.

He pulls his bike from the garage and checks the tyres; he hasn't ridden it since last summer but it seems to be okay. He quietly slips out of the driveway and starts peddling toward Smestad, then Majorstuen and downtown, with a million thoughts racing through his head. Perhaps this is a mistake – he has no recollection of ever meeting his grandparents and all of a sudden he just shows up?

He slows down as if to convince himself that he can still turn around and forget about the whole thing. Images of his mother come to him, a montage of the photographs he's recently come to know. He knows them inside out, every crease, every worn corner where he's held them – they're all he has. And meeting his grandparents could open up a whole new world of information about his mother. Who she really was and what she loved. It could be like finally bringing what he knows of her life from monochrome to Technicolor.

After a long while, Storm turns down the cycle lane that runs alongside the beach from Ulvøya to Bekkelaget. The access road to the house is narrow and rocky, making it difficult to cycle, so Storm jumps off his bike and pushes it past row upon row of houses. He stops in front of his grandparents' property – he instantly recognizes it from the Google Street View images. The house is surrounded by a small white picket fence and a perfectly manicured lawn to the front where a small apple tree throws shade against the window.

Storm swallows hard and looks up at the house: the lights are on and there is an old Volvo in the driveway. He opens the latch on the gate, pulls his bike inside and lays it on the lawn. He watches the house for a few minutes, his feet fixed to the path that leads to the front door. A figure walks past the window and it jolts him back to his senses. He walks toward the house, his heart racing and with no real sense of how this is going to play out. A flurry of emotions starts rising in his chest and he has to fight back the urge to turn and run. He knocks hesitantly on the front door.

The door opens and a grey-haired woman smiles kindly at him, her face blank and friendly. Then she steps forward and takes a closer look at him, her eyes locking on his, and now she does a double take before her hand reaches for her mouth in disbelief. She stumbles toward him and pulls him into her arms, letting out a deep wail as she squeezes him tightly.

'Storm, is it really you?' she cries. 'You came,' she says as she grabs his shoulders, squeezing them as if to check he isn't a mirage or a visitor in a dream. She turns and ushers him into the house.

'Einar, come quickly, Einar... Einar, where are you? Hurry!' she looks around, searching for her husband. They find him sweeping the terrace at the back of the house. She takes Storm by the hand and leads him through the living room and dining room which opens up onto a terrace where an old man stands bent over a dustpan and brush.

'Einar,' she says softly. 'Look who's come.'

Einar slowly gets to his feet and looks up at Storm

standing awkwardly in front of him. He looks at Frida and back to Storm.

'Einar,' says Frida, 'it's Storm.'

'Storm?' whispers Einar, his eyes clouding over with a sheen of tears, and Storm feels his own eyes blur. '*Herregud.*' Oh, my God.

Storm swallows the lump in his throat and smiles at his grandfather, who steps forward to ruffle his hair like he's still three years old. A silence falls between them all as they just stare at each other, Frida still holding Storm's hand, realizing that she needs to wipe the tears that are rolling down her face but not letting go of his hand clamped in both of hers.

Eventually they go inside and settle down on the sofa in the living room, which has huge floor-to-ceiling windows overlooking the water, the light reflecting on the surface of the fjord, giving it a silvery sheen, like a mirror.

'I'm sorry,' Storm says. 'I should have called.'

'No, you mustn't apologize,' Frida says. 'It's so lovely to see you. It's more than we dared hope for, though we have always hoped you would come someday, and here you are. I can't quite believe it.'

'I got your letter,' Storm says, rubbing his hands together nervously. 'It's the first one I got.'

'Oh, dear boy, we wrote to you so many times but we never had a reply. We weren't sure any of them even reached you. We thought about just turning up, too, of course, but we didn't want to do anything that might traumatize or upset you,' Frida says.

'Yes,' Einar adds. 'We must have written monthly for many years and we sent cards and gifts on your birthday and Christmas. We wrote when you were first selected for the Norwegian youth team, when you won at Chamonix and at St Anton. Did you not get any of them...?'

'No,' says Storm.

'We never stopped writing,' says Frida, fresh tears appearing in her eyes. Einar gets up from the sofa and opens an antique cupboard in the corner of the room, from which he pulls out a large scrapbook, placing it in Storm's lap. It's filled with newspaper clippings of Storm's skiing success, pages upon pages of photographs, tickets stubs where they've watched, each one dated with a little note beside each picture detailing his time and position.

'I didn't get any of them. I'm so sorry, I had no idea you were trying to contact me. Why would they have stopped me seeing your letters? I don't understand—' Storm says through tears.

'It's not *they*, dear boy, it's *her*,' Frida said, a touch of anger in her voice.

'Do you think so?' asks Storm. 'But why?'

Now Frida stands up and takes out another photo album from the same cupboard. She flicks through the pages quickly, stopping at a photo of a young Mia standing outside the old Viking Museum in Oslo. She can't be more than eighteen or nineteen. Beside her is another girl of around the same age, her blond curls hanging into her face, her right arm draped affectionately over Mia's shoulder, and looking at Mia and laughing.

'Bianka?' Storm repeats, still confused. 'Bianka knew my mother?'

'Didn't you know that Bianka and your mother were best friends?' Frida asks. 'They were completely inseparable for years. Until Mia met your father she did absolutely everything with Bianka.'

'Why did I not know that? Why keep it a secret?' Storm asks.

'Who knows?' Einar says, stroking the white beard on his face. 'Perhaps, for Bianka, it was easier to erase the past when your mother died, or maybe Emil didn't want you to know he'd married your mother's best friend. They made a lot of decisions after Mia died that made little sense to us.'

In the photo album there are so many pictures of his mother that he has never seen before, early shots of her and Emil, young and in love. They chat for several hours until it starts to get late, and Storm promises to come back and visit soon. They swap numbers and hug tightly when he leaves. The wind has picked up a little and though it is late, the night is bright with a sleek white sky stretched low above Oslo. He messages his father to say everything is okay at summer camp and then pops his AirPods in and calls Madeleine, who picks up almost immediately.

'Hey you,' she says, clearly pleased he's calling.

'Hi. I was wondering if we could meet? Like, now?'

'Umm, yeah, sure. Is everything okay?' He feels momentarily silly for having called her. Though they've bonded quite intensely they don't yet know each other very well, but he knew instinctively that it was her he wanted to talk to about his mother and Bianka, not one of his friends.

'I don't know. I just found out that Bianka knew my mother, and not just knew her – they were best friends. Nobody has ever told me that.'

'What the fuck?'

'I know. Can you get away? Meet me at the lake behind

the middle school in Vinderen in twenty minutes? I think it's right around the corner from your uncle's house.'

Madeleine holds her arms out as soon as she sees him approaching through the trees, and he walks into her embrace, tears of bewilderment and confusion blurring his vision. They hold each other very tight for a long time and as his nervous system begins to regulate itself, Storm realizes that the last time he was hugged close like this by a woman other than Madeleine, it was by Mia. Bianka has never hugged him, not once, or shown him any physical affection. He feels it, then, the contours of a memory beginning to take shape inside him; his body remembers being held like this, close, and he holds Madeleine even closer. And Mia, too.

Twenty-Two

Charlotte

The day after the party at Sa Capricciosa mercifully passed in a blur. I lowered the blinds and went from almost an hour in the shower to bed and stayed there until it got dark outside, sleeping and crying with shame and exhaustion. I ignored the intermittent and insistent knocking on the door; I knew it was Bianka and I had no intention of speaking to her. I messaged the girls and said I had a migraine. Late in the evening I went downstairs for a snack; even I can't go for days with no food at all, and the evening before at the vegan restaurant I'd only had a couple of pieces of steamed cabbage, blaming intolerances to gluten and pulses for not indulging in any of the other food. I listened out for a long while before venturing downstairs. I wanted to make sure I was definitely alone but, as I stood looking into the refrigerator trying to decide between some slices of cucumber and a boiled egg or some chorizo, a voice spoke from the corner of the room.

'How are you feeling?' It was Linda, sitting with her feet

drawn up beneath her on the sofa, quietly reading a book. 'Is the migraine any better?'

I nodded, knowing I just wasn't ready to talk – I still felt so overwhelmed and in need of time to myself. I retreated back upstairs to my room with three chorizo slices and a quarter of a cucumber. No need to go overboard just because I felt a little fragile.

Back in bed, I decided that when I woke up again, I would think of the new day as a fresh start, a brand-new Charlotte, entirely untouched by the seedy and inappropriate lifestyle choices made by that other Charlotte, who'd lived in another time. I'd think of her as a stranger, a woman that was nothing at all to do with me.

The truth is, it works. So many of the things that happen to us in life reach their potency not in the unfolding of the situation itself, but in the meaning we assign to it in hindsight. To some it may seem preposterous or ruthless to insist that we can control everything, but that isn't the point; the point is to take control of the narrative that is unfolding. I have decided that I will not let anything that has happened on this trip impact or destroy my marriage and my life. It no longer has the power to, because I've left it behind in the past and am interested only in looking forward.

Today is a stunning day, the most beautiful so far. I place my feet on the cool marble floor and take several very deep breaths before standing up. Outside, a flock of birds sweeps across the sky in a perfect arrow, pointing west. I wonder how they reach an agreement among themselves, about who takes the lead. Perhaps it's just obvious to them in ways we cannot understand. I slide the floor-to-ceiling doors open and step outside onto my balcony. From here, I can see that the blinds in Bianka's bedroom are still down. I consider a swim, a cold lurch from one side of the bay to the other, but I worry that Bianka will spot me from up here and come rushing down, trying to strike up conversation and reconcile. I could ask Anette to come down to Cala Azura with me and act like a human buffer, but she'd know exactly what I was doing and I don't want to give her that satisfaction just yet. She'll get the picture soon enough. Besides, Anette can barely walk after her glass-slicing incident. At least it didn't stop her from having a bit of fun with that gorgeous twenty-something catering boy.

The thought of a hot twentysomething drags my mind back to Max, and the way he was with us in bed – hungry, patient, appreciative. I immediately wrench my mind away from the man child and remind myself of my *new day, new Charlotte* strategy. I think about Andreas instead, handsome in his three-piece suit at Madeleine's confirmation this spring, how our eyes met across the round flower-laden table during the speeches, and how I'd noticed that day that other women's eyes also naturally sought out my husband.

I lie back down in the bed, leaving the sliding doors open so that a fresh breeze enters the room. I try to call Andreas, first once and then again, but it goes to voicemail. It's Thursday, I think; yes, it must be, because we are going home on Saturday. Only two more days and then my life will be sweet, orderly, normal, and incredibly privileged again, though not quite the same as before. I've learned my lesson on this trip and I intend to nurture it – the realization that I am beyond lucky.

A message from Anette flashes on WhatsApp on my phone, still in my hand from trying to call Andreas.

Hey, the three of us are downstairs and have made breakfast. Hope you've had a proper chance to rest and feel up for joining us.

I don't especially want to sit down for a drawn-out chatty breakfast with the girls right now; I'd prefer the cool solitude of the sea, but I wouldn't dream of letting on that I might be feeling a little off.

Breakfast consists of what seems to be a mountain of carbohydrates. I simply can't understand where they came from: baguette, French toast, croissants, *pain au chocolat*, even cereal. It goes without saying that I don't keep any such things in my home, so one of my companions must have popped out early to one of the village bakeries. Someone has flipped a couple of eggs around in a frying pan for me, and I half-heartedly eat these, or at least a couple of parts of them.

I make a huge effort to seem like my normal controlled self, and though I'm in no doubt that this will come easier with a bit more time, I won't lie – I find it a little taxing to be in the company of others just now, trying to keep up with tongue-in-cheek conversations. Every time someone asks me something, I simultaneously pop a sliver of egg white in my mouth and chew dramatically so I don't have to answer, or at the very least get away with a headshake *no* or a nodded *yes*.

Throughout, I feel Bianka's eyes on me. I don't meet her gaze a single time, but I almost want to, to gauge whether it's intense and suggestive as it usually is, or chillier now since our big blow-up. The atmosphere between us feels undeniably strange now, and I wish Bianka had never come here with us, that it was just Anette, Linda, and me as usual, that we could spend the last couple of days in our comfortable, familiar rhythm of complete relaxation.

Just before noon we head down to Cala Azura. Perhaps it would have been easier to ride the Vespas south to one of the beach clubs where we could settle in on comfortable beds, waiters hovering around us like bees, but it is our tradition to spend at least one full day at Cala Azura. We carry collapsible chairs and mattresses and cooler bags filled with cold cuts and cheese and wine down the meandering, narrow path to the sea in the increasing heat. I pretend to fumble with something in one of the bags when we get there so the others naturally take their places while I'm preoccupied. Anette is in the middle so I have to choose between placing my mattress next to Linda on the one side or Bianka on the other, the side closest to me. To draw the moment out and seem less weird, I walk down to the surf and take a couple of pictures of the bay with my phone; that way, when I come back up to our spot, I am equidistant from both Bianka and Linda, making it more neutral where I choose to sit. I choose Linda, of course, and casually throw my mattress onto the pebbles. I feel Bianka's gaze on me but I pull a book about food starch I've been meaning to read from my bag and flick it open, shutting the chatter of the others out.

We swim and sunbathe and drift in and out of conversation.

'It's too hot. I think I'm going to head back up to the house,' says Linda after we've finished.

'Yeah,' says Anette. 'I'd like a proper nap before we go out this evening, too, so I'll come back up. Ibiza better watch out – first night back out without that ugly bandage.'

'I guess tonight is the last night we'll go for dinner and drinks,' I say. 'Our flight is at the crack of dawn on Saturday so maybe it's a good idea to have a quiet night in tomorrow.'

'And maybe that catering boy could return with his meat,' says Bianka, making everyone laugh, even me. Our eyes meet for a brief moment and I feel it again, the energy between us. I didn't imagine it, that's for sure, but it belongs in the past and not in the present or the future. Now, it scares me as much as it used to thrill me. I look away and out to sea, where a jet ski is speeding in a straight line, heading north. I can make out the outlines of two people on the back of it, and am reminded of all the Vespa rides up and down the dusty, rolling hills, my arms closing around Bianka's waist, her hair fluttering into my face.

'I'm going to stay down here a while longer,' says Bianka. 'Who knows if I'll get to go to Ibiza again, so I'd better maximize my tan. What about you, Charlotte?' She winks at me and I smile coolly back, aware of Anette and Linda's eyes travelling from Bianka to me and back again. It feels like an overt dig, and a way of putting me on the spot in front of my friends; asking whether she will be included in the future. I know she wants to be met with a gushing response about how of course she'll be invited back, we must make this a yearly occurrence, the four of us, how unbelievably fun it has been.

'I'm heading back up, too,' I say. 'I want to sort through some stuff before this evening and a nap sounds like a really great idea.'

Anette, Linda, and I start on the laborious return journey back up to Can Xara, a solid ten minutes' walk up the path which is pleasant at times, and almost vertical at others. We reach the top of the stairs that connects the beach to the cliff above, alongside which the path runs before it climbs upwards past the finca and to the new house. I glance back down at where Bianka is lying on the beach, stretched out on her stomach, her body a smooth, even brown, her feet moving rhythmically to the beat of the music she's listening to.

I move my gaze from Bianka to the beautiful rolling hills and I'm about to follow the others up the path when I notice some movement on the lower part of the Dubois-Joseph property – I happen to be standing in one of the few spots where it can be seen from below. A man is walking fast down toward the bottom of the property, probably toward the gate in the hedges where Bianka and I emerged on our morning walk of shame. I feel a dull ache in my stomach at the thought of that walk through Sa Capricciosa's groomed gardens, the sound of Bianka's footsteps behind me, my heart lurching, the nasty aftertaste of the coke at the back of my throat.

'Charlotte?' Anette has stopped on the path ahead and is waiting for me. I look from the neighbours' property to Anette and back again but the man is gone. Seconds later I watch as a square patch of the hedge opens, then closes again, and the man appears at the top of the path that leads nowhere but directly towards us. Though he's still far away,

I know the man is Max – I can tell by the way he holds himself.

'Sorry,' I say, pulling my phone from my bag and pretending to press the home button. My heart is suddenly pounding so hard in my chest it feels as though I could have an actual seizure, but I use all my focus to breathe properly through my nostrils and give Anette a casual smile, while watching Max head toward us out of the corner of my eye. 'I've had a couple of urgent emails this morning,' I continue, 'so I'm just going to sit down for a half hour or so and answer them.'

'Surely they can wait for, like, five minutes until we're back up at the house?'

'Ah, actually, no. This is, uh, urgent…'

'Charlotte, it's not like you're a surgeon or a pilot. Whatever could be so urgent in the low-carb universe?'

Linda laughs at Anette's little quip and I do too, trying to seem relaxed and good-natured. They need to keep moving, right now, or they'll walk straight into Max on the path. If they hurry and move along, I have a chance of quietly intercepting him. I smile at Anette as they turn to keep walking, but she raises an eyebrow and glances pointedly back down to the beach toward Bianka, as though to say *I know what you're really doing. You just want more time with Bianka alone,* when really, the absolute opposite is true.

As soon as they go, I rush back down to the beach.

'Hey, Bianka, quick. Max is coming here. Right now.'

Bianka sits up, shielding her eyes from the sun, peering up and down the deserted beach. 'What…?'

'I saw him coming down the path from the top of the stairs. God, how awkward, what could he possibly want?'

'Well, he might just be heading down to the beach. Isn't the only access across Can Xara?' This is true. And people do have the right to access the beach, which isn't private, only the land surrounding it. We stare at the stairs and the cliffs above, and sure enough, Max appears moments later, wearing smart dark-blue jeans and a white linen shirt, an 'H' Hermès belt completing the look – hardly the outfit for a day at the beach. And wouldn't he have come with some of his buddies if he was intending to spend the afternoon here? I vaguely recall his two burly friends with the matching interlinked 'o' neck tattoos. Max had joked about them having mafia connections, and I believed him – they'd probably have to, to afford to rent out a house like Sa Capricciosa from the Dubois-Josephs, or even move in those circles. I know the type; I've seen them plenty over the years in Ibiza – the sons and daughters of billionaires, who call themselves 'nomads and philanthropists', who found cute little so-called sustainable businesses selling craft bracelets made by locals, or handbags made from recycled plastic, while they simultaneously jet around the world on Daddy's plane.

'Hi, beautiful ladies,' says Max. 'I saw you guys from the house and figured I'd pop down and say hello. Actually, to formally introduce myself. I think we skipped that part when we last met.' He winks at me and I try to return his smile but my face won't quite comply. Seeing him stone-cold sober and in full daylight, he's hardly the mega-hunk Bianka and I must have felt he was. I feel bile rising in my stomach just looking at him; he has a sleazy, cocky attitude, evident even in the way he's standing, feet planted widely apart as though to inform us that a certain part of his anatomy needs a very excessive amount of space. His arms are crossed across his wide chest, sleeves rolled back to show off the intricate tattoo on his right hand. I remember that same hand cupping my breast and have to suppress a shudder. His hair is slicked back and rigid, like a shiny helmet.

'We were just leaving actually,' I say.

'Maybe you could give me a little tour. I've been wanting to take a proper look at Can Xara for some time.'

'Excuse me?'

'Forgive me. How rude of me,' he says, taking a step forward and extending his hand, the one with the tattooed eagle. 'Maxime Dubois-Joseph. Max for short.' I am literally speechless; wave after wave of horror crashes over me at the ugly realization that Max is the son of my neighbours. I'd vaguely known that they had a son, I remember seeing a young boy down on the beach years ago, when I first came to Can Xara. It actually makes sense that if that was twenty years ago and the boy was five or six at the time, then it could be the same person as the man now standing in front of me.

'Wait, who did you say you are?' Bianka asks, having gotten up from where she'd been lying on her stomach. She stands next to me, looking Max up and down, a flirtatious glint in her eyes as though she may at any point invite him to join us for a repeat. I wouldn't put it past her. I shoot her a firm glance and give her a curt nod, but Bianka just looks confused.

'I'm the neighbour.'

'You *own* that place?'

'My parents do, yes.'

'I think I mentioned Mr Dubois-Joseph's parents to you, Bianka. You know, they're the ones who have repeatedly tried to get me to sell most of Can Xara's land, including my mother's finca, in spite of the property not being for sale.'

At this, Max smiles graciously, as though the relationship between his parents and myself hadn't deteriorated to the point where we only spoke through lawyers.

'Ah. Yep.' Bianka realizes it's probably best to stay out of the conversation at this point and walks back over to her stuff to start packing up.

'You really had no idea who I am, did you?' Maxime says to me.

'Perhaps you could have let me know?'

'I'm not sure we would have had so much fun if I had.'

'Fun.' I turn around and glance longingly up the path toward the house but I know I can't just run away from this – I have to find a way to figure out what this guy wants and make sure that, whatever it is, he won't be able to negatively impact my life more than he already has.

'Frankly, I'm a little surprised you didn't realize. I didn't even give you a fake name.'

'Well, it's hardly surprising, I haven't seen you since you were a little kid. And I never knew your name.'

'I think you babysat me once or twice.'

'No, that wasn't me. I would have remembered it if I'd come to the house.'

'It was definitely you. My father said. Maybe they brought me to you at Can Xara before your mother died. I missed her, you know. I used to like coming to see Ximena with my father. Even though she was a little, you know...'

'A little what?'

'Nothing. Never mind.'

'No, say it.'

'Crazy. She was a little crazy, let's face it. No. More than a little.'

'Like I said, we were just about to leave. Anything else I can do for you this afternoon, Mr Dubois-Joseph?' I feel like hitting the guy in the face for having the nerve to even mention my mother, and consciously draw my breath very slowly to calm down.

Maxime chuckles and kicks at the sand, then runs his fingertip across the carefully curated stubble on his chin.

'Actually, yes, there is. As I said, I'd quite like a proper tour of this place.'

'A tour?'

'Yes.'

'Of my property?'

'Yep.'

'I'm sorry, enlighten me – why would I give you a tour?'

'So I can start getting my bearings and plan what I'd like to do once it's returned to my family.'

I let out an incredulous laugh at the sheer nerve of this guy. I can't believe I have actually done what I've done with him; regret and disgust course through me as instantaneously as though they'd been injected into my bloodstream.

'You heard what Charlotte said, Maxime. I think it's probably time to leave.' Bianka has inserted herself in between myself and Maxime, as though there might be a physical altercation, and judging by the fury I feel just looking at him, there may well be. I feel suddenly grateful for Bianka and that I'm not here by myself with this guy.

'I want to see the house, Miss Vinge.' He pronounces my name 'whinge' rather than the correct 'vin-gay'. 'I have a bit of a proposition for you.'

'I know what your parents want and I've already said no. I'm sorry to confirm that no part of Can Xara is for sale but you, like everyone else, are of course entitled to cross the land to reach the cala.'

'That's not what this is about.'

'So what is it about?'

'It's about returning to my family what was always rightfully ours.'

'Excuse me?'

'Ximena swindled my father for the finca and its land in the first place. The entire coastline has been in my family for generations.'

'Swindled?'

'I think you know what I mean. Used her charm. Got him to sell the finca and its land to her for basically nothing. Well, nothing but a few blow jobs.'

'How dare you,' I whisper, my voice trembling.

'If you won't give me a tour, I suppose I'll just have to show myself around. Now, if you'll excuse me, ladies.'

Maxime spins around and charges up the stairs, Bianka and I following close behind him. I just can't believe the sheer nerve of this guy.

'You need to leave,' I shout.

'No, I don't, really.'

'This is my property. I'll call the police if I have to, believe me.'

'It won't be your property once we're done with you.'

'I will call them.'

'And tell them that the guy who made you come three times a couple of nights ago and who is trying to give you several million euros for a little strip of land worth a fraction of that, which is part of an estate your mother swindled off my family, is such a baddy?'

'Please just leave.'

'Maybe I should just call your husband. In fact, that's what I should have done to begin with. Trying to do business with Ximena's daughter was always going to be a challenge. Lives up to the family reputation in other ways, though, I'll give you that.' Maxime has come to a momentary stop on the steepest part of the path, just before it branches in two – one leading to the finca and the other to the main house at the top of the property. Bianka and I stop just below him.

'My husband has nothing to do with this.'

'Charlotte, don't let this douchebag trigger you,' says Bianka, and places a hand lightly on my shoulder but I shake it off.

'Of course your husband has something to do with this. Are you seriously telling me he wouldn't be a little weirded out by what happened between us at Sa Capricciosa?'

'Well, it would be your word against mine. My husband trusts me one hundred per cent, as I do him.'

'Brave guy. Would he trust you if I showed him the footage of you giving me a blow job?' Maxime fishes his phone out and dangles it from his fingertips. 'Got me some great porno the other day,' he says.

'I'm sure you're aware it's completely illegal to record someone without consent?' says Bianka.

'It's also illegal to steal other people's property,' Maxime retorts. 'We can make this easy, or we can make it really fucking difficult.'

'I'm going to call your father.'

'Yeah? Please do. In fact, why don't we call him right now. He wouldn't believe his luck if I told him you and your lesbian lover stopped by my party, basically drooling all over my dick. He'll get even more excited when I tell him I caught a couple of your tricks on camera. I mean, what do you think all your wholesome fans are going to say when you break the internet with your oral skills?'

'This is blackmail and emotional extortion, both punishable offences,' says Bianka, and it's the first time I've ever seen her look truly flustered. I feel another wave of gratitude for her but then I remember this is all thanks to her in the first place – if I'd never involved myself with her, or succumbed to the sheer insanity she instigated at Sa Capricciosa, I wouldn't be in this position at all.

'Like I said, we don't have to go down that road. We can settle this nice and easy.'

'Oh, really? By threatening me with illegally obtained footage, saying you'll end my career and bring my husband into this unless I sell my land to you? You've got some fucking nerve.'

'You should be careful. You don't want to end up like your mother, do you?' Maxime laughs and I want to kill him with my bare hands for making light of my mother's death.

'Are you actually threatening me?'

'Wouldn't dream of it. Your problem, Madame Vinge, is that you and your life both look shiny and perfect on the outside but none of that matters when it's built on lies.'

'Lies?'

'Indeed. I looked at your Instagram, as one does. Impressive number of sheep who feel the need to follow you and your endless low-carb reels, but I was mostly interested in your cute description of yourself. Happily married Keto Queen. What a fucking joke. As far as I know, happily married suburban mums don't feel the need to engage in threesomes with their girl friends and guys young enough to be their sons. As for Keto Queen, I mean, what is that even? Or is it *Viking Keto* these days? Maybe Streamstar will be impressed by your adult movie skills, too.' He laughs.

'Fuck you,' I say, but Maxime just laughs more, and louder. Then he turns around and continues onto the path that leads to the finca. Bianka and I follow behind him but have to break into a run to keep up. He turns back briefly and chuckles at the sight of us, only a couple of steps away from the finca's front door. Then he wrenches it open and disappears inside.

'No,' I scream, lurching after him.

Twenty-Three

Bianka

30 minutes later

'Thank God you've come to,' says Bianka. 'I've been so worried.'

'I...' The look in Charlotte's eyes is wild, desperate, and miles away, as though she isn't really here in her mother's finca in Ibiza with a dead body, the murder weapon ice cold and terrifying in the palm of her hand. She must realize what she is holding and where it has been, deep in the jugular vein of the man on the floor, and she drops it so it rolls noisily on the crude stone slabs, its silvery length glinting sharply in the meagre light streaming in. 'I... no...'

'Yes,' says Bianka. 'Do you remember what happened?' Charlotte shakes her head forcefully, sending more tears scattering.

'Anything?'

'No,' whispers Charlotte.

'I have an idea,' whispers Bianka urgently, shooting

nervous glances at the door. 'We're going to fix this. But you have to listen to me. And do what I say. Okay?' Charlotte looks from the dead man to Bianka and back again, too shocked to speak. She nods.

Bianka reaches across to cup Charlotte's face in her hand and strokes it gently. Then she gets up and pulls her to her feet.

The Charlotte Bianka knows has disappeared, or at least receded into herself, leaving behind this shell-shocked, trembling woman with a deep frown and scratchy, whispered voice.

'I don't think I—' she says, stopping herself and releasing a little gasp as they stand over the dead man lying on his back. He has a gaping, deep slash on his neck. Charlotte has been unconscious for quite a while, probably around fifteen minutes, after striking the side of her head as she fell after Maxime lunged at her. Bianka grew increasingly hysterical as Charlotte remained unresponsive and Max charged around the finca trying to stop the bleeding, crashing into furniture and Ximena's many trinkets which still sit in their places on wooden shelves. Then he slumped to the ground on his knees, muttering and crying, and Bianka remained over by the door, holding unconscious Charlotte in her arms as he began pleading with her.

'Please,' he'd said. 'Call a doctor. Please. I'm not a bad guy. I don't want to die here, please...' He grappled with his phone, but dropped it and was in no state to recover it.

Bianka didn't move. She didn't for a moment entertain the idea of calling for help. She could tell from the state of him that his wound would be imminently fatal – the amount of blood he was losing was beyond anything she could have imagined. He wasn't even able to complete the sentence before he slumped forward and began convulsing. The cramps went on for a long time and Bianka tried to focus on helping Charlotte come to rather than on the rhythmic thumping of Max's shoe on the wooden floor during his final moments. Then, finally, he went quiet.

'I don't think I did this,' Charlotte whispers. 'It's… It's not possible.'

'You had no choice,' says Bianka, sending Charlotte a gentle look intending to convey her full empathy.

'It's him,' says Charlotte. 'Max. From the other night.'

'Yes. Do you really not remember?'

Charlotte closes her eyes, winces a little, and shakes her head as if dispelling rather than evoking a memory. Bianka watches her carefully; she's good at reading people and uncovering whether they are telling the truth. Charlotte is lucky if she really can't remember what happened to Maxime, unlike Bianka herself. She can feel the little hairs at the back of her neck stand up at the horror of it, the moment the hairpin was plunged full force into Maxime's neck.

'What is the last thing you remember?'

'Uh. It was evening. We went to dinner. Me and you down by the beach. We swam in the moonlight.'

'Nothing since then?'

'No. Oh wait. Yes. This morning, we all had breakfast together. After, I sat in that little wicker chair in the garden answering emails because reception is better down there. You came and found me. Then we went down to the beach.'

'Yes. Then what?'

'Nothing.'

'That guy, Max, came here. You saw him approach on the path, I think. The others had already gone up to the house.'

'Oh.'

'Can you remember the conversation?'

'No.'

'None of it?'

'No.'

'He threatened you. He said that he was going to make you sell the property or else he'd publish footage from the other night. *That* night. You... You do remember the other night, right?'

Charlotte nods, and blushes. She looks so uncomfortable Bianka almost feels sorry for her. Almost.

'He said he'd tell Andreas,' Bianka continues. 'And he insulted your mother. He said the most disgusting, horrible things. That was when you—'

'Jesus,' whispers Charlotte, no doubt struggling to build the images in her mind.

'He literally marched up the path from the beach, making us run after him, saying it would all be his property soon enough anyway. He wrenched the door to this house open and when you tried to stop him, he lunged at you. He struck you across the face and you pulled out the hairpin from your bun, and... and...' Here, Bianka pauses and lets a couple of tears drop from her eyes. It wasn't hard to make them appear, replaying the full horror of the situation; the wild look in Maxime's eyes as the shaft of the hairpin dagger was buried in his neck, the thump, thump, thump of his foot trembling uncontrollably as he was overcome by cramping as he died.

'And you killed him. He tried to hit you again but he was injured and you stepped aside. Then you tripped and fell and it was the fall that knocked you unconscious – you struck the side of your face...' Bianka gently runs her fingertip across the deep-blue bloodied ridge above Charlotte's cheekbone. Charlotte winces – it must be swollen and tender to the touch, pinprick bursts of blood bruising her milky white skin. 'You saved us both,' Bianka whispers. 'God knows what he might have done. You had no choice, Charlotte.'

'I can't believe it. I just can't. What do we do now? I mean, we have to go to the police. We'll tell them it was self-defence. It *was* self-defence, clearly—'

'No.'

'No? Bianka, what? Seriously?'

'Think about it, Charlotte. What do you think will happen if we do that?' Bianka realizes she's practically hissing and Charlotte retracts, tears springing to her eyes again. She has to be careful with Charlotte; they'll both go down if one of them loses it. Bianka hasn't seen this version of Charlotte before, this meek, frightened woman who seems completely bewildered and unable to get a grasp on the situation. She has seen calm, controlled, alpha Charlotte, the woman who has everything. And the Charlotte with the cool edge, the one who was seemingly quite fine to just cast Bianka out in the cold when she'd decided everything they'd shared no longer meant anything to her. But now, everything is different. Charlotte needs her, Charlotte depends on her entirely; Charlotte will owe her big time if Bianka helps her to make this go away.

'Well, I don't think I'd get convicted of murder, if that's what you mean,' says Charlotte, her voice thin and weak.

'Really? But, Charlotte, that's what this is. Murder.'

'In self-defence.'

'Well, yes. Absolutely. But do you really want to spend the next couple of years in Spanish courts trying to prove it, while your marriage and your career burn to the ground? I mean, can you imagine what Streamstar would say?' Charlotte falls still and silent, probably seeing those flames licking at the foundations of her hard-earned respectable life.

'So what do we do?'

'Get rid of him.'

'No—'

'Think about it. The guy's dead. It is what it is. Nothing can ever bring him back. It would be insane to let what happened to him drag us down with him. Do you think Emil and Andreas would see any mitigating circumstances in this situation? Do you think they'd forgive us when the full picture emerges? Because it would. He had footage, he said. If we go to the police, they're going to start digging and they won't stop until our lives are ruined, even if it didn't end in a murder conviction. Hell no. And what about your career? Imagine the headlines. Your viewers. Not to mention the catastrophic effect on your poor kids.'

'Stop. Stop it, Bianka.'

'Their childhoods would be ruined.'

'Stop. Please.'

'Fine.'

They sit for a long moment in the deep-violet afternoon light seeping into the little farmhouse, the dead man on the floor between them. Bianka had slid his eyes shut before Charlotte regained consciousness, which was harder than she might have imagined. They kept slipping back open, revealing terrifying white slits beneath. Charlotte reaches out and lightly touches the eagle tattoo on the back of the man's hand, encrusted with drying blood; he'd held his hands up to his neck to stop the bleeding after pulling the metal blade of the hairpin out. Charlotte releases a little sound, a soft whimper, and her body trembles as she cries at the shock of this terrible new reality. Bianka knows she'll never forget these moments, and that Charlotte won't either. They'll be bonded by this, and bound by it, too, forever. In spite of the gruesome way it happened and the horror of watching Maxime die, Bianka couldn't actually have wished for a better outcome.

Their eyes meet and Bianka tries to convey strength and support to Charlotte – it is imperative that they are completely and fully united in this situation or it will ruin both of their lives and many others, without doubt. Charlotte nods and takes several deep breaths, and Bianka sees the contours of controlled, calm Charlotte return.

The only sounds inside the finca are the waves crashing against the rocks at the far end of the bay far below, and the lazy squawks of gulls in the distance.

'How would we even go about getting rid of him?' asks Charlotte, her fine-featured face contorting into grimaces as she seems to imagine what that would entail. She shoots a quick glance at the body over by the door, and winces, tears springing to her eyes again at the sight of the lifeless young man.

'Well. We'd have to think about making sure he'd be difficult to identify in case the body ever was found. And we'd have to make sure that absolutely nothing points to us. I think… I think we'd need to find a way to make it look like he'd gone somewhere voluntarily.'

'How would we do that?'

'We'd come up with a cover story. Dispose of his phone. Then him.'

'But… how?'

'Let's think. But we have to be quick. Anette or Linda could come back down to the beach to look for us or, God forbid, come here. We're both covered in blood. We need to get cleaned up and hide him for now, then return tonight, after the dinner.'

'The dinner? We can't go to dinner!'

'Why not? Charlotte, we have to. It will be our alibi. We'll probably be there for hours, hopefully around the time Maxime's friends will raise the alarm. Here's hoping he didn't tell them where he was going when he came here.'

Charlotte hesitates, then nods.

'And then, after, we'll come back here and drag him down to the boathouse. I assume you have the key? And can we launch the boat easily?'

Charlotte nods again, frowning.

'And then?' she asks.

'We dump him at sea. We'd need to weigh him down. Figure out the best place to do it. Somewhere deep and open, not in the bay where he might be spotted or dragged in on a strong current.'

'I know a place,' says Charlotte. 'It's not far, but the sea is very deep there. I remember someone told me not to use the paddleboard out there because of strong outward currents. I don't think we'd risk him appearing on a beach somewhere, especially if we find a way to weigh him down properly.'

'I can't… I just can't believe we're having this conversation,' whispers Bianka, making her voice low and anguished. It's time to make sure Charlotte knows how lucky she really is to have someone like Bianka, who is willing to do anything for her, even get rid of a dead man. 'I never thought I'd find myself in a situation like this. Never.' Bianka buries her head in her hands and cries.

'I—' says Charlotte, placing a light hand on Bianka's bare shoulder. 'I don't know what I'd do without you. Thank you.'

'You don't have to thank me for anything.'

'No. I do. I was horrible to you, before. After that night. I was just so completely overwhelmed. And now this. I just can't believe you're willing to help me right now, I don't deserve it. I wouldn't blame you in the slightest if you wanted to just leave and I can figure this out somehow by myself. We don't both have to risk our entire lives for this.'

'Charlotte. Stop. I'm not going anywhere. We're in this together. And I'm going to help you. But you have to promise me one thing.'

Charlotte nods. *Anything*, her deep brown eyes say.

'No matter what, literally for the rest of our lives, we never tell anyone what happened here today. Never.' Charlotte stares at Bianka, taking in the enormity of what they're pledging. Then she nods.

'Of course.'

'Because the only way to make this go away is to act as though it never happened at all.'

'Yes.'

'Okay. Are you ready for this?' They both glance back at Max, the side of his face lit up by a shaft of golden afternoon sun pooling into the room and, for a moment, it looks like he's just relaxing in a yoga pose, or sleeping. Bianka imagines she catches a glimpse of what he might have looked like as a child in this moment, when his features were relaxed and softer, when his hair was bleached and curled at the tips after weeks in Ibiza. When a long life seemed so likely it was basically a given for this boy born into unmatched privilege.

'You're right,' whispers Charlotte. 'Let's get rid of him.'

Twenty-Four

Storm

It's past midnight when Storm lets himself into the house, having talked the situation through with Madeleine for hours. This simply can't wait and he presses *Call*. Emil answers after several rings, sounding disorientated.

'Storm. Hi. Is something wrong?'

'You tell me.'

'What's that supposed to mean? It's the middle of the night. Are you okay?'

'I know about Bianka, Dad.'

'What do you mean?'

'That she was my mother's best friend.'

Emil sighs heavily down the phone.

'I'm sorry, Storm. Let me explain.'

'Is that code for coming up with more lies?'

'Storm. That's quite enough.'

'So, it's not true then?'

'Well. Yes. It is true that they were best friends.'

'And why the actual hell did you never tell me that?'

'I guess I worried you'd find it, uh, upsetting.'

'Of course it's upsetting. It's totally fucked-up.'

'I'm not sure how much of a difference it would have made for you to know about that—'

'What? That you married my mother's best friend six months after she died?'

Emil doesn't say anything. Storm focuses on a patch on the floor rug, waiting for him to speak again.

'Who told you about this?'

'My grandparents. Who, by the way, have spent the last decade trying to get in touch with me. Unsuccessfully. More lies. You told me that they stopped writing.'

'They did.'

'Like hell they did. They never stopped trying. Their letters were returned unopened. I've seen them. I found one.'

'Storm. You need to calm down.'

'Calm down? I've just found out that the stepmother who treats me like crap was my mother's best friend. Don't you think there's something super creepy about that?'

'You need to stop right now. Bianka does not treat you like crap. That's very unfair. Bianka loves you. She—'

'Do you really not see it? Or do you just pretend not to see it? She's a bully and a fucking narcissist. I've never met anyone as empty inside as Bianka.'

'That's quite enough, Storm.'

'Tell me the truth. She didn't want me to know, did she?'

'And what good would that have done?'

'It's about the truth, Dad! Not about always manipulating every single fucking situation to suit your own narrative!'

'I said, that's enough!' Emil suddenly bursts into tears, giant hoarse sobs, and it's the first time Storm has ever heard his father cry. Most of the time, he's unreadable at best. 'She saved me, Storm,' he whispers down the line when he regains some composure.

Storm clutches the phone to his ear but doesn't continue.

'I'm sorry, Dad,' he says, when Emil's sobs finally subside.

'I'm sorry, too, Storm. I should have told you these things years ago. I just didn't know how. The truth is that I fell in love with her, and she fell in love with me. I believed it was what Mia would have wanted, for someone she knew and loved to raise you like her own.'

Storm nods. He's too tired to fight. He's old enough to understand that more than one truth can exist. He also knows that while Bianka is the adult in the relationship, he's made it difficult for her over the years and she's only human. Listening to his father, Storm realizes that he must have been very lonely and fragile after his mother's death, and Bianka brought him some happiness. Can he really begrudge him that?

'I know,' Storm says. 'I'm sorry. I guess it's been overwhelming to, uh, find out more stuff about my mum.'

'I know. I figured. And that was the main reason Bianka and I wanted to wait until you were older before dwelling too much on what happened. We felt it was important to properly anchor you in the present. But we might not have gotten it quite right, Storm. It's not like we have all the answers.'

'Yeah. I get that.'

'I just couldn't think straight back then. I was in a daze for years, if I'm honest. And it was Bianka who cared for you then, I want you to know that. And very gently. She was the one who pieced you back together. You were so traumatized when your mother died, and it was both bittersweet and beautiful to watch her help you find your feet again.'

It's past 2 a.m. when Storm is getting ready to sleep. He has the strange sensation of touching upon something long-forgotten, not unlike trying to remember a fading dream.

He gets into bed and thinks about the strange sensation of coming almost within grasp of a memory, though not quite. He knows there must be a whole vault locked up inside him and he's not sure he'd want to unlock them even if he could. And yet, deep down, Storm knows that while he doesn't retain conscious memories of his mother, she's very much there underneath, remembered in his body, his subconscious, his heart. And the voice inside, when he needs it the most, is hers.

Twenty-Five

Charlotte

I watch Bianka cover Maxime Dubois-Joseph with a tarpaulin we've found behind the finca. She moves fast around the open-plan living space, cleaning up the worst patches of pooling blood with some old beach towels stored in Ximena's bathroom, but there is just so much of it, seeping in between the cracks in the oak floorboards and gathering in sickening, sticky puddles. I feel dazed and violently nauseated, and my mind is entirely blank, as though my brain is shutting down to protect me from the unfolding scene and this new reality.

'Charlotte. Are you ready?' Bianka's voice cuts through my thoughts and I glance around, surprised to find myself in my mother's farmhouse, now a murder scene. The sickly metallic smell of blood lingers on the air. I nod, then shake my head. I'm confused and dazed; my head hurts badly. How will I get through dinner?

'Yeah. Are we doing it now?'

'Doing what?'

'Getting rid of him.'

'No. Charlotte, what do you mean? We've just made a plan, haven't we? I'm worried that you might have concussion.'

'I remember now. Tonight. When the others are asleep. After dinner.'

'Yes. No one will find him here in the meantime – I've dragged him further into the corner beneath the window and covered him pretty well with that tarpaulin.' I nod. 'I found his phone,' continues Bianka, holding an iPhone with a gaudy jade marble case pinched between her index finger and thumb. 'I unlocked it with his fingerprint and got rid of the videos. He wasn't bluffing. He had three, and one was over four minutes in length. One of them was especially bad, of you snorting coke off of me… Thankfully it doesn't look like he'd passed them on to anyone, I checked his socials. The guy has over twenty thousand followers on Instagram, though – people will definitely notice his absence sooner rather than later.'

'Oh, my God,' I whisper. As much as I don't want to, I think back to the night at Sa Capricciosa, and can't remember ever noticing him recording us. I suppose there are very discreet ways around that kind of thing, though, and we should just be glad we discovered it before it was too late. I can't even bear to contemplate the consequences if Maxime had actually sent something to Andreas. Or put it on the internet.

'Okay, let's head back up to the house. One more thing, though. Change of clothes. We're both literally drenched in blood. Is there something here we can use?'

And so I find myself in Ximena's bedroom for the very

first time in all the years I've been coming to Can Xara. The dust is thick on the surfaces, but other than that, it looks as though she might have been here just days ago. The bed, narrow and deep and carved from mahogany, is made and above it hang several pictures in silver frames, all of me as a child and teenager. I look away and scan the room for a closet or chest of drawers. It's quite dark – the shutters are closed and the only light I have to navigate by is what streams in through the wooden slats, projected onto the floor in lines of light. There is a large wooden armoire, painted aqua blue and peeling. I open it and inside I find some neatly folded clothes and a couple of storage boxes. I pull one out and it's overflowing with scraps of paper, letters, and photographs. I recognize my own handwriting on many of the letters and feel a surge of grief at my mother keeping them all, perhaps rereading them occasionally, cherishing my words. I pick a random photograph from the pile – it's of Ximena as a young woman with a man. At first glance, he bears a faint resemblance to my father, but it definitely isn't him. They are sitting closely together at a table in a restaurant, gazing at each other, not the camera. I put it back face down. Maybe someday I'll venture back in here and deal with it, but most definitely not today.

There are some white, plain linen tunics similar to the ones I often wear myself, and when I pick one up and draw in its scent without thinking, nothing could have prepared me for the fact that the garment would hold the lingering scent of my mother all these years later. Hers was a distinct scent I'd know anywhere – sandalwood, fleur d'oranger, sea salt. Instead of feeling devastated and unable to cope with it, it feels like a beacon of light in this exact moment. I grab the tunics – if we bump into Anette and Linda back up at the house, I don't think they'd notice any difference from what I usually wear during the day at Can Xara, and it's not strange that Bianka might have borrowed a cover-up after a long afternoon on the beach.

We go to the bathroom together, neither of us wanting to be left alone with the gruesome reality of the dead body in the next room. I look at myself in the mirror and realize I have a spray of blood across my forehead. My stomach turns violently and I swallow back mouthfuls of bile. I don't know if it's my own blood from when I fell, or *his*. I take a quick shower and scrub myself meticulously with a sponge while Bianka sits on the closed toilet lid, scrolling on her phone, then we swap. It's past six when we finally close the door to the finca behind us, and I lock it for the first time I can recall with an old iron key that hangs from a string above the door, slow to turn in its lock. Bianka had the foresight to message the others hours ago to tell them we'd decided on a coastal walk. Now all we have to do is stick to the story and somehow act normal.

At the house, we both pad quietly upstairs, and I feel a wave of relief not to bump into the others. I send them a WhatsApp message on our chat.

> The cava is ice cold in the fridge downstairs, I hope you know to help yourselves... Will be down in around an hour, I had a bit of a funny accident on the way back up from the beach so going to get a bit of rest.

Then I get straight back in the shower. I feel woozy and confused one moment and pretty normal the next, like drifting in and out of sleep and not being sure what was a dream and what was not. I catch a glimpse of myself reflected back in the mirror and my expression alone makes me burst into tears again. It's frightening how much of a stranger the woman looking back at me appears to be. The beads of water on my face remind me of the spray of blood I washed off earlier and I feel like it's still there on my skin, so I start to scrub myself harder and harder. The grazed skin on my cheekbone opens again and I watch in horror as blood seeps down my face and merges with the flowing water. I want to scream but the others would hear me. I want to run from the room and from the house and from the island, but where would I go? Is home even an option anymore, when I can't ever again become the woman who belonged there? Eventually I stumble from the shower into my fluffy bathrobe and back into the bedroom, where I lie down on top of the white linen bedspread, my hair wrapped in a towel. I have a pounding headache and need to close my eyes, if only just for a moment.

'Charlotte. Charlotte!' says a voice. 'Jesus Christ, you gave me a fright. What's happened to your face? I thought you were kidding about having an accident! But this is, like, bad. Oh, look, you've bled all over that beautiful bedspread.'

I sit up. It takes me a long moment to recognize my surroundings as Can Xara and the woman speaking as Anette. My head hurts so much. Then I remember the rest.

The party. Bianka and me. Maxime dead and waiting in my mother's finca. I groan loudly.

'Charlotte? Shit, are you okay?'

'Yeah. Yes, sorry, I'm fine. I just needed to lie down for a bit.'

'What the hell happened to you?' Bianka and I have practised this, every last detail of the story.

'I stumbled on the steps back up to the path,' I say.

'Oh, God. Haven't I been saying for years that someone is going to break their neck on those stairs?'

'Yep.'

'And now look at you. Your face all smashed up and bloody.'

'I know. You're right. They're very dangerous.'

'Was Bianka in front of you or behind you when you fell?' It's a strange question. Why would Anette ask me that? It makes me wonder if she's already heard the story from Bianka and for some reason suspects it to be untrue. I immediately feel ridiculous – Anette wouldn't play those kinds of games with me.

'I don't remember,' I say, deciding it's actually most likely that I wouldn't remember anything – and that is the actual truth, at least. 'I came to and Bianka was cradling my head, gently splashing my face with water.'

'That's so awful. Thank God she knew what to do.' I nod. Thank God for Bianka, it would seem.

'But what's happened to your skin?' I follow Anette's gaze to my chest where the bathrobe has slipped open, revealing long, bruised streaks where I've dragged the wiry shower brush across my skin over and over, trying to clean myself of blood stains.

'I must have scraped myself when I fell on the steps.'

'Let me see.' Anette moves forward, tugging at the bathrobe as though it were a curtain obscuring a window she wants to look through.

'Anette. No.'

'Show me. Please.' I feel admonished, like a child, and the truth is I often do by Anette. I can feel my skin stinging and every muscle in my body aching. I don't know how much I might have hurt myself with the intense scrubbing and I am not about to show Anette without having a chance to see for myself first.

'Anette. I've told you what happened. I don't want to show you. You do need to respect that. Why don't you head downstairs and grab some cava and I'll be down really soon.'

'I don't mean to be rude, but it's going to take more than a little while to cover that up,' she says, pointing to my face. I sigh and make as if to get up, but the room begins to spin and I have to lie back down. I try to stop the tears that sting in my eyes but I don't have the strength.

'Anette, would you mind grabbing me a couple of ibuprofen from the second drawer in the bathroom?' Anette gets up and in the moment it takes for her to locate the pills and return to the bedroom with them, I fling the bathrobe open and take a quick look at my body. It looks like I've been mauled by a tiger: long streaks of bruising crossing my arms and stomach. I cover myself as Anette appears, and hands me the pills and a glass of water.

'Charlotte. Look. I hope this isn't overstepping but I just can't not ask... What is going on with you and Bianka? The whole thing, it just feels weird. One minute, you two are behaving like you're crushing on each other. The next, the vibe is cold and obviously contentious. She's perfectly pleasant and everything, but she follows everything you do with her eyes, laughs at absolutely everything you say, always makes it so that she's sitting by you. If anyone else is speaking, she literally glazes over. I swear, it's like she's in love with you.'

'Anette—'

'I know what you're going to say. That I'm just jealous and you're allowed to have other friends. And of course you are. I know I've been possessive in the past but that is not where I'm coming from when it comes to Bianka. This is a completely different thing.'

'She's one of my best friends.' She was, anyway. I know that Anette is right about how Bianka gravitates toward me; I was probably flattered at first but now I find it stifling and inappropriate.

'You've just met, Charlotte. Of course she's not your best friend. *I'm* your best friend, since we were five years old. I can see it's intense, but that isn't necessarily friendship, is it?'

'You're right,' I say. I need to tread carefully here, making Anette feel validated and like I agree with her observations while simultaneously starting to pave the ground for distancing myself from Bianka after we return home. After what has happened, that is going to be difficult and I have to tread carefully; I absolutely cannot afford to anger her, not now, not ever. At the thought of this I feel as though I can't breathe and I'm loosening the already loose bathrobe to get more air but I momentarily forget that I've hurt myself with the scrubbing and Anette lets out a gasp when she sees the marks on my skin, like lashings.

'Oh, my God. Charlotte, you have to tell me the truth about what's happened. Please. Did someone do this to you?' I shake my head but I still can't breathe properly unless I hunch forward and take tiny little panting breaths the way I was taught to in labour, and I sit like this for a long while until the feeling of panic subsides and I can breathe slightly more normally again, Anette rubbing my back and making soothing noises.

'I have to tell you something,' I say, at last. 'I've done something awful.'

Anette nods and reaches across to squeeze my hand. I glance at the door, which is firmly shut, and lower my voice. Even if someone – Bianka – pressed her ear to the door, she wouldn't be able to hear what I'm saying. I don't know how she would react to me telling Anette what I'm about to, but I know that I need to speak to somebody.

'I know this is going to shock you. And I just can't – I can't explain how it even happened, it's so unbelievably out of character. You know what I'm like, I'm not exactly a risk-taker—'

'You slept together.'

I can literally feel my mouth drop open in surprise.

Anette squeezes my hand again and lets out a little nervous laugh, followed by a mouthed *woah*.

'Yes. How…'

'Charlotte. Come on. It wasn't that much of a surprise. She's *all* over you, like I said. It's literally like you're the sun and she's a little fucking planet orbiting it.'

'I can see how it might have seemed a little much.'

'I was a bit surprised you don't seem to mind. She's so touchy-feely. You're not, usually.'

'Well. I guess I was flattered.'

'But were you really attracted to her?'

I think back to that night at Benirràs, when I grabbed Bianka's hand because it felt impossible not to. 'Yes. At the beginning I was. But I don't think it was really about that. I think it was more a case of needing to feel alive and desired again.'

Anette smiles empathetically and takes my hand. 'I know that feeling. It's not strange to feel like that sometimes, especially when you've been married a long time.'

I nod. 'I just felt new again, you know? Young. Sexy. Like I could be anything. Sometimes I feel that if I just keep doing what I'm doing, the rest of my life will be wasted. Even though it's a good life. Comfortable.'

'I'm not sure a good life should be summed up as comfortable. It's not unreasonable to want to feel alive again.'

'The thing is, it's not going to happen again. I'm going to tell her. But... But, Anette, it's more than that. Worse than that.' I wish I could tell her everything. About the party. Even about the dead man in the finca. I wish I wouldn't have to keep those things to myself for the rest of my life. And maybe worse, that Bianka knows and thereby wields some real power over me. But perhaps I'm being cynical – it feels ungrateful to second-guess her motives for helping me this afternoon after everything that's happened.

'What do you mean?'

'Andreas and I... We've had some issues.'

'What kind of issues?' I open my mouth to speak, again wishing I could tell Anette the truth, wishing that a parallel universe existed in which she would understand and still be my best friend. But there isn't and there is simply no way to tell her. What I've done is unthinkable. Unforgivable. Unexplainable. I killed a man today. I took his life and now he is dead. It was self-defence, of course it was; according to Bianka he was completely wild and I had no choice but to defend myself and get him off me, but still. I *killed* him.

I start to cry, huge sobs escaping me like bursts of steam from a pressurized container.

'I...'

'Oh, sweetie. I'm so sorry. This must all feel very strange and confusing for you.'

After a long while, I manage to stop crying. I pull back from Anette's embrace and make myself look her in the eyes. If she guesses what I have done, I will tell her the truth. I feel as though I have 'murderer' carved into my forehead, but of course I don't and Anette just squeezes my hands in her own and smiles gently at me.

'Try not to worry too much. This is just one indiscretion after years and years of fidelity. Your secret is entirely safe with me. We're going home in just a couple of days. Just turn your focus to fixing stuff with Andreas, I know you can. You two are such a rock-solid couple.'

I nod. I try to summon to mind an image of that life I have to preserve at any cost. Madeleine, Oscar, my husband and me. But I can't.

The clock in the hallway strikes eight and Anette glances at it.

'We should get ready, I guess,' I say.

'Are you sure you feel up for going out?'

I swallow hard, panic rising at the idea. Then I nod. I know Bianka's right and that it's better to go out and act normal than to cancel and fall apart here, rousing suspicion. Bianka and I have to just somehow hang on until we've gotten rid of Maxime and we can go back to London and pick up our lives as though none of this ever happened.

Anette gets up and bends back down to where I'm sitting on the bed to give me a hug. Before she heads for the door, she gives my hand a long, hard squeeze. I feel so stupid, suddenly, for having thought that my newfound and intense friendship with Bianka was any match for Anette. I've neglected her for weeks now, spending every free moment with Bianka. I stare at Anette as she opens the door to leave, at the fiery red hair pouring down her back, and I feel lonelier than I have in all my life. I can tell her everything but not this. Not that I killed someone. My mind is overrun with thoughts and questions, questions I'll never have answered. Wouldn't almost anyone have done what I did in those moments, to protect themselves? Can I ever truly become the same person again after this?

'Oh, hi,' says a voice – Bianka. She's opened the door at the same time as Anette and awkwardly manoeuvres her body into the room, meaning Anette has to take a step back.

'Hi,' says Anette in a pleasant, neutral voice. Bianka looks past Anette to where I'm sitting on the bed, my face still no doubt bloated and distorted from the crying. Bianka, too, looks different. It's as though her usual peppy, high-energy way of moving and talking now just makes her seem nervous.

'Everything okay?' asks Bianka, her eyes still flitting

between me and Anette. Anette shrugs and leaves the room, shutting the door with a soft click. Bianka moves softly across the floor toward me. I avoid her eyes; I don't need to look into them to know they are steely and cool.

'Yeah,' I say, my voice coming out in a sore whisper.

'Why am I getting the feeling you told her something?'

'I didn't.'

'Oh, come on. Please. The look on her face. She knows something.'

'Of course I haven't said anything. I'm not completely insane.'

'I'm glad you fully understand that,' says Bianka, and I am filled with fury at her tone, as though I'm some dumb kid who doesn't grasp the implications of what has happened.

'I need a little space right now, Bianka. I'll see you downstairs in half an hour.'

'You're not going to do anything stupid, are you?'

'Like what?'

'I don't know. You tell me. You just seem… I don't know. Not yourself.'

'I just killed someone.'

Bianka looks stricken, like she wasn't there when it happened and has just been told.

'I know. Just… I want you to know that I'm here for you. We're in this together. I am going to make sure nothing happens to you. We're going to make this go away.' I look her in the eyes, and nod. Whether I like it or not, I need Bianka now and have to play my cards very carefully.

'Why are you putting your own life and safety on the line to help someone who's just committed murder?'

'Why do you think?' Bianka smiles softly at me and

picks up my right hand which was resting in my lap. She cups my chin with her hand and tilts my head so I am forced to look her in the eye. Her smile is the same as it always has been, curling upwards almost cartoonishly, and her sparkling blue eyes grow narrow, sunken beneath thick, arched brows, but now I no longer find her slightly quirky look endearing or cute. After everything that's happened, I find her sinister.

'Because we're friends.'

'Best friends,' she says, giving my chin a little squeeze before letting go. 'Girlfriends.'

I nod, bile shooting into my trachea again, making me swallow, then cough.

'What happened to your skin?' She's still holding my hand and picks up the other one, too, angling them so that they catch the light from the overhead lamp. They are bright red and visibly sore from the scrubbing.

'I – I scrubbed a lot. To get the blood off.' I deliberately avoid looking at my right hand, the one that did the deed and plunged the hairpin into Maxime's neck. I swallow hard. 'I can't remember anything, Bianka.'

'I think that's probably a good thing, considering,' says Bianka. For a moment I feel sorry for her, for the moments she spent alone with Maxime as he lay dying and I'd blacked out.

'I've heard before that with things like this, memory quite often returns eventually. I guess I'll have to hope it doesn't. I just want to forget all of this ever happened.'

'All of it?' asks Bianka, caressing the pale skin of my wrist with a long, slim index finger. 'Even me and you?'

'Well. No,' I begin. I instinctively know that I can't afford to say or do anything to anger her. The truth is, I'm afraid of her. It's strange how quickly things have changed. I look away and feel a sudden chill chase up the length of my spine at the intensity of her gaze. 'I just can't think of any of that right now.' When I get home to Andreas and Madeleine and Oscar, I hope this will all seem like a hazy nightmare eventually, and I will find a way of dealing with Bianka. I can't see us maintaining any kind of closeness but I equally can't anger her.

'That's understandable, sweet Charlotte. Let's just focus on getting through tonight. Luckily I brought you something to take the edge off the next couple of hours.' Bianka slowly and theatrically places her hand inside her floaty midnight blue top and fishes for something in her bra. She pulls out a little pink pouch – cocaine. I shake my head. Then I remember how it made me feel a couple of nights ago: in control and capable and calm during some of the strangest, most nerve-racking moments of my life. And I want to feel like that again.

I take the pouch from Bianka's hand and pour the white powder onto the gold-veined marble surface of my bedside table. I cut four lines with the narrow spine of a little notebook on mindfulness I keep by the bedside. Then I bend down and draw a line into each nostril before handing the fifty-euro bill to Bianka.

'That's better,' she says, gazing at me admiringly from where she has settled atop my bedspread. The coke makes its way through the pathways of my brain and it's as if it clears out all the old debris and brain fog and leaves a delicious, brilliant clarity in its wake.

'I'll see you in half an hour,' I say, glancing pointedly at the door. Bianka gets up and leaves, but not before kissing me hard on the cheek, leaving a patch of wetness that I wipe away with my sleeve as soon as she's out the door. I go to the bathroom and run a face cloth under the hot water tap and rub hard where her lips touched my skin. I also scrub my hands again even harder with the cloth, making the little cuts bleed afresh.

I look at the woman in the mirror. I imagine watching her, like in a movie, or rather – like Bianka did in real life – releasing her hair from its topknot and stabbing someone to death with the long, thick silver pin that had held it. I go back into the bedroom and retrieve the hairpin from my handbag. It's still encrusted with Maxime's blood and I hold it for a long while under the hot tap, watching the rusty stains fade, the silver gleaming again. I work soap into a lather and massage the pin with it until I feel satisfied not a single trace of blood remains, my hand shying away from the terrifying sharpness of its tip. I hold the pin in my fist the way I must have done in the moments before I plunged it into Max's neck. I imagine it would have met firm resistance as soon as it was embedded in the skin; I must have had to use real, furious force to actually sever the jugular vein and kill a man with it.

I brush my hair with a couple of brusque strokes and then I twist it round and round into a coil and secure it with the pin. It meets resistance and I push harder until I'm sure it's deeply buried in my densely wound, thick hair. I feel a wave of panic course through me like a hot flush but realize that, actually, it's fury. I imagine stalking through the house, screaming at the top of my lungs, smashing everything into splinters, violently shoving anyone who gets in my way until every last bit of this crazy energy is gone.

Are you that angry, deep down? I ask her, the murderer, in the mirror.

Yes, say her eyes.

Twenty-Six

Bianka

It's not going to be easy to get away and call it an early night; both Anette and Linda seem livelier than usual this evening, as if it's taken them all these days to fully wake up to the joys of Ibiza's nightlife. And tonight of all nights, thinks Bianka. She's itching to get back to the finca, so the grisly deed will be done.

Anette insisted on going on to Els Horizonts for cocktails after dinner in Santa Eularia, at a cute beachfront brasserie whose name Bianka has already forgotten. Bianka decided it was probably a good idea to head on to a crowded bar – it would be much easier to get rid of Maxime's phone there than in a restaurant. At dinner she kept seeking out Charlotte's gaze across the table but the moment their eyes met, Charlotte would avert her eyes as though a shared glance held the power to burn her. She barely took part in the conversation, nodding here, laughing half-heartedly there, and Bianka could tell how high she was by the glassy, distant look in her eyes. When they arrived at Els Horizonts,

Bianka pressed the pink pouch into Charlotte's hand and she disappeared into the bathrooms for a long while.

Bianka watches Anette and Linda in an animated discussion about the merits of outdoor kitchens in their mountain cabins – Linda seems to be of the opinion that there's little point as it's so cold, but Anette reassures her that it really is *the* smartest thing she has ever done – her daughters simply adore barbecues on reindeer hides under the stars. Bianka has to stop herself from rolling her eyes and imagines Anette's teenage daughters, probably as annoying as their mother, with shiny auburn hair and those weird, pale snake-like eyes. She focuses on Charlotte instead.

'What do you think, Charlotte?' asks Linda about something neither Bianka nor Charlotte caught.

'About what?' says Charlotte, a mellow, confused little smile on her lips. Bianka wonders whether Anette and Linda might suspect she's taken something, but she assumes not; though these girls are heavy on the wine, they seem resolutely disinterested in drugs.

'Are you feeling okay, Charlotte?' asks Linda.

Charlotte looks great in a black organza silk dress. It's high-necked and short, with a big bow tied at the side of her neck. She's clearly good at makeup; the bloody ridge where she struck her face beneath her right eye has been carefully concealed, a line of highlighter dabbed alongside the top of it, reflecting the light.

'Yeah. I just took a bit of a knock earlier. I don't feel quite myself.' Charlotte reaches across the table and takes a piece of the fluffy rosemary-and-salt encrusted focaccia Linda ordered 'for nibbles'. She breaks off a chunk, dunks it into the truffle olive oil and pops it in her mouth, closing her eyes as she chews.

'What in the actual hell are you doing?' asks Anette. 'Earth to Keto Queen?'

Charlotte keeps chewing, her eyes half-open and red-rimmed, as though she were actually asleep, and only now does Bianka realize how high she really is. Time to get this show on the road, she thinks, before Charlotte says or does something stupid.

'Just having a nice piece of bread,' says Charlotte, giggling, but her voice sounds hollow and strange.

Bianka pulls her phone from her handbag and pretends to check a message but carefully takes a picture of Charlotte, her eyes half-closed and strangely shiny, carbohydrate pinched between thumb and index fingers, as though she's never held a piece of bread before, her teeth sinking again into the soft tissue of the focaccia. Then Bianka stands up.

'Service is pretty slow here, I'm going to the bar to get some water for the table,' she says. 'Does anyone else want anything?' Nobody does; Bianka has chosen this moment when everyone already has drinks.

She slips her phone back into the inside pocket of her handbag, a vintage Azzedine Alaïa bag she treasures, and it sits snug against Maxime's Samsung. She's already changed the access code.

She crosses the room and inserts herself into the dense throng of people clustering around the long mahogany bar. In the ceiling, huge fans whir, their wingspans as wide as rotor blades. Buddhas peruse the crowd from several vantage points throughout the large space. The bar is packed with the usual crowd of hip international types and Bianka picks out a medley of languages on the buzzy air: French, Catalan, German, and English, among others. Bianka glances over to the table where her friends sit, and, satisfied she can't easily be seen from there, fishes Maxime's phone from her handbag and swiftly unlocks it. She opens the Instagram app and selects *Story*, then takes a picture of the crowd, hashtagging it #ElsHorizonts and #IbizaNights before posting it. She scans the crowd for a suitable candidate for the next step but decides to step outside for a quick breath of fresh air and a chance to order her thoughts first. Els Horizonts has huge wraparound terraces as well as its enormous indoor bar area, and is right on the Port de Sant Miquel harbour front, where superyachts moor up out in the bay, sending their fancy guests in for dinner and drinks in nippy little speedboats. One such boat is just pulling up to the jetty in front of Bianka, the sound of laughter from its passengers rising above the engine's rumble as the boat moors. Its bow reads 'Soraya, Porto Cervo', and it's carrying six people dressed to the nines, three men and three women. A beautiful blonde carrying a pair of skyscraper heels in her hands hops onto the pier, cheered on by her friends who follow behind her. Bianka suddenly recognizes one of the men as one of Maxime's burly friends from the party at Sa Capricciosa. She can't recall his name. He doesn't even glance at her as the party passes her on the way in to Els Horizonts; his eyes are glued to the blonde's posterior, graphically outlined in a gold Hervé Léger dress, but Bianka spots the interlinked 'o' tattoo on his neck and shudders. Then she has an idea.

She waits for a couple of minutes, then goes back inside. She sees the Soraya yacht party in a private area adjacent to the bar. By a stroke of luck, one of the women, a leggy, pouty brunette with cartoonish feathered eyelashes, makes her way over to the bar and begins to talk to a woman already standing there, who could pass for her identical twin.

Bianka orders a large bottle of Acqua Panna and while she waits for it to arrive she discreetly fishes Maxime's phone from her handbag and slips it into the wide Christian Dior handbag flung over the shoulder of the brunette. The girl shifts a little and flicks her curly bouncy hair over her shoulder so Bianka pushes against her, then apologizes, in case the girl felt the shift in weight as the phone landed in her bag. When Bianka returns to the table with the water and a thundering, erratic heart, she's pleased to see Linda attempting to conceal a yawn.

When Bianka sits back down, Charlotte shoots her a quizzical look. Bianka nods very slightly, trying to convey that everything went to plan. She can't wait to tell Charlotte what an incredible stroke of luck she's just had seeing Maxime's friend if it plays out as she hopes. The phone will leave Ibiza on the *Soraya*, and in the company of someone who actually knew the dead guy. And even better, someone who has known mafia connections.

Charlotte looks like she is about to burst into tears, though she is nodding enthusiastically in all the right places as Anette tells a story about a vile colleague. After she's finished, to a collective murmur of agreement about the horrible colleague, Linda jumps in and changes the conversation.

'Hey, did you guys hear about the body they found off the coast of Formentera? Well, head rather than body. It was severed.' Linda's face is twisted into a horrified grimace, but Bianka also detects a hint of excitement.

'What? No?' says Charlotte, her face appearing even whiter than before.

'Yeah, I read about it online this afternoon. Isn't that just the most awful thing you've ever heard? Imagine you were out there swimming and suddenly a head is bobbing around next to you,' says Linda.

'Oh, eww,' says Anette.

'Stop,' says Charlotte, visibly shuddering. 'I just can't even...'

'Well, they say the Mediterranean is full of bodies,' says Anette, her face cracking into a gleeful smile as though this were a juicy piece of gossip and not a human tragedy.

'Yes,' continues Linda. 'Full. Like, apparently you're never more than a hundred feet from a body at any given time, statistically speaking.'

'What? No, that can't be true,' says Charlotte.

'The article said.'

Charlotte looks like she might throw up all over the table. Bianka also feels nauseous and chilled imagining a beautiful azure blue sea full of dead people in various stages of decomposition drifting around within its depths.

'Where is the rest of the body?' asks Anette.

'They don't know. Apparently, heads are often severed from the rest of the body by fish because they eat the eyes and the lips first.'

'Stop,' whispers Charlotte. Her thin fingers are gripping the water glass so hard her knuckles are white and Bianka fears it will shatter in her hand. She wants to reach across and uncurl her hand and take it in her own, squeezing it, reassuring Charlotte that everything will be okay eventually, it *has* to be.

'Seriously, are you okay?' asks Anette.

'Yeah, I'm just tired.' Charlotte takes a sip from her water glass but her hand trembles violently. Anette stares at her, her weird serpentine eyes narrowed, and Linda suppresses a yawn.

'Sounds like we could all use an early night. Shall we get out of here?' Bianka asks, forcing a yawn, too. She feels a surge of anticipation mingled with dread.

'Yeah,' says Linda. 'With all these drugs in my system, it's like I'm constantly sleepy. Not only do the hormones make me chubby and depressed, but apparently exhausted too.' She yawns dramatically again as they stand up and begin to move through the crowd toward the door. Bianka scans the room for signs of the yacht party but their private area is now occupied by someone else and when they step outside she sees the little speedboat leaving the harbour, its lights blinking as it crosses the bay to one of the superyachts, taking Maxime Dubois-Joseph's phone off Ibiza.

It's past midnight by the time Bianka and Charlotte quietly walk down the path from the house to the beach through scraggy, steep fields that carry the scent of lavender and sage and thyme, cicadas loud in the air, their sound constant and insistent. At the far end of the beach stands the boathouse, barely a house at all, more a shack with a corrugated tin roof, built to house Ximena's rowing boat during the winter storms. Bianka remembers how, only this afternoon,

Maxime had stood here, in this very spot, in his jeans and his fancy belt, shielding his eyes against the sun and talking to Charlotte.

They walk in silence – there is nothing more to say. There needs to be absolutely nothing to connect Maxime to Bianka or Charlotte now that Bianka has managed to get rid of the phone. Hopefully the police will be thrown off scent by its signal as the *Soraya* and her passengers continue onwards to wherever they are heading next.

If the body is never found, and no link is ever established to either of them, Maxime Dubois-Joseph will become just another missing person like the smiling faces you might see on a poster in the underground in big cities. His memory will fade in the minds of the public, who may initially engage with the mystery of the vanished playboy heir, cooking up all kinds of theories about his whereabouts. Then he will gradually be forgotten, as missing people inevitably are. And Bianka and Charlotte will be safely back home in Wimbledon, moving on and forgetting, together.

Charlotte unlocks the boat shed with a loud metallic clang, and they stop in their tracks for several long moments, scanning the headlands and the beach for any signs of life, but there is none. Together they slide the door open enough to slip through the gap. It groans loudly and they pause again, listening out, as if someone might be out there in the night. But the beach is deserted. Suddenly, her mind returns to the severed head bobbing in the water near Formentera. She pushes the thought away, but it won't quite fade and she imagines the little horseshoe bay full of floating heads, nudging against each other, dozens of unseeing eyes staring, Cala Azura's clear, shallow water running red with blood.

No, she tells herself. She must have shaken her head because when she looks up at Charlotte, she's staring at her, frowning. She glances around at her surroundings – the beach, the wide expanse of sea beyond the cape, the little boathouse – and re-centres herself. *Come on, Bianka, get a grip.* The moon is high in the sky and the sea is calm, whispering onto the rocks on either end of the bay. The first night, when Bianka came down here, she'd envisioned a much younger Charlotte on this same beach, arriving back at Can Xara after her mother had unexpectedly died. She wouldn't have possibly imagined that some day, she'd return to this place, a killer.

Bianka opens the torch function on her phone when they have both stepped inside the boathouse and shut the door behind them. The boat fills most of the space in the shed and though it's old, it looks well-maintained and seaworthy – Charlotte had explained that it would be, that Andreas sometimes likes to take it out to fish beyond the cape. Its hull sits atop a metallic launch track that leads through the shed, outside and all the way down to the water's edge. Together, as quietly as possible, Bianka and Charlotte release the catch holding the boat in place and urge it down and out, a laborious task because the track is old and rusty, but eventually they manage to shove the boat into the calm, black water, and Charlotte secures it to an iron hook on the rocks with a rope.

For a moment they stand there, the pointed bough of the boat between them, staring at each other, before quietly heading back up to the finca for the next step toward ensuring Maxime Dubois-Joseph's body will never resurface. Bianka considers herself a woman with a steely constitution but the thought of this next step brings the bitter taste of bile to her mouth.

Charlotte, she tells herself, watching Charlotte nimbly move up the path in front of her. *You're doing this for Charlotte. You'd do anything for Charlotte. Anything at all.*

Twenty-Seven

Storm

For the next few days, Storm and Madeleine spend most of their time together, sometimes at the lake, sometimes at Storm's house, up in the bedroom in the eaves, chewing the marijuana gummies, laughing at everything and nothing, cuddling and kissing but nothing more, not yet, at times sharing silly jokes, and other times, their deepest thoughts and dreams. He feels himself return to himself after the upset of the other day, and relishes his freedom, away from his father and Bianka, away from school, in the company of Madeleine.

They go for walks in the evenings, endless loops around the murky lake. Sometimes they walk only a little and kiss a lot. Other times they walk for hours, in the rain or when it's stiflingly hot, like today.

'The thing is,' he says, 'now that I've started looking back and asking questions about my mother, I want to know more. Everything. But I just can't remember. It's so weird. And frustrating.'

'I think it's trauma,' says Madeleine. 'I've read about it. We need to recover more of your memories. It's all there, inside of you.'

'Yes, but how?'

'I have an idea. We need to reintroduce you to the things you knew. When your mother was alive. They call it exposure therapy. At some point, something, some random little thing, will trigger a memory. And then that memory will dislodge other memories until you have access to a whole ton of them.'

The next day, a warm but rainy day, they take the number 19 tram across town to Saeter, where Storm used to live with his parents when Mia was still alive. It's not far from where his grandparents live, set high above the city and its fjord on a rocky promontory. The house is blue and semi-detached, set in lush gardens, the trees heavy with deep-red apples, but Storm has no instant recollection of it. He stares at each of the upstairs windows in turn. One of them must have once been his bedroom, where he'd slept, not knowing that soon, his family as he'd known it would break apart.

'Nothing?' asks Madeleine, placing a light, warm hand on his arm. Storm shakes his head.

The nursery is just down the road in a low building by a roundabout; it was easy to find with a simple Google search. It's only a couple of minutes' walk from the blue house and Storm feels oddly unsettled at the complete blank of his memory. Storm and Madeleine cross the road, exchanging a little smile as they approach the dark-brown timber bungalow with an ornate wraparound terrace, set in large gardens – it looks more like a mountain cabin than a nursery. In spite of the light rain, children are playing in the garden, running around and shrieking, one little boy squirting water from a plastic bottle after the other kids.

He must have stood here, in this exact spot, every morning as Mia slid the metal bolt of the gate open, perhaps turning back to smile at him. It can't be normal to have chunks of your early life just deleted, though Madeleine says she's the same; she barely remembers a thing before she started school.

'Can I help you?' says a voice. A woman is standing on the building's terrace and smiling quizzically across the soggy strip of trampled lawn on which the children chase each other.

'Uh…' says Storm, feeling as if a big mushy lump has suddenly slotted into place in his throat, closing it almost completely. He's seen this woman before. 'Uh.'

'My name is Madeleine Vinge. And this is Storm Langeland – he used to go here. We wondered if anyone has worked here, like, a really long time?'

The woman's eyes narrow as she takes Storm in and she appears to recognize him, smiling widely and touching her hand to her chest above her heart.

'Oh, my goodness. Storm Langeland. Of course. How fantastic to see you. You're all grown up. And as lovely as always.' The woman rushes off the terrace and across the patchy, mud-streaked grass to the gate. She slides it open and then holds out her arms to him. When she sees him hesitate, she immediately drops the gesture and gives him a fist bump instead.

'I've seen you on TV, of course, making all of us very

proud indeed. But to have you drop in here at the Blueberry Patch… Oh, how very special. You must come inside. I'll fix us a nice drink and we can have a chat in my office.'

The woman shows them down a long corridor decorated with children's scratchy drawings and smelling of boiled meat and disinfectant, then into a cosy office with book-laden shelves and a pleasant view of the peaceful suburban neighbourhood outside.

'Do you remember me, Storm?'

'Uh. No. Well… I think I remember your face. And maybe your voice.'

'My name is Lone. I was your key worker when you attended the Blueberry Patch. Oh, Storm, it really is wonderful to see you again.'

'Yeah. It might seem a little, uh, strange to just stop into your old day-care like this. I just wanted to see it again. To see if I might remember something from when I was small. We moved across town to Slemdal and I don't think I've been to Saeter at all since then. Since around the time when my mother died, so thirteen years.'

'Yes. Oh, you poor boy. It was a tragedy, what happened to your mother. I knew her well.'

'You did?'

'Well, yes, but only from here, of course. But you do get to know some of the parents properly, and Mia was one of them. She was just so sweet. So proud of you. She loved being your mother.' Lone pauses for a moment, probably because of the look on his face. Storm can feel it twisting into a grimace as though he has no control over it. He wants to say something but the lump in his throat is so thick he knows the words couldn't possibly form around it.

Lone appears to sense this, and continues speaking. Storm glances at Madeleine sitting next to him, her sweet face focused on Lone's words.

'Sometimes you can get a lot of closure from going back and getting a sense of who you were back when something traumatic happened to you.'

'Yeah. Did you, uh, notice a big change in me, you know, after she'd died?'

'Well, yes. Naturally. You were very affected by it.'

'I don't actually know how long I was here for after she'd died.'

'Less than six months.'

'Yeah, that makes sense, we moved to Slemdal around the time I turned four. Because my dad remarried. Quickly.' Lone purses her lips together in sympathy, and Storm realizes his words came out tinged with bitterness.

'Yes. I remember. I sent your file over to your new nursery. I actually had quite a few conversations with the new place in the year or so after you moved. You found it difficult to transition into a new life. No wonder, after what you'd been through. Between you and me, I think it was very soon after Mia died for you to also change your environment. But I hope your stepmother and father were able to create a very loving and safe home for you. You've done incredibly well for yourself, Storm. I'll be crossing my fingers for you next year in Vail.'

Storm nods slowly. 'Did you ever meet my stepmother?'

'No, I didn't.'

'In what way, specifically, did you think I was affected or traumatized after Mum died?'

'I think, because you were there when it happened, you

really needed to work through your memories of that day, and—'

'Wait. I'm sorry. I was there?'

'Well, yes—'

'I...'

'I don't think Storm knew that,' he hears Madeleine say, and he can feel her tugging at his hand to sit back down. He hadn't realized he'd gotten up. It's as though all the blood in his body has rushed into the confines of his skull, making it feel like it might actually explode.

He lets himself be pulled back down onto the chair. He does his breathing exercises, counting slowly to five when he inhales and seven when he exhales. It takes him a very long time to angle his head toward Madeleine, such is his shock; it's as though it has struck him still, trapped inside his own body. When he manages to move his head the last inch so that their eyes meet, Madeleine's are wide in horror.

'I didn't know that,' he says, and his voice breaks, making him sound like a young boy again. How will he get up, walk out of here, make small talk with Madeleine, go home? How will he ever look his father in the eye again? What else has he lied about? It seems to be one thing after another and Storm feels certain that it's Bianka's doing – she's always discouraged any questions about what his mother was really doing up there that day so many years ago. But to not tell him that he had been with his mother on that mountain when she suffered a fatal accident, it was unforgivable.

'I'm not sure I should tell you this, Storm. But you are almost seventeen now and seem like a very sensible and clever boy. And I think you've come here looking for something, some insight into your own self, which is something I believe everyone deserves.' Lone pauses, her eyes searching his. Storm makes himself hold her gaze level and steady. 'I reported your family to Barnevernet, Oslo's social services, a month or so after your mother passed away. I felt I didn't have any choice. You can imagine it didn't go down well with your father, which, of course, I understand – it must have felt like an extra burden in the thick of grief. But I was extremely concerned for you. Shortly after, your father made the decision to move to another part of the city, and as far as I'm aware, the case was left unresolved as most cases unfortunately are. But I made sure to get in touch with your new day-care to make them aware of the things that had caused me concern, in the hope that they would follow you up and pay extra attention to you when I no longer could. I want you to know that I really tried to do right by you.'

A thick silence separates them for several long moments. Storm tries to recall any memories about what Lone just told him, but there simply aren't any. All he remembers from those early years in Slemdal is playing out by the edge of the forest with a couple of boys from the neighbourhood. They'd trap baby frogs in their hands and hold competitions over who could resist releasing them for the longest, relishing the disgusting, thrilling scramble of the sticky little animal trapped in the cave of their cupped hands. And he remembers Bianka's shrill voice as she'd call him in for supper; he'd run so fast, his pulse sounded in his ears just to make her exaggerated singsong voice stop. *Stooo-ooorm. Stooo-ORM. Stoooooooorm.* The other kids would pause whatever game they were playing and stare at him open-mouthed as he raced toward the strange sound. Nobody else's mother screamed like that.

Storm makes himself return to the present moment. Madeleine on the plastic chair next to him, close, her warm hand snug in his own. Lone across the desk, looking at him with her hooded, maroon eyes shining with kindness and concern.

'What was it that made you so concerned?'

'You said some terribly disturbing things. And I believed you.'

Twenty-Eight

Charlotte

I unlock the door to the finca and Bianka shines the light from her phone around the main space, letting it dwell for a long moment on the gruesome sight of the tarpaulin-covered bundle beneath the window. A new wave of panic surges through me at the feeling of standing here in an enclosed space in the dead of the night with Maxime's body in the room with us, and I have to swallow hard several times to stop a scream rising in my throat. Still, in spite of the feeling of panic, I feel somehow ready for this – it's as though I've come to accept that it has to be this way. It's me or Maxime now, and it's too late for him anyway.

The coke has worn off by now and I'm simultaneously jittery and exhausted, plagued by a terrible cold that seems to be originating in my bones. In the past few weeks I've almost entirely removed myself from all the ideas I ever had about myself and how I live my life.

'I'll go get the weights,' says Bianka. I nod and follow her back outside into the night; I can't bear to wait inside, alone with Maxime's body. While I wait for her to return I realize it might not be any better to be left alone with my own thoughts. I try to tame them, to streamline them into controlled and useful ones the way I usually do. I think about standing on the sidelines, watching Oscar play football, his young, agile body lurching across the pitch like a puppy's. And about brushing Madeleine's hair in the evenings, helping her ease out the stubborn knots at the nape of her neck, our eyes meeting in the mirror. This is the life I have to focus on, to stand a chance of preserving it. And yet, it feels so distant and elusive to me, like watching someone else's great life on TV and knowing you can never have something like it yourself.

I stare down the path, past the cliffs and out at the black, moonstruck sea. Down there, on the beach, my mother's boat lies in wait. I'll pick up the oars worn smooth by Ximena's hands and slice the water swiftly until we reach the open sea. We'll do what we have to do and then we'll return without Maxime and pull the boat back up.

Bianka takes a long while and by the time she finally returns, the sound of her feet crunching lightly on the stones of the path that leads from the house, I have convinced myself that she's been injured, or that the police have come and are asking questions up at the house, or that she has run away, leaving me to deal with Maxime by myself.

I breathe a sigh of relief at the sight of her, though Bianka looks and seems like a different woman from just days ago. Her eyes, which usually shine with a combination of quick wit and mischief, look dull and distant, and she carries herself differently, more slowly and considered, like she's constantly bracing herself.

'Okay?' I whisper, and she nods, motioning to the eight-kilo kettlebells swinging from each hand.

'Fuck, these are heavy.'

'Good,' I say, and we exchange a tight smile.

Back inside the boathouse, by the light of the phone torch, angled so its glare is unlikely to be spotted through the gaps in the tightly drawn curtains in the almost inconceivable event of someone walking along the path on my property in the middle of the night, we uncover Maxime's body. In the hours we've been gone, he has started to grow slightly rigid – though his limbs still bend, they seem unnaturally leaden and stiff.

We slowly drag him into the middle of the room so we have more space to move around. Then we begin to take his clothes off. I'm not yet sure what we'll do with them, but we've agreed that we need to do absolutely everything we can to get rid of as many possessions and identifying features as possible. It takes us a long while to get him out of his blood-soaked white linen shirt – he's heavy and his head is lolling around grotesquely as we lift his torso. We place him back down on his back when the shirt is off and quietly take him in, exchanging glances. The gash in his neck has dried up and looks like a terrifying black hole. The large eagle tattoo on the back of his hand, which I'd thought looked sexy when that same hand cupped my breast, now fills me with intense pity. He's so young.

Was.

Not even thirty.

He behaved badly and I had to defend myself, but can that justify what I've done, what I've taken from him? He'll never have children, will never laugh or travel or make love or hug his mother, ever again, because of me. He's an only child and at the thought of his elderly parents, who in this moment don't yet know that they are childless, I feel as though I've been punched in the gut.

We might have had our differences with the Dubois-Josephs, but I'd never wish the death of their only child on them, or anyone. And yet, I caused it.

'You okay?' whispers Bianka.

'Well, no. Obviously.'

'Hey. Hang in there, okay? If you can pull his jeans down, I'll try to lift his lower back up a little.' I do as she says, and unbuckle his belt, then his jeans, one tough metal button at a time. I can't help but think back to the party, of Maxime taking his trousers off then hungrily watching Bianka and me on the bed.

Bianka manages to hoist Maxime up and I pull hard at the jeans, but they are tight and stuck to the skin. I manage to roll them down little by little until they gather at his feet.

'Now his underpants,' says Bianka. I swallow hard and go straight for them, classic black Calvins, the same kind as the white ones he wore the other night. I feel myself blush and brusquely cover his genital area with one of the blankets we found in Ximena's cupboard.

'Anything else that can identify him easily?' I ask, shining the torch across the dead man's naked body.

'Well, the tattoos,' says Bianka. He has six in total.

'Not much we can do about that,' I say. 'Besides, I think after long enough in the sea, they'll become indistinguishable.'

'Unless… Unless we burned him first,' says Bianka.

'Oh, God.'

'I know. But… It might make the difference between getting caught for this, or not.'

'How, though?'

'We could do it on the beach.'

'No. It would draw attention to us. Besides, it's illegal to light an open fire on Ibiza between May and October. The police would be here in five seconds.'

'I see.'

'Let's just stick to the original plan. I think the most crucial things are that we make sure he is extremely unlikely to resurface and that the family and the police are made to believe he's done a runner, at least initially.'

'What about forensic evidence, though? Once it's obvious that the guy's gone missing, don't you think the police are going to be poking around everywhere? Maxime's the son of very rich people. They're not going to leave a single stone unturned,' says Bianka.

'You're right. Which is why we have to make damned sure that there simply is no connection between us and Maxime.'

'Lots of people saw us at the party. He might have bragged to his friends after what happened. A lot of guys probably would.'

She's right. Could it be that he initiated what happened between us to create a situation where he could blackmail me to begin with, after Bianka told him I'm the owner of Can Xara? Of course he did. How could we have been so stupid as to think that an attractive man in his twenties was just desperate to sleep with a couple of bored, undersexed fortysomething women? I can't help the tears that rush from my eyes and drip onto Maxime's bare skin.

'Hey,' says Bianka, placing a hand on top of mine. I pull it away irritably.

'Let's just get this done.'

'I had an idea,' says Bianka. 'When we were in the bar I saw a friend of Max's – the shorter one with the green eyes, do you remember? He was one of the two guys with those interlinked "o" tattoos on his neck. Max made some joke about them being mafia. And then something occurred to me. I think we mark him. Maxime. So that in the event he were to resurface the police would hopefully assume that he was killed by whatever mob branch his buddies belong to.'

'Mark him.'

'Yes.'

'But – how?'

Bianka picks up the thick carving knife we'd found in Ximena's kitchen and we exchange another glance, both wincing at the reality of cutting the dead man's skin open.

'Where?' she says. I shake my head; I'm not sure it matters where. But it's a good idea.

Bianka takes a deep breath, then she begins to run the knife across the smooth skin below his collarbone, already bloodstained from the gaping wound on his neck directly above it, but it doesn't pierce the skin.

'More pressure,' I whisper. She tries again and this time she produces a curved line, her face contorting with concentration and disgust. I expect blood to squirt out but nothing happens – of course – he's been dead for almost eight hours at this point. When Bianka has carved an almost perfect 'o', she starts on another, linking it in with the first. When she's finished we both sit in silence for a while, the knife on the floor between us.

'I had another idea, too,' says Bianka. 'The weights and the rocks are all well and good but I think we should' – she pauses here, her voice shaky – 'disfigure the tattoos. As in, smash them with the kettlebells. There will be massive bleeding beneath the skin.' I'm shocked and disgusted at the idea, but I realize she's right. As horrible as the thought is, it might be the thing that makes the difference between being caught and running free if his body is ever found.

'I'll do it,' I say. Bianka raises an eyebrow but says nothing, merely watches as I pick up one of the kettlebells and raise it above my head. *Come on*, I tell myself. *You can do this*. I tighten my grip but my palm is slick with sweat and my heart is beating so hard I can hear its thud as loudly as if it were a separate entity in the room with us. The weight is very heavy and my muscles twitch with the effort. All I have to do is let go and let my arm follow its natural trajectory downwards onto the back of his hand. I try to summon the fury I felt earlier when I stood on the path with Maxime and he insulted my mother. But in its place is just deep, bleak exhaustion and fear. I can't do it. In the split second before I was going to bring the weight down full force onto Maxime's immobile hand, I slowly lower it and place it upright next to his body. I feel an intense wave of nausea and quickly stand but don't make it to the bathroom before I start throwing up, mouthful after mouthful of foul vomit splashing onto the tiles.

'Lie down over there for a bit,' says Bianka, pointing to the slouchy sofa, across which one of Ximena's hand-crocheted blankets is flung. I could lie down and cover myself with the throw. I could turn my back to Bianka and stick my fingers in my ears, leaving her to do the dirty work. But in the end, I slump down onto the floor and sit with my back against a kitchen cabinet, watching as Bianka continues our grisly job with a determined look on her face. She's quick, now, not hesitating for a moment. Over and over she brings the kettlebell down onto Maxime's hand, then his shoulder, and his thigh, its sickening thud filling the little space as she crushes his tattoos and the bones underneath.

I'm dizzy and feel as though I'm not really here on the floor but hovering somewhere above the unfolding scene, safely tucked away among the dark wooden beams reaching across the vaulted ceiling space. I close my eyes every time she brings the weight down but its sound reverberates through me. I keep my eyes mostly closed as she cuts Maxime's stomach open and places the iron kettlebell inside, followed by the second unused one, the way we planned it. She motions for me to come back over and together we tape his stomach closed with the heavy-duty gaffer tape I found up at the house.

'Almost there,' whispers Bianka. She inserts a finger into Maxime's half-open mouth, and tries to prize his jaw open but it won't budge much and she has to use real force, her biceps growing taut in the meagre light from the torch. I worry that his jaw will snap and that I'll never forget the sound, but she manages to open his mouth enough to wedge a round pebble we brought from the beach between his teeth, propping it open. She then places stone after stone into his mouth as though she were feeding coins into a slot machine until no more will fit. Then we tape his mouth shut, and his eyes, too.

'Are you ready?' asks Bianka, standing up and looking down on Maxime with an odd look of satisfaction at the final result. I nod, trying to avoid looking at the dead man any more than I have to.

'Let's go.'

It takes us over twenty minutes to drag Maxime down the path and the stone steps onto the beach, still wrapped in the tarpaulin, his feet sticking out and dragging behind us as we go. We manage to get him onto the boat and he crashes into the forward space of its hull. My hands tremble violently as I release the rope from its metal hook and throw it into the boat, where it lands on top of Maxime with a wet slap. We take turns rowing and this is the easiest part so far, though it's heavy and dark, because we are outside, breathing fresh air, not the stale air of the finca with its sweet stench of blood, and in spite of everything, it is beautiful out here on the water underneath the stars. We can more easily choose to avoid the sight of the dead man slumped at the bottom of the boat.

I manoeuvre the boat past the towering sentry rocks at the entrance to the sheltered little cala, keeping it calm even when strong winds whip the island. The moon is high in the sky and shines its crystalline light onto the sea, highlighting the lines of a current. This is well known for being an especially perilous spot due to the riptides. And it's deep. Again my thoughts return to all of the other bodies in the Mediterranean, and I wonder where the next closest one is, whether it might be right around here, held still in the chilly depths beneath us. I glance at Maxime. He looks like a black mummy, covered almost entirely by duct tape. His longish brown hair partly sticks up in messy tufts, and partly lies matted to his scalp with blood. I recall how meticulous and sleek it was in life.

My thoughts move on to his parents. Soon, I imagine, they'll come here amid the ongoing investigation into their only child's mysterious disappearance. They'll be over the worst shock by then, and they'll still be buoyed by hope that someday, somewhere, their wayward but adored boy will turn up. The hope will fade as months and then years go by, but perhaps it will never die completely when a body isn't found.

Something interrupts my thoughts, a voice – Bianka is speaking to me.

'Charlotte. Are you okay? You're miles away. Come on. We need to get him overboard. It's almost three o'clock.'

I nod, pulling the oars from the water and resting them in the oarlocks. It takes us several minutes to figure out a way of heaving Maxime overboard – he's heavy and the boat is small, rocking so hard as we shuffle about that I worry it might actually overturn. We also have to be quick – both Can Xara and Sa Capricciosa have sea views and someone could potentially spot us if we're unlucky. Though I feel confident we're shielded by the limestone rocks at the cape, I can't be totally sure. In the end we manage to roll him overboard and it happens so quickly and almost soundlessly that I can't quite grasp that we've done it.

'What if the police come knocking, asking questions?' We're only metres from shore now and I can make out the pinprick lights from Can Xara high up on the hillside, separated from the stars by a narrow patch of trees.

'They won't.'

'They might, though. He could have told his friends about

what happened between us and that I own the neighbouring property. He could even have told them he was going over here for a little chat. Of course they'll be suspicious when the guy just doesn't return.'

'Listen to me. If you really want to get away with this, Charlotte, you need to assume that nobody suspects you because then you won't come across as suspicious. People like you don't kill random men with whom they have no provable connection. They just don't. So rest assured, nobody is going to look at you and be like *Oh, yes, I bet that keto chef lady in the five-million-euro neighbouring house killed that young, rich dude that went missing in Ibiza*. Believe me. His reputation is going to work in our favour. I'm sure he has one. He was a total playboy. I bet he has a long bad-boy history of drugs and various women and all kinds of issues. You have to remember that only you and I know that he's dead. People will not automatically assume murder. Besides, he posted on Instagram from Els Horizonts, remember? Police will trace his phone to that yacht and assume he must have gone wherever it did. Then they'll hopefully uncover that at least one of his friends was on that yacht.'

'Yeah, but what about his friends, though? How do we know they won't point the police in the right direction?'

'Because they're mafia, Charlotte. Criminals. Do you really think they're going to call the police and be like *Oh, hi, my friend's gone missing, could you come here and have a poke around?* They're probably dealing drugs and all kinds of stuff and absolutely not interested in having police come calling. I'm totally sure they're going to scarper and cover their tracks when they realize Maxime is missing, which is great for us because it makes them look suspicious as all hell.'

'I guess.' The boat scrapes against the pebbles on shore and we pull the oars back in before I jump onto the beach. 'I can't stop thinking about what we've – I've – done, though. The brutality of it. That I actually *killed* him. He was just a kid, you know? How can I possibly live with this?'

'Look. Cry for five more minutes, while we get the boat back into the boathouse. Then never cry over him again, ever. Promise me? No need to cry about something that never happened or someone you never provably even met.' I nod and allow the tears to flow freely while we begin to manoeuvre the boat onto the metal track. She's right, of course – again.

'Let's make a pact,' I say. 'We never speak of this again. It's done now.' Bianka nods and we solemnly shake hands, her hand lingering in mine for a long while.

It's almost four a.m. when we start on the final stretch of the path from the finca back up to the house. We've changed back into our party dresses which we left in the finca while we got rid of Maxime wearing old sweatpants and plain T-shirts. If we happen to run into Anette or Linda, we'll say that we've been down on the beach, talking and drinking. They'd believe it; it's not like it would be the first time. We're just coming up to the final twist in the path, directly beneath the yoga platform, when Bianka takes my hand.

'Hey. I just want to say that I really feel it's important that we try to return to how we were, before all of this terrible stuff happened.'

'Bianka—'

'I'm serious, Charlotte. I can't bear the thought of things changing between us. I just can't.'

'Well, obviously things have changed. We just threw a dead body into the Mediterranean.'

'It doesn't have to change the amazing thing between me and you, though.'

I know I have to be careful here but at the same time, I just can't believe she'd stand here, looking as though she'd quite like to kiss me in the moonlight, knowing what we've just done. I can't help but release an incredulous little sigh. 'Seriously? You seem completely unaffected by what we've just done. I find that unbelievable. I need some space.'

'And I need you. Please.' Bianka looks desperate and unhinged suddenly, like she might go absolutely crazy if I don't give her what she wants. But what she wants is me, and she can't have that. I take my hand back, and have to pull quite hard to release it from Bianka's clammy grip. I keep walking up the path, but Bianka seizes my arm and yanks me back.

'Hey, that hurts.'

'What you just said hurt.'

'Bianka, will you please stop? You're freaking me out. You can hardly blame me for wanting some space considering what has happened in the last couple of days.'

'And you can hardly blame me for feeling a little used, Charlotte.'

'Look. Can we just forget it, all of it? We agreed we would.'

'That's what I just suggested. Let's just leave this behind

now and remember what it was like… It can be like that again.'

'No. It can't.'

'Yes, it can. And it will.' She has a look of defiance and triumph and I realize that she's actually threatening me.

'What exactly do you mean by that?'

'Well. I think it's fair to say that I've helped you out tonight. Big time. Perhaps show a little appreciation. I mean, why would I keep your dirty secrets if you're going to cut me off like that?'

'I'm not cutting you off. I need space, Bianka.'

'Space!' Bianka practically shouts the word and I instinctively glance around to make sure nobody heard. Through the branches of the olive trees that grow on the slopes surrounding us I can make out the glass-walled terraces by the pool and become aware of a slight movement up there, then a flash of copper red – Anette. Bianka is standing with her back facing the house and I most certainly don't want her to realize someone is watching – in her aggravated state I just can't be completely sure she wouldn't say something that would give it all away. She might not even have to – we both look pretty dishevelled, I imagine, and Anette might grow suspicious of what we've been up to if she sees us in this state, especially later on, in hindsight, when news of Maxime Dubois-Joseph's disappearance makes international headlines, which I have no doubt it will. I need to throw her off the scent and make her go away. The best way to do that is to make this look like a lover's tiff, an intimate and awkward moment you wouldn't want to intrude on.

'I'm sorry, Bianka,' I say, loudly. 'You're right. Come

here.' She looks up at me, confused. I take a step closer. Then another. I close the gap between us and kiss her hard on the mouth, burying my hands in her hair, and she responds eagerly. It clearly doesn't matter to her at all that I was throwing up an hour ago or that the hands playing with her curls are encrusted with blood.

Part Two

'When people show you who they are, believe them.'

–Maya Angelou

Part Two

Twenty-Nine

Charlotte

On my first day back I drive slowly around Wimbledon Village running errands, looking at all the familiar places I go to all the time. Everything is exactly the same and yet nothing is. I pull over several times simply because my heart is racing so badly I have no choice.

A police car is parked outside the Rose and Crown and, as I drive past, I'm convinced the officers catch a glimpse of me and instantly knew the truth – that I'm a killer. A ruthless and violent woman. I actually slow down and wait for the blue lights to sweep across the road, the loud beeps alerting all of Wimbledon to the murderer among them. Of course, nothing happens, and I continue home, my hands trembling violently on the wheel. I feel the need to check all the news channels for any mention of Maxime going missing, as I have done numerous times a day since *that* night, but there is nothing.

At home, too, everything is the same; the pristine, beautiful garden, the plumped-up cushions on every beige sofa, the total absence of a single speck of dust. Ayla knows dust drives me insane.

Everything is the same, except Madeleine is still in Norway, not due home for almost another week. I'm glad she's away. She's so perceptive, she'd take one look at me and realize something big has happened. Now, at least I have a week to fully regain my composure, move past the horrors of Ibiza and properly rebuild my life.

I get into bed to wait for Andreas. I've asked him to turn off whatever he's watching and come upstairs to speak to me – we have to start having real conversations about our lack of intimacy. I muster up all my courage; it's not like I haven't tried to instigate these conversations before but this feels different. The stakes are higher.

Andreas appears in the doorway, looking drawn and pensive. I pat the bed and try to give him my best seductive look. He looks like a mouse that's been deposited inside a hungry tiger's cage. I try to build the image of what sex with my husband used to be like and find that I can't. I actually don't clearly remember. But I do remember what it was like with Bianka, how she moulded her entire body into mine, how she just fitted, all curves and dips and softness, and how she wouldn't stop kissing me and laughing and kissing me more, like it was impossible not to. Before we met, I'd forgotten what it feels like to be wanted like that. I try to recall when Andreas was last like that with me, like he couldn't get enough, but it's so long ago, since before we had Oscar. He's thirteen now and I don't think we've had sex more than a handful of times since he was born. Is it so strange that I couldn't resist the feeling of being wanted?

'I missed you, honey,' I say.

'I missed you too.'

'The whole thing with Anette and Mads' divorce has made me think about how lucky you and I are.'

'Yeah,' he says, reaching across to squeeze my hand pleasantly but chastely, the way a father might.

'But I think we need to start thinking about how we can re-establish more of a physical relationship.' I've practised this conversation in my head all afternoon and Andreas reacts precisely how I assumed he would, wincing then dropping his gaze. It astonishes me that a man this conflict-shy and evasive could be as successful as he is in business. 'Seriously, babe, it's time we talk properly about it. I feel like you just don't want to sleep with me. You don't initiate sex and you turn me down when I do. I've tried to understand that you have a lot of stress at work. And that your needs might be different to mine, though it didn't seem that way before. But I have needs, too. It's been years, Andreas. Literally years. And I need you to hold me, you know? To touch me, and—'

'Charlotte... Look. You're right. I'm not sure how it's happened this way. Just, when the kids were little, it was all just so crazy. It felt like you didn't want me to touch you. And then, later, when they were older, it just felt like that part of our relationship was over.'

'It doesn't have to be, though.'

'Maybe not. I'm sorry, Charlotte.'

'I'm sorry, too. I just want to feel close to you.' Andreas nods pensively, and runs a hand through his hair, then he moves a little closer to me on the bed. Then he kisses me.

His kiss is hungry and hard and my heart begins to race as he tugs at my top and then my bra. We break apart for a moment and both laugh before kissing again. It happens so fast it's almost as if my head can't quite keep up, but for a few delicious minutes I forget everything except the feeling of being close, really close, to my husband, and I clutch him to me so hard I don't immediately notice when he stops moving. I want him to keep going but it's quickly obvious that he's done. He flops over on his back next to me and we lie side by side staring up at the ceiling.

'Wow, honey,' he says, and leans across to kiss me again. 'That was amazing.' Then he gets up and puts his clothes back on and makes for the door. 'I'm going to sleep down the hall. Early meeting with the guys from Zurich tomorrow.' I smile at him and nod, in spite of feeling disappointed with the ending – at least it's a giant leap in the right direction. I go back over the sex in my mind, how he felt, the way he kissed me and pinned me down beneath him.

And in spite of everything I suddenly miss the intensity and intimacy with Bianka. I bring myself to a quick but powerful climax at the thought of her beneath me in bed, wanting and laughing and available, always so focused on my pleasure. After, I feel ashamed and confused and dirty, and it takes me ages to fall asleep.

Thirty

Storm

He runs as fast as he can but he feels whoever is pursuing him getting closer and closer. He screams, but even in those moments he knows that nobody can hear him. The sounds are of his boots stomping on a gravel path, towering trees being shaken by a howling wind, the crunch of footsteps getting closer and closer, his wild screams. He turns around to see how close the baddy is now but he doesn't get a chance, because the baddy is a giant looming above him, right there, and has managed to grab him by the hair on the back of his head and is flinging him to the ground like a ragdoll.

The last thing he hears before he wakes up, sweating and shaking in his bed, is a menacing voice hissing into his ear.

'Listen to me, you little pig. I will snap your neck like a twig if you don't do exactly what I say. Do you understand?'

The ping of an incoming text message jolts him awake. Just his dad, checking in. He hadn't intended to fall asleep, it's only five o'clock in the afternoon, but he was exhausted to the bone after a long run up to Tryvann this morning.

Storm puts his phone down and stares into the soft afternoon gloom of his bedroom for a long while. He finds the drawings Lone handed him as he left the Blueberry Patch from where he keeps them in his bedside table and sits up in bed. She'd managed to uncover them along with his file in the nursery's digital filing system. He stares at them, moving his gaze slowly from one to the next, for what seems like the hundredth time. And still, he can't quite make sense of them.

In the first drawing is a little boy – himself – running through the woods alone. At the time he'd told Lone that he was running away from the baddy who threw his mother off a cliff. She'd found it very strange and had asked him gently about it several more times, and every time his story had been the same. Storm and his mother were in the woods on the crest of a mountain, walking on a narrow path when a baddy came and shoved his mother off the path. As Lone spoke, Madeleine's hand closed tightly around Storm's and he'd felt a rising panic in his chest at her words. But he remembered nothing.

In the second drawing, he's still running but there is someone in the distance, though it's just a stick figure. Storm had told Lone that the baddy was in the woods with him and that he'd had to hide. But then, in the third drawing, he's drawn himself holding a curly-haired blond woman's hand. Bianka. 'I hope you're still close,' Lone had said as she hugged him goodbye, 'I had the impression that she gave you a lot of love and affection after your mother died.'

He feels guilty, all of a sudden, for all his criticism of

Bianka. It was there on paper for anyone to see – his own childhood interpretation of an adult who'd clearly stepped in to take care of him.

Perhaps it hadn't been so easy for her, either, though he's never thought about it like that before. He pores over the drawings again for a long while. He tries to recover a sliver of memory from the moments the drawings came into being, where was he sitting, how did the pencil feel in the crook of his hand, if he was angry with himself for not managing to draw any straight lines. But no memory remains.

He feels so lonely and cut off from everything that when the sky has weakened into shades of violet and pink, Storm gets up on impulse. He runs all the way to Slemdal station, passing a few boys he knew from his old school, barely slowing down to high five them as he goes. Since St Anton, Storm rarely walks down the street in this part of Oslo without being recognized or congratulated.

He rides the subway to the central station, then changes for the southeast-bound number 19 tram. He slumps back in his seat, mindlessly scrolling on his phone. He feels unhinged, like he could burst into tears at any moment, and for the first time he can remember, a visceral yearning, specifically for his mother, washes over him. Now he touches upon something resembling a memory; it's a feeling rather than an image, of her presence, her love, of finally bridging something of the distance between them.

When he arrives at the house in Mosseveien, all the lights are off, and Storm realizes that his grandparents have of course gone to bed. He lifts his finger to the doorbell – he has no choice, but he hesitates at the thought of his grandmother being startled awake and frightened at the sound of the bell, and his grandfather painfully and slowly making his way down the stairs. But Storm has nowhere else to go. Just as he's about to press it, the door opens and his grandmother is standing there, a faint smile on her face. She pulls him inside, then into her arms.

Thirty-One

Bianka

In the three days since they returned from Ibiza, Bianka has barely slept. Not even the sleeping pills she stockpiles from America succeed in lulling her into a state of real rest. Long into the night she lies tossing and turning until Emil groans and mumbles, 'Come on, B, I have to get up in a couple of hours,' then moves further away from her. Sometimes she gets up from the bed and sits a while downstairs, scrolling on her phone, checking her messages. Nothing from Charlotte today. Bianka has messaged her several times and the messages have the little blue ticks next to them showing they've been read by the recipient, but still no response. She finally responded to something yesterday, basically fobbing her off with a vague promise of a 'coffee next week', but Bianka isn't stupid. She knows what's happening.

Every time Bianka thinks about it or checks her phone only to find she still hasn't heard back from her, an immense fury continues to build, filling all that empty space inside her. She watches Charlotte's most recent Instagram reel, lifted from the UK Streamstar release, which is already proving a big hit, posted the day after their return, another vacuous rant about the unparalleled dangers of low-fat products, seed oils, and carbs. She's a natural on camera, smiling and joking, and so very beautiful, appearing completely unaffected. One wouldn't have thought she'd thrown a dead man into the Mediterranean just days before.

But Bianka isn't as unaffected as she assumed she would be. Bianka feels as though she is dying herself, poisoned from an invisible pinprick wound that has unleashed deadly bacteria into her bloodstream. She feels constantly sick to her stomach, her head hurts so badly it's as though she's banged it repeatedly against the wall, and she's tortured by a nonstop stream of mental images of the final hour before Maxime went to his ocean grave. The sound of the kettlebell striking bone, the disgusting cool stickiness of his insides as she shoved the weights into his stomach cavity. Bianka wants to take a pill that will make her sleep for a week. Or forever.

She endlessly replays the last moments with Charlotte, how she'd driven both Bianka and Anette home from the airport and deliberately dropped Bianka off first to avoid being alone with her even though she actually lives closer to the Vinges than Anette does. The telling thing was the screech of tires that hollered down Dunstall Road as she drove off in her gleaming Range Rover – she just couldn't get away from her fast enough, that was obvious. Bianka had stood on the curb, clutching the handle of her wheelie bag in her clammy fist, fighting off both waves of nausea and frustrated tears, and feeling the instant hot sting of fury.

You might think you can dump me like a hot potato,

but it doesn't work like that, she'd thought to herself. Emil had opened the door and helped her inside, kissing the top of her head and fussing over her, and she'd let herself be held, if only to gain some time to recover an acceptable facial expression. Since she's been back, she's helped herself to wine even more liberally than usual at dinner; Emil notices but says nothing. On the second day, she took the train to Vauxhall and walked up to a quiet residential street bordering Vauxhall Pleasure Gardens where she met with a young man who waited for her in a red Alfa Romeo, his long legs stretching out of the open door and resting on the pavement. He handed her a generous measure of cocaine and some amphetamines, too. It's the first time in many years that she has bought drugs, and the first in London, and it wasn't easy to find a drug dealer when you're trying to look like a respectable lady in Wimbledon Village. In the end, she'd asked a couple of gangly youths smoking in an alley near the Odeon in town, reassuring them she wasn't a cop or from social services, and slipped them two rolled-up twenty-pound notes, and they'd given her the number for this guy, who went by the name Dinky.

Today is the third morning since she's been back and she wakes feeling even worse than the other two days. Slowly, last night comes back to her in fragments. She and Emil had eaten together in the kitchen – lasagne, still in its aluminium tray, not from one of the chichi delis but from Tesco, and Emil had glanced at it, visibly surprised. Bianka stared back, challenging him to say something, but he didn't, he merely shoved his fork into the bubbling, cheesy top layer and wrenched it apart. It was slightly burned on top and lukewarm in the middle, but Emil made a point of saying it was delicious, perhaps sensing her downcast mood and fearing an explosion.

'I'm going to go into the library to Skype Storm,' Emil said afterwards. He'd been doing this most evenings since they'd been in London, leaving Bianka alone with the housework. She felt a stab of annoyance.

'I'll join you,' she said. She had the feeling something was up and she usually made sure she stayed in the loop. 'It feels like ages since I've seen Storm.' Emil looked momentarily horrified, then swiftly arranged his features to amenable and bland.

'Ah. Sure, honey. That's great,' he said. 'Storm will be pleased.'

Bianka could tell Storm was surprised to see Bianka sitting next to his father on the sofa when the screen flickered to life.

'Oh. Hi. How was Ibiza?' he asked.

Bianka made the effort to arrange her face into a little smile. 'Good,' she said. Though she was slightly tanned and her hair was even lighter, Bianka knew she didn't look especially well. Even in the little window on the video chat showing her and Emil, she could see she looked gaunt, her complexion sallow, a sprinkle of acne studding her jawline.

Storm appeared to feel emboldened by this meek, quiet Bianka.

'So,' he began. 'I have some pretty exciting news. I've been trying to find out more about my mother. To remember her. Dad's helped me, and Madeleine, too, and I've even met my grandparents—'

'What? Emil—' Bianka's voice came out shrill and edged with hysteria.

'Storm,' said Emil. 'Maybe you and I should—'

But Storm doesn't stop there. 'Bianka, I was hoping you might help me too. I'm older now and I have some questions about her. I didn't even know that you guys knew each other, that you were friends.'

Bianka stood up abruptly, making her chair squeak loudly. 'We agreed a long time ago that we don't talk about her in this house,' Bianka said. She stood up and left the room quietly, but upstairs she slammed the bedroom door violently shut, its sound reverberating down the stairwell.

That fucking boy just doesn't get it, Bianka thinks now, lying in bed and staring up at the uneven plaster of the ceiling. His father, too. They think that she objected to talking about Mia and displaying pictures of her around the house because it might be too hard for Storm, when really, Bianka knew that looking at Mia's smiling face every day in her own home would break her heart into even smaller pieces.

Bianka sits up in bed, propping a pillow behind her back for support, then checks her phone yet again. She cancels her therapy session scheduled for the next morning by sending Dr Matheson a text message. She has no choice – if she makes herself dial in, meeting Dr Matheson's earnest, intelligent gaze, Bianka just knows she'll divulge something of what happened in Ibiza; in this state it might be as though everything she's ever done is written on her face. It has been hard enough, over the years, not to sit on that couch and tell her the truth. Dr Matheson answers almost immediately.

Bianka, we can reschedule for the same time on Friday. But you know these sessions are mandatory and I have to report it if you miss more than one session. Please confirm.

Best, Dr M

Bianka goes downstairs the next morning, trying to ignore the lurching feeling in her stomach at the thought of having to make conversation with her husband. She can hear him downstairs, rummaging in the kitchen like he always does, looking for stuff, and wonders why he isn't already at the office. She intently hopes he doesn't intend to work from home; usually she likes it when he does but today she needs space and quiet. She sets about making herself coffee, fiddling with the fancy new machine Emil insisted on when they moved here. Emil acknowledges her with a nod and a tight smile, and they both stare out at the light rain falling. The warm, serene mornings at Can Xara feel as far away as a dream.

'So. Ah,' Emil begins. 'I just had a call from Storm's school. They called about some equipment stuff, but it turns out he hasn't turned up for the training camp all of last week. He forged an email in my name. And now he's not picking up. He, uh, was pretty upset yesterday when you walked out of that call—'

'What the hell?'

'I sent Mia's parents a message. He's there, at their house. But God knows what he's been getting up to all week when we thought he was in Lillehammer.'

'Jesus Christ.'

'Yeah.'

'Well, he needs to go back to school immediately.'

'I agree, but at least he's not bunking off mandatory stuff or endangering his education. The summer camp is voluntary. Besides, he won't talk to me; he's not answering messages or picking up the phone. I suppose it could be worse. At least we know where he is.'

'I'm not sure it could be much worse. Mia's parents are batshit.'

'Well, he's sixteen. I'm not sure it's that terrible if he spends some time with his grandparents if he feels the need, to be fair.'

'Clearly I can't ever go away. You're unable to control that boy.'

'Is that the goal, though? To control him?' Emil sits down at the kitchen table and peers into his coffee as though he might find the answer there.

'Isn't it? You and I both know he'd have gone off the rails years ago if I hadn't understood he needs a firm hand. And look at him now. VM gold, Euros silver, Olympics next.'

'I'm not talking about his achievements. I'm talking about how he *feels*. You can't control that. You have to try to understand him.'

'I do understand him. What I don't understand is, the one time I'm away I come back to this bullshit. Why is he suddenly asking about Mia? We both know it will only bring more hurt. You need to shut it down. And, seriously, running away from school and forging his father's emails? This is bad. But the most interesting thing of all is that he gets away with it.'

'So what do you suggest I do? Fly to Oslo, turn up at Mia's parents' house and take him back up to Lillehammer?'

'Obviously. It's called parenting.'

'Wow. That's pretty rich, Bianka. Giving me a lecture on parenting. Maybe we should talk about what's going on with you. You've been weird since you got back.'

'It's not weird to feel upset about coming home to this level of bullshit.'

'What level of bullshit, though, Bianka? Embellish?'

'Last night. Him asking about Mia. The fact that he's run away.'

'Look. You seem jittery. You haven't been sleeping much. Maybe just take some time to look after yourself this week? I imagine Ibiza was pretty full-on.'

'It was more sedate than I'd thought it would be, actually. But don't change the subject. Seriously, how dare you insinuate I don't parent? I've raised your son since before he can remember.'

'I think he remembers more than you think.'

'What the hell is that supposed to mean?'

'Bianka. Please. Let's stop this, right now. I'm sorry for my contribution. I don't want to fight with you.' She opens her mouth to say, *well, perhaps you should have thought of that before you said what you said*, but she stops herself. Bianka works hard at her self-control these days. It's something she's had to learn. Picking her battles, too.

'Ok, fine,' she says.

'Can I ask you something?'

Bianka feels suddenly irrationally stressed, as though he's going to ask her something to do with Maxime, although it is, of course, impossible. Every time she closes her eyes, there he is. The long hair floating up toward the surface. The tattoos, smashed to a pulp. The gaping abdomen taped shut. The violence of it seems to have become part of her, constantly inserting its imagery into her mind.

'Sure,' she says, focusing on looking calm and relaxed.

'Did something happen between you and Charlotte?'

'Excuse me?' Bianka's voice bursts out shrilly and she can feel her face burning with the sudden adrenaline.

'Yeah, sorry, I felt like I needed to ask—'

'What do you even mean by that, *Did something happen*?' Could Charlotte have come clean to Andreas? An image appears in her mind, of gently twisting Charlotte's hard nipples beneath her fingertips. *Yes,* she thinks to herself as she makes herself meet Emil's eyes defiantly, *something happened between me and Charlotte.*

'As in, did you have an argument or something?'

'Oh.' Bianka consciously backsteps after jumping down his throat, making her voice soft to disguise her racing heart. 'Of course not. Why would you think that?' Emil avoids her eye. 'Emil? Talk to me, what made you think that?'

'Just… I'm sure it's nothing. And I know you don't need me to tell you to tread carefully with one of my employee's wives—'

'Indeed. I don't.' Emil looks stricken, and exhausted.

'I heard they had a, uh, thing, on Sunday night and I thought it was a little weird that we weren't invited.'

'A thing?' The fury again, like a beast roaring to life. Sunday night – the day after she got back.

'Yeah. It was only a barbecue I think but a couple of other guys from work were there, and Linda with her husband. And Anette. So it struck me as a little odd.'

'Oh. Of course, the barbecue. Oh, honey, did you think we

weren't invited to that? Of course we were.' Bianka releases a loud, trilling laugh, but even she feels its unpleasant pitch.

'But – why didn't you tell me?'

'To be honest with you, you're right – I'm exhausted after Ibiza. They're quite wild those girls, you know. Nothing sinister; they just know how to party. Charlotte called me a couple of times to try to change my mind about going, but I simply couldn't face it. And the truth is, I wanted some time together, just me and you.'

'I guess I just thought it was odd that Andreas didn't mention it at work, not yesterday or the day before. In fact, he was a little cool with me today.'

'Honey. You know what they're like. I don't think Andreas gets much of a say in the party planning in that house, do you? Seriously, don't worry about it. Charlotte and I are like *this*.' She winks at him and holds up her intertwined index and middle finger.

'I'll see her tonight, actually, at Scandi ladies' drinks.'

'Oh, is that tonight?'

'Well, yes, it's every other Wednesday.'

'Ah, yes, of course. I'll drop you off.'

'Seriously, I think you need to go to Oslo. You have plenty of time to catch one of the evening flights. Surely you can work from home tomorrow?' Emil nods pensively.

Bianka picks her freshly made cortado up from the kitchen counter and smiles at Emil before heading back upstairs. She closes the door to the bedroom softly, and locks it – she'd insisted to Emil when they got to Wimbledon that they get locks fitted, like they had at home in Oslo, though he'd objected, saying he hadn't grown up in a family with locked doors.

Well, I didn't grow up in a family at all, Bianka had thought to herself, *so forgive me if I get it wrong sometimes.* She crosses to the window and looks out at the rain-lashed park across the street. She's still trembling with fury and knows she needs to bring this under control before drinks this evening. She'll come face to face with Charlotte then and will have to find a way to speak with her alone. How dare she pull back from Bianka after what she did for her in Ibiza, and after the incredible closeness they'd shared?

She wants to open the window and unleash a blood-curdling scream, or better still, to jump from it; if she were lucky she'd strike her head on the stone slabs of the paved front garden and die instantly. *No,* she whispers, using her full focus to regain control of her shallow breathing. *Not yet,* she thinks, finally managing to slow her breath down to even, deep inhalations. *It's not me who's going to bleed.*

She walks the couple of hundred metres up the road to the cosy iconic pub on the edge of the common beneath a pink umbrella, trying to save her blown-out hair from stray droplets of rain. There are patches of indigo blue in the early evening sky in spite of the rain, and a fading rainbow stretches across the sky above the village. People are smoking and laughing outside the pubs, the air is heavy with incoming planes, cars crawl up Parkside toward Putney, and in spite of everything, Bianka loves this place, a beautiful village surrounded on all sides by the metropolis.

She had to psych herself up to coming out tonight, to sitting across from Charlotte, Anette, and Linda and the other Scandinavian ladies now that she knows they have wilfully excluded her from their little fucking barbecue. She did a line of coke in the bedroom and thank God for it – she feels ready to hold her head high and put these bitches back in their boxes. She's wearing a fabulous outfit – a tight royal blue silk trouser suit which shows off her slender frame and long legs; Bianka has always found it's better to power dress than to dress to blend in.

It's her third time at these drinks with the other expat wives, and the other two occasions were surprisingly fun – she'd been pleased to see that there were all kinds of people, from the posh, groomed crowd including Charlotte, to a couple of scientists, a group of doctors on exchange with Kingston Hospital, as well as many stay-at-home wives like herself. She pushes the heavy door to the pub open and scans the room for the group. The pub is completely packed, but she can't make out anyone she knows. A girl working at the front of house comes over carrying a clipboard.

'Hi, there. Do you have a reservation?'

'Ah, yes, I think so, but not sure which name it would be under.' Bianka cranes her neck to look past the girl into the far corners of the pub, but there is definitely no sign of Charlotte or the other Scandi ladies. 'It's the Scandinavian Ladies group? We meet every other week on Wednesday at eight.'

The girl scans her list, then seems to remember something. 'Just a minute,' she says, disappearing behind the bar, where she confers with a man pulling beers at the tap. 'I'm terribly sorry,' she says when she returns, the pale skin on her neck reddening with embarrassment, 'my boss just told me that, uh, the Scandinavian ladies' drinks were moved this week and took place last night...'

Bianka stares at the girl for several long moments, as though her words hadn't quite registered, then the enormity of what has happened dawns on her. She turns away from the girl and is about to storm from the pub when she stops in the doorway and takes a picture of the heaving room on her phone. She sends the picture to Charlotte on WhatsApp with the caption *fuck you*, then she blocks her number. She runs all the way home, not bothering with the umbrella now, and the rain has gotten heavier, dragging her mascara down her face in black streaks.

At home, the house is empty – Emil texted to say he caught the seven o'clock flight to Oslo. She begins to sob and pours herself a huge glass of red wine, drinking it in gulps. She goes through to the living room and picks up the TV remote control, opens Streamstar and selects *Viking Keto*. She clicks on Charlotte's beaming face, proudly proffering a huge, bloody steak in the preview picture. Bianka clicks past the intro with its infuriatingly upbeat theme song, to the start of the newest episode. She mutes it, but watches Charlotte's face, and is entirely transfixed by the way she moves and speaks and throws her head back in laughter, as though depriving yourself of essential nutrients for a living is that fucking funny.

After a while, Bianka gets up and, without pausing *Viking Keto*, goes back in to the kitchen and pours the other half of the Malbec into her glass. With the extra alcohol, she feels bold and unhinged, so she grabs her phone and scrolls through her camera roll until she finds the video she's looking for. It's over three minutes long and it shows herself and Charlotte in bed with Maxime, which she sent to herself from Maxime's phone after he'd died in the finca and Charlotte was still knocked out. She's watched it many times already but it never fails to captivate her. She stands up again and draws the curtains firmly shut.

Then she plays the video on the TV. The people on the screen leap into action. Maxime is lying reclined on the bed, stroking himself and watching as Charlotte and Bianka meet in a kiss, tongues visibly flitting in and out of each other's mouths. Bianka hits pause at exactly the right moment, when they break apart and look into each other's eyes. Rather than the more sexually explicit parts that follow, it's this moment Bianka watches over and over, the dull ache of loss filling her entirely. And now it's even worse than the first time.

She begins to cry again, throaty sobs echoing around the little lounge. She rewinds over and over and over; their lips locked together, eyes closed, the slow move apart, the eyes opening, that beautiful look of utter adoration. She gets back up and opens another wine bottle, pouring almost half of into her glass, then downs it while still standing at the kitchen counter. Then she lies down on the sofa and blacks out.

Thirty-Two

Charlotte

It's seven a.m. and a later start for me than usual, but I have a whole day off except for a Zoom call with my Norwegian network this afternoon. I do my stretches for a while, like Linda has taught me and insists I must do every day or otherwise I'll end up 'prematurely aged', and only when I'm done do I look at my phone. I do an instant double take when I glance at my notifications. After a two-second scroll, it's clear that my world is on fire.

'You're a fucking meme,' says Caty, my manager and a no-nonsense New Yorker, pointing to the image which has been massively enlarged and projected onto the screen in the middle of the room. I nod, keeping my head down because there is nothing I can say that can undo this damage.

'I mean. What were you *thinking*?'

'I don't think I *was* thinking,' I say.

'Our publishers are going to freak the fuck out. Probably

Streamstar, too. And I can't say I blame them. We're going to have to issue a grovelling statement. Elly, you deal with that?' Caty directs this last request at my publicist, a young and serious girl with a morose face and limp mousy brown hair. She nods. Caty paces around, back and forth in front of the photograph, which really only shows a woman taking a bite out of a piece of focaccia but no doubt has the power to ruin my career.

'Do you have any idea who took this picture? We are going to sue their ass so bad.' Judging by the angle it was taken from, it leaves no doubt that it was Bianka who took the picture; she was sitting directly opposite me at the restaurant. I can't say that because I don't want to risk an even worse situation with her. When I went through my phone, she'd also sent me a picture message from the pub with the caption 'fuck you'.

I shake my head. 'No idea. Sorry. The bar was super crowded. It could have been anybody.'

'You're supposed to be wholesome and trustworthy. That's, like, your entire USP. You're not the sexy, fun one who just does whatever the hell she wants; you're the one people can aspire to. Your success comes from making keto work for normal people. Wholesome and trusty keto gurus don't eat focaccia in public and get caught.' When Caty says 'hell' she screams it. She screams 'focaccia', too. *Fuck-atcha*.

When I finally leave the meeting to address focacciagate, I have two new calls from Anette and three from Andreas. I call Andreas back first, shielding the microphone from a chilly wind sweeping in from the Thames as I walk away from the office building at the riverfront and head toward the parking garage. I've taken to driving everywhere, even in central London; since the show launched in the UK I feel as though I'm getting stared at wherever I go, even though I know that isn't really the case, you'd have to be an A-lister for that, not just a carb-hater on TV.

'Seriously, what the hell, Charlotte?' Andreas says when he picks up.

'Oh, hi to you too, honey,' I say sarcastically.

'Someone just sent me a picture of you. You're a meme. You look high as a kite – please tell me you weren't actually taking drugs in Ibiza? You know the kinds of people I work with. This could be very damaging.' I reassure him that of course I wasn't taking drugs and the picture must have been manipulated by a crazy, jealous troll. I hang up, but immediately the phone starts up again, vibrating in my pocket, and I could scream with frustration at how it just hasn't stopped – it's probably yet another journalist calling to confront me with one of my own numerous punchy quotations about the dangers of bread. I get in the car and simultaneously attempt to answer the phone and manoeuvre the car from the parking garage and into the flow of traffic.

'Hello?' I shout into the phone, but just then something catches my attention. It's a sweep of blue across the tarmac, followed by the wail of the siren. Police. They know. They must have taken one look at me and they just *knew*. For a crazy moment I entertain the thought of just stepping on the accelerator, of tearing down the streets until I can get no further, boxed in by a traffic jam or a dead end by the river, but at least I'd have those wild moments, the last moments of freedom…

I pull over and a stern-faced female officer waits for me to roll down the window, a walkie-talkie ready in her hand to call in her big arrest. *Stop it*, I tell myself. Maxime hasn't even been reported missing. No one knows. But I'm convinced my face tells a different story. I open my mouth to speak, to tell her that I didn't do it, it was all a mistake, I'm just a nice low-carb lady from Norway, but no words will come and to my horror I burst into tears.

'Ma'am?' says the officer. 'Do you know why I've pulled you over this afternoon?' I nod but still no words will come because I'm full-on ugly crying now. 'Ma'am? Are you feeling okay?'

'I didn't do it,' I whisper, but thankfully my words don't carry out through the window and into the world.

'You touched your phone while operating the vehicle,' she continues. 'It's against the law.'

I stare at her, my face contorted into a grimace. 'I...' I begin. 'I'm sorry, I...'

'Are you okay? Are you feeling unwell?'

'Apologies, officer, it was a family emergency.'

She looks me up and down and the sternness is gone now, she actually looks concerned. 'I'm going to have to give you a formal warning and a fine, as well as a mandatory traffic safety course, to be completed in Lambeth borough by end of July.'

I nod and cry some more, now mostly with relief. When I'm about to roll up my window and drive away, she asks, 'Don't mind me asking, but are you that bread lady off TV?'

I don't even dare glance at my phone on the long rush-hour drive home, and when I finally do, I see I have over twenty missed calls from Bianka. I feel another surge of anger, then turn my phone off. How could she have betrayed me like this? I know I'll have to deal with her at some point but I can't right now. Now I have to make a plan.

Thirty-Three

Bianka

Same day

The next thing Bianka knew, it was morning outside. It had to be, judging by the sharpness of the sun's rays and the angle that they fell across the floor. She was on the sofa and when she sat up, she had to lie back down; her head was aching terribly and she had a foul, indeterminate taste in her mouth. She must have been out for almost twelve hours, a rather worrying feeling. Pieces of last night came back to her: the pub full of strangers, the humiliation she'd felt, the run home in the rain, the drinking.

She grappled with her phone that was lying face down on the table where she'd left it. She squinted at the impossible information on its screen and sat back up, mouth dropping open in shock. Fifteen missed calls from numbers she didn't recognize, and... 6,803 new likes on Instagram. With an onslaught of dread, Bianka tried to remember what happened last night before she passed out. She remembered watching the video. Then what? Had she opened another bottle of wine? She glanced into the kitchen – there were two empty bottles, their corks on the floor.

She opened the Instagram app and found it still logged into an account she didn't recognize. @VikingKetoFanGirl was the handle and it only had a single post. She immediately recognized the picture because she'd taken it herself at Els Horizonts. She must have created the account last night in her rage and posted the picture that is apparently breaking the internet, or at least the low-carb corners of it. It was immediately obvious to Bianka that this image could end Charlotte's career. It was taken close up; Bianka remembered how she'd angled the phone to pretend she was responding to a message, while actually zooming in on Charlotte's face in the exact moment she bit into the thick, moist focaccia, her eyes closed and her face beaming with pleasure. Her hand began to shake as she read the hashtags. One read #TheRealKetoQueen and the other #CokedUpMuch? She'd even linked it to Charlotte's official @ketoqueen account with over three hundred thousand followers. Immediately, she pressed *Delete* and disabled the account, though it was, of course, much too late.

Bianka sank back into the sofa, fresh tears stinging her sore eyes. How could she have done something like this? She'd lost any chance at all, however small, of reconciliation with Charlotte. She tried to call her over and over, then realized she'd blocked her number. She unblocked it and tried again and again, but got no answer. By early afternoon, she was going stir-crazy and realized she had to do something.

★★★

For the first time, Bianka wishes she had a dog; that way it wouldn't appear so weird to be lurking around other people's neighbourhoods. She looked Linda up on the very helpful Scandi ladies call list and found her address easily enough. She lives on a very exclusive street out in Cobham with vast villas and preened lawns. She'd assumed that Linda was Wimbledon-rich, like the rest of them – big house and a decent sized garden, privileged by London standards certainly – but this is next-level rich. The house looks like a miniature Cannizaro Hotel, with two distinct wings and lawns perfectly suited for helicopter landings, the kind of home that no doubt keeps several members of staff. Linda is clearly as loaded as Charlotte, if not more so.

Bianka allows herself one discreet walk-by and stares up at the house, mostly concealed behind tall hedges like a wrapped gift. It's almost 3 p.m. and it's unlikely that anyone is at home. Linda lives alone with her husband who presumably goes to work, and Linda herself keeps very busy indeed with a tight schedule of yoga, coffee dates, and eyelash appointments. When she reaches the end of the road, Bianka discovers to her great pleasure that there is a little coffee shop on the corner.

She orders a latte and sits at a table on the pavement. Yesterday's rain has let up and the air is nippy but fragrant in its wake, the scent of freshly cut lawns, coffee, and wet earth filling Bianka's nostrils as she draws her breath.

Linda's street is one-way so if she leaves by car, Bianka will see her. If she is already out and heading back home, she'd have to take the parallel road, meaning Bianka would miss her. She's barely taken a couple of sips of her admittedly glorious coffee when a slight woman pulled along by a very big, panting Bernese mountain dog appears from Linda's street, her face partially concealed behind enormous sunglasses, expensive blond hair scraped into a high ponytail. Bianka can't believe her luck; it's Linda. She feels suddenly unprepared, though she'd hoped to bump into her. When Linda realizes that Bianka is sitting at the café, directly across from her, her mouth drops open in surprise and she gives a little half-hearted wave.

'Bianka. Hi. Such a surprise. What are you doing here?'

'Oh, I come here occasionally. The *best* coffee. How lovely to bump into you.'

'What, since they opened like a month ago?' Linda pushes her sunglasses off her face and lets them perch on her forehead. Beneath, her eyes are slightly narrowed, taking Bianka in, and Bianka thinks there's something quite confrontational in her demeanour. Could she have gotten Linda all wrong?

'Well, about time there was a good neighbourhood café.'

'Except this isn't your neighbourhood.'

'Yes, but I'm a really big walker. I'm actually just stopping here on my way to Painshill Park. I just *love* walking around that lake.'

At this, Linda smiles tightly and raises an eyebrow. 'Right, well, I'd better move along. Miso here needs a bit of a run around.' She motions to the enormous dog, which lies panting at her feet and looks like he most certainly wouldn't be able to run around.

'I assume you've heard the awful news about Charlotte

being trolled on Instagram,' Bianka says, making sure her expression is that of horrified and concerned friend. Linda looks uncomfortable, then she slides her sunglasses back down so Bianka can no longer read her expression.

'Indeed. Very unfortunate.'

'I mean, who would do that?'

'Bianka. Please.'

'Excuse me?' Bianka's heart is racing but she manages to keep a mock-pleasant, steady voice.

'I know it was you. It was obvious as soon as I saw the picture. I sat next to you at the bar, remember? From that angle, it could only have been you or me. And it obviously wasn't me.'

'It seems like you've gotten this all wrong, Linda. I believe the picture must have been taken by someone standing directly behind us.'

'And why would they do that? It seems more likely that it was you. Let me guess. Feeling cast out in the cold since we've come back from Ibiza, can't handle Charlotte distancing herself, and—'

'Shut up.'

'Wow.'

'I want to know why I wasn't invited to the barbecue at Charlotte's, Linda.'

'You'd have to ask her.'

'I'm asking you, though.'

'And I'm telling you, quite clearly, that I don't want to get involved.'

'Then perhaps you can tell me why in the actual hell Scandi ladies' night was moved from Wednesday to Tuesday? It's always on a Wednesday!'

'Stop being ridiculous. It was because it clashed with the tennis party at Cannizaro and the email went out to everybody on the mailing list, including you, I imagine.'

'I never got an email.'

'So then you set about trying to destroy Charlotte's career. Unbelievable.'

'How dare you insinuate that it was me? You know, Linda, you've always seemed a little bit jealous of Charlotte.' At this, Linda lets out an incredulous laugh and pulls on the lead so Miso slowly gets back on his feet.

'Wow. You really are mad.'

'I imagine it's to do with the successful career. And the beautiful children, perhaps. But Linda, it's a really nasty thing to do, to suggest that I might have posted that picture. I hope you don't go around saying things like that to Charlotte.'

'Bye, Bianka.'

Bianka has the sudden urge to throw the hot coffee straight into Linda's face and actually has to place her hands beneath the table to make sure she doesn't. Charlotte has clearly said something to Linda and Anette, perhaps at the barbecue, perhaps a little mention that things had gotten a little 'intense'.

'Oh, wait,' says Linda. 'One thing. Out of curiosity, what happened last Thursday night?'

Bianka feels herself grow entirely still, like every cell in her body stands to attention.

'Thursday night?' Rule number one, buy more time. Rule number two, never ever admit to anything, not even in the face of confrontation, or straight-up proof. Thursday night, *the* night. Nobody saw anything; they'd made sure. Hadn't they?

'After we got back from Port de Sant Miquel, I went to bed but came back downstairs for some water. And I saw you, in the hallway, coming out of the gym, carrying two kettlebells, then disappearing outside.' Deep breaths, no reaction, just a bland little smile.

'Oh, that.' Bianka laughs. 'I went down to the yoga platform and did a weights session underneath the stars. Like I said, I like working out.'

'In the middle of the night, after five or more mojitos? Impressive.'

'Yep.' Bianka stands up abruptly, turns around and walks away, leaving Linda standing there, open-mouthed. Bianka knows that if she stayed another moment, the wild fury coursing through her would overpower her entirely and she would risk losing control and actually hitting Linda straight in the face.

'Bianka!' Linda calls out, but Bianka doesn't turn around. 'Painshill Park is that way, actually.'

Thirty-Four

Charlotte

At first, I didn't feel bad for not including Bianka and Emil at the barbecue – I just wanted it to feel like it used to, before I'd ever even met her. It wasn't like I'd planned it especially, it just happened at the last minute, a casual little neighbourhood event. I lied to Andreas and told him that Emil and Bianka were busy. I didn't want to make it awkward for him; Emil is his boss, after all. The truth is that I desperately felt the need for some space, but equally, I'm terrified of her. And now, after what she's done on Instagram, it's very obvious that I have reason to be.

Like the barbecue, tonight wasn't planned. I messaged Linda and Anette an hour ago asking them to come over – I need to feel out the situation with my friends before I speak to Bianka herself. Anette, Linda, and I briefly touched on Bianka at the barbecue but couldn't really continue the conversation with husbands and kids hovering around us. And now, after what's happened on Instagram, we'll definitely have plenty to talk about.

I carry a bucket full of ice with a bottle of Perrier-Jouët plunged into it from the kitchen and into the living room where the girls are sitting. I obviously haven't even slightly alluded to what really happened in Ibiza, but I have made it pretty clear that I've been feeling a little overwhelmed by the intensity of the friendship with Bianka. Anette and Linda didn't seem surprised, though I was intrigued that Anette didn't mention that she'd seen me and Bianka on the moonlit path that night.

Perhaps she actually didn't see anything, merely a rustle among the trees, but I know Anette, and I know Can Xara like the back of my own hand, and from where she stood on the terrace, I'm in no doubt that she would have seen or – at the very least – heard something.

'So,' I say, sitting back down and unpeeling the foil covering the champagne cork. 'That insane picture on Instagram. Of me eating the focaccia. It must have been Bianka who posted it.' The girls nod sagely and exchange a quick glance. They've clearly had this conversation already.

'That was insane all right,' says Linda. 'They're calling it *focacciagate*.'

'But...why?' asks Anette.

'Bianka has been calling and messaging me quite a bit since we got back, but I haven't seen her. I think she's mad about the barbecue. I feel bad, but I needed a bit of space.'

'I mean, *I* need some space from her and I'm not the one who is super close to her,' says Anette, chuckling.

'I wouldn't call it super close...' I wonder whether Anette might have told Linda about my sexual relationship with Bianka. Perhaps not directly, but all she'd have to do is insinuate that it might have crossed over into that.

'I think *she* would,' says Linda, and they laugh as I wrench the cork loose from the bottle's neck with a soft pop. 'I bumped into Bianka today, by the way.'

'What? Where?'

'Literally down the street from my house. I was walking Miso and she was sitting at the coffee place at the end of my road.'

'That's miles away from her,' I say.

I have the sudden feeling that there is no such thing as 'bumping into' Bianka.

'She behaved really weirdly. She flat-out denied posting focacciagate, and basically insinuated it was me.' At this, Anette's mouth drops open. 'She's definitely mad about the barbecue. And she also ranted about Scandi ladies' night, how it was moved to freeze her out or something.'

'But that's crazy,' I say. 'It seems like she blames me for that. It didn't even have anything to do with her. None of it makes any sense,' I say.

'God, how awkward,' says Anette, who suddenly looks a little sheepish. 'But... I wasn't kidding about needing a break from her after Ibiza. So I took her off the mailing list when Scandi ladies' night was rescheduled.'

'Anette, no!' I say. 'Seriously? She posted the focaccia picture after that happened. She... She's furious with me. You might have told me.' I pick up my phone and show her the picture Bianka sent from the pub with the charming 'fuck you' caption.

'Sorry,' Anette says, 'but I just wasn't in the mood to deal with her. And you said it yourself – how lovely it was that she didn't turn up.'

'Yes, but... Anette, that's mean and she's clearly furious.

And it's me she blames for it. I mean, she's literally tried to ruin my career.' God knows what she might do next. Bianka can take me down, and we both know it. I have to find a way to fix this.

'Look, I'm sorry,' says Anette. 'I guess I didn't think it would blow up into this big thing. She does seem pretty unhinged, though. And how weird that she "bumped" into you in Cobham, Linda,' she adds. I feel a chill run up my spine at the thought of Bianka out there, looking for Linda.

'Yeah, it was. I also asked her about this odd thing that happened one of the last nights at Can Xara and she, like, freaked out and just walked off. Just like that. Not even a goodbye.'

'Wait, what?' My heart picks up its pace. 'What odd thing at Can Xara?'

'Maybe I should have mentioned it before. I did think it was strange, but I guess I forgot. It was so late. I didn't think about it again until this afternoon when I saw her.'

'What?' I ask, careful not to shout, though I want to – Linda has a rather infuriatingly slow way of getting to the point.

'I saw her in the middle of the night, walking around the house with a pair of kettlebells and then she disappeared outside with them.'

'That *is* weird,' says Anette.

'Well, not necessarily,' I say. 'I sometimes work out pretty late.'

'Yes, but Bianka doesn't really strike me as the type to, though,' says Anette. 'She's a total hedonist.'

'Do you think so?' I ask, trying to keep my voice neutral. 'See, I'd say that she's also actually quite sporty.'

'Umm, I don't want to be mean, but did you *see* her when we did yoga? Definitely her first time,' says Anette.

'Exactly,' says Linda.

'Okay, well. I know I brought her up but let's talk about something else. I feel a bit mean,' I say, and refill everyone's glasses.

'I think maybe you should call her, though,' says Linda. 'You know, touch base, and if you need clearer boundaries, then state them.' Linda has had a lot of therapy. She's right, though, I do need to speak to Bianka. I simply can't afford for her to be out there, furious and feeling rejected – not after what we've done and what she holds over me. She's not going to go away and I absolutely need to find a way to keep her sweet and simultaneously at arm's length.

'On a different note, did you guys hear about that young guy going missing in Ibiza? Charlotte, I think it's literally right by Can Xara. They said the hills south of Sant Miquel,' says Anette, sending a bolt of sheer shock through my body. I happen to glance down at my hand holding the stem of the champagne glass and for a split second I see the hairpin in its place, drenched in blood. I place the glass on the table. I must have somehow missed the news breaking.

'What?' I say.

'Yeah,' says Linda. 'What happened? That's awful.'

'It came up on my Ibiza Live Facebook group. The police are looking for information. Here, I'll find it.' I hold my breath as Anette laboriously scrolls through her phone, avoiding both her and Linda's gaze.

Get a fucking grip, I tell myself. *They can't read your mind. Nobody can.*

'Ah, here it is,' says Anette, glancing up as if to ensure

she has our full attention before sharing an especially juicy piece of gossip. I simultaneously want her to shut up and to continue. 'Ibiza police today released the identity of the young man who has gone missing after his stay near Port de Sant Miquel in Ibiza. The man is twenty-six-year-old Paris native Maxime Dubois-Joseph, whose parents own an estate on the north coast of Ibiza. His family are increasingly concerned for his well-being and are extremely anxious to get in contact with anyone who may have information about his whereabouts.'

'God, I wonder if we might have seen him, if he was staying in Port de Sant Miquel,' says Linda. 'We could have sat next to him in a restaurant.' She pulls out her phone and starts tapping away eagerly, and within moments she produces a picture of a smiling Maxime Dubois-Joseph, his perfect white teeth glinting, his hair slicked back and shining.

'Wow,' says Anette. 'I'd definitely remember if we'd seen him. He looks like a young Johnny Depp.'

'Let's hope he ages better,' says Linda, and they both titter.

'Oh, my God,' I whisper. 'That's my neighbour's son. The couple at Sa Capricciosa. That's him.' I'm confident that I've managed to convey both surprise and horror.

'What, the godawful Parisians suing you?' asks Anette.

'Yeah. What does it say about what they think has happened?'

Linda scans the text again. 'They're not sure whether he went missing on the island or after leaving. No reason to suspect foul play.'

'The guy is obviously dead, though,' says Anette.

'Why would you think that?' Linda asks.

'Hmmm,' I say. 'He looks like one of those loaded, troubled types to me. The kind with more money than sense and probably a drug problem. Maybe Daddy's pulled the plug on the money and he's run off somewhere.'

'Yeah, or he's pissed someone off and they got rid of him,' says Anette.

'I don't really think Ibiza is that kind of place,' I say, and pick up my glass, draining it.

'Oh, I do,' says Anette.

'How well do you know the parents? And have you met the guy?' asks Linda.

'I don't think I have, no. I've met his parents once or twice over the years. My mother was quite friendly with them at one point, but it really soured over the beach access situation.'

'Well, I imagine they'll stop hounding you with their pit bull lawyers now they have something else to think about,' says Anette.

I feel a twinge of anger at her careless comment; as if I'd have wished for the Dubois-Josephs son to die so they wouldn't sue me. 'Excuse me for a moment,' I say, and stand up.

I walk out of the living room and upstairs to our bedroom, where I sit down on the bed. Andreas is still out at a work dinner, and I know he won't rush home when he knows I've got the girls over. Oscar is somewhere in the house, on his screens probably, or maybe Ayla has put him to bed by now. I can't remember whether I said goodnight or not but I must have – it's past eleven. I pull out my phone and glance at the long list of notifications. Hundreds of questions and furious comments from fans on Instagram about focacciagate. A message from my father saying food delivery never turned up. A message from my son saying *Goodnight, Mom*, with a confusing smiling emoji with a tear, sent twenty minutes ago. Nothing from Madeleine, but when I send her a text saying *You okay?* she replies instantly – *yep*.

There are also four new missed calls from Bianka, one from just moments ago – I keep my phone on silent or I'd never get a moment's peace. I press *Call* and she answers almost instantaneously, her voice thick and strange. It sounds like she's crying and then I realize she definitely is.

'Hey,' I say. 'I'm glad you called. We need to talk.'

'Yeah,' she whispers, exhaling with an audible shudder. 'Have you heard the news about Maxime? The police are appealing for information.'

'Yeah. I heard just now. I don't think we need to worry, though. They're saying they don't suspect foul play.' Bianka doesn't answer, but I can tell by her hiccupy breathing that she's still there. I feel claustrophobic and anxious talking to her. In my mind it's like I've already completely cut myself loose from her and everything that happened in Ibiza. 'But Bianka. Linda saw you that night. With the weights.'

'Did she tell you that?' Bianka's voice goes from whispered and low to its usual firmness.

'Yes. And she told me that she randomly bumped into you this morning by her house. In Cobham! That wasn't a coincidence, I imagine?'

'I wanted to speak to her, yeah. Since I haven't been able to speak to you.'

'But, Bianka, that seems a little extreme. And we need to talk about that picture on Instagram. I'm not sure I can overstate how unbelievably damaging something like this can be.'

'It wasn't me.' *Of course it was you*, I want to scream. But I don't. Instead I take a deep breath and remind myself that I have to keep Bianka on my side, no matter what.

'Okay. I believe you. It just seemed like it was you, considering you're clearly upset with me.'

'Charlotte. Why didn't you invite us to the barbecue?'

I sigh. I knew this was coming. That fucking barbecue. I should have been more careful. I knew even as I was standing there in the garden sipping Pimms, watching Andreas flip burgers, that it was a bigger mistake not to have invited Emil and Bianka than to invite them – it was very noticeable and I knew they'd hear about it, and I wish I'd realized then that it wasn't the most strategic way to handle things.

'I'm sorry.'

'I was really hurt and confused by that.'

'Bianka. Look. It wasn't a planned thing. It just happened like that, last minute. I care about you and our friendship—'

'Friendship.' Bianka snorts incredulously. 'Some friendship.' I ignore her. 'I just want to see you,' she eventually continues, her voice softer now. 'I feel like you're trying to get rid of me.'

'Bianka, that's not true, okay? I don't want you to think that. It's just, I have a full life with lots of work and lots of social stuff going on and I can't always be with everyone all the time. Why don't we get a coffee in the diary sometime soon, and sort things out then.' Sometime soon means never, as we all know.

'A coffee. Wow. Here's the thing, Charlotte. I just don't

understand. One minute in Ibiza you're telling me you regret everything, that it all meant nothing and you need space. And the next, you kiss me out of the blue. That kiss changed everything for me. It made it all worth it. It made me feel as though we have a future.'

'We'll talk about all of it and more. I have to go. But I'm worried that Linda could have seen something. Are you sure nobody followed behind you on the way back down to the finca? And how can we know if she wasn't standing at one of the windows upstairs with binoculars? She could have seen us out there, on the boat.'

'That's all you care about. Getting caught or not. I care about *us*.'

Us. Just the word makes me feel repulsed. 'Of course I care about… us.'

How I wish I could return to that night at Benirràs and the split second before I took Bianka's hands, lacing my fingers in hers. I wish with all my might that I could undo it.

'I think whatever happened between us is very secondary to the situation that happened after,' I hiss.

'You were the one who placed us in that absolutely insane situation by doing what you did. And now, you and I are bound together.'

'Bound by what? It never happened, and that's how I intend to live,' I say. 'We agreed,' I add. Bianka doesn't speak for a long while and I know I was right to return her call and attempt to diffuse the situation. 'Listen, let's get together this week, I'll try to move some stuff around in my diary. I'll text you tomorrow, I really want to see you.'

Eventually, after agreeing that I'll definitely make it happen this week, not next, I manage to get off the phone.

I'm mentally exhausted and shaken up by the conversation. I stay here in my bedroom for a long while, remembering my own gaze in the mirror at Can Xara, when I truly realized what I'd done, that I'd murdered Maxime. Could I do it again? I almost laugh out loud at the sheer insanity of even entertaining this thought, but only almost, because there is an underlying seriousness – would I rather go to prison for Maxime Dubois-Joseph's murder, losing my family and absolutely everything else, or would I kill Bianka to keep her quiet? There is no doubt in my mind that I would get rid of her.

But only if I have to.

I breathe a sigh of relief and head back downstairs to the living room. Linda and Anette fall silent again as I enter.

'We're out of wine,' says Anette, meaning *she's* out of wine, as my glass is still full and Linda's not drinking.

'I think we're going to have to call it a day,' I say.

'What's going on?' asks Linda, concern etched across her face. 'Where were you?'

'Oh, just in the bathroom. I've been feeling a little queasy.' Anette and Linda exchange a pointed glance. I'm so tired. Tired of acting and performing and achieving and pretending and masking and lying. The girls leave and I trudge upstairs heavily, stepping out of my dress and crawling into bed. I'm exhausted but I need to know more about what the police are saying about Maxime's disappearance. I go to the Ibiza Live Facebook group and find the post toward the top of the page.

Police appeal for information in baffling disappearance of Ibiza holidaymaker, reads the headline.

It remains unclear whether French national Mr Maxime Dubois-Joseph has voluntarily or involuntarily disappeared, and whether he went missing on Ibiza or shortly after having left the island. Dubois-Joseph is last believed to have been at Els Horizons in Port de Sant Miquel on Thursday June 24th, likely in the company of friends. Police are interested in speaking to anyone who may have observed, or been in the company of, Mr Dubois-Joseph on the night in question. There is no suspicion of foul play at the present time, but the young man's family are growing increasingly concerned for his well-being after being unable to establish contact with him since the 24th. Dubois-Joseph had spent a week at his parents' private property, and according to witnesses, numerous parties had taken place during this time.

I scan the big international news sites, from BBC to *VG* to *The Guardian* to *El País* to *Dagbladet*, but there is nothing more. Not yet. I don't for a moment doubt that it will come.

The next morning I wake before six and am in the makeup chair at the TV studio in Clapham by seven. I have been invited here to take part in a panel discussing the government's official dietary outlines, which in my opinion amount to slow suicide: *Want to die? Eat this.*

Usually, this is the kind of thing that gets me really excited – I'm good at debating and am competitive enough to want to change the opinions of my fellow panellists, as well as the audience's. But today I don't feel right; I have a terrible headache spreading out from the base of my skull, and the swelling on my cheekbone from when I fell in Ibiza is strangely more tender now than when it first happened. I bite my lip as the makeup artist, an annoyingly talkative girl with an impressive number of facial piercings, spends a long while on the area, firmly dabbing a silicone-based concealing agent over the top of it, then blending it to give the illusion of smooth, unblemished skin.

All I can think about is Maxime, and where he is at this moment. What does he look like by now? And his parents – what are these days like for them? *Stop it*, I tell myself. I'm not going there. I was doing so well. This shouldn't change anything. When they move on from my face to my hair, I return to Google to see if anything new has come up but, still, there is nothing. I hope it will just go away, that the police will stop looking when nothing suggests foul play. But my hands still shake as I finish getting ready.

'We're rolling,' says the producer, giving us a thumbs-up.

I'm on camera, sitting on a high yellow leather chair, wedged in between the two other panellists, a man who works for a British oatmeal company and a woman who works to promote healthy eating habits in young people. Both naturally hate me.

'The problem is when someone like you, who is a trained medical professional, spreads lies, because you're in a position of trust,' says the man, his face red with indignation before we've even properly started.

'Excuse me – *spreads lies*?'

'The diet you are promoting to vulnerable people has repeatedly been linked to elevated cholesterol, strokes, heart disease, and bowel cancer.'

'I'm sorry, but this is simply untrue. If it were true, why would a ketogenic dietary approach be used extensively in treating epileptic patients? It's because it regulates insulin response and actually cures insulin resistance, which is the main cause of obesity and a wide host of lifestyle-related cancers.'

'It is also directly in breach of the government's dietary guidelines—'

'Which are wildly outdated.'

'Isn't it morally wrong, though, to promote a diet that is financially inaccessible to a large portion of the population?' he asks, and at this both the host and the woman next to me nod sagely.

'I agree that this is a real problem, but shouldn't governments be working to make the food that truly nourishes us more accessible for everyone by subsidizing food prices, rather than funding big pharma medicines that treat symptoms that arise as a result of a poor diet?'

Both the host and the woman nod at this, too. I'm smashing it, like I always do. The man says something in response but I don't catch it, because suddenly, I spot Bianka in the crowd. She's sitting in the front row, wearing the garish red trouser suit she wore the first time we met, and she is staring straight at me, a wild look in her eyes. I squint to see her better in the bright glare of the spotlights, and shift in my seat to lean forward a little. As I do, my angle of view changes slightly and I see that it's not Bianka at all, but a slight young man with a yellow baseball cap I mistook for Bianka's light blond hair.

'Charlotte? Umm, Charlotte?'

The audience titters.

'I'm sorry. Can you repeat that?' I feel the beady eyes of the so-called experts on either side of me, the air of superiority and perhaps pity. They must think the lack of carbohydrates has prevented oxygen from reaching my brain.

'I said, do you not think that it's harmful for your thousands of young followers to be told that a regime as restrictive as the ketogenic diet is the best way to eat?'

'Why would the truth be harmful?'

The man says something else, some mumbled old crap about people having had grains as the main staple of their diet for thousands of years and why would European life expectancy be so high if bread was so very terrible? When it's my turn to speak again, I completely lose my train of thought and stammer an inarticulate half-sentence about the diminishing quality of grains and the overuse of pesticides, because I've spotted Bianka in the crowd again and this time, it's definitely her. She's sitting to the side of a pillar, her hair piled on top of her head, scrutinizing me with a sarcastic little smile on her face. I crane my neck and lean across the woman next to me to get a better view. She coughs uncomfortably and shifts in her seat. But again, it's not Bianka.

'Right,' says the host. 'Okay, I think we'll round off there. The debate will continue in our online chatroom.'

Being backstage is an awkward experience and I rip the

microphone from my cheek and hand the transmitter to one of the technicians before storming out and down the long bare corridors to the elevator which will take me down into the parking garage.

I drive fast south toward Wimbledon but then I remember that Andreas is working from home today. I pull over in a miraculously available parking spot alongside Clapham Common and sit a long while, just trying to manage my breath, staring out the window absentmindedly at dog walkers and runners sluicing in and out of the park. And there she is again – Bianka – walking full speed toward me, this time pushing a baby in a stroller, her unruly curls rising and falling as she powers in my direction, but of course, it isn't her at all. Is this what it's like to go crazy? I watch my hands resting on the steering wheel. They are slim, brown, and laden with big diamonds on three fingers. These hands have killed someone. I begin to cry.

Tears pour down my face, and again I feel like someone else, someone certifiably insane, who has no control over themselves and their emotions. I stay in the car for a long while, over an hour. Then it begins to rain heavily and the common empties as people take cover in the many cafés lining the street running alongside it. I leave the car and cross the first wide stretch of grass and sit down on an empty bench, letting the rainwater rush across my face, taking the heavy TV makeup and my tears with it.

It's early afternoon by the time I let myself back into the house, drenched to the bone. I head straight up to bed and am surprised to find Andreas standing there in the bedroom, bare-chested and about to put on a fresh light-blue shirt.

'Charlotte. You're back early… Jeez, what's happened to you? You look terrible.'

I shoot him a glance and wrench my clothes off, kicking them in a soggy pile into the corner. Andreas raises an eyebrow. I never do this kind of thing, being as controlled as I am.

'Where are you going?' I ask, burying myself beneath the comforter.

'I have to head into the City for a few hours. I need some files for a meeting tomorrow morning.'

I stay in bed, with a neat vodka in a water glass for company. In the mirror opposite the bed, the woman looking back at me is glassy, cold, frightening, unfamiliar. At one point, when I head downstairs for a refill, I meet Oscar in the hallway, carrying a lacrosse stick, sweat plastering his dark hair to his skull, and he looks at me strangely when I say 'Hi, honey.'

I return to the bedroom, drawing the summer duvet up to my chin. Then I compulsively google Maxime Dubois-Joseph, and see that a couple of new articles have appeared on French sites. I run them through Google Translate and learn more about the man I've murdered. *He loves dolphins*, says his girlfriend of four years, a chic Parisian brunette with full lips and kohl-rimmed almond-shaped eyes named Elodie. *He'd never go off without telling me where he'd gone*, she continues. Elodie likely believes her boyfriend would never indulge in cocaine-fuelled threesomes, either. Maxime's father, Louis Dubois-Joseph, is now offering two million euros for information, whether he's found dead or alive. *My wife can't stop crying*, he says.

Heir feared dead, says *Paris Match*, and *link to Sicilian mafia discovered*.

When I wake again, it's morning and in spite of a slight headache from the vodka, I feel better. I cringe at the thought of yesterday's train wreck behaviour; to think that I imagined seeing Bianka so many times – it was frightening. But now, I feel truly rejuvenated. Sometimes all we need is a good night's sleep and a chance to recover. I go down into the kitchen and my stomach sinks at the realization that I've gone downstairs too early – it's not yet seven and my husband and son are there, shuffling around and making breakfast.

'Oh, hi, Sleeping Beauty,' says Andreas, winking at me. 'Are we still having the Langelands over for dinner on Saturday?' he asks. 'Do you remember we said we'd do a lobster party? It's been in my calendar for over a month.'

'Oh, no,' I whisper. 'Definitely not. Cancel it.'

'How come?'

'I just can't right now. I'm really behind with work.'

'Ok, well, would you mind cancelling it? Crazy day today, with people flying in from Houston and Singapore and all kinds of places.'

'Fine.' I fiddle with the coffee machine for several long moments before continuing. How best to phrase what I'm about to say? 'Look. About them,' I begin, trying to find the best words to make myself clear but with a degree of discretion. Emil is, after all, Andreas's boss. My husband and son watch me carefully as I continue, and I can feel Ayla's eyes on me, too, from over by the window, where she's sitting and folding linen serviettes. 'They're lovely people. Marvellous. And yet, I think we might take just a tiny step back. On a social level, if you see what I mean.'

'How come?' asks Oscar.

'Yes, why is that?' asks Andreas, looking at me.

'I think that maybe Bianka is quite a complicated person. It might be good to maintain a degree of distance from her, if that makes sense. In fact, I'm pretty sure she has... depression.'

'I don't think Madeleine's going to distance herself from Storm anytime soon,' says Oscar, barely glancing up from his phone.

'Oh? What do you mean?' I ask.

'Uh, he's her boyfriend. Duh.'

'What? No, of course he isn't. They've only met once.'

'No, Mum. It's not like something isn't happening just because you don't know about it. In fact, I'd bet they're together right at this moment, all snuggled up.'

'Oscar,' says Andreas, in warning, but I can tell from the look on his face that we are both having the same terrible realization at the same time, that neither of us have had any idea what's going on while Madeleine has been in Oslo. Oscar is tapping into his phone and then triumphantly turns it around to show us the screen.

'Look,' he says. 'Here she is on SnapMaps. That's her avatar and this is Storm's. Both in the same location in Slemdal. Isn't that where they lived in Oslo?'

'Oscar, you're being ridiculous. Madeleine is at Uncle Fredrik's house. It's seven in the morning, for God's sake,' I say, but even as I speak I realize it's wishful thinking.

'My point exactly. He's her boyfriend and they've had a nice little sleepover,' Oscar says, laughing. I have to turn away but meet Andreas's horrified gaze as I do. The last thing I need is for my daughter to be dating Bianka's stepson.

'Oscar, you can stay out of this. I'm calling my brother,' says Andreas.

'I forbid her to see that boy!' I shout.

'You *forbid* her? Lol.' Oscar laughs incredulously. 'Seriously, what the hell is going on?'

'I'm concerned for Bianka. I'm finding ways to be there for her. In the meantime, I worry that Storm is being exposed to all kinds of things at home and, for that reason, I feel it would be healthier for your sister to spend less time with him.'

'Wait. So you're saying that Storm is going through a hard time at home, and for that reason you forbid his girlfriend to spend time with him?'

I open my mouth to answer, but even I can tell how unreasonable it sounds. Andreas is staring at me, one eyebrow elevated. Andreas and I work well together as parents usually – we don't challenge each other's decisions or authority in front of the kids but I can tell he is naturally interested in how I am going to weasel my way out of this one.

'I thought you were best friends,' says Oscar.

'Oh. Oh, no. We're very new friends, Oscar. She's a lovely person but Anette is my best friend.'

'But you're friends.'

'Yes, of course.'

'Like, aren't friends supposed to be there for each other if one has depression?'

I leave the room and immediately start calling Madeleine, but she doesn't pick up.

Thirty-Five

Storm

Storm stands at the window and watches the sun rise above the eastern forests, its bright light dropping onto the fjord outside the window. From here he can see most of Oslo, held snug in its grey hollow. In the winter the city centre is often covered entirely by a lid of smoke and when he used to train up at Holmenkollen Ski Centre it would look as though the capital had been swallowed whole by a murky brown cloud.

His father has flown to Oslo and is coming here to pick him up, he just messaged to say. Storm doesn't want to leave but knows he has little choice. He'll have to get creative to get himself out of all the trouble he'll be in.

'The thing you should remember is that Bianka really loved Mia,' his grandmother said last night, when he sat closely beside her on the sofa, drinking hot chocolate and looking through the photo albums again. 'Maybe more than we realized,' she added softly. 'I think her death must have broken her completely.' This makes some sense to Storm, though he still can't understand why Bianka's always so angry. He just hopes his father hasn't brought her to Norway, and that he and his dad will have the chance to spend some time together, just the two of them. There's a knock on the door, and then Frida pokes her sweet, weathered face into the room and lights up at the sight of him.

'Your father will be here any minute, Storm,' she says. He glances out the window again and now he spots Emil's Tesla coming to a stop at the end of the road leading to his grandparents' house. He waits for Emil to emerge from the car and walk up to the house, but he doesn't, and when several minutes have ticked past, Storm realizes he isn't going to. He understands, suddenly, that Emil is embarrassed to come face to face with his grandparents.

He goes downstairs and hugs Frida and Einar goodbye, promising to come back soon. In the car, nobody speaks, though Storm can sense that Emil is frustrated and probably angry about everything he's done. He can only imagine the hell Bianka must have given him.

Finally, Storm breaks the silence. 'I'm sorry, Dad. Uh—'

'It's okay, Stormy. I didn't mind a weekend in Oslo and I wanted to make sure you're okay. It seems like a lot has been going on and I need you to tell me everything.'

Storm nods.

'Let's sit down together this evening and you can talk me through your decision-making over the past couple of weeks.' Storm catches a glimpse of what his mellow father must be like at work; kind but firm.

His phone beeps, and it's a message from Madeleine. He perks up. He messaged her a couple of times last night but didn't get an answer, which is unusual – he guessed she fell asleep.

> Hey do u know if something weird has happened between my mom and Bianka?
>
> Nope. Why?
>
> My mom's being extra crazy.
>
> Ok will try to find out.
>
> Same. She says I have to come straight back to London.
>
> What?? When? Can we meet later? At the lake?

No response. The whole rest of the day and afternoon passes without a response from Madeleine, even though Storm messages her twice more and they're marked as read. He feels irritable and restless and even a long run up to Kobberhaugen, deep in the woods, fails to take the edge off. After a shower, he attempts a game of Fortnite but can't concentrate at all, Mio and Felix's laughter hollering down the earphones as he misses shot after shot and they beat him for once.

He knocks on his father's bedroom door and waits. He knows he's in there because he bumped into him earlier in the hallway, and Emil had looked dishevelled and stressed and pointed to the earbuds in his ears as he headed down the corridor saying 'uh-huh,' and 'no, we stay on one-seven-five,' and 'yes, I'll be in KL on the twentieth.' He'd felt sorry for his dad for a moment – he's a busy man and now he's had to drop everything to fly here to deal with his wayward son. He must have popped out because when Storm eventually pushes the door open after more knocking, the room is empty, the bed messy and unmade.

In the end he can't stand it anymore, and cycles over to Madeleine's uncle's home on Frognerseterveien. He knows the route, because he's walked Madeleine there several times, kissing her goodbye by the gatepost. The gate is locked but Storm can see two identical, gleaming black Range Rovers in the driveway. He presses the intercom button but nobody answers for a very long time. Then the gate swings open with a soft whirr. Thankfully it's Madeleine herself who comes to the door, but not the Madeleine he has come to know. This is someone else entirely, a nervous, sad being who looks ready to bolt back into the huge house.

'Hey,' she whispers, glancing behind her, as though someone is standing in the shadows, listening. 'You can't just turn up here, Storm.'

'You haven't answered my messages. Sorry, I felt worried, can we talk—'

'No. I'm sorry.' Her eyes are wet with tears and she looks like she's having to use every ounce of her energy not to start sobbing. 'I can't see you anymore, Storm. I'm sorry.' She glances dramatically around again, then lowers her voice to an almost inaudible whisper. 'My mom is so fucking crazy. I'm positive it has something to do with what's happened between her and Bianka. I think she's going to make me fly back to London tonight or tomorrow. I'm sorry, Storm.'

'Madeleine?' calls a voice from inside the house. Madeleine quickly shuts the door after another 'I'm sorry,' and Storm stays there for several minutes, staring at the oiled, dark wood with its ornate brass knocker like a creepy little hand. Then he walks slowly back over to his bike, as if in a daze. He bikes all the way uphill back to Slemdal, his feet pedalling furiously. He's humiliated and upset and his heart feels like it might stop in his chest. He'd started to thaw ever so slightly toward Bianka, mostly because of what Lone and his grandmother had said, about the gentle way she'd looked after him when he was small and motherless. But every time he even remotely entertains the idea that she's not so bad, she goes and shows him that she is, in fact, worse. And whatever it is that Bianka has done that's cost him his relationship with Madeleine, she's going to fucking fix it, he'll make sure of that.

His father is back from wherever he went when Storm walks back in. He takes one look at his son, then pulls him into a close embrace.

'How about you and I drive up to the cabin?' Emil says. 'We haven't been there since the snow melted. And we can get some training in, too.' Storm ponders this for a moment – a whole weekend away with his father. When Storm was a little boy, he realized that the only way to get his father to himself was to ask to go to the cabin because Bianka hates it there. He consciously went for the ski team when his friends were choosing sports and put all of his efforts into it when he realized that the training it would require to get really good meant he got to spend most weekends away from Bianka. So, really, it's thanks to his stepmother that he became a pro skier.

He pictures the cabin sitting on its own, overlooking the narrow valley, and in his mind its roof is laden with a thick layer of snow, the jagged peaks of the Jotunheimen mountains tearing at the sky in the distance. The cabin was the last place his mother had been seen alive. In this moment, Storm feels the discombobulated parts of his life grow clearer and he has the sensation of almost being able to grasp a memory lurking in the depths of his mind. What his father has suggested is just right – they need to go there, now.

Thirty-Six

Charlotte

I'm working from Caffe Nero in the village today, looking through shades of pink samples for the packaging tube of my upcoming seed-oil-free béarnaise sauce. I'm here to show myself that life moves on; it has to. Soon, everything will feel totally normal again, and I'll slip back into my routine of work, calorie restriction, and family life. Before that I'll need to get through the gruelling social schedule of the Wimbledon tennis tournament with all its wild parties, and then several weeks at Can Xara with my family, but I won't focus on what that might feel like now. I need to decide between 'ballet slipper', 'blush', or 'taffy.'

My phone begins to vibrate on the table. It's a Spanish number. I've prepared myself mentally for this. Of course they were going to call me at some point; I'm the next door neighbour. I might have heard or seen something. Over the course of the last twenty-four hours, numerous news articles about the 'disturbing disappearance' of Maxime Dubois-Joseph have appeared online, though mostly in the same vein, focusing on his suspected connections to Sicilian mafia, as well as previous drug convictions now uncovered by the media.

I knew this was coming; all I have to do is answer and make my voice friendly and slightly surprised. But I can't do it. Though I thought I was prepared, shock and panic washes over me and I can't move a single muscle. The woman at the next table shoots me a quizzical then annoyed glance; my phone is making a grating repetitive sound against the wooden tabletop. Then it stops. I've barely caught my breath before it starts up again. And again, I don't answer.

'Excuse me,' says the woman in an American drawl. 'Your phone is ringing.'

I manage to flip the button on its side to silent, then quickly stand up and gather my laptop and the colour samples together before rushing out the door. I've parked around the corner on Lancaster Road and I throw my things onto the passenger seat and slam the door shut. I wait several minutes before looking at my phone, doing the single-nostril breathing routine Linda has taught me for moments of severe stress. There's one new message, from the same Spanish number.

Hi, can you please return my call at your earliest convenience?

Inspector Juanes Fuentes, Comisaria de la Policia Nacional de Ibiza.

I steel myself and return Inspector Fuentes' call. He sounds like a pleasant enough guy and asks a couple of standard questions about when I was last in Ibiza, what I was doing there. He asks whether I am aware of the fact that my neighbours' son has gone missing. I hesitate for a moment, and then decide to pretend I had no idea because otherwise it must seem suspicious that I haven't already been in touch. We agree that I'll sit down with Fuentes on Zoom for an 'informal chat' tomorrow morning. He says he wants to speak to all of the guests who were staying at Can Xara during the week prior to Dubois-Joseph's mysterious disappearance, so I give him the contact details for Anette, Linda, and quickly decide to give him Bianka's details too – not like I have any choice.

'Have you ever met Maxime Dubois-Joseph?' he asks.

I chance being vague, saying I'm not sure, that I might have, years ago. A long silence ensues and I can hear the furious scratch of Inspector Fuentes' pen in the background. Scratch, scratch, scratch.

We hang up and I text the girls to say the police will be getting in touch.

I drive fast over to Bianka's house on Dunstall Road. All the blinds upstairs are down but her ice-blue Range Rover Velar is in the driveway. I knock on the door but the house is completely silent. I realize I haven't spoken to Bianka since our phone call the other night and I said I'd message her the next day to make plans to meet this week. I haven't. My stomach turns again at the thought of what happened between us. That I've actually jeopardized my entire, big life for this woman I barely know; now, in hindsight, it seems completely insane. My only excuse is that my hunger for touch and attention was so powerful that it disabled my better judgment. And now we find ourselves in a situation where we need to make sure our stories are watertight for the police.

I start as the door opens a crack and Bianka stands in front of me, her face very pale, her usually wild hair greasy and pulled back into a tight ponytail.

'Charlotte. You came.' She looks pathetically grateful to see me.

'Hi. Yes. Can I come in? We need to talk.'

Bianka lets me into the house and I lean in and give her a hug, but even though I do my best to act normal, she must feel my coldness.

'The police called,' I say.

'Oh, my God,' says Bianka.

'I know. That's why I'm here. We need to make sure we tell them exactly the same thing. As close to nothing as possible.'

'Obviously. But I feel like you've just drifted away completely. You said you were going to call. That we'd meet up this week. This would be so much easier to deal with if I felt we were on the same team, like before.'

'We are on the same team. Of course we are.'

'Well, since we've been back it certainly hasn't felt like it. It feels like you're keeping me sweet to make sure I don't tell everyone what happened between us or that you killed Maxime.'

'Hey.'

'That's how it feels.'

'We made a pact. We agreed to never talk about it again. So don't say things like that.'

'I can't cope without you, Charlotte,' says Bianka, bursting into tears. I am so repulsed by her and by this entire shitshow of a situation that it takes all my mental and emotional energy to pull her close until her sobs subside. I pat her back and try not to think about the tears slipping from her eyes into my hair and onto my clothes as we embrace. Eventually I pull back.

'Look. We both need to focus on not freaking out. I need to know that we are both fully in agreement about what we say to the police. As little as possible. Then, when all this has gone away, we can, uh, maybe we could go away together. Reconnect.' I don't know why I say it; even as I speak, my words sound hollow and contrived, like they prove exactly what Bianka is accusing me of – that I'm trying to keep her sweet so she won't ruin my entire life. Which is, of course, the truth.

'Really?' she asks. 'You'd want that?'

I nod, then I squeeze her shoulder, another odd and awkward moment, and then I step back outside.

Thirty-Seven

Storm

They've turned off the main road and are heading down the smaller gravelled track toward the few cabins scattered across the remote valley of Nissedal, when Storm turns to his father.

'Can we drive up to that parking lot at the end of Fyresdal, just where that really steep path leads up onto the mountain?'

'What? No, why would we—'

'I want to see where it happened.' Ever since the thought occurred to him, Storm had known he had to go there himself. Could it be that returning to the exact place would recover his memory so he could move forward? He knows what happened to Mia. She went out hiking as she often did and fell down one of the steepest parts of the mountain and died instantly. As of recently, he also knows that he was there and saw it happen. But he doesn't remember any of it, and maybe seeing the spot could change that.

'Storm. Look. I'm getting increasingly concerned with

your focus on this. I understand that you're hurting and that it must be very difficult to not be able to remember much, but—'

'I do remember some stuff, Dad. I just need to understand my memories. You guys lied to me. I have a right to know what really happened that day.' Storm thinks about the drawings and what he'd told Lone.

Emil sighs, then nods dejectedly.

'Please. I just want to see it. I looked on Google Earth and it seems like it's only about ten minutes' walk from that parking spot. Please, Dad.'

Emil reverses the car back up the track and then makes a three-point turn. Within fifteen minutes he parks the Tesla in the empty parking spot beneath the heavily forested southern face of Rasletind mountain, where twelve years ago, Mia Langeland fell to her death with her little boy as the only witness.

'Show me where it happened,' says Storm, walking away from the car up the steep rocky path. Emil hesitates and rubs absentmindedly at the stubble on his jaw, then he follows behind Storm. The path is too narrow to walk side by side and very badly eroded, sending chunks of mud and rocks crumbling as Emil and Storm slowly labour their way upwards. *Any steeper, and we'd have to climb*, thinks Storm. After less than fifteen minutes, the path merges with another more solid gravel path rising toward the summit from another access point in the valley, and after a couple of sharp bends, they reach a spectacular viewpoint giving wide, dramatic views of the empty, silent valley. From where they stand, they can see the path continuing along the shoulder of the mountain further up in a treacherous stretch, and though there is a rope fence nailed to the rockface intended to hold on to, it's obviously a dangerous spot.

'Up there,' whispers Emil. 'That's where it happened.' Storm nods and turns his gaze from where he and his mother must have stood, to the rocky slope where she must have landed, dizzyingly far below. Storm envisions Mia down there, broken and bleeding and how he would, no doubt, have been able to see her. What must it have been like for him, standing there, in those moments after she'd tripped and fallen? Did Mia scream, her voice hollering up the mountainsides? Storm doesn't miraculously recover his memory of those moments, or what happened next. He feels sobered and deeply disturbed by seeing the place his mother died. He wants to lie down in his dark, safe room and regain control of his thoughts.

'Dad. I want to go home now.'

'Okay. I'm sorry, I can only imagine—'

'Now, please.' Storm walks as fast as he safely can along the track back down to the car, his father hot on his heels.

'I was thinking we could grill hot dogs over the firepit,' says Emil, restarting the car engine, avoiding looking at Storm. 'If it doesn't start to rain.'

'I don't want to go to the cabin. I want to go home.'

'But we've driven all the way here. It's over two hours back to Oslo, and—'

'Please, Dad.'

Emil is likely taken aback by the stream of tears rushing down Storm's face because he doesn't protest further, just turns back around in the direction they'd come. They don't speak for a long while, Emil's eyes are trained on the road, and Storm's are closed as he tries to make sense of his chaotic thoughts.

'I went to the Blueberry Patch, Dad,' Storm says when they're nearing the capital, moving slowly through a slow stretch of traffic. 'I met Lone. She told me that I used to say strange things at nursery after... After what happened to Mum.' Emil keeps his eyes on the road, but Storm can tell by the pulsating clench and unclench of his jaw that he is affected by this information. 'I drew stuff.'

'I know. I've seen. You were terribly traumatized, unsurprisingly.'

'I don't know why I drew Bianka, though.'

'I think you felt loved and taken care of by her in the aftermath of Mia's accident.'

'Lone says I kept mentioning a baddy.'

'There was no baddy, Storm.'

'How do you know? I... I actually remember some stuff, though I feel as though there's this haze covering the memories. But the other day, in my dream, I was running on a path, and it was *that* path, the path we were on earlier, and someone ran behind me and—'

'Storm. Stop. Please.' Emil indicates and pulls off the motorway, bringing the car to a stop in the forecourt of a gas station. 'There is something I have to tell you.'

Thirty-Eight

Bianka

It was the shoulder squeeze that did it. The humiliation of being used and simply discarded burns so fiercely in Bianka's stomach that she knows that now, all bets are off. She watches Charlotte walk confidently down her driveway to the car parked on the curb, a self-satisfied spring in her step, Bianka imagines, as though she's entirely convinced that everyone around her will perform to her narrative if only she awards them with the occasional empty promise. Or shoulder squeeze.

Now it's time for Bianka to take control of the narrative. Over the years she's learned that people don't always know what's good for them, even when the option of a better life is right there in front of them. But Bianka knew, from the very first time she laid eyes on Charlotte Vinge, that they were meant to be together, and that everything that had happened in her life up until meeting her had just been a dress rehearsal. Even Mia. As they've gotten to know each other, Bianka has come to realize that Charlotte is a victim of her own obsessively controlled world and her empty marriage, and won't allow herself to be happy. So Bianka needs to help her along a little. It's time to raise the stakes.

'Thank you for getting back to us, Mrs Langeland,' Inspector Juanes Fuentes says, an attractive, bearded guy in his late forties with soft hooded eyes. Bianka had expected him to wear a uniform, but he isn't – he's dressed casually in a denim shirt. She angles the screen and glances at her own reflection in the smaller frame on the side bar. A second man is in the room with Fuentes, behind him by the door.

'Of course,' she says. 'I'm happy to help in any way I can.'

'Firstly, can you please confirm the dates you spent in Ibiza this month?'

'Yes, it was from the seventeenth until the twenty-sixth of June.'

'And can you confirm that your place of residence while on Ibiza was Can Xara, near Port San Miquel, the property owned by Charlotte and Andreas Vinge?' Fuentes pronounces Vinge as *Binge* and Bianka has to suppress a smile.

'Yes,' she says.

'Also, can you confirm when you last spoke to Mrs Vinge prior to this conversation?'

'It was the day before yesterday,' Bianka lies.

'I see. And how would you describe your relationship with Mrs Vinge?'

'Very close.'

'Have you known each other long?'

'No. Less than two months.'

'But you're very close.'

'Yes. At least we were.'

'Were?'

'Well. Yes. I suspect Mrs Vinge is angry with me.'

'Why would she be angry with you?'

Bianka knows that if she is to stand any chance of her plan working, she needs to do what she said she would and make sure they really get away with Maxime's murder. And she needs to ensure Charlotte has no convenient marriage to fall back on at the end of all of this...

'I... Because something happened between us in Ibiza. Our relationship became sexual.'

'I see. And for what reason is she upset with you?'

'Well, the truth is that I wanted to end our sexual relationship when we returned to London, but it's my impression that Charlotte, uh, Mrs Vinge, wanted to continue it.'

'Right. Tell me. What did you do in Ibiza? Did you party a lot?'

'Quite a lot.'

'Meet any interesting people?'

'Some, yes.'

'Did Mrs Vinge at any point mention her neighbours to you?'

'Yes. She said there was an ongoing legal dispute with the French neighbours to do with beach access. It sounded stressful.'

'And did she mention the son of the neighbours at any point?'

'No.'

'Are you under the impression that Charlotte knew Maxime Dubois-Joseph?'

It occurs to Bianka that the police must already know they were at the party. 'No, but she met him at one of the parties we went to. At their property.'

'Sa Capricciosa?' Fuentes' eyes twinkle at this information and Bianka senses he is a man of deep and intuitive intelligence.

'Yes.'

'On which day did you go there?'

'I think it was the night of the twenty-second.'

'And you met Dubois-Joseph at the party.'

'Yes.'

'Did you speak to him?'

'Yes.'

'At length?'

'Yes.'

'Who was Dubois-Joseph with at the time?'

'Two guys. I think he said they were brothers. Pretty sure they were Italian. They had the same tattoos on their necks, big ones and very noticeable, of interlinked "o"s. I believe one of them was called Matteo or Marco.'

'What did you talk about?'

'I... I made up a story. About me and Charlotte being a couple. He seemed to enjoy hearing about it. He asked several questions about us. How we met, where we live, that kind of thing.'

'And did he tell you much about himself?'

'A little. He said that he lives in Paris. And that he likes to come to Ibiza because his father puts so much pressure on him to achieve, but on the island he feels free.' Bianka is careful to keep any mention of Maxime in the present tense. She once watched on TV that many murderers reveal themselves by referring to their unfound victims as though it was a given they were dead.

'What kind of pressure?'

'He didn't say.'

'Were you aware of who he was at this time?'

'No.'

'Did Mrs Vinge know, do you think?'

'No.'

'Did Dubois-Joseph mention any future plans, such as what he was planning on doing next?'

'He said that he wanted to go to Sardinia with some friends the following week. No, Corsica. Oh, wait. Sorry, no, I think it was Sardinia. Or maybe it was Sicily?'

'Did he mention who he was planning on going with?'

'No, I don't think so.'

'This is very important, Mrs Langeland. It is our theory that Dubois-Joseph left or attempted to leave Ibiza the day after the party in question. We've been unable to establish where he went after that but any little bit of information might contribute to shining some light on what has happened and where he went.'

'I think... I think he said that he and the guy called Marco had planned to go somewhere on a yacht. Yeah, that's it. He definitely said that. Sorry I can't be more specific, I'd had quite a lot to drink.'

'How did the conversation end?'

'It didn't, really. It changed nature, rather.'

'What do you mean by that?'

'Charlotte and I had sex with him.'

Fuentes' mouth twitches and he seems to clamp it shut. Bianka gets the impression that he almost allowed it to drop open in surprise before regaining his composure.

Thirty-Nine

Charlotte

I sit down with a glass of champagne in the VIP lounge at the airport, but unsurprisingly, I can't relax at all. I send Bianka yet another message but only a single tick appears – she's either blocked me or turned off her phone – the tables have well and truly turned. I don't understand why she isn't responding, I feel like I managed her quite well when I went to her house, she was certainly appeased at the mention of going away together to 'reconnect.' But now I have no way of knowing whether Fuentes has been in touch with her, too. What if he has, and she told him all kinds of lies? Or, even worse – the truth. I have seriously considered coming clean at this point, because how can I live with this hanging over me for the rest of my life? In the end I concluded that it won't, because I truly believe what I said to Bianka the other day. We can still make this go away; we just have to be smart about it. And that depends on her keeping her fucking mouth shut. When the call came, I realized that I needed to get smarter, and that is precisely why I'm here. I asked myself, what would an innocent person do?

'Hi, Mrs Vinge. Pardon this inconvenience but I'm calling as we've had some new and relevant information come in about Maxime Dubois-Joseph since we spoke this morning.'

'Okay, no problem. I'm happy to be of any help I can, of course.'

'I'd like to ask you whether it might be possible for you to come in in person.'

'To Ibiza?'

'Well, yes.'

'Can I ask what this is about?'

'We'd like to ask a few more questions about the nature of your relationships with the Dubois-Joseph family.'

'I see.' I realized they must be aware of the feud with the neighbours. Or – could Bianka have said something to the police? 'When?'

'As soon as possible. Could you be here by tomorrow afternoon?'

I board the plane and sink back into my seat in row 1, thanking my lucky stars that the rest of the row appears to be empty as the flight attendant shuts the aircraft door with a hollow clang. Because I had to travel as quickly as possible and it was already afternoon when I decided to leave immediately, I have to change planes in Frankfurt and won't get in until gone two o'clock in the morning. As the plane begins to taxi, I switch my phone over to flight mode and it's actually a relief to make myself unavailable for several hours. It's comforting to think that I'll be unreachable and free to think about what exactly I will say to the police. As we take off, the plane rolling on the brisk wind, I close my eyes and think about how surreal it is, that it's just a few weeks ago that I sat there clutching Linda's hand in mine as we took to the sky, excited for the week ahead, not knowing that those were the last moments that my life as I knew it was intact.

Forty

Charlotte

For the first time I wake at Can Xara with no real appreciation for my surroundings; even the sight of the deep-blue sky and shimmering sea as I open the blinds fills me with dread. I deliberately avoid even a glance down toward the finca. My heart is thundering in my chest as I go downstairs and prepare a coffee, and my eyes flit around the room as though someone might leap forward, though nobody is here. I am all alone here for the first time. I stand a while at the window gazing out at the unblemished horizon. Will the sea ever look uncomplicatedly beautiful to me again, now I know what it holds beneath the surface?

My stress levels are so high ahead of the police interview this afternoon that I just don't know what to do with myself for the next few hours. I try Bianka again and again, but she doesn't pick up. I even message her husband asking him to ask her to get in touch with me. I consider going for a run but decide against it, settling instead on a heavy weights session in our home gym, but as soon as I enter the airy, large space at the back of the house, I remember where the kettlebells are, inside the abdomen of the man I killed, taped shut, and I feel violently nauseous. I pace back and forth in the living room, trying to calm my racing heart and mind. I didn't work so hard for so long to get everything I wanted only to lose it.

I decide to do something I've put off for so long, my entire adult life – the one thing I can think of that will undoubtedly take my mind completely off the insane and stressful situation at hand.

I'm crying before I even reach the finca, not for Maxime or for myself now, but for my mother; I'm imagining her walking along this same path, shielding her eyes from the sun, smiling to herself at the incredible beauty of Can Xara, and I let myself remember how radiant she was, how alive. I hope that she was happy here, even when I wouldn't come. She'd begged me to, telling me of the olive groves and the scent of the waxy leaves of the citrus trees, and of a wonderful little international school I could go to, of Can Xara itself – the place she called the home of her heart. But I couldn't see beyond my safe little life in the house I'd grown up in. I must have thought there would be second chances.

Today, I will spend my time until the police interview sorting through my mother's stuff, breathing in her scent still stored in them. I might look at some of the pictures I noticed in the box in her bedroom, and perhaps finally decide which items of her jewellery to keep and which to sell; I've never been able to face these tasks, until now. My father has never come here; in fact we have never once discussed Can Xara other than to talk about my newly constructed house, which he was interested in seeing pictures of.

I unlock the door to the finca and move quickly through the main living space without looking at any of the places where Maxime Dubois-Joseph's dead body lay, hurrying instead to my mother's bedroom at the back of the house. I open the shutters and let light flow into the room. I make myself look at the deep, narrow bed in which my mother was found dead. In just a few short years, I will surpass my mother's age, and this is a strange and upsetting notion, that I'll be older than she'll ever be. If I'm still alive, then, that is. Just weeks ago, I would have naturally assumed I'd still be here years down the line but I'm no longer so sure. I've seen too much death now.

I sit down and try to breathe deeply and, for the first time today, I'm actually able to. I decide to go all the way and imagine Ximena's final moments in this room. She must have had a few drinks and come in here hoping to sleep it off. She would have pulled the covers up to her chin and lay shivering as the toxins coursed through her system. The autopsy report was inconclusive as to cause of death, though most likely a heart attack caused by 'excessive intoxication'. The toxicology report had found alcohol, painkillers, and a sedative in her blood. It was strange, because my mother was never a big drinker, but the doctors concluded she had an unusual and unfortunate reaction to the exact combination of those drugs with alcohol.

I feel overcome with a thick sadness and get up off the bed and get the box of photographs and letters from the cupboard. I've steeled myself for this: most of the pictures are of Ximena and me. Me as a laughing little girl, perched on the arm of my mother, gazing adoringly at her child. My mother and five-year-old me on the wintry beach in Bygdøy, throwing rocks at the frozen Oslo Fjord. My mother alone in a formal photograph as a young girl. I study her face for a long while and it occurs to me that I know almost nothing about her childhood and youth here on the island. Her parents had moved to a village near Valencia after Ximena's marriage to my father, and I vaguely recall going to see them as a child, but there might still be family living on the island; I've never tried to find out. What I would give to be able to ask her now.

There are several photographs of a very young Ximena, probably in her mid to late teens, with a handsome young man. I briefly recall having seen him before, in the picture I picked up while looking for something to wear after Maxime had died.

There are dozens more; in one, they're in a vintage car, Ximena looking chic in a duck-egg blue crepe suit, the man looking at her the way a hungry man might look at a bloody steak. In another photo, they are at a party, surrounded by other young people, and Ximena is sitting on the man's lap, her thin arm flung casually around his neck. There's a photo of them on the beach, probably taken in the seventies when Ximena was sixteen or so, judging by her beehive hair and thick black eyeliner flicked like wings at the corners of her eyes. Like in all the pictures, they are laughing, droplets of water studding their smooth, bronzed skin. I focus on the young man in the picture – there is something familiar about him. Then I see it – he looks a bit like Maxime Dubois-Joseph. It's something about his nose, sharp at the end, and the thick eyebrows, set low above expressive, mischievous eyes.

I go through the rest of the photos in the box, and among

the last few I find what I'm looking for. It's another picture of my mother with the same man, only now they are several decades older. In fact, it's one of the few pictures I've seen of Ximena taken in the years after she left Norway – her hair is streaked with silver and she's grown even more beautiful as her face has softened with age. Though her skin is still supple and radiant, she has becoming laughter lines at the corners of her eyes. In this picture, they are outside the finca, on a wooden bench I threw away years ago, as it was ruined by rot and termites. And the man in the picture is unmistakable – it's Louis Dubois-Joseph, Maxime's father, and he's looking at her in exactly the same way he did when they were very young – like he'd die for her.

I stand up and walk slowly and unsteadily outside; I feel the sudden need for fresh air. There is something disturbing about these pictures, which clearly show that my mother was affiliated with Dubois-Joseph from a very young age, and that whatever their relation was, it continued in some form until fairly close to her death, judging by the last picture. As far as I knew, she'd merely bought the land from them and set about restoring the finca. That was all I'd known until after Ximena's death, when the Dubois-Josephs became increasingly insistent on buying the land back as it became obvious that I wouldn't sell Can Xara, as they'd probably assumed I would.

Something occurs to me and I go back inside to the bedroom and rifle to the bottom of the box with pictures; I'd noticed letters, too, lots of them, but hadn't stopped to look. There are several from me, both from childhood and later. And several from Louis, all professing his love for my mother. My Spanish is nowhere near fluent but I can understand the gist of them. *Soon, my love*, reads one. *I can't wait to be with you*, says another. *You and me forever*, a third. I fold them carefully and place them in my pocket, then head back outside. I need to think. Suddenly a disturbing memory comes back to me. I'm standing on the path leading to the finca and Maxime is standing above me as the path climbs the final stretch up to the house. He's laughing at me and I have the distinct recollection of intense fury coursing through my system. Then I remember his words.

You should be careful. You don't want to end up like your mother, do you?

I sit down shakily on the ground where the bench in the photograph had once stood, leaning my head against the wall of the house, closing my eyes and trying to make some sense of the thoughts churning through my head. I try to remember something else from the exchange with Maxime, but there is nothing. Where was Bianka in those moments? I can't recall. I breathe deeply, drawing in the scent of all the plants Ximena had loved so much: citrus, roses, frangipani, belladonna, thyme, rosemary, and the earth itself. I think, with a pang of sadness, of my mother's final resting place. I can see it from where I'm sitting, on a natural promontory at the end of the garden, in the spot with the best sea views, entirely at one with the landscape, like she would have wanted. You would never find it unless you knew it was there; it's impossible to spot from the path or the garden. I've made sure the gardener has kept it beautifully over the years, but I never go there myself – I can't bear it. Now, I stand up and walk slowly toward the spot, stumbling a couple of times through a haze of tears. It feels as though

I'm being steered by an invisible hand intent on making me come entirely undone.

Ximena's headstone was brought up from Cala Azura and is a beautiful, large, uneven rock with metallic-specked patches, and white dusty traces from centuries of being drenched in saltwater still visible on its sides. It would seem the gardener hasn't been for a while and I tear furiously at the brambles and weeds partly covering it, brushing it clean of earth with my white linen sleeve, until the two lines are revealed; her name and the dates of her birth and death inscribed in gold.

Ximena Antonia Bizes Marí

01.10.1957 – 22.04.2002

When I've entirely cleared her headstone, I rush back to the garden to the side of the finca, and pick a thick bunch of flowers, mostly roses, some lilies, and several beautiful leaves. As my hand tears loose one of these leafy greens, a memory appears in my mind, as clear as though it had happened yesterday.

I'm in a garden somewhere with my mother. It's probably Spain because I can see the long shadows of palm trees falling across the grass, and we're surrounded by an explosion of colours. I'm small, maybe five or six, and I can see my own tiny, dimpled hand reaching out to pick a kiwi from the tree. I can practically feel the firm, hairy fruit filling the palm of my hand, the brief resistance of its host plant as I yanked it loose. My mother crouches down and peruses the fruit, smiling and kissing my cheek loudly.

Never forget the beauty and abundance of this earth, my

darling, she whispers in my ear. *It will give you everything you'll ever need.*

We walk around in slow circles and Ximena points out a wide variety of trees and plants, saying and repeating their Latin names – *this one for luck, this one for love, this one for a quick death…* My mother suddenly becomes alive to me again and I regain memory of details that were lost to me; a little scar by her eyebrow, the charming bump on her nose, how long her eyelashes were, how she used to coil her hair up into a tightly wound bun, securing it with a dagger hairpin, like the one she gave me.

It's this that rouses me back to the present moment, standing in the brilliant afternoon sun at my mother's grave, finally cleared and bearing fresh flowers – the image of the hair dagger. I run inside and like I remember, I find one almost identical to the one that killed Maxime among her things in the bathroom drawer. I pick it up and a memory rushes through me, its images as vivid as if it were unfolding in real time; Bianka yanking the hairpin from my hair in the split second before I fell… No. Before I was shoved out of the way. And then, after, turning me over, her face edging close to mine, checking to see whether I really was unconscious. I must have opened my eyes a sliver because now I clearly remember a hand, *her* hand, pulling the dagger from Maxime's neck as he crashed around the room, blood erupting from the gash in his neck. Then Bianka slid the pin into my hand and closed my fist around it. I clearly recall the warm press of her hand squeezing my own shut, the cool metal pin inside.

It was Bianka who killed Maxime, not me.

I feel a scream rising in my throat and a compulsion

to leap from the bed and call the police, or the Dubois-Josephs, and tell them that I know everything, including exactly where Maxime is. But I can't, because I'm more than complicit to the crime and I'm even less willing to go down for a murder I didn't commit.

Like most people, I've known fury and rage but only occasionally. And never like this. It's like a searing white heat tearing through me, burning my insides and exploding in my stomach. I want to kill Bianka, like Bianka killed Maxime, mercilessly and without hesitation. How dare she make me believe I'd taken a man's life and then use it to coerce me? And why? *Why* did she do it? I can only think of two plausible explanations – she either totally snapped in the moment and acted impulsively, in which case she's clearly straight-up dangerous. Or she did it more deliberately, as a way of ensuring a continued bond with me. *We're bound together now*, she'd said. In which case she's even more dangerous.

It must be the intense adrenaline rushing through me that provides the crystal-clear clarity that's eluded me before. I'm not going to let Bianka take me down.

Forty-One

Bianka

Bianka feels like the walls are encroaching on her, like the world is closing in and will soon crush her. After the conversation with Fuentes she turned off her phone, took some American sleeping pills, and went to bed. All she can do now is wait for Charlotte's perfect life to begin to crumble and then make sure it's her who's there to pick up the pieces. But waiting is brutal. And there might be a lot of drama before she gets her happy ending. But this time she will.

When she woke again it was just past ten p.m. and Bianka turned her phone back on. As expected, she had many missed calls from Charlotte, the last one in the late afternoon. She considered calling back but decided to wait until morning. She tried to go back to sleep, but the hours stretched out bleak and unfilled and now, at seven a.m., she decides to stop trying and get up. She's about to call Charlotte and explain the reasoning behind what she's done but decides it's better to have this conversation in person.

She takes a long shower and it feels good to cleanse herself of the long, dark night and its looping, scary thoughts.

As she's about to leave the house, she checks her phone and notices a new message from Dr Matheson.

> Bianka, you know I have to report when you miss more than one session. Our work together is mandatory, as per your sentence, you know this. Please get in touch.
>
> Dr M.

She'll have to deal with her later. Bianka gets in the car and drives the short distance over to Charlotte's house and just as she parks outside, Andreas emerges from the gates, wearing a suit and carrying a sleek brown leather briefcase.

'Oh, hi Bianka,' he says, as she emerges from the car and gives him a brilliant smile. She can tell he finds her attractive, he's the kind of guy who shows his feelings on his face. *Poor guy,* she thinks, *he has no idea what's about to hit him. The house, the wife, the kids, the swanky Wimbledon life, it's all going to be gone.*

'Hi there,' she says, offering her cheek for a kiss. 'I've just popped over to see Charlotte.'

Andreas looks confused and awkward. 'Oh, hasn't she told you? She's gone back to Ibiza. Last night. She was asked to, by the police. Apparently, a young man has gone missing under mysterious circumstances and turns out he's the son of our neighbours, so they wanted to speak to her. He went missing while you guys were out there, apparently.'

'Right.' Bianka feels the hot impact of shock spread out in her stomach. She says her goodbyes, gets back in the car and picks up her phone to call Charlotte, only to find she's just had a message from her. She opens it and it's a selfie of the two of them taken that night at Benirràs; Bianka is standing behind Charlotte, hugging her close. Charlotte's arm is stretched out in front of her to take the picture, the sky is a deep indigo behind them, and they are both beaming. Bianka stares at the picture in confusion. Why would Charlotte send her this now? A long message follows below.

Hey B,

I've tried to call you. Please call me back if you feel able to, we really need to talk. I'm back at Can Xara and I've been hit by the clearest of realizations – being here without you is unbearable. You were right all along. What we have is special. I've just been freaking out so, so much since everything happened. But we only live once and I want to do this life with you. Please let's forgive each other. Let's move forward, properly – together. I love you.

Bianka's hand trembles violently and tears spring to her eyes. The hurt and confusion of the past week fades in her heart and mind and she wants to just scream with joy. Charlotte loves her. She knew it. It's different this time, different from Mia. She wasn't crazy; it did all happen the way she felt it did, and what could have been so beautiful was only derailed by what happened with Maxime. It should never have happened and Bianka has searched her own mind constantly since, trying to understand why she instigated it that night at Sa Capricciosa. The only answer she's come up with is that she was high – on life, on Charlotte, on alcohol, on Ibiza; she'd felt truly alive for the first time in years and it had seemed like a fun, wild idea at the time.

She understood that it had ruined everything as soon as she saw Charlotte sitting in that chair the next morning, a look of pain and horror on her face. And then, the murder. Looking back, Bianka can't believe just how much of a disaster she managed to create on that trip. But here in front of her, in the most beautiful message she's ever received, is a second chance. She presses *Call* and this time Charlotte answers straight away, her voice full of warmth again, the way she was before.

'I'm sorry,' says Bianka, before Charlotte can even speak.

'I'm sorry, too. For everything. Now, let's fix this. Together.'

'Do you want me to come out there? I know you're in Ibiza. I could come now.'

'I'd love that. Oh, Bianka, I've missed you so much.'

Bianka drives fast back to the house, with Charlotte still on the line, and while she packs a weekend bag, they come up with a watertight plan. Charlotte asks Bianka what she said to the police, and she tells her everything. Charlotte thankfully understands Bianka's reasoning and they come up with a solid and coordinated story. They agree how they are going to move forward. Step one: get the police off their backs. Step two: begin a new and beautiful life together. Bianka finds a flight leaving in less than two hours from Gatwick and buys it in spite of its exorbitant cost. She looks back at the house as she leaves – they've only been there a couple of months and now she's leaving forever. In leaving Emil, she's leaving Mia, too. Finally. And it feels good.

Forty-Two

Storm

'Your mother. Mia...' The words don't come. Storm softens when he sees his father's knuckles grow white on the wheel. 'She killed herself.'

'No.'

'Yes. Storm, I'm so sorry.'

'But it didn't happen like that.'

'Storm. I can only imagine how much this must hurt. But I think you're old enough, and smart enough, to hear it straight. Perhaps I should have told you years ago, but I, uh – we, felt that it would be harmful for you to know the exact circumstances. It was enough, to take in the loss of your mother at such a young age.'

'It was Bianka, wasn't it? She didn't want me to know.'

'Bianka is very protective of you, Storm.'

'I think Bianka is very protective of herself.'

'What do you mean?'

'That she'll do and say whatever serves her. Even if it's a lie.'

'Stop it, I'm quite serious.'

'How do you even know it was suicide?'

'It was pretty obvious, Storm. You were the only people there. The weather was perfect; she was extremely used to mountainous terrain.'

'What kind of mum would do something like that in front of her kid? She wouldn't. I don't buy it.'

'Storm. You didn't really know her. She—' His father stops speaking and his face is etched with raw grief. 'She really, really suffered in the year leading up to her death. After you were born, she had postnatal depression, very badly. She wasn't herself for months and months, it was like the light in her had just been switched off and everything was dark. She loved you so much, she was completely besotted with you, and still, she couldn't take care of you in the way that most mothers do in the first year of a child's life.

'Then she got better. So much better that we started talking about having a second child, and about six months before Mia died, we started trying. When it didn't immediately work, Mia became frustrated and withdrawn and I sometimes felt like she shut down completely from me, preferring to speak to her friends – uh, Bianka, specifically – instead of me.'

'What about her other friends?'

'She had a few. Nice people. But she and Bianka were like this.' Emil holds up his intertwined index and middle finger.

'But none of what you've told me sounds that bad, not bad enough to kill yourself—'

'Storm, believe me when I say her postnatal depression was bad. She'd lock herself in the bathroom for hours, howling. I'd stand on the outside cradling you while you also howled. You wouldn't take a bottle and she wouldn't breastfeed. She'd cut herself on the soles of her feet and when she eventually emerged, she'd walk around the house, leaving a trail of blood—' Emil stops and wipes at the tears brimming in his eyes. 'I'm sorry, Storm. I'm not sure I should be telling you this.'

'You should absolutely be telling me this. You should have told me everything a long time ago.'

After a while, Emil starts speaking again. 'She got better and then she got worse. But it was different to the first year after you were born, which literally felt like a profound hormonal breakdown. When you were almost three she became incredibly withdrawn, from both of us. She'd barely engage with you and not at all with me. It was heart-breaking. I tried everything from couples' therapy to encouraging her to get back on medication, but nothing worked. Of course, in hindsight, I should have had her sectioned. She might still have been with us.'

'Did she ever speak of being suicidal?'

'Not to me, no. In fact, I never would have thought she'd do something like that, because no matter how low she'd get, she'd always plan ahead. She'd say things like "In five years, when Storm's eight, we should get a puppy". She even instigated us booking a really expensive holiday to Greece. But people are complicated. Sometimes, she'd plan ahead, other times she wouldn't get out of bed for a week. And she said some very disturbing things to Bianka. She warned her the weekend it happened. She even said she was afraid of what she might do to you. I'm so sorry to even say this. But it's the truth. And that's why Bianka headed there that day, to stop her. But it was too late.'

'Wait, what?'

'Yes. It was why she went up there. And thank God she did, because she found you, running along the path, hysterical. I've thought about that so many times, how incredibly lucky it was that you didn't fall, trying to help, or—'

'So she only warned Bianka.' Storm's voice is thick with emotion and his heart is thundering in his chest.

'Well, I don't know, but—'

'What about my grandparents?'

'I don't know. I didn't stay in touch with them afterward, as you know…'

'Which in itself is fucked up. As you know.'

'Storm. It was just so difficult. I didn't have any answers back then. It's easy to be wise in hindsight. I barely slept for years, from stress and anxiety and worry for you. I just tried to make things as easy as possible for both of us.'

'As easy as possible, according to Bianka. Did you tell my grandparents to keep her suicide secret from me?'

Emil hesitates and keeps his eyes trained on the damp dark concrete of the gas station's forecourt. 'Yes. It was something we all agreed between us adults. That your life would probably be easier if you could process your mother's death in the belief that she'd died in an accident rather than a suicide.'

'I think the truth might have been easier for me.'

'You're almost seventeen. It's different now. It wasn't a conversation I could have with you when you were five or ten or twelve.'

'What, the truth?'

Eventually, Emil begins to drive again and less than ten

minutes later, they pull up at the house. His father is about to open the door, having snapped his seatbelt off and shut down the engine.

'Dad. Wait. This can't be right. I think... I think Bianka did something to my mother.'

Emil looks stricken, and his eyes travel from Storm to the house and back to Storm.

'I...'

'Dad, I'm serious. You say Mum mentioned feeling suicidal, but the only person she apparently warned was Bianka. The person who then turns up at the scene and quote unquote *saved the little boy*. The person who then married the husband left behind. Think about it. It's so fucked up. Even the stuff I drew was fucked up. Lone agreed. She reported us to Barnevernet based on what I said, talking about a baddy throwing my mom off a mountain. She gave me the drawings. This is too much of a coincidence.'

'Storm, there was no baddy who threw your mom off a mountain. The psychiatrists all agreed on that.'

'Dad, I even drew the baddy for all to see.'

'No, you just drew pictures of Bianka. Holding your hand.'

'Bianka *is* the baddy, Dad.'

A stunned and heavy silence fills the air. Father and son look at each other, then outside, as though for clues as to what to do. It's still raining, though not as heavily as earlier, and the sky is slate grey and gloomy. Tears run down Emil's face and Storm feels numb and disorientated. What are they supposed to do now? Emil's phone pings loudly, breaking the tension. They look at each other.

'Where is Bianka?' whispers Storm as Emil unlocks the phone.

'What the… I just had a notification from my bank app that Bianka bought a two-thousand-pound flight on my Amex card this morning.'

'I don't understand…'

Emil starts stabbing furiously into his phone and Storm gets out of the car and walks in the direction of Slemdal, calling Madeleine over and over, so that she'll understand it's an emergency and he has to speak to her, whether or not the batshit crazy adults that surround them both have forbidden her to. Finally she picks up.

'Meet me at the lake.'

'What, now?'

'Yeah. Please. Just find a way.'

She hesitates and he waits for her to say she can't – won't – come, but she doesn't. She whispers 'Okay,' her voice tender.

Forty-Three

Bianka

It's not true what Bianka told Charlotte and basically everyone else about her early life. Her mother didn't die as she'd insinuated; she left her for a man named Joel in America, and went to live with him in his big house in Fort Lauderdale. Joel didn't want any more kids, so Bianka's mother left her to be raised by her great-aunt, Edna. Aunt Edna gave up after a couple of years and sent her to a Christian boarding school on the west coast of Norway, after her early teens were marred by uncontrollable behaviour and substance abuse.

She walked out of the school after three weeks and she can still see herself as the lone figure she must have been then, running through the wet, dark night to the main road, feet slipping on trampled orange leaves, black mountains swept in drifts of fog blocking the moon from reaching the narrow, remote valley. She didn't see her mother again until her twenties, and by that time she had become an unrepentant day-drinker who rarely returned her daughter's calls. Bianka suspects that deep down, she is very angry. No wonder Bianka panics whenever people pull away from her. Everything would have been different if her mother hadn't abandoned and rejected her. She wouldn't have been drawn to others who'd repeat that pattern, like Mia. But now, everything is different. The cycle is broken and Bianka is about to discover a different kind of life, one defined by genuine love and connection.

Bianka walks as though in a haze through Gatwick Airport, going through the motions of the security check point on autopilot – her weekend holdall bag on a tray. That's it – it's all she carries as she travels toward her new life. She tries to rid herself of the thoughts of her early life but finds that she can't quite; her brain keeps wanting to go back, to understand. She realizes she has to process the past to release it and move forward, like Charlotte said.

How did we get here, Bianka? She asks herself the question as she heads through the winding duty-free shop and catches sight of herself in the mirror of the Dior makeup counter.

Who is this woman? It feels as though she's entirely created herself, as if she came from nowhere at all, with nothing to root her or keep her moored. She thinks of Emil, and as much as he's a good man and a loving husband, their marriage is entirely based on performance, on Bianka constantly acting to perform the part she had to play to save herself. And Storm… Storm has been a difficult chapter from the beginning. Bianka has always known she's walking on eggshells with the boy, that if anyone was going to tear her down, it would be him.

Bianka has the sensation that her life has been lived uphill but that she's always had to pretend otherwise. Or chosen to. But now, she's tired. She's tired of pretending, lying, conforming, aspiring, concealing. Once, she was in love and filled up inside by it, and once she'd had it, everything else seems like a lie by contrast. But Mia took it all away from her. She questioned the very reality on which Bianka's world rested. She said she was delusional and wrong and to stay away, or else, but nobody speaks to Bianka like that. Nobody hurts her and gets away with it, as Mia learned the hard way. Bianka just hadn't counted on a witness.

On the plane, she sits in her seat at the back, leaning her head against the headrest and closing her eyes, letting the cool air from the funnel rush across her face. She lets herself go back in her memories again as the plane begins its cumbersome taxi toward the runway, and the future. She's surprised by how easy it suddenly feels to look back, and how rarely she's attempted it over the years.

People don't usually *want* to lie and fuck people over, they do it because they feel they have to, and Bianka is no different. She'd never planned to do it, but once you go down the road of building a life from lies, then you are going to be maintaining them forever. To herself, Bianka justifies it all simply as doing what she had to do. It just wasn't going to cut it to turn up in Oslo as a teenage runaway, an empty shell of a kid, wanted by nobody, so Bianka created another version of events. The boarding school in the deep, rain-lashed valley became a top Swiss private school. Her mother became a vague and tragic reference, and always brought sympathy.

The lies kept coming, one after another, and with time, she came to find that people almost always believe what you tell them, because why wouldn't they? The vast majority of people who look like Bianka and speak like Bianka and fit into the world Bianka inhabits, really are who they say they are.

At the beginning, when she first arrived in Oslo and began to build a life for herself, she realized that she was good at befriending people and not so good at keeping people in her life; it was a repeat pattern and one that grew increasingly devastating with time. It brought up all the old trauma of her mother suddenly deciding one day that life would be better without Bianka in it. She decided to break the cycle and create a beguiling persona that nobody would ever reject or abandon again. At the beginning, it was difficult. But Bianka knew even then that nothing worth having comes easily. She would meet someone and they'd be drawn in by Bianka's effusiveness and contagious energy, but inevitably, weeks or months later, they'd drift away, giving one vacuous excuse or another. But Bianka took something from each of them and made it her own; a gesture, a look, a subtle honing of her carefully studied Oslo West accent, a stolen anecdote that reflected the person she was constructing.

By the time she met Mia in her late teens, she had had plenty of practice creating herself and knew she came across as successful, thoughtful, and charismatic, often described as a real breath of fresh air, someone who made other people feel special and brought a burst of energy to her surroundings. She'd learned that the trick with people was to reflect back what people themselves wanted to be. Most people wanted to be confident, to feel seen and interesting, qualities that are remarkably easy to emulate – it's simply a case of making the other person feel that *they* are those things.

Then she met Mia, Mia who was so good at seeing beneath the surface, who just seemed to gently crawl into the most hidden of places, her very core. Things began to change for Bianka, she went from nightclub promotion to PR to marketing, and friends no longer constantly dropped out of her life – she was popular and seemingly well liked.

Mia was confusion and conflict and connection and love, passionate love. Mia was deep water. Mia was everything. Sometimes Bianka couldn't be sure if she loved her or wanted to be her; it was probably a case of both. They slept together, but only once, and what had seemed to Bianka to be a natural and beautiful progression, filled Mia with regret.

Mia began to distance herself. She met a man and said she was in love. And Bianka couldn't handle it when she lost her. Even now, so many years later, Bianka can't bear to think of what happened next, and who she had to become without her. She pretended like it was all fine but set about trying to dismantle Mia's new life. Coercion, manipulation, bullying – these had all seemed like acceptable strategies to Bianka.

She wrenches her mind off Mia and replaces the image with Charlotte. This is easy; they look remarkably alike, a source of endless amazement for Bianka. When she first laid eyes on Charlotte it felt like Mia was back, that it could all be undone. She couldn't believe her fortune when she realized how fundamentally insecure Charlotte was. She comes across as so powerful and confident, but she was easy game, someone who constantly craves reassurance and attention – a classic avoidant narcissist. Charlotte just doesn't see other people or understand that they are real independent beings with their own needs and agendas – as long as her ego is stroked sufficiently, she purrs like a cat.

When she realized that she'd truly lost Mia, that Mia would report her for harassment, she did what she had to do. It wasn't easy but it had to be done. The rejection brought back the searing heat of grief and rage that Bianka had felt when her mother left her; violent storms of emotion that were eventually internalized and replaced with that numb, white haze. Bianka simply snapped, after months of pleading and what Mia called emotional blackmail. She wasn't planning to kill her, of course not, she'd gone to the cabin to reason with her. She hadn't meant to come across as threatening. She just wanted to talk. But Mia wasn't there, the cabin was empty. The farmer down the road had told Bianka that Mia headed up to Rasletind most mornings, so Bianka drove there and parked her car right next to Mia's. She walked fast up through the woods on the gravel path which grew narrower as it looped around the neck of the mountain, the valley opening up far below. They came face to face on the path and Bianka will never forget the look of sheer shock and horror on Mia's face as she took her in. Up until that moment Bianka must have believed on some level that Mia loved her and that it was merely a matter of convincing her of that, but as she stood there in front of her on the path with a look of disgust on her face, the truth was very obvious. The truth was ugly. And it hurt so much. *I just want to talk to you*, Bianka said. But Mia didn't want to talk; she ran away from her as she approached, rushing down the narrow path, dragging the little boy alongside her. And Bianka snapped.

Months later Emil got in touch to ask whether she might help him make sense of some drawings little Storm had been making, since she'd been the person who knew Mia best, apart from him. He wanted to hear about the moment Mia had leapt from the path; was Bianka really sure it was intentional? Could she perhaps have tripped? Bianka shook her head sadly and let her eyes fill with tears. Emil had placed his warm hand atop hers and something about him suddenly felt safe and irresistible, like coming home to the parent she'd never had.

By this time, Bianka had lost her grip on her life completely. Haunted by what she'd done, she spent her days in bed, high or drunk or both. She was shocked when she saw Storm's drawings. Could it be that he'd be able to articulate what had really happened? Emil, too, looked exhausted and terrorized, and his warm eyes searched hers. Bianka realized the solution was there. Right in front of her. If she couldn't be with Mia, she could become her and allow herself an idyllic, comfortable life. Two birds with one hell of a large rock. Marry the money, get the life she'd never had growing up, and shut the kid up. It was all better than expected for a while; Bianka found she enjoyed being idolized and taken care of by Emil, who was probably beyond grateful to get a second chance at marriage, and not having to raise his son by himself. It was easy to pretend to be there for him; he was so naïve and unquestioning. Bianka spent time sorting through most of Mia's possessions, getting rid of her diaries where she whined pathetically about her 'delusional friend' stalking her and harassing her to the point of a nervous breakdown in the years after she married Emil.

Bianka did what she could to be a good wife to Emil and a stand-in mother for Storm, but the truth was she found them both repulsive and annoying, and it took all her effort to achieve just a vague semblance of family life. There were upsides, too – Emil was the first person Bianka had ever met who she didn't think would ever leave her, and she grew to cherish the secure, almost parental relationship that developed between them.

There were other indiscretions before Charlotte – after all, Bianka is only human. A couple of women, one she met through work who turned out to be boring and not worth the effort, and another, a Swedish singer who also bore a vague resemblance to Mia. Bianka pursued her relentlessly, which eventually ended in a formal charge of harassment and a restraining order, with two years of mandatory therapy sessions with Dr Matheson. But all of that is water under the bridge now. Charlotte loves her and she is on a plane moving fast toward the future.

Forty-Four

Charlotte

I sit across from Inspector Fuentes, a man with a misleadingly pleasant demeanour, considering his job is essentially to expose liars and criminals like myself. Behind him sits a woman with a buzz cut and cool eyes, pen poised above paper to take notes. I feel like she can tell what I've done just by looking at me. *Nobody can see inside of you*, I tell myself. This is something Ximena often told me. *It's your job to show them.*

Or not.

'As briefly discussed on the phone, you're aware of the disappearance of Maxime Dubois-Joseph?'

'Yes.'

'We're at a stage of our investigations into his disappearance where we are building a picture of Dubois-Joseph's days leading up to when he went missing. It is of utmost importance that we know who he was with, what he was doing, what his plans were.'

'Of course.'

'We've spoken to a number of Dubois-Joseph's friends, as well as your guests at Can Xara. I'm glad you could come in in person, as these conversations have left us with more questions than answers.'

'Oh,' I say, swallowing nervously – a lump has appeared in my throat. *Stop*, I tell myself, *you're prepared for this.* I smile what I hope is a slightly confused, uncomplicated, law-abiding-citizen smile.

'Can you confirm whether you have ever met the missing man, Maxime Dubois-Joseph?' asks Fuentes, speaking slowly.

'I'm not sure,' I say. 'I can't recall.'

'Perhaps it would be most helpful for us to start off with a run-through of your activities during your recent trip to Ibiza. Can you confirm you were with three friends, and their names?'

'Yes. It was Anette Young, Linda Wagner-Cantrell, and Bianka Langeland.'

'What was the purpose of this trip?'

'A girls' trip. A breather from real life. We go every year.'

'And this year, you were joined by an extra guest, is that correct?'

'Yes. Bianka.'

'How would you describe your relationship with Bianka Langeland?'

'We're friends.'

'Just friends?'

I shift in my seat. 'No,' I say.

'Can you explain in detail what happened between you?'

'We met in May, at a party at my house in London, to celebrate the release of my Streamstar show.' I pause to give Fuentes a chance to express some admiration at this extraordinary achievement, but he doesn't bat an eyelid. I ignore a stab of annoyance and continue. 'We spent quite a lot of time together after we first met, but it escalated during our trip to Ibiza.'

'Escalated?'

'Yes. It turned sexual.'

'Instigated by whom?'

'By me. But it was very much a mutual thing. We, uh, I believed we were in love. She showered me with attention and affection. I was very taken with her; I've spent many years in what can only be described as a dead marriage. But since we've been back, things have cooled off between us. It feels as though Bianka has basically dumped me. She doesn't contact me, or answer my calls.' The lady with the buzz cut writes something down in her notebook. I look Fuentes in the eyes and try to make myself look harmless and a bit confused. So far, I've carefully stuck to the narrative agreed with Bianka. I almost have to chuckle at the thought that she bought it, that right now, she believes that I'm dutifully running through the motions, with the aim of riding off into the sunset with Bianka. But that was never my plan. And now it's time to take this to the next level. 'And the other thing is, I've discovered that she lies.'

At this, Fuentes raises an eyebrow. 'What does she lie about?'

'Lots of different things. It's hard to put a finger to one specific thing, but it's constant little inconsistencies, embellishments, and half-truths. She told me that she lost her mother in childhood. Then, later, she casually mentioned to Anette that her mother lives in Fort Lauderdale with her husband. Just one example, but it's exhausting to be around. I feel sorry for her, really.'

'I see. Back to your trip. What did you do? Where did you go? Did you attend any parties?'

I list the restaurants we ate at, places this guy has probably never even heard of, that cater to women like me and my friends, who bring foreign money and a host of eating disorders disguised as 'dietary requirements' to Ibiza.

'We mostly relaxed at my property,' I continue. 'That's what we come here for, year after year. To do yoga and swim in the sea. To really connect with the island. We're not really big party girls.'

'So, no parties?'

I hesitate here, and I can tell that both inspectors notice. The room feels claustrophobic and too hot and I have to fight the urge to bolt from the room. But there is nowhere to go, nowhere to hide, and we all know it. All I can do is hope that Bianka has been fully honest with me about exactly what she's said. The story is we met, we went to Ibiza, we had a fling, we partied a little too hard and ended up in bed with a man who I had no idea was Maxime Dubois-Joseph, an episode I didn't even recall the next day, and we haven't seen him since. We returned home and saw each other occasionally, though not much.

'Actually, Bianka Langeland and I ended up at a party at the neighbours' after the noise was disturbing us at Can Xara. We went over there to see if they could keep the noise down, it was already very late. And we got carried away. It was a nice atmosphere, lots of young people having a good time, and I suppose I felt a little ridiculous coming over to complain. I had a couple of drinks, some tequila, I believe, and I don't remember much after that.'

'Nothing?'

'No.'

'Mrs Vinge. Can I respectfully remind you that everything that is said here today is recorded and used as part of an ongoing police investigation into a missing persons case? It is of utmost importance that you tell us everything and anything that could be of relevance to the investigation. And believe me, it doesn't look great to be caught in lies. Or embellishments. Or half-truths. Does this picture help jog your memory?' From a folder on the table, Fuentes extracts a photograph and slides it across to me. For actual fuck's sake. I swallow hard; my throat is so dry I couldn't speak if I wanted to. The photograph is of Bianka and me on the dance floor by the vast infinity pool, kissing, my mouth curling upwards in a smile beneath Bianka's lips, watched on by Maxime Dubois-Joseph and the gangster twins, who are seated on a daybed by the side of the pool.

'Do you know who the men in the picture are?'

'No. Well, not their names. Except for Dubois-Joseph.' I focus on looking innocent and helpful and point to Maxime. 'And the two others were brothers, I believe. Italians.'

'I need to ask why, in our original conversation, you said you didn't recall having met Dubois-Joseph, when you clearly had, or attending this party before now.'

I try to make myself cry again but it doesn't work, and Fuentes watches me with a mix of fascination and surprise as I contort my face and make some gargled, throaty sobs, rubbing hard at my eyes in an attempt to produce tears. In the end I think of my mother's face, lighting up at the sight of me, the way it did absolutely every time she saw me, and this does the trick – tears begin to stream down my face.

'I'm sorry,' I say. 'I'm very sorry. I wasn't aware at the time that the man we spoke to was the son of the Dubois-Josephs. We've had an ongoing dispute with them for several years, it's been pretty inflammatory, and I didn't want my husband, who has paid so much money in legal fees, to find out we'd been to their party. He'd be furious. As you can see from the picture, things got carried away, though, like I said, I can't remember this... this unsavoury display with Mrs Langeland. I was inebriated.'

'How inebriated?'

'Very, clearly.'

'What can you recall after this picture was taken?'

'Not much. But I do remember the next morning. I woke up with this man and Bianka. I believe she had sex with him while I was passed out.'

'Do you think it's possible that you engaged in sexual activity with them?'

'No, absolutely not.'

'If you don't remember, how can you be sure?'

'You asked if I think it's possible. I don't, but naturally I can't be totally sure as I had passed out.'

'How did you get home?'

'I – I don't remember.'

'Nothing?'

'No, nothing.'

'Have you heard from any member of the Dubois-Joseph family since that night?'

'No.'

'What about Bianka Langeland?'

'Well, yes. We've been in touch, naturally. And the thing is—' I pause, making my voice shaky and low, 'she's behaved very badly toward me.'

Fuentes raises his eyebrow incredulously again. 'Badly how, exactly?'

'Well. To begin with, she was literally all over me. Other people noticed and commented. Anette and Linda found it super weird. Like I said, I hardly remember anything from that night – I'm not a big drinker as I'm on a strict keto diet. You might have heard of me, actually, the *Viking Keto Queen*? On Streamstar? No? Anyway. So, I barely drink and clearly got smashed as I have no recollection of this picture being taken. But it makes a lot of sense considering how Bianka behaved after we returned home, just... ice cold. It's as though what we had meant nothing to her. And then she threatened to tell my husband that we'd had some kind of sordid fling. She kept saying she'd expose me and ruin my life, unless...'

'Unless what, Mrs Vinge?' asks Fuentes, and he's smart enough to make himself look soft and harmless here, like someone you might feel safe to confide in.

'She wanted money.'

'And did you give her any?'

'No.'

'Correct me if I'm wrong. Is Bianka Langeland not married to the CEO at Norbank in London?'

'Well, yes—'

'Would she not have access to plenty of funds herself?'

'She plans on leaving her husband. Maybe that's why she needed money. I don't think it's about money, though. I think it's about ruining my life and marriage.'

'Why would Mrs Langeland wish to do that?'

'Jealousy. She strikes me as a pretty jealous person.'

'I see,' says Fuentes, but I feel like he doesn't see at all. He looks extremely sceptical, and his eyes keep darting to the horrible photograph of Bianka and me at Sa Capricciosa. It isn't the kiss itself that bothers me the most, but the foolish grin on my face. Now it's time for the grand finale. This was definitely not part of the script agreed with Bianka.

'There's one more thing,' I say. 'Just speculation, really, but in light of all this I think you should probably know about it. As I say, I believe that Bianka Langeland is planning on leaving her husband. But you should know that the person she's leaving him for is Maxime Dubois-Joseph. I believe they have planned his disappearance together and she'll run away to join him. I'm assuming trying to pressurize me for money is part of that plan. I bet she'll swindle her poor husband first.'

'Why would you believe such a thing?'

'It was something she said, after we were back in London. I went to her house to try to talk to her. I missed her so much and I needed to understand why she'd gone so cold toward me. I mentioned that I'd heard Dubois-Joseph had gone missing, it was the same day I first spoke to you so I'd just heard it from you and it was naturally on my mind. I remember she laughed a little and said that if you had parents like his, you'd make yourself disappear too. I thought it was odd and asked her if she'd been in touch with him since Ibiza. She wouldn't answer and basically shut the door in my face. But I wouldn't be surprised if she knows where he is.'

Fuentes twirls his pen around and around between his fingertips and sighs heavily.

'What are your plans moving forward, Mrs Vinge?' He pronounces my surname '*binge*' which really seems to be astonishingly ironic.

'Well, I thought I might spend some time clearing out my mother's old house on my property. You know, rethink its use. I don't often get time away from my family.'

'I see. We're going to conduct some more interviews and investigations in the coming days. A lot of questions remain unanswered, so if you can think of anything at all that might cast some further light on the whereabouts of Mr Dubois-Joseph, give me a call without hesitation. In the meantime, I'd like to ask you to let us know if you plan to leave the island.'

'What? I can't come and go as I please?'

'Of course you can. We are merely speaking to you as a neighbour and member of the public who came into contact with the missing person in the days leading up to his disappearance.'

'You know, just my two cents, of course, but I do think that boy kept some bad company. Those Italian brothers, bad news in my opinion.'

'You said you didn't recall speaking with them.'

'I don't. But look at them, they look like criminals. Mafia, I imagine. Perhaps Mr Dubois-Joseph has gotten himself involved in some dirty business with them.'

'Officer Gutierrez here will show you out now, Mrs Vinge. Thank you for your time. We'll be in touch.'

★★★

Back at Can Xara, I pace around the terrace in the shade, playing the interview over and over in my head. It felt disastrous, like they knew they had something on me and I kept walking into little traps. I think I managed to turn it around by planting the idea that Bianka had continued to be involved with Maxime, and very soon it will all make perfect sense to the police.

Someday, I'll look back at this time and it will seem distant and almost impossible that I once killed someone and got away with it. I suddenly see Maxime in my mind again, and the cruel glint in his eyes as he said I should be careful. *You don't want to end up like your mother, do you?* I stop dead at the far end of the pool and look down the hillside toward the finca, and beyond, where my mother's grave lies, sheltered from view. I begin to run.

Standing in the brilliant afternoon sun at my mother's grave, finally cleared and bearing fresh flowers, I try to bring order to my churning thoughts that are now descending wildly into ever crazier territory. I pull the letters and one of the smaller photographs from my pocket and stare at them. My mother was a beautiful woman. Too beautiful, dangerously beautiful.

And it's these words, 'beautiful woman', that prompt the realization that slots all the pieces together. Bella Donna. *Atropa belladonna*, the plant of choice for instant death.

I stand here for a very long time, rooted to the spot by what I know to be the truth: my vivacious, otherwise healthy mother didn't die at forty-six from an unfortunate mix of alcohol and painkillers – she was murdered by a simple plant from her own beloved garden, common across the Mediterranean regions. But why?

I sink back down onto my knees in the crumbling earth and place my hand on the cool stone.

'I'm sorry,' I whisper, and it's as though Ximena whispers back in a sudden sweep of salty air rushing at me from the sea. *Charlotte*, she says, *my darling Charlotte*.

'I'm so sorry, Mama. I'm going to get to the bottom of this.'

I feel foolish whispering into the wind, but it feels good and like the right thing to do. Then I turn back toward the path and the faintly visible glass structures of my house high up on the hill, reflecting the golden late-afternoon sun. My phone vibrates with a message from Bianka.

There in 5, she writes, followed by a long string of excited-face and heart emojis. Time to get this show on the road.

Forty-Five

Charlotte

'm outside, reads the message from Bianka. *Can you open the gate?*

I stand a while in the white, empty hallway, staring through the thick expanse of the glass wall at the bronze gate across the yard, on the other side of which Bianka Langeland is standing. I hear the sound of a car engine revving and then disappearing, heading back south. Before I press *Open* on the intercom, I take a picture of Bianka standing there on my phone. As I watch her walk up the path to the house as the gate slides shut behind her, I shake off a sudden bolt of fear rushing through me at the thought of being alone at Can Xara with her. I have a plan and I know what I'm going to do, or what I *have* to do, rather, but that doesn't make it easy.

I feel a fresh surge of anger and fear at the thought of the things this woman has done as I open the door and she stands in front of me. I don't doubt for a second that she'd ruin my whole life if I let her. And still, there is a part of me that must be in thrall to her, because in spite of everything I can't help be disarmed by her, even now, as she gazes up at me with those wide-set pale eyes, her smile slow but warm and only ever exactly like this when she's looking at me.

'Come here,' I say, pulling her into the house, glancing past her to make sure no cars or cyclists have passed at exactly this moment, catching a brief glimpse of a blond curly-haired woman arriving at Can Xara just as the sun dips behind the western hills. She reaches for me and I give her a long hug, forcing myself to bring conviction and a feeling of passion to it.

We go through to the kitchen and I hand her one of the cocktails I've prepared for us.

'Wow,' she says, drawing its fruity scent in deeply. 'What is this?'

'Voilà,' I say. 'It's my newest recipe, a low-carb kombucha mojito with berries and thyme from the garden.'

Bianka takes a long sip, then another.

'You have to tell me everything about the interview. God, I hope it went well. Now our stories are totally in alignment, this is all going to go away soon, baby,' she says, raising her glass to me in a toast. I nod, smile, and raise mine in return, touching it to hers.

'Bianka,' I say. 'Why did you let me believe I killed Maxime, when really, it was you?' She grows pale. I can't be sure if it's shock at my words or the drink. I'd imagine it works quite quickly, and especially at this concentration. Her face changes from relaxed and expectant to uncertain.

'I'm sorry, what?' She lets out a shrill laugh that ends in a spluttery cough. 'That's not true. You killed him and I've done everything I can to help you after it happened—'

'No, *you* killed him, Bianka. Not me. And you let me believe that I'd committed murder. You're really fucking twisted. And you've dragged me into your universe where everything seems to be something other than what it actually is. And poor, poor Mia. You know, when I saw the picture of her I was in total shock. No wonder you were so obsessed with me. And that you couldn't handle it when I told you there is no such thing as us. Was it your plan that I'd end up like her?'

Bianka drains her drink and places her empty glass hard onto the marble surface of the kitchen island, then laughs loudly again, her eyes now strangely glazed.

'Wow,' she says, and chuckles. 'I should have realized. I can't believe I fell for your fucking games, Charlotte. Well, good luck trying to prove it. You're going to jail for murder.'

'No, I'm not.'

'Charlotte. I'm going to the police right now. I'll tell them everything. Who do you think they're going to believe? I have pictures of you. With the murder weapon in your hair. I even have footage of you having sex with the victim. Yep. Oh, please, don't look so shocked. Did you really think I'd wipe his phone clean without sending the evidence to myself first? Remember, Charlotte, that crucially, you're the one who had motive.' Bianka reaches out and steadies herself on the kitchen island. A dark rash has appeared on her collarbone. She must be starting to feel rather bad.

'Bianka, you did know I'm a doctor, right?'

'What?' she whispers.

'Your pupils look a little extended. Oh, wait. That must be the belladonna. I don't believe you have more than two or three minutes to live. Your mouth must feel really dry.

Yeah? I can tell. Atropine and scopolamine are rushing through your veins right now, shutting down your vital organs. Did you know that once, a king slayed a whole army with this stuff? Your eyes are crossing, I'm guessing your vision is pretty blurred. Soon, you'll experience circulatory collapse, swiftly followed by death from respiratory failure. I don't believe you have more than two or three minutes to live.' Bianka tries and fails to say something, before she crumples to the ground. And for two minutes and thirty-nine seconds, I stand there watching as Bianka convulses and struggles for breath. Then she's quiet.

Many hours later, when I have done things I wouldn't have imagined myself capable of, I do a final sweep of downstairs. Everything is as it should be, perfect, except for the blood trickling down my face from underneath my crudely bandaged forehead, where a deep, self-inflicted gash will serve forever to remind me of Bianka and this evening. There is no trace of the splashes of projectile vomit that splashed from Bianka's mouth when she hit the floor. And there is, of course, no trace of Bianka herself.

It's three a.m. and I am exhausted, having worked for hours since Bianka died just after nine p.m. And now, it's time. I dial the number for the police with a violently trembling hand and chase my voice into a high-pitched wail when a voice answers.

'I've been robbed at knifepoint,' I sob, and the tears and the shock and the pain and the blood – they're all real.

Forty-Six

Charlotte

Eighteen months later

I got my life back. No, that's actually not true at all – I got a new life, one infinitely better than the one I left behind. I came home, to Ibiza, to my mother, and to myself. I won, like winners always do. It was mayhem, of course. Utterly so. I can only imagine the shock waves that reverberated through the privileged upper echelons of the Scandinavian expat society of Wimbledon in the aftermath of everything that happened, but thankfully I wasn't there to watch it unfold. Andreas filed for divorce after the video from Sa Capricciosa was leaked to the internet, but he got nothing apart from half of the house. Anette really is the best divorce lawyer in town.

My popularity surged to new heights after my armed robbery ordeal at the hands of Bianka Langeland. The police search for Bianka remains active and urgent, and Inspector Fuentes tells me they feel confident they will track her down eventually. The picture I took of her on my phone as she arrived at Can Xara circulates the island and indeed Europe on wanted posters.

She managed to escape Ibiza most likely on a yacht, possibly one procured for her by members of the Sicilian mafia, with whom Bianka had proven ties. Her phone was eventually traced to such a vessel, one that had spent the previous weeks crisscrossing the Mediterranean. One can imagine she might have gotten quite far with the cash she stole from my safe, after she threatened me to open it at knifepoint. At least that's how the story goes. In reality, she didn't get far, poor thing. She made it to the industrial-sized freezer in my pantry, where she spent several weeks underneath the mountain of organic steaks I'd ordered to tide myself and my family over for the summer holidays, which we naturally had to cancel due to the terrible trauma I'd suffered and the added shock of my callous husband filing for divorce.

I disposed of Bianka's phone the same night she died, in a similar way to Maxime's, though a little more hands-on. Why fix something if it ain't broke, right? I'd been pleased to spot several large yachts out in the bay that night, not unusual in July. I waited until past midnight when I was mostly done with the clean-up and then I placed Bianka's iPhone, which had been in her back pocket, back into her small clutch bag that also contained her passport. I left the bigger weekend bag at Can Xara. I'd let the police take care of that – it would serve to back up my story that she'd come to the house.

I sealed the little canvas envelope clutch into a wrap of two Ziploc bags, duct-taped shut. I covered my hair with a black swimming cap and put my wetsuit on, with the plastic parcel inside pressed to my chest, then hurried down to Cala Azura, walking silently to the far point and across the rocks until I could slip into the sea as far out as possible from the beach. The moon was a narrow sliver and the sea was inky and calm. I swam as quietly as I could, much of the time under water, until I reached the hull of one of the yachts, a large one with a long row of cabin portholes, all dark. I pulled myself onto the wide, teak afterdeck as quietly as I could and waited for several long moments before proceeding – had I heard a single sound I could have easily slipped back under the surface undetected. But there was nothing, only the gentle slap of the water against the hull and a distant throb of music from somewhere far away on the island.

I unwrapped the parcel and placed Bianka's clutch bag onto the deck, in a corner where it might go unnoticed for a while. I hoped that the boat was full of rich playboy types and their silly girlfriends, and that all the silly girlfriends would just assume that the little bag belonged to one of the other silly girlfriends. The odds were in my favour, knowing the crowds that flock to Ibiza on yachts in the summer.

The children chose to live with me, though they see Andreas in London from time to time. Oscar and Madeleine enrolled at a beautiful international school in an old converted olive mill near Sant Joan de Labritja. Every few weeks Storm comes to visit and I encourage his relationship with Madeleine now, he's a good kid, and he loves my daughter.

Next year, after graduation, they talk about going to university in Vancouver together.

I set about building a new life for us, vowing it would be beautiful, and it is, though it has thrown some interesting curveballs my way. I knocked down the finca and in its place a new villa is taking form, this one smaller and less fancy than the main house, but I envision it as a space I can eventually retreat to, when all four kids have grown up. Yes, four. I'll get back to that.

It felt good to watch the bulldozers raze the finca to the ground, all its secrets and violence and history obliterated, leaving an empty space behind that just felt peaceful. My poor mother was exhumed from her grave and, with the improved medical technology of the present day, it was possible to discern traces of *Atropa belladonna* in her remains. Anne-Marie Dubois-Joseph is awaiting trial for her murder, apparently motivated by obsessive jealousy prompted by her husband's first love returning to Ibiza and her husband securing her retirement by selling her Can Xara at a fraction of its value. Honestly, I can see why she went mad; it must have felt rather humiliating to have the love of your husband's life on the doorstep. Note to self: never confess to murder in your diary.

Before my mother was returned to her grave, a second body was buried in a shallow layer of earth beneath where hers would lie and there is no reason at all to believe they won't both lie there forever. It wasn't easy to do, of course, but easy is seldom worth it. Besides, we can do hard things, this I've learned. And as much as I hate the idea of that vile woman sharing a grave with my beloved mother, I've accepted it was the price I had to pay for my freedom.

Maxime Dubois-Joseph never turned up and I often say a little prayer that he never will. His father tells me that both they and the private investigators they've hired over the past eighteen months to look into the case, believe that he is likely still on the run with Bianka Langeland, a woman considered both manipulative and extremely persuasive. There have been several reliable sightings, most recently in Lisbon. Louis Dubois-Joseph, who is very old and ailing, never went back to Paris after his wife's arrest, preferring to remain in Ibiza, staring out at the sea, totally unaware of what it holds beneath its surface. We visit him most afternoons, and for Louis, some gentle blessings have appeared in the autumn of his life. One of the last things Maxime did before he vanished without a trace was father a child. A girl. A sole heiress – discreetly confirmed with DNA – not only to Sa Capricciosa and the vast property portfolio her grandparents possess, but her share of Can Xara, too. Her existence is, in all effect, a marriage. The marriage of Louis Dubois-Joseph and Ximena Marí that never was.

Today is another beautiful day on the most incredible island on the planet and I woke to the sound of my baby's furious wail. Xara Ximena is ten months old now and it's fair to say she takes after me. She's an early riser, a go-getter, and a fiery little thing with soulful dark eyes like her namesake and a glorious, dimpled smile. I won't lie, the initial discovery of Xara's existence was a little challenging to wrap my head around. After all, I was a married forty-two-year-old anorexic murderer with quite enough problems on my plate – the last thing I needed was an unplanned baby with a dead man child. But she was the one who saved me.

I found out after the nausea didn't disappear and it dawned on me that it wasn't necessarily just an immediate response to seeing dead bodies, but rather a physiological manifestation of something wrong inside of me. I went to the doctor and he ran some tests. He said a pregnancy test was routine and I assured him it wasn't necessary as I'd had the coil fitted after the birth of my son and replaced it bang on time ever since, but even as I spoke, the gruesome reality that this was untrue occurred to me. Some months previously I'd experienced intermittent bleeding and terrible period pains and so I decided to take a six-month break from the coil to see if my symptoms improved. This seemed fair enough, since I hadn't had sex with my husband for years at that point. And I simply forgot, having been so used to having the coil for almost two decades. If there had been a single moment of rational thinking around contraception that night at Sa Capricciosa, it must have been instantly eviscerated by a tsunami of cocaine and raw, ridiculous desire.

I lift my baby from her cot and carry her downstairs. I kiss the top of her head for each step and she giggles merrily. When Oscar and Madeleine see Xara, they shriek and pull funny faces at her, though they obviously weren't initially as enthusiastic. But here's the thing – people mostly come around. We adapt and grow and accept. Sure, people talked – in fact, I'm sure people did nothing *but* talk for the first few months. But then they found other things to talk about than the car crash personal life of that lady who won't eat carbs. People forget. The kids were mad, and now they're not mad – they're thriving. It just took a bit of time and therapy.

My career doesn't appear to have suffered at all – in fact it is going from strength to strength and *Mediterranean Keto Queen* is launching next month on Streamstar. Must be true what they say, that all publicity is good publicity.

'Hey, babe,' says a voice, and I turn around in surprise to see Alessio sitting there at the far end of the kitchen island – usually my man child boyfriend isn't up before eleven. He's scooping spoonfuls of beef jerky into his plush mouth and I pad over, Xara perching on my hip, and kiss him hard on the mouth. We chat for a while, laughing and discussing that afternoon's logistics like any normal family, as if there ever was such a thing.

The kids are picked up by the school bus and rush off in a flurry of goodbyes and chatter and high fives for Alessio, who they've concluded is 'pretty cool'. Then he and I go and pick mint leaves from the garden for our tea. Xara goes down for her ten o'clock nap. Alessio lifts me onto the marble island which is so cold beneath my bare skin that I wince, pulls my underwear to the side, and then he's inside me moving hard. I clutch onto the back of his neck, my hand closing around the double 'o' tattoo protruding slightly from his collar.

Acknowledgements

Like the characters in this novel, I wanted a breath of fresh air when I set out to write *Girl Friends*, and I wanted to infuse the book with the beauty and hedonism of Ibiza. So, like the ladies in this book, I went to Spain, and Spain worked its magic in making me reconnect with everything again, and I hope something of all the beautiful experiences I had there found its way into *Girl Friends*.

I had the fantastic support and encouragement of many, many people whilst creating *Girl Friends*, both personally and professionally. A special thank you is due Laura Longrigg, my amazing agent for many years – I'll never forget our many wins, and wish you all the best for your future adventures. A big thank you also to my new agent, Federico Ambrosini – I am very excited to work with you and for the future. Thank you also to everyone at Salomonsson Agency for the warm welcome.

A very big thank you to Susan Smith, Tim Webb and Andrea Mitchell – I so appreciate your hard work, and am excited for what lays ahead.

I've been fortunate enough to work with two fantastic

editors on this book, whose instinct and wisdom have benefitted it greatly – thank you so much to both Madeleine O'Shea and Bethan Jones. Our mad plot conversations really are a highlight of my professional life. Thank you also to all the other wonderful people at Head of Zeus – I always feel lucky to be published by you. Thank you to Louis Greenberg for the pitch-perfect insights, again. A very big thank you is also due Sophie Ransom – I feel very lucky to be working with you.

A huge thank you is due to my writer's group in Spain – Ida, Kendra, Raquel, Sara and Terese. You've really made my year and I am so grateful for all of you. A special thanks to Terese, my 'friendsick' expert, whose forensic insights were invaluable as *Girl Friends* took shape.

This novel centres around the power and pitfalls of close female friendships, and there is no doubt I have been especially fortunate in that department. So thank you to all my amazing, empowering, interesting, wild girl friends – you know who you are and you enrich my life on so many levels. A special thank you is due Charlotte and Bianka, who have shown amazing levels of chilled-outness whilst lending their names to the protagonists of this novel.

A huge thank you to the booksellers who read and talk about my novels to readers all over the world – I appreciate you so much.

Thank you to Lisa Lawrence, for all the hours and all the insights. We're nearing a point when I almost totally trust that you'll never put a fly in my wine glass.

Thank you to Chris and Judy, for everything – we appreciate you so much. Thank you to Lana del Rey for the sweary ballads I love to write to. And to Tricia Wastvedt, for everything, always.

Last, but definitely not least, thank you to my family: my mother Marianne, my sister Emmanuelle, my queen Laura, and my children Oscar, Anastasia and Louison – you really are everything and I love you. Thank you for putting up with the radical opposite of a nine-to-five and for your endless belief and support.

About the Author

ALEX DAHL is a half-American, half-Norwegian author. Born in Oslo, she studied Russian and German linguistics with international studies, then went on to complete an MA in creative writing at Bath Spa University and an MSc in business management at Bath University. A committed Francophile, Alex loves to travel, and has so far lived in Moscow, Paris, Stuttgart, Sandefjord, Switzerland, Bath, and London. She is the author of five other thrillers: *After She'd Gone*, *Cabin Fever*, *Playdate*, *The Heart Keeper*, and *The Boy at the Door*, which was shortlisted for the CWA Debut Dagger.

Follow Alex on:
X (@alexdahlauthor)
Instagram (@authoralex)
Facebook (alexdahlauthor)